D1325429

THE EDINBURGH EDITION OF THE WAVERLEY NOVELS

EDITOR-IN-CHIEF
Professor David Hewitt

VOLUME TWENTY-FOUR
THE SHORTER FICTION

EDINBURGH EDITION OF THE
WAVERLEY NOVELS

to be complete in thirty volumes

Each volume is published separately but original conjoint publication of certain works is indicated in the EEWN volume numbering [4a, b; 7a, b, etc.]. Where EEWN editors have been appointed, their names are listed

WALTER SCOTT

THE SHORTER FICTION

Edited by
Graham Tulloch and Judy King

EDINBURGH
University
Press

© The University Court of the University of Edinburgh 2009
Edinburgh University Press
22 George Square, Edinburgh

Reprinted 2009, 2014

Typeset in Linotronic Ehrhardt
by Speedspools, Edinburgh
and printed and bound in Great Britain
on acid-free paper by CPI Group (UK) Ltd, Croydon, CR0 4YY

ISBN 978 0 7486 0589 7

A CIP record for this book is available from the British Library

The publisher acknowledges support from the Scottish Arts Council towards the publication of this title.

Scottish
Arts Council

FOREWORD

THE PUBLICATION of *Waverley* in 1814 marked the emergence of the modern novel in the western world. It is difficult now to recapture the impact of this and the following novels of Scott on a readership accustomed to prose fiction either as picturesque romance, 'Gothic' quaintness, or presentation of contemporary manners. For Scott not only invented the historical novel, but gave it a dimension and a relevance that made it available for a great variety of new kinds of writing. Balzac in France, Manzoni in Italy, Gogol and Tolstoy in Russia, were among the many writers of fiction influenced by the man Stendhal called 'notre père, Walter Scott'.

What Scott did was to show history and society in motion: old ways of life being challenged by new; traditions being assailed by counter-statements; loyalties, habits, prejudices clashing with the needs of new social and economic developments. The attraction of tradition and its ability to arouse passionate defence, and simultaneously the challenge of progress and 'improvement', produce a pattern that Scott saw as the living fabric of history. And this history was rooted in *place*; events happened in localities still recognisable after the disappearance of the original actors and the establishment of new patterns of belief and behaviour.

Scott explored and presented all this by means of stories, entertainments, which were read and enjoyed as such. At the same time his passionate interest in history led him increasingly to see these stories as illustrations of historical truths, so that when he produced his final *Magnum Opus* edition of the novels he surrounded them with historical notes and illustrations, and in this almost suffocating guise they have been reprinted in edition after edition ever since. The time has now come to restore these novels to the form in which they were presented to their first readers, so that today's readers can once again capture their original power and freshness. At the same time, serious errors of transcription, omission, and interpretation, resulting from the haste of their transmission from manuscript to print can now be corrected.

DAVID DAICHES

EDINBURGH
University
Press

CONTENTS

ACKNOWLEDGEMENTS

The Scott Advisory Board and the editors of the Edinburgh Edition of the Waverley Novels wish to express their gratitude to The University Court of the University of Edinburgh *for its vision in initiating and supporting the preparation of the first critical edition of Walter Scott's fiction. Those Universities which employ or once employed the editors have also contributed greatly in paying the editors' salaries, and awarding research leave and grants for travel and materials.*

In addition to the universities, the project could not have prospered without the help of the sponsors cited below. Their generosity has met the direct costs of the initial research and of the preparation of the text of the novels appearing in this edition.

BANK OF SCOTLAND
The collapse of the great Edinburgh publisher Archibald Constable in January 1826 entailed the ruin of Sir Walter Scott who found himself responsible for his own private debts, for the debts of the printing business of James Ballantyne and Co. in which he was co-partner, and for the bank advances to Archibald Constable which had been guaranteed by the printing business. Scott's largest creditors were Sir William Forbes and Co., bankers, and the Bank of Scotland. On the advice of Sir William Forbes himself, the creditors did not sequester his property, but agreed to the creation of a trust to which he committed his future literary earnings, and which ultimately repaid the debts of over £120,000 for which he was legally liable.

In the same year the Government proposed to curtail the rights of the Scottish banks to issue their own notes; Scott wrote the 'Letters of Malachi Malagrowther' in their defence, arguing that the measure was neither in the interests of the banks nor of Scotland. The 'Letters' were so successful that the Government was forced to withdraw its proposal and to this day the Scottish Banks issue their own notes.

A portrait of Sir Walter appears on all current bank notes of the Bank of Scotland because Scott was a champion of Scottish banking, and because he was an illustrious and honourable customer not just of the Bank of Scotland itself, but also of three other banks now incorporated within it—the British Linen Bank, Sir William Forbes and Co., and Ramsays, Bonars and Company.

Bank of Scotland's *support of the EEWN continues its long and fruitful involvement with the affairs of Walter Scott.*

THE BRITISH ACADEMY AND THE ARTS AND HUMANITIES RESEARCH BOARD

Between 1992 and 1998 the EEWN was greatly assisted by the British Academy through the award of a series of research grants which provided most of the support required for employing a research fellow, without whom steady progress could not have been maintained. In 2000 the AHRB awarded the EEWN a major grant which ensured the completion of the Edition. To both of these bodies, the British Academy and the Arts and Humanities Research Board, the Advisory Board and the editors express their thanks.

OTHER BENEFACTORS

The Advisory Board and the editors also wish to acknowledge with gratitude the generous grants and gifts to the EEWN from the P. F. Charitable Trust, the main charitable trust of the Fleming family which founded the City firm Robert Fleming Holdings, now incorporated within J. P. Morgan; the Edinburgh University General Council Trust, now incorporated within the Edinburgh University Development Trust; Sir Gerald Elliot; the Carnegie Trust for the Universities of Scotland; the Modern Humanities Research Association; and the Robertson Trust.

THE SHORTER FICTION

The editors wish to thank the Australian Research Council which assisted this work with a grant for a number of years, and are grateful for the financial support of Flinders University.

The manuscripts of the stories in this collection and other relevant manuscript materials are to be found in a number of libraries, and the editors would like to thank in particular: the staff of the Sterling Library, University of London; Mike Kelly and the staff of the Fales Library, New York University; Iain Gordon Brown and the staff of the National Library of Scotland, especially Yvonne Carroll; the staffs of the Edinburgh University Library, the British Library, and the Bancroft Library, University of California, Berkeley; and the staff of the National Archives of Scotland.

For additional manuscript materials they would like to thank: the Beinecke Rare Book and Manuscript Library, Yale University; the Folger Shakespeare Library; the Historical Society of Pennsylvania; the Houghton Library, Harvard University; the Huntington Library; Iowa University Libraries; Lincolnshire Archives; McGill Library, McGill University; the Morgan Library and Museum; the New York Public Library; and the Watkinson Library, Trinity College, Hartford, Connecticut.

For printed materials they are grateful to the staff of the Aberdeen University Library; the staff of the Flinders University Library, especially Lynda Clarke, Ann Sigston, Jessica Raeburn. Gillian Dooley, Aliese Millington and Andrew Tuft; Cheryl Hoskin of the Barr Smith Library,

University of Adelaide; and the staffs of the State Library of Victoria and the Baillieu Library, University of Melbourne.

For specialist advice on various points the editors thank Eric Bouvet, Alan Cadwallader, George Couvalis, Javier Díaz Martínez, Patricia O'Grady, and Michael Tsianikas. They must also thank Roy Pinkerton, the Edition's consultant on classical literature. They have also had the assistance in Aberdeen of Rachel McGregor and Sally Newsome who undertook part of the boring but essential task of checking references and quotations. In particular, the editors wish to express their warmest thanks to David Hewitt, whose vast knowledge of Scott and experience of editing his works have added so much to this volume, particularly in its final stages, and to their own enjoyment in preparing it.

Finally, Graham Tulloch would like to thank his wife, Sue Tulloch, for being there with help and encouragement from the very beginning of his obsession with Scott's short stories; and Judy King would like to thank her husband, Alan Mayne, not only for his loyal support during the preparation of this volume, but also for the inspiration provided by his own work.

The General Editor for this volume was David Hewitt.

INTRODUCTION

This book gathers together for the first time all the stories and sketches contributed by Scott to periodicals. The first collected edition of Scott's fiction, the *Waverley Novels*, was published in forty-eight volumes between 1829 and 1833. It is familiarly known as the Magnum Opus, the great work, and is apparently complete, but it includes only three of the eight pieces to be found here.

The original plans for the Magnum had envisaged forty volumes covering the novels from *Waverley* (1814) to *Woodstock* (1826) but it proved so enormously popular that there was every reason to continue it beyond *Woodstock*, the only question being how many volumes it would eventually comprise. On 3 June 1830 Scott's publisher, Robert Cadell, suggested that it should be forty-eight or fifty volumes, and should include all the novels Scott had already published, as well as those yet to appear.[1] In his journal entry for 20 December 1830 Scott notes that Cadell had proposed 'assembling all my detachd works of fiction [and] Articles in annuals',[2] in other words all the stories and sketches Scott had published in literary periodicals. Scott is apparently accepting of the proposal: there is no sign or suggestion of dissent. However, in a letter of 3 August 1831 Cadell lists only those stories included in *Chronicles of the Canongate* (1827) and *The Keepsake for 1829*,[3] and he seems unaware of those which had appeared anonymously earlier in Scott's career in *The Edinburgh Annual Register*, *The Sale-Room*, and *Blackwood's Edinburgh Magazine*. Thus the Magnum's omission of five 'detachd works of fiction' does not appear to have been deliberate, and the Edinburgh Edition of the Waverley Novels now collects them all for the first time. This collection takes in the five which were omitted from the Magnum, namely 'The Inferno of Altisidora', 'Christopher Corduroy', 'Alarming Increase of Depravity Among Animals', 'Phantasmagoria', and 'A Highland Anecdote', as well as the three which did appear in the Magnum, 'My Aunt Margaret's Mirror', 'The Tapestried Chamber', and 'Death of the Laird's Jock'.

Even so, it might be argued that this collection is incomplete. It omits unfinished works: two of these, 'Fragment of a Romance which was to have been entitled Thomas the Rhymer', and 'The Lord of Ennerdale', originally published as appendices to the General Introduction to the *Waverley Novels* of 1829–33, together with Scott's conclusion to Joseph Strutt's romance *Queenhoo-Hall*,[4] will be found in Volume 25a of the Edinburgh Edition, *Introduction and Notes to the*

Magnum Opus. Two other unfinished works, *Private Letters of the Seventeenth Century*,[5] and 'Bizarro',[6] were published for the first time in 1947 and 2008 respectively.

Secondly, this volume omits three tales of the supernatural which could be considered as short stories detachable from the novels in which they appear: 'The Fortunes of Martin Waldeck' in *The Antiquary* (1816),[7] 'Wandering Willie's Tale' in *Redgauntlet* (1824),[8] and 'Donnerhugel's Narrative' in *Anne of Geierstein* (1829).[9] Of these 'Wandering Willie's Tale' has frequently been anthologised and discussed as an independent work, rather than an inset tale, but although the other two have not been treated this way they might have been. Each story is set up with a narrator and audience, and this facilitates their being 'detached', and makes them similar in some respects to 'Phantasmagoria', 'My Aunt Margaret's Mirror', and 'The Tapestried Chamber' which are included in this collection. This volume also omits a further two from *Count Robert of Paris*, 'The Retreat from Laodicea' and 'Zulichium',[10] which illustrate opposing attitudes to chivalry. The stories in *Chronicles of the Canongate* are rather different in that they were nominally collected and retold by Chrystal Croftangry; of these two have regularly been treated as detachable stories or novellas— 'The Highland Widow' and 'The Two Drovers'.[11] However, although these pieces have often been discussed as short stories, and sometimes treated as such, they belong to greater wholes, and because they appear elsewhere in the Edinburgh Edition of the Waverley Novels they have not been included in the present book.

Many anecdotes, often very similar to 'A Highland Anecdote', are to be found in the introductions and notes Scott wrote for the Magnum (which appear in Volumes 25a and 25b of the Edinburgh Edition), and many more in his notes to *Minstrelsy of the Scottish Border*, to his poetry, to his many collections of historical documents, and to the works of Dryden, Seward, Swift, and Carey which he edited. Anecdotes may be found throughout his letters and journal. All these have been excluded from this volume not because they are not short stories (an untenable distinction in that the boundary between the short story and the anecdote is undefined and fuzzy), but because Scott did not treat them and publish them as formal 'works'. Scott's imagination may be said to be narratological: he tends to frame things as stories, and any reader of Scott must feel that there is no end to the storytelling habit. His lives of Dryden and Swift, his shorter, Johnsonian, lives of the novelists, and his account of Robert the Bruce in *Tales of a Grandfather* (to choose but a few examples) are full of anecdotes, some of which might be 'true', and others of which represent aspects of the lives of his subjects in the ways of traditional stories. It would be impossible to provide a comprehensive list of anecdotes because anecdotes are so pervasive in his writings, and because normally they cannot be easily detached from their literary and historical contexts. The present volume confines itself to those works that Scott published as 'detachd pieces'.

The sketches and stories to be found here (unlike those which have been excluded) first appeared in periodicals, in *The Edinburgh Annual Register*, *The Sale-Room*, *Blackwood's Edinburgh Magazine*, and *The Keepsake*. Scott's response to the new demands of periodicals for short fiction, and his contribution to the development of the short story as a form, await proper study. Meanwhile, the reader of this collection is more likely to perceive the connections with the novels. The stories cover the span of Scott's career as a novelist. The earliest, 'The Inferno of Altisdora', was probably written in the autumn of 1810, around the same time as some of the early chapters of *Waverley*;[12] the pieces in *The Sale-Room* and *Blackwood's* were written in 1817–18, in the period of *Rob Roy* and *The Heart of Mid-Lothian*; the *Keepsake* stories were completed in 1828, with the last, 'A Highland Anecdote', coming some time after March 1828, just possibly between his finishing *The Fair Maid of Perth* and beginning *Anne of Geierstein*. Like the novels, the stories employ framing devices and fictional narrators, which emphasise their origins in, and connections with, traditional tales and 'urban myths'. The range of subject matter is typical of Scott's fiction as a whole: there are three satiric sketches ('The Inferno of Altisidora', 'Christopher Corduroy', and 'Alarming Increase of Depravity Among Animals'); there are three ghost stories ('Phantasmagoria', 'My Aunt Margaret's Mirror', and 'The Tapestried Chamber'); and there are two tales, one from the Borders ('Death of the Laird's Jock') and the other from the Highlands ('A Highland Anecdote').

The texts of the stories in this volume are based on the first published version in each case, and, when manuscripts are extant, readings from them which were lost through accident, error, or misunderstanding have been incorporated. In this respect *The Shorter Fiction* follows the textual policy of the Edinburgh Edition of the Waverley Novels as a whole, which reflects the fact that the manuscript of each novel is a starting point, not a culmination: Scott relied on his printers to give his texts their public, normalised, and pointed form, and he corrected and revised the resulting proofs. For these reasons the editors of the Edinburgh Edition normally choose the first edition, rather than the manuscript, of a novel as base-text. But they also recognise the failings of the first editions, and thus after the careful collation of all pre-publication materials, and in the light of their investigation into the factors governing the writing and printing of the Waverley Novels, they incorporate into the base-text those manuscript readings which were lost in the production process through accident, error, misunderstanding, or a misguided attempt to 'improve'. In certain cases they also introduce into the base-texts revisions found in editions published almost immediately after the first, which they believe to be Scott's, or which complete the intermediaries' preparation of the text. In addition, the editors correct various kinds of error, such as typographical and copy-editing mistakes including the misnumbering of chapters, inconsistencies in the naming of characters, egregious errors of fact that are not part of the fiction, and failures of sense which a simple emendation can restore. The result is an 'ideal' text, such as his first readers might have read had the production process been less pressurised and more considered.

The manuscripts of most of Scott's major works are largely extant (he is the first novelist of whom this is true), and the textual policy of the Edition responds to this fact. Unfortunately, the manuscripts are missing for four of the stories in this book, 'The Inferno of Altisidora', 'Christopher Corduroy', 'Alarming Increase of Depravity Among Animals' (although for this there are fragmentary drafts), and 'My Aunt Margaret's Mirror'; in other words there are no manuscripts for material making up about two-thirds of the volume. However, this does not affect the textual policy, although it does affect editorial practice: the first published versions are again the culmination of a creative process, even if the evidence for the earlier parts of that process is missing for four of the stories. Furthermore, no later editions could have been used as base texts. With the novels, a case can be made for basing the text on the Magnum, though the Edition has rejected this option primarily because the texts that Scott was working with had, unknown to him, become very corrupt. But Scott was not involved in the republication of two of the stories and sketches that did appear again in his lifetime—namely 'Alarming Increase of Depravity Among Animals' (in the second printing of the relevant issue of *Blackwood's*), 'Phantasmagoria' (in *Literary Gems* and *Tales and Essays*)—and only cursorily with 'My Aunt Margaret's Mirror', 'The Tapestried Chamber', and 'Death of the Laird's Jock' in the Magnum. There is minor variation in the texts of the republished stories of the kind that any textual critic would expect, and the result is that some obvious errors in the first published versions are corrected (these corrections are of course adopted in the present volume), but new mistakes arise. The choice of the first published versions of the stories as base texts is thus unavoidable.

Nonetheless, the first published versions of the stories may not have the authority of the first editions of the novels, or that authority may be there for some of the pieces, but not for others. As Scott wrote his novels he normally sent off batches of manuscript which were copied, and these copies were then sent to the printer, typeset, proof-read, and corrected. A fresh proof was pulled, which went to James Ballantyne, the master printer, who corrected and annotated, and sent his corrected and annotated proof to Scott, who revised and added further corrections. James Ballantyne normally copied all the corrections, his and Scott's, on to a new set of proofs and these went back to the compositors. From time to time Scott demanded revises. For the novels this was a standard set of processes; the copyists were normally men used to reading Scott's hand; James Ballantyne edited the text of every novel written by Walter Scott. With the possible exceptions of 'The Inferno of Altisidora' and 'Christopher Corduroy', the stories must have been sent to editors, and printers, who were not accustomed to Scott and his ways.

It can be argued that authorial proof-reading sanctions whatever procedures were followed in the production of the stories. As the editors of this volume show in the Essay on the Text, Scott revised 'Alarming Increase of Depravity Among Animals' very substantially in proof, and he corrected proofs of the *Keepsake* stories. Whether he saw proofs of the other stories has not been determined. But even in the pieces whose proofs Scott is known to have read there are some glaring errors, and the present editors have identified many mistakes in the eight pieces published in this book, which probably indicate printers' and publishers' unfamiliarity with Scott. When there are no manuscripts, authorial readings lost in the process of printing and publication cannot be recovered. No doubt had the missing manuscripts been available the editors would have been able to realise Scott's intentions more perfectly in the texts in this volume, but, in partial compensation for their absence, the whole experience acquired in editing Scott's fiction has been applied to the mistakes in the stories. Emendations, admittedly based on a hypothetical reconstruction of what may have gone wrong, have been made as a result of editorial understanding of Scott' hand and writing habits. For example in 'Alarming Increase of Depravity Among Animals' knowledge of Scott's handwriting permits the emendation of 'arts' to 'acts' (Scott was a lawyer, and crimes in his work have to be *acts*, not arts), and of 'unwillingly' to 'unwittingly' (he usually left his t's uncrossed, and 'unwittingly' makes better sense). Had it been a novel, James Ballantyne would have sorted out the muddle of whether Captain Falconer is a captain or a major in 'My Aunt Margaret's Mirror', which appears uncorrected in *The Keepsake*, and he would have corrected the manuscript's 'localities of the detail' to 'detail of the localities' instead of letting the nonsense of a simple transposition appear in the print of 'The Tapestried Chamber'. Scott's quotations from ancient and foreign literatures are usually grammatically correct in the manuscripts of novels (even when adapted to their context), but often wrong in print: thus the mistakes in the Spanish quotation from *Don Quixote* in 'The Inferno of Altisidora' are errors.

The editorial policy of the Edinburgh Edition of the Waverley

Novels has generated remarkable changes. *Rob Roy* is a startlingly different novel when it appears in its first-edition form, shorn of the Magnum's huge Introduction which converts the story of Frank Osbaldistone, Englishman, Presbyterian, and Hanoverian, into the history of Rob Roy MacGregor, Highlander, outlaw, and Jacobite. The emendations to each and every text have revealed Scott to be a much better writer than was previously recognised; they dispel utterly the old view that Scott was careless. Even in this volume of shorter fiction, readings recovered from manuscripts turn the pedestrian into something sharp and apposite. In 'Phantasmagoria' is it not better that a witch should die on 'pitched faggots' than on faggots alone, that the correspondent's father should be 'Sir Mickelmast' rather than 'Sir Michaelmas', and that it should be 'curious' information that is to be saved from 'the darksome bourne', not 'current' information? In 'The Tapestried Chamber', the 'particolour towers' of the old castle are vivid, while 'particular towers' makes no great sense, and it is typical of a ghost to return 'by habit, to her old haunt' rather than 'by twelve', an error which involves a literal-minded response to the 'castle clock striking one' which follows. The changes are slight, but cumulatively transformative. They recover for the twenty-first century one of the great masters of tale-telling. The Edinburgh Edition of the Waverley Novels has revolutionised Scott.

DAVID HEWITT
August 2008

NOTES

1 MS 21043, f. 77r.
2 *The Journal of Sir Walter Scott*, ed. W. E. K. Anderson (Oxford, 1972), 613.
3 MS 3919, f. 77r–v.
4 *Waverley Novels*, 1.xli–xc.
5 Walter Scott, *Private Letters of the Seventeenth Century*, ed. Douglas Grant (Oxford, 1947).
6 Walter Scott, *The Siege of Malta and Bizarro*, ed. J. H. Alexander, Judy King, and Graham Tulloch (Edinburgh, 2008).
7 Walter Scott, *The Antiquary*, ed. David Hewitt, EEWN 3, 137–46.
8 Walter Scott, *Redgauntlet*, ed. G. A. M. Wood with David Hewitt, EEWN 17, 87–101.
9 Walter Scott, *Anne of Geierstein*, ed. J. H. Alexander, EEWN 22, 106–22.
10 Walter Scott, *Count Robert of Paris*, ed. J. H. Alexander, EEWN 23a, 47–62, 117–21.
11 Walter Scott, *Chronicles of the Canongate*, ed. Claire Lamont, EEWN 20, 68–122, 124–46.
12 Walter Scott, *Waverley*, ed. P. D. Garside, EEWN 1, 376–80.

THE SHORTER FICTION

From

THE EDINBURGH ANNUAL REGISTER

THE INFERNO OF ALTISIDORA

Á uno dellos nuevo flamante y bien encuadernado, le diéron un papirotazo, que le sacáron las tripas, y le esparciéron las hojas.—
DON QUIXOTE, Part II., lib. viii, cap. 70.

They tossed up a new book fairly bound, and gave it such a smart stroke, that the very guts flew out of it, and all the leaves were scattered about.—MOTTEUX' *Translation.*

TO THE PUBLISHER OF THE EDINBURGH ANNUAL REGISTER

SIR,—

The character of your present correspondent is perhaps very little to the purpose of his communication; but who can resist the temptation of a favourable opportunity for speaking of himself and his own affairs? I am, then, a bachelor of fifty, or, by'r lady, some fifty-five years standing, and I can no longer disguise from myself, that the scenes, in which I formerly played a part of some gratifying degree of consequence, are either much altered, or I am become somehow less fitted for my character. Twenty years ago I was a beau garçon of some renown, escorted Lady Rumpus and Miss Tibby Dasher to oyster parties, danced with the lovely Lucy J——, and enjoyed the envied distinction of handing into St Cecilia's Hall the beautiful and too-early-lost Miss B——t. But, as the learned Partridge pathetically observes, *non sum qualis eram*; and now, far from being permitted to escort the young and the gay through that intricate labyrinth, entitled the Entrance to the New Theatre Royal, I observe it is not without obvious reluctance that I am selected as a proper beau to the General Assembly. Nor indeed can I disguise to myself, that I owe even this humble distinction to the gravity of my physiognomy and habit, which the discerning fair consider as peculiarly calculated to overawe the beadles, by conveying the impression of a Ruling Elder. My apartments in Argyle's square, those very lodgings where my *petits soupers* were accounted such desirable parties, have now acquired a certain shabbiness of aspect, and seem to me contracted in their very dimensions. Nay, what is worse than all this, my annual income, though nominally the same, does not produce above half the comforts it used to compass. Amid these disconcerting circumstances, one would have thought that I might still have derived some benefit from a smattering of literature, which, having decorated my conversation in my better days, might be supposed still in some measure to recommend me to society. But I know not how it happens, that even in this respect matters seem strangely altered to my disadvantage. The time has been, when I could thrust my head over the threshold of Mr Creech's shop, and mingle in the first literary society which Scotland then afforded, and which (no disparagement to the present men of letters) has hardly been equalled since. I was personally known to Adam Smith, to Ferguson, to Robertson, to both the Humes, and to the lively Lord Kaimes. At a later period, my company was endured by the Man of Feeling, and other distinguished members of the Mirror Club. I have talked on prints and pictures with Johnie M'——n, have shaken my sides with the facetious Captain Grose over a bottle of old port, and one evening had the superlative distinction of hearing the tremendous Dr Johnson grumble forth wit and wisdom over a shrinking band of North British literati; so that I may say, with the magnanimous Slender, "I have seen Sackerson loose, and taken him by the chain." These, sir, are pretensions to a respectable place in literary society, and might entitle me to some deference from my juniors, who only know most of these great men in their writings or by tradition. Yet now I find my opinions in taste and criticism are almost as much out of fashion as my toupee and my small silver buckles. Every stripling, whom I remember an urchin at the High School, seems to have shot up into an author or reviewer, for the purpose of confuting my sentiments by dogmatical assertion, or overwhelming my arguments by professional declamation. This is so melancholy a truth, that I have learned to rank myself in conversation according to the rule of precedence settled at processions; and never attempt to declare my own opinion till I am sure all the younger members of the company have given their sentiments. But, notwithstanding every compromise which I have endeavoured to make with the spirit of the time, I feel myself daily becoming more and more a solitary and isolated being; and while I cook my little fire and husband my pint of port, I cannot but be sensible that these are the most important occupations of my waking day.

I was thus whiling away my evening, with a volume of Don Quixote open before me, when my attention was caught by the account which Altisidora gives of the amusement of the devils in the infernal regions. "I got to the gates of hell," says she, "where I found a round dozen of devils in their breeches and waistcoats, playing at tennis with flaming rackets; they wore flat bands, with scolloped Flanders lace, and ruffles of the same; four inches of their wrist bare to make their hands look the longer, in which they held rackets of fire. But what surprised me most was, that, instead of tennis-balls, they made use of books, that were every whit as light, and stuffed with wind and flocks, and such kind of trumpery. This was indeed most strange and wonderful; but what amazed me still more, I found that, contrary to the custom of gamesters, among whom the winning party is at least in good humour, and the losers only angry, these hellish tossers of books of both sides did nothing but fret, fume, stamp, curse, and swear most horribly, as if they had been all losers." "That's no wonder at all," quoth Sancho, "for your devils, whether they play or no, win or lose, they can never be contented." When I had proceeded thus far in my author, the light began to fail me. I finished my last glass of wine, and threw myself back in my easy chair to digest what I had read. The ludicrous description of Cervantes became insensibly jumbled with my own reveries on the critical taste and literary talents of my contemporaries, until I sunk into a slumber. The consequence was a dream, which I am tempted to send you as an introduction to some scraps of poetry, that, without it, would be hardly intelligible.

Methought, sir, I was (like many of my acquaintance) on the high-way to the place of perdition. The road, however, seemed neither broad, nor flowery, nor easy. In steepness, indeed, and in mephitic fragrance, the place of my peregrination was no bad emblem of the descent of Avernus; but, both in these and in other respects, it chiefly resembled a deserted *close* in the more ancient part of our good city. Having been accustomed to the difficulties of such footing in my younger days, I picked my way, under low-browed arches, down broken steps, and through miscellaneous filth, with a dexterity which no iron-heeled beau of the present day could have emulated. At length I came in sight of a very large building, with a court-yard in front, which I conceived to be the Tartarus towards which I had been descending; I saw, however, neither

Minos nor Æacus, neither Belial nor Beelzebub; and, to speak plainly, sir, the building itself seemed rather to resemble your own Pandemonium, than either that of Milton, the Erebus of Virgil, or the dread abode of Hela. Cerberus was chained near the door; but, as he had got rid of two of his heads, and concentrated their ferocity in that which he retained, he did not greatly differ in appearance from an English bull-dog. Had it not been for certain whips, scourges, gorgon-faces, and other fearful decorations of infernal architecture, which were disposed on its front by way of architrave, like the fetters and chains in front of Newgate,—had it not been, I say, for these and similar emblems of disappointment, contempt, and mortification, and for a reasonable quantity of flying dragons and hissing serpents that occasionally flew in or out of the garret windows, I should rather have taken the place for an immense printing-house than for the infernal regions. But what attracted my attention chiefly, was the apparition of a body of fiends, of different stature, size, and ages, who were playing at racket with new books, exactly in the manner described by Cervantes in the passage I have quoted, and whose game was carried on and contested with most astonishing perseverance in the court-yard I have mentioned. The devils, being, I presume, of real British extraction, were not clad in the Spanish costume of laced bands and scolloped sleeves, and they seemed to have transferred the pride which Altisidora's fiends took in the length of their wrists, as mine more demoniacally piqued themselves on the longitude and sharpness of their claws. Neither was the party equipped in the same livery, but exhibited all sorts of dresses, from the priest's to the soldier's, and from that of a modern fine gentleman to the rags of a *polisson*, whose cloven hoofs peeped through his second-hand boots. They all wore vizards, however, which, although not complete disguises, (for the by-standers pretended to distinguish them by their mode of playing, and I heard them whisper, "That's Astaroth," "that's Belphegor," and so forth,) yet served, like the wire masque of a fencer, to save their faces from the awkward accidents incident to so violent a sport. I did, indeed, remark one old gentleman, and, 'twas said, he had been a notable man in his day, who made a match to be played barefaced; but whether, like Entellus of old, he had become stiff and unwieldy, or whether he was ill-seconded by his few and awkward partners, so it was, that he was soon obliged to give up the game, which the rest continued to prosecute with the utmost vigour.

As few of the volumes, which it was their amusement to buffet, stood many bangs with the racket, the whole ground was whitened with their fragments; and it would have grieved your very heart, sir, to see the waste of good paper and pica. The incessant demand of the players for new materials was as constantly supplied by a set of little ragged urchins, no-wise differing from printers' devils, except that each had at his back a small pair of bat's wings, which, I suppose, were only for shew, as I did not observe the imps make any use of them. The books, which they brought in quantities from the interior of the building, they tossed one by one into the air, and it seemed their object (but which they rarely attained,) to throw them out of the reach of the gamesters' rackets, and, if possible, over the low boundaries of the court-yard. On the other side of these limits waited an immense and miscellaneous concourse of spectators, whose interest seemed to be excited by the fate of each volume. The general appearance of the game resembled tennis, or rather battledore and shuttle-cock; but I was unable to trace the various and apparently complicated principles acted upon by those engaged in it. This I observed in general, that when, by its natural lightness and elasticity, or by the dexterity of the *diablotins* by whom it was committed to the air, or by the stroke of some friendly racket, or, in fine, by a combination of these causes, a volume was so fortunate as to clear the barrier, it was caught up like a relique by the spectators on the outside. You have seen, sir, boys at a review chace each other for the fragments of smoking cartridges, which may give you some idea of the enthusiastic regard with which these fortunate books were received by this admiring multitude. On the contrary, when any one was struck to the ground, or shattered to pieces within the inclosure, its fall was solemnized by whooping and hisses and groans from the good company. So far I could understand the game well enough, and could easily comprehend further, that the imps by whom each book was thrown into the air, had deep bets in dependence upon its being struck across the line. But it was not so easy to comprehend the motives of the different players. Sometimes you beheld them anxious to strike a volume among the spectators, sometimes equally industrious to intercept its flight, and dash it to the ground. Often you saw them divide into different parties, the one attempting to keep up a favourite book, the other to bring it down. These partialities occasionally gave rise to very diverting bye-games. I sometimes saw a lubbard fiend, in attempting to give an impulse to a ponderous volume, strike it right up into the air, when, to the infinite delight and laughter of the beholders, it descended with added momentum upon his own noddle, and put him out of combat for some time. I also observed the little bat-winged gentry occasionally mix among the racqueteers, and endeavour to bias their game by bribing them to play booty. Their offers were sometimes accepted with silent shame, sometimes rejected with open contempt; but I observed in general, that those whom these bustling but subordinate imps were able to influence, were the worst players, and most frequently exposed to the ridiculous accidents which excited the contempt of the spectators. Indeed, the gamesters were incalculably different in strength, activity, and dexterity; and one of superior address was very often able, by a well-timed back-stroke of his racket, to send in, or to bring down, a book, which all his comrades had combined to destroy or to save. Such a game, it may be easily believed, was not played by such a description of beings without infinite noise, clamour, and quarrel. Sometimes a book would be bandied between two of them without any further regard for the volume than as they could strike it against each other's face, and very often one party seemed determined to buffet a work to shivers, merely because another set had endeavoured to further it on its journey over the lists. After all, a great deal seemed to depend on the degree of *phlogiston* which each manufacturer endeavoured to throw into his volume, and which, if successfully infused, afforded an elasticity capable of resisting the downward impulse of the most unfavourable racket. In some few cases, the mob without made a scramble for a favourite, broke in, deranged the play, overset the racqueteers, and carried off in triumph, works which apparently would never have reached them according to the usual practice of the game. These cases, however, were uncommon; and when, through a violent and unfair blow, some tome, which had been waited for with anxiety without the barrier, was beat down and trampled on by the players, its fall only occasioned slight murmurs among the respectable part of the expectants, without any desperate attempt to rescue it. A single friend or two sometimes essayed to collect the fragments of a volume, and to raise an outcry against the usage which it had sustained; but, unless supported by the general voice of the exterior mass, they were usually jostled down by the players, or silenced by a smart knock with a racket. The fate of a volume, also, *cæteris paribus*, depended in some degree on its size. Your light *twelve-mo*, sir, (to use your own barbarous dialect) flew further with a favourable impulse, and afforded a less mark to the assailant, than the larger and more ponderous quarto. But neither was this rule without exception. Some large volumes spread their wings like wild swans, and went off triumphant, notwithstanding all the buffets of opposition; and, on the other hand, you might see a whole covey of crown octavos, and duodecimos, and such small deer, drop as fast as a flight of plovers who have received a shower of hail-shot while upon the wheel. In short, the game depended on an endless complication of circumstances and principles; and although I could easily detect many of them when operating singly, they were yet so liable to be balanced and counterbalanced, that I would sooner have betted on throwing doublets thrice running at backgammon than upon the successful escape of any single volume from the rackets, and its favourable transmission to the other side of the court-yard. But, after I had long watched this extraordinary scene, I at length detected a circumstance which altogether confounded the few calculations which its uncertainty had previously permitted me to form.

I observed that there mingled among those engaged in the game, as well as among the gazing crowd, a man in the extremity of old age. His motions were as slow as the hour-hand of a watch, yet he seemed to be omnipresent; for, wherever I went, I saw him or the traces of his footsteps. Wherever I turned my eyes, whether upon the players, or upon the populace who watched their motions, I beheld him; and though I could with infinite difficulty find out his occupation while gazing upon him, yet, by watching him from time to time, I discovered that his influence was as powerful as its operations were slow and invisible. To this personage, whom I heard them call *Tempus*, various appeals were made on all hands. The patrons of the wrecked volumes claimed his protection almost unanimously; the defeated players themselves, though more coldly, desired him to do justice between them and their more successful opponents, or to make register of the undue violence by which spectators in some cases rescued their lawful prey. The old gentleman, to do him right, was as impartial as the justices of peace in a small debt court, when none has a tenant at the bar, and as inexorable as the same bench when dinner-time draws near. He continued his tardy but incessant manœuvres, now crawling among the feet of the gamesters to collect and piece together some of those volumes which had suffered the extremity of their fury, and now gliding unseen and unnoticed among the spectators, to wile out of their hands certain works which they had received with the loudest jubilee; and he succeeded in both cases, as nurses do in securing the play-things of children, which they have either broken in a pet, or admired to satiety. The use which he made of his power and his perseverance, was very different in these different cases. When he had slyly possessed himself of some of these works which had been most highly applauded, I detected him stealing towards a neighbouring ditch (the Lethé of the region) into which he discharged his burthen, without the least regret on the part of those from whom he had abstracted it. On the other hand, in his slow and impercept-ible manner, he would every now and then unfold to some of the more grave and respectable among the by-standers, fragments and favourite passages out of books he had rescued from among the feet of the racket-players, and, by the impression these made, he gradually paved the way for a general and brilliant reception of an entire volume. And I must observe of the books thus brought into notice, that they were said to be rarely liable to a second declension in public favour, but, with a few worthies, who, like them, had stood the test of *Time*, were, I was informed, deposited in an hon-ourable and distinguished place in his library, for the admiration and instruction of future ages.

The general feeling of surprise and consternation, with which I had hitherto regarded this extraordinary scene, began soon to give way to curiosity and to the desire of making more minute observa-tions. I ventured to draw as near as I durst to the old father I have described, who was then employed in collecting and piecing a huge quarto, which had received an uncommonly severe buffet from a racket, and on the front of which I could spell the word MADOC. "Good father," said I, as respectfully as I could, "do you account that volume a great treasure?" "Since I saved," answered he, "a poem in the same measure, the work of an old blind man, out of the hands of some gay courtiers, I have hardly made a more valuable acquisition." "And what then do you purpose to do with it?" pursued I, emboldened by his affability.—"Reserve it under my mantle, as I did the former, for an age worthy of it."—"Good Tempus," resumed I, "if I do not entirely mistake your person, I have some reason to complain of hard measure from you. Is it not you that have thinned my hair, wrinkled my forehead, diminished my apart-ments, lessened my income, rendered my opinions antiquated, and my company undesirable; yet all this will I forgive you on one slight condition. You cannot have forgot a small miscellany, pub-lished about twenty years ago, which contained some copies of verses subscribed Amyntor?"—The old personage protested his total want of recollection.—"You will soon remember them," rejoined I: "suffer me but to repeat the verses to Lydia, when a fly settled on the tip of her ear."—"I have not time," answered the obdurate old brute, although he was Time itself—"Yet promise me," cried I, endeavouring to detain him, "that you will look back among your stores for this little volume, and give it that interest in the eyes of posterity, which was refused to it by contemporary stu-pidity and malevolence." "My son," replied he, gliding from my grasp as he spoke, "you ask of me impossibilities. Yon ditch, to which is consigned all the refuse of this Pandemonium, has most assuredly received the volume in which you are so much interested. Yet do not be altogether disconcerted. A set of honest painstaking persons have erected gratings upon the common-sewer of oblivion, from one interval to another, for the precise purpose of gathering the scraps of printed paper thrown into it, without being deterred by the mean and nameless purposes which they have served. No lame beggar rakes the kennel for stub-nails with half the assiduity that these gentlemen fish among all sorts of trash for the names and offal of forgotten rhymers; for Love esteems no office mean, or, as the same old friend has it,

> Entire affection scorneth nicer hands.

If thou hast any luck," continued he, looking at me with infinite contempt, "thy fragments may be there fished up by some future antiquary, and thy name rendered as famous as the respectable sounds of Herricke or Derricke, or others that are only now remembered because till now they have been most deservedly forgot." With that, his usual constant though imperceptible motion conveyed him out of my hold and out of my sight.

I endeavoured to divert the mortification which this colloquy had excited, by turning my attention once more to the game of racket, which was continued with more fury than ever. These hellish tossers of books, as Cervantes calls them, curst, swore, threatened, roared, and foamed, as if the universe depended on the issue of their gambols. Verse and prose, sermons and stage-plays, politics and novels, flew to pieces without distinction; nor (what you, sir, would probably have felt afflicting) was more respect paid to the types of Bensley or Bulmer, or to your own, than to those employed on half-penny ballads and dying speeches.

In observing the manner and address of the different players, my attention was at length powerfully fixed by the dexterity of one individual dæmon. He was, in stature and complexion, the identical "wee reekit devil" of my poor friend Robert Burns; but, being ambidexter, and possessed of uncommon activity and accuracy of aim, he far surpassed all his competitors. He often shewed his dexterity by striking the same volume alternately in different directions, leaving the gaping crowd totally at a loss whether it was his intention to strike it over the lists, or to shiver it to atoms; and he had an unlucky back-handed blow by which he could sometimes intercept it, while all hands were in the air to receive it with acclamation. Sometimes he seemed to repent him of his severity, and, in one or two instances, endeavoured to give a new impulse to works which had suffered by it. But this seemed to defy even his address; and indeed I observed of the players, that they were not only, as might be expected from the philosophic observations of Sancho upon their diabolical nature, much more prone to assault a book than to favour it; but even when they made the latter attempt, they went about it awkwardly, and were very rarely successful. But, in shattering calf-skin and letter-press, the dexterity of this champion was unequalled, which produced him much ill-will from his less successful brethren; till at length, like Ismael, his hand was against every one, and every one's against him. A dæmon, in particular, who had exchanged a jockey whip for the racket, seemed to bear him particular spleen, and I generally observed them and their followers attempt to strike the books at each other's noses. The latter gamester, although he played some capital strokes, and was indisputably the second-best in the field, could not at first be termed equal to the other in agility, although, as he grew warmer, he evidently improved in his game, and began to divide the opinion of the spectators, chiefly aided by some unknown individuals closely masked, but who, like the disguised heroes of romance, were easily distinguished from the vulgar. I observed that the rivalry between these two leaders was attended with some acts of violence, especially after either of them had taken a cordial out of a small dram-bottle, to which they occasionally applied. These flasks, I was informed by a by-stander, contained an alcohol called *Spirit of Party*; infamous, like all ardent spirits, for weakening the judgement, dazzling the eyes, and inflaming the imagination, but rectified in a different manner according to the taste of those who used it. "It is a pity that they are so much addicted to the use of it," added he; "but, were you to ask them its nature, the one would pretend that his was pure *Pit-water*, and the other protest that he himself only used a little genuine and salubrious *Hollands*; although his enemies pretend that he, or at least that some of his followers, preferred a French liqueur double distilled, *a la Burdett*."

My curiosity now became ungovernable; and, as the lively genius aforesaid was standing near the court-yard wall leaning on his racket, after having played, as we used to say at the High-school, a very hard *end*, I could not help addressing him for some explanation. "I see, sir," said I very respectfully, "upon some of these loose leaves with which your dexterity and that of your companions has been sheeting this area, certain works to which our upper world is no stranger. But, what greatly surprises me is, to behold fragments of some books bearing the names of well-known authors, who, I am pretty confident, have not yet given such productions to the public." "My friend," replied he, in a very peculiar tone of voice, which I have certainly heard somewhere about Edinburgh, "you must know that what you now behold is an emblematical representation as well of what is to happen, as of what has befallen in the earthly walks of literature and criticism. You remember, I doubt not, the occupation of Anchises in the shades?" "I rather think I do not," replied I. The goblin proceeded:

"Inclusas animas superumque ad lumen ituras
Lustrabat——

"In something the same manner our sport announces the reception of the future labours of the press, the fates and fortunes which books yet unborn are to experience both from the critics and from the world in general. In short, as critics play the devil upon earth, so we devils play the critics in hell. I myself am the image, or emblem, or *Eidolon*, of a celebrated"——Here his discourse was interrupted by a quarrel among the gamesters. A racqueteer, whom I had observed playing my obliging informer's back-game, and who, though in a parson's band and gown, had distinguished himself by uncommon frisks and gambols, was complaining loudly that one opponent had given him a black eye with his racket, and that another, in the trencher-cap of an Oxford student, had torn and dirtied his band. My friend went with all speed to his assistance, leaving me to regret the interruption of his communications. Indeed the urbanity of this goblin seemed so great a contrast to his diabolical character, and to the inveteracy with which he pursued the game, that I could not help concluding in his favour, like the liberal-minded Sancho Panza on a similar occasion, that there may be some good sort of people even in hell itself.

I became aware, from his kind explanation, of the opportunity afforded me of collecting some literary intelligence from so authentic a source. I hastened to gather some of the scattered leaves which bore the mark or signature of celebrated living names; and while I glanced them over, I exulted in the superiority which my collection would afford me in the conversaziones of the upper world. In the midst of this task my ears were assailed with a discordant sound, which imagination, with its usual readiness to adapt external impressions on the senses to the subject of a dream, represented as proceeding from a battle royal of the fiends. But, as the din predominated over my slumber, I plainly distinguished the voice of my beldame landlady screaming to her noisy brats in the tone of a wild-cat to its litter, that their caterwauling would disturb the "old gentleman's afternoon nap."

I was no sooner thoroughly awakened by her ill-judged precautions in favour of my repose, than I took pen and ink, and endeavoured to secure the contents of the fragments which yet floated in my imagination. I am sensible I have succeeded but indifferently; nor can I pretend to have made by any means an exact transcript of what the visionary fragments presented. In this respect I am in exactly the same predicament with the great Corelli, who, you know, always insisted that his celebrated piece of music, called from the circumstances, the Devil's Concerto, was very inferior to that which his satanic majesty had deigned in a vision to perform upon his violin. As, therefore, I am conscious that I have done great injustice to the verses from the imperfections of my memory, and as I have, after all, only the devil's authority for their authenticity had I recollected them more accurately, I will not do any respectable author the discredit to prefix his name to them, trusting that, if my vision really issued from the Gate of Horn, these fragments will retain traces of resemblance sufficient to authorize their being appropriated to their respective authors. I retain some others in my budget, which it is not impossible I may offer to you next year.

Meanwhile, I am, sir, (for any nonsensical name will suit as well as my own) your humble servant,

CALEB QUOTEM.*
Argyle's Square, April 1.

Fragment First

THE POACHER

Welcome, grave stranger, to our green retreats,
Where health with exercise and freedom meets!
Thrice welcome, sage, whose philosophic plan
By Nature's limits metes the rights of man;
Generous as he, who now for freedom bawls,
Now gives full value for true Indian shawls;
O'er court and custom-house, his shoe who flings,
Now bilks excisemen, and now bullies kings!
Like his, I ween, thy comprehensive mind
Holds laws as mouse-traps baited for mankind;
Thine eye, applausive, each sly vermin sees,
That baulks the snare, yet battens on the cheese;
Thine ear has heard, with scorn instead of awe,

* The Editor, in the plenitude of his conviction that honest *Caleb* is entitled to all the honours of the Gate of Horn, doth fervently entreat the continuance of his visionary lucubrations.

Our buckskin'd justices expound the law,
Wire-draw the acts that fix for wires the pain,
And for the netted partridge noose the swain;
And thy vindictive arm would fain have broke
The last light fetter of the feudal yoke,
To give the denizens of wood and wild,
Nature's free race, to each her free-born child.
Hence hast thou marked, with grief, fair London's race
Mock'd with the boon of one poor Easter chace,
And long'd to send them forth as free as when
Pour'd o'er Chantilly the Parisian train,
When musquet, pistol, blunderbuss, combined,
And scarce the field-pieces were left behind!
A squadron's charge each leveret's heart dismayed,
On every covey fired a bold brigade—
La Douce Humanité approved the sport,
For great the alarm indeed, yet small the hurt.
Shouts patriotic solemnized the day,
And Seine re-echoed *vive la liberté!*
But mad *Citoyen*, meek *Monsieur* again,
With some few added links resumes his chain;
Then, since such scenes to France no more are known,
Come, view with me a hero of thine own!
One, whose free actions vindicate the cause
Of sylvan liberty o'er feudal laws.
    Seek we yon glades, where the proud oak o'ertops
Wide waving seas of birch and hazel copse,
Leaving between deserted isles of land,
Where stunted heath is patch'd with ruddy sand;
And lonely on the waste the yew is seen,
Or straggling hollies spread a brighter green.
Here, little-worn, and winding dark and steep,
Our scarce mark'd path descends yon dingle deep:
Follow—but heedful, cautious of a trip,
In earthly mire philosophy may slip.
Step slow and wary o'er that swampy stream,
Till, guided by the charcoal's smothering steam,
We reach the frail yet barricaded door
Of hovel formed for poorest of the poor;
No hearth the fire, no vent the smoke receives,
The walls are wattles, and the covering leaves;
For, if such hut, our forest statutes say,
Rise in the progress of one night and day;

Though placed where still the Conqueror's hests o'erawe,
And his son's stirrup shines the badge of law;
The builder claims the unenviable boon,
To tenant dwelling, framed as slight and soon
As wigwam wild, that shrouds the native frore
On the bleak coast of frost-barr'd Labrador.*
    Approach, and through the unlatticed window peep—
Nay, shrink not back, the inmate is asleep;
Sunk mid yon sordid blankets, till the sun
Stoop to the west, the plunderer's toils are done.
Loaded and primed, and prompt for desperate hand,
Rifle and fowling-piece beside him stand,
While round the hut are in disorder laid
The tools and booty of his lawless trade;
For force or fraud, resistance or escape,
The crow, the saw, the bludgeon, and the crape.
His pilfered powder in yon nook he hoards,
And the filch'd lead the church's roof affords—
(Hence shall the rector's congregation fret,
That, while his sermon's dry, his walls are wet.)
The fish-spear barb'd, the sweeping net are there,
Doe-hides, and pheasant-plumes, and skins of hare,
Cordage for toils, and wiring for the snare;
Barter'd for game from chace or warren won,
Yon cask holds moonlight,† run when moon was none;
And late snatch'd spoils lie stow'd in hutch apart,
To wait the associate higgler's evening cart.
    Look on his pallet foul, and mark his rest:
What scenes perturb'd are acting in his breast!
His sable brow is wet and wrung with pain,
And his dilated nostril toils in vain;
For short and scant the breath each effort draws,
And 'twixt each effort Nature claims a pause.
Beyond the loose and sable neck-cloth stretch'd,
His sinewy throat seems by convulsions twitch'd,
While the tongue faulters, as to utterance loth,
Sounds of dire import—watch-word, threat, and oath.
Though stupified by toil, and drugg'd with gin,

---

* Such is the law in the New Forest, Hampshire, tending greatly to increase the various settlements of thieves, smugglers, and deer-stealers, who infest it. In the forest courts the presiding judge wears as a badge of office an antique stirrup, said to have been that of William Rufus. See Mr William Rose's spirited poem, entitled "The Red King."
  † A cant name for smuggled spirits.

The body sleep, the restless guest within
Now plies on wood and wold his lawless trade,
Now in the fangs of justice wakes dismayed.—
"Was that wild start of terror and despair,
Those bursting eye-balls, and that wilder'd air,
Signs of compunction for a murdered hare?
Do the locks bristle and the eye-brows arch,
For grouse or partridge massacred in March?"—
    No, scoffer, no! Attend, and mark with awe,
There is no wicket in the gate of law!
He, that would e'er so slightly set ajar
That awful portal, must undo each bar;
Tempting occasion, habit, passion, pride,
Will join to storm the breach, and force the barrier wide.
    That ruffian, whom true men avoid and dread,
Whom bruisers, poachers, smugglers, call Black Ned,
Was Edward Mansell once;—the lightest heart,
That ever played on holiday his part!
The leader he in every Christmas game,
The harvest feast grew blither when he came,
And liveliest on the chords the bow did glance,
When Edward named the tune and led the dance.
Kind was his heart, his passions quick and strong,
Hearty his laugh, and jovial was his song;
And if he loved a gun, his father swore,
" 'Twas but a trick of youth would soon be o'er,
Himself had had the same, some thirty years before."
    But he, whose humours spurn law's awful yoke,
Must herd with those by whom law's bonds are broke.
The common dread of justice soon allies
The clown, who robs the warren or excise,
With sterner felons trained to act more dread,
Even with the wretch by whom his fellow bled.
Then,—as in plagues the foul contagions pass,
Leavening and festering the corrupted mass,—
Guilt leagues with guilt, while mutual motives draw,
Their hope impunity, their fear the law;
Their foes, their friends, their rendezvous the same,
Till the revenue baulked, or pilfered game,
Flesh the young culprit, and example leads
To darker villainy, and direr deeds.
    Wild howled the wind the forest glades along,
And oft the owl renewed her dismal song;

Around the spot where erst he felt the wound,
Red William's spectre walked his midnight round.
When o'er the swamp he cast his blighting look,
From the green marshes of the stagnant brook
The bittern's sullen shout the sedges shook!
The wading moon, with storm-presaging gleam,
Now gave and now withheld her doubtful beam;
The old Oak stooped his arms, then flung them high,   ⸌
Bellowing and groaning to the troubled sky—
'Twas then, that, couched amid the brushwood sere,
In Malwood-walk young Mansell watched the deer:
The fattest buck received his deadly shot—
The watchful keeper heard, and sought the spot.
Stout were their hearts, and stubborn was their strife,
O'erpowered at length the outlaw drew his knife!
Next morn a corpse was found upon the fell—
The rest his waking agony may tell !

𝔉ragment 𝔖econd

Oh say not, my love, with that mortified air,
        That your spring-time of pleasure is flown,
Nor bid me to maids that are younger repair,
        For those raptures that still are thine own!

Though April his temples may wreathe with the vine,
        Its tendrils in infancy curled,
'Tis the ardours of August mature us the wine
        Whose life-blood enlivens the world.

Though thy form, that was fashioned as light as a fay's,
        Has assumed a proportion more round,
And thy glance that was bright as a falcon's at gaze,
        Looks soberly now on the ground,—

Enough, after absence to meet me again,
        Thy steps still with ecstacy move;
Enough, that those dear sober glances retain
        For me the kind language of love!

                *   *   *   *   *

[The rest was illegible, the fragment being torn across by a racket stroke.]

Fragment Third

THE VISION OF TRIERMAIN

I

Where is the maiden of mortal strain,
That may match with the Baron of Triermain?
She must be lovely and constant and kind,
Holy and pure and humble of mind,
Blithe of cheer and gentle of mood,
Courteous and generous and noble of blood—
Lovely as the sun's first ray
When it breaks the clouds of an April day;
Constant and true as the widow'd dove,
Kind as a minstrel that sings of love;
Pure as the fountain in rocky cave,
Where never sun-beam kiss'd the wave;
Humble as maiden that loves in vain,
Holy as hermit's vesper strain;
Gentle as breeze that but whispers and dies,
Yet blithe as the light leaves that dance in its sighs;
Courteous as monarch the morn he is crown'd,
Generous as spring-dews that bless the glad ground;
Noble her blood as the currents that met
In the veins of the noblest Plantagenet.
Such must her form be, her mood and her strain,
That shall match with Sir Roland of Triermain.

II

Sir Roland de Vaux he hath laid him to sleep,
His blood it was fevered, his breathing was deep.
He had been pricking against the Scot,
The foray was long and the skirmish hot;
His dinted helm and his buckler's plight
Bore token of a stubborn fight.
    All in the castle must hold them still,
Harpers must lull him to his rest,
With the slow soft tunes he loves the best,
Till sleep sink down upon his breast,
    Like the dew on a summer-hill.

III

It was the dawn of an autumn day;

The sun was struggling with frost-fog grey,
That like a silvery crape was spread
Round Glaramara's distant head,
And dimly gleam'd each painted pane
Of the lordly halls of Triermain,
    When that baron bold awoke.
Starting he woke, and loudly did call,
Rousing his menials in bower and hall,
    While hastily he spoke.

IV

"Hearken, my minstrels! Which of you all
Touch'd his harp with that dying fall,
    So sweet, so soft, so faint,
It seem'd an angel's whisper'd call
    To an expiring saint?
And hearken, my merrymen! Whither or where
    Has she gone, that maid with her heav'nly brow,
With her look so sweet and her eyes so fair,
And her graceful step and her angel air,
And the eagle-plume on her dark-brown hair,
    That pass'd from my bower e'en now?"—

V

Answer'd him Richard de Brettville; he
Was chief of the baron's minstrelsy,—
"Silent, noble chieftain, we
    Have sate since midnight close,
When such lulling sounds as the brooklet sings,
Murmur'd from our melting strings,
    And hush'd you to repose.
Had a harp-note sounded here,
It had caught my watchful ear,
    Although it fell as faint and shy
    As bashful maiden's half-form'd sigh,
When she thinks her lover near."—
Answer'd Philip of Fasthwaite tall,
He kept guard in the outer-hall,—
"Since at eve our watch took post,
Not a foot has thy portal cross'd;
    Else had I heard the steps, though low
And light they fell as when earth receives,

In morn of frost, the wither'd leaves,
    That drop when no winds blow."—

VI

"Then come thou hither, Henry, my page,
Whom I saved from the sack of Hermitage,
When that dark castle, tower, and spire,
Rose to the skies a pile of fire,
    And redden'd all the Nine-stane Hill,
And the shrieks of death, that wildly broke
Through devouring flame and smothering smoke,
    Made the warrior's heart-blood chill!
The trustiest thou of all my train,
My fleetest courser thou must rein,
    And ride to Lyulph's tow'r,
And from the baron of Triermain
    Greet well that sage of pow'r.
He is sprung from druid sires,
And British bards that tuned their lyres
To Arthur's and Pendragon's praise,
And his who sleeps at Dunmailraise.
Gifted like his gifted race,
He the characters can trace,
Graven deep in elder time
Upon Helvellyn's cliffs sublime;
Sign and sigil well doth he know,
And can bode of weal and woe,
Of kingdoms' fall, and fate of wars,
From mystic dreams and course of stars.
He shall tell me if nether earth
To that enchanting shape gave birth,
Or if 'twas but an airy thing,
Such as fantastic slumbers bring,
Fram'd from the rain-bow's varying dyes,
Or fading tints of western skies.
For, by the blessed rood I swear,
If that fair form breathes vital air,
No other maiden by my side
Shall ever rest De Vaux's bride!"—

VII

The faithful page he mounts his steed,
And soon he cross'd green Irthing's mead,

Dash'd o'er Kirkoswald's verdant plain,
And Eden barr'd his course in vain.
He pass'd red Penrith's Table Round,
For feats of chivalry renown'd,
Left Mayburgh's mound and stones of pow'r,
By druids raised in magic hour,
And traced the Eamont's winding way,
Till Ulfo's lake beneath him lay.—

VIII

Onwards he rode, the path-way still
Winding betwixt the lake and hill;
Till on the fragment of a rock,
Struck from its base by lightning shock,
    He saw the druid sage:
The silver moss and lichen twined,
With the red deer-hair check'd and lined,
    A cushion fit for age;
And o'er him shook the aspin tree,
A restless rustling canopy.
    Then sprung young Henry from his selle,
      To greet the prophet grave,—
    But, ere his errand he could tell,
      The sage his answer gave.

*   *   *   *   *

THE SHORTER FICTION

From
THE SALE-ROOM

CHRISTOPHER CORDUROY

Ἑως, οτφαιει θελει ειναι, ην.

THE MOTTO which we have put at the head of our paper, forms
the conclusion of a beautiful fragment of Menander, in which that
elegant comedian held up to the ridicule of his countrymen one of
those strange and fantastical systems in his time so prevalent among
the philosophers of Greece. According to this theory, the materials
of which the universe is composed had lain from all eternity in an
inert state of dullness and chaos, without form and void, not, however, without certain feelings of dissatisfaction on account of the
long continuance of this their uninteresting condition, and certain
vague aspirings after shape and activity. These feelings, it seems,
increased every moment in fervency, till at length the suffering
became intolerable, and the wish so strong, that it accomplished its
own end. The rude materials became what they had wished to be,
and the result—the αυτοποιητον παν—is before us.

Although this theory of creation has now, like its author, become
entirely forgotten, it is founded upon the observation of a principle
in human nature, which is not likely so soon to go out of fashion.
So much of the misery which flesh is heir to, depends upon that
innate spirit of laziness which makes us prefer remaining as we
are, to working our way out of the evils with which we are surrounded; so many of the successful adventurers, in every mode of
life, have owed their fortunes to nothing more than a robust constitution and an elasticity of animal spirits sufficient to make them
easily overcome petty difficulties, and forget petty mischances; in

short, to keep alive and stedfast within them the strong wish of success, that it is no wonder the fanciful speculators of Greece should have carried the matter a little farther, and ventured to account for the great phenomena of nature, on a principle whose operation in things of less importance was perpetually before their eyes. The oracles of Delphi and Dodona, so long as their authority was believed in, worked not unfrequently their own accomplishment; and were consulted by designing princes, who, possessing themselves the best possible reasons for incredulity, were willing to make use of the confidence, and resolution, and earnestness of desire, which they well knew a favourable response could not fail to create in the instruments of their ambition. And, in like manner, the fond presages and prophetic dreams of a doting nurse, have, without doubt, more than once pointed the way to the after greatness of her bantling.

But even when the strong desire *to be* does not manifest its power by any external change in the *mode of being*, the fancy of the wisher sometimes comes to his assistance, and supplies, with a lavish hand, the deficiencies in the realities of existence. There is an admirable history in the Arabian Nights of one Abon Hassan, who became somewhat in this way convinced that he was Caliph, and went through all the forms and duties of his office with great gravity, to the infinite amusement of the real Haroon al Rasheed and his court. Not even the teeth of Mesrour, the chief of the black eunuchs, could bite him back to a knowledge of his true condition; and when he awoke in his own bed, he began, to the great displeasure of his wife, to call about him for *Soul's Torment, Cluster-of-pearls, Morning-star,* and *Moon-face,* as if he had been the actual Lord of a thousand sultanas. Aristotle, in his book *De Mirabilibus Ausculta-tionis,* gives an account of another visionary of this sort, who was found one morning sitting by himself in the vast theatre of Agrigentum, enjoying the whole amusement of a dramatic exhibition, without feeling any want of either scenery, actors, music, or dialogue, applauding and hissing as the imaginary performance pleased or displeased him. Nay, we have read somewhere or other of a person, whose whole life was coloured by the strength of his imagination. He had carried his powers of self-deception to such a pitch of perfection that he considered himself as Lord of all the land within view of his house, paid high premiums for the insurance of merchandise which did not belong to him, and got drunk every night upon hornfulls of small-beer, in the belief, (like a *bonâ fide* Lord Peter,) that he was quaffing Chateau-Margout, or Champaigne. The tale which we have at first coined, after we have told it a hundred times, begins to appear true. The Quack becomes in the end a convert to himself, and swallows his own nostrums; witness the well-known story of a late celebrated High-German Doctor who went so far as to lose his nose out of an improper confidence in the authority of a forged letter in one of his own advertisements. Don Quixote has always appeared to us the most moderate of all caricatures. Cervantes himself, before he had finished writing it, seems to have become almost as mad as his hero. Dr Spurzheim, we have no doubt, is a believer in his own doctrines, and would never think of choosing a wife on any other ground than the shape of her skull.

These observations have been suggested to us by the following letter from a commercial town at no great distance. The strange species of insanity which it commemorates is by no means uncommon in the city, where the *novi homines* very frequently illustrate the vanity of human wishes, by making that the prime object of their ambition, which is in fact the only one of the external distinctions with which all their riches can never invest them.

TO THE CONDUCTOR OF THE SALE-ROOM

——————, January 26, 1817.

SIR,

I hope you will be so good as to insert this letter in the first number of your paper, as I have no expectations, except through your means, of seeing my poor uncle's judgment restored to him, and an end put to the ridicule which his late strange behaviour has drawn upon him and our whole family. My uncle, whose unhappy condition is the cause or my troubling you at present, is the elder brother of my late father. My grandfather was a very respectable tailor in this town, and gave his sons a good education, by means of which they both met with considerable success in life. My uncle, in particular, arrived some years ago at the dignity of the magistracy, and has bought several substantial tenements in this neighbourhood, which have, in the main, turned out very good purchases. But all his education, as you will shortly perceive, has not been sufficient to hinder him from falling into one of the strangest delusions that ever entered into a man's head. It is now about six years since I left this country, being obliged to spend some time in the West Indies in the way of my business, so that it is only of late, that, on my return home, I have been fully informed as to my uncle's real case. From all that I can hear, very shortly after I left Scotland, he had, somehow or other, fallen in with a book called Nisbett's Heraldry;

and the first strange symptom that appeared, was the wonderful affection he soon began to entertain for this author, entirely giving up all other reading, and sitting in his back-shop studying coats of arms and crests, when he should have been attending to customers or balancing his accounts. This was remarked by a neighbour of his, a hatter, from the Highlands, who, it seems, is the proper chief of his clan, although his great-grandfather was cheated out of his birthright by the management of his great-great-grandfather's second wife, who managed to get the estate settled on her own children, the marriage of his own great-great-grandmother, who was cook in the family, having been kept secret, and all the witnesses being dead. My uncle was at first contented with being a patient listener to all the puffing stories of this Highlander, whom he considered as one of the most nobly-descended men in the world. But by degrees he began to lay claims to gentility for himself; and being, by the hatter's interest, admitted into a club of respectable trades-men, who call themselves the Genealogical Society, and spend most of their evenings in adjusting questions of pedigree among them-selves, he there got acquainted with a celebrated antiquarian, by name Moses M'Crae, a glover, who suggested to him an idea which has given a new colour to his existence ever since. Our family name of Corduroy had, as I always supposed, been bestowed on some of our forefathers on account of their being instrumental in introducing the use of that particular kind of stuff in the neighbour-hood; but Mr M'Crae hinted that the name ought, in his opinion, to be written *Cœur du roy*, and that, in all probability, my uncle was the male representative of some ancient branch of the house of Douglas, as Cœur-du-roy means a king's heart, and the Douglasses wear a heart with a king's crown on it in their arms, instancing the clan of the Macgregors, who had all been obliged to change their names for the best part of a century. Mr M'Crae, at the same time, advised my uncle to employ an acquaintance of his, in the Register-office in Edinburgh, to search all the old records for proofs of this connection between the Corduroys and the Douglasses. I have never heard that his fees to the Register-office produced any thing very satisfactory, but by dint of constant talking about this matter over his punch with the hatter and Mr M'Crae, what at first appeared barely possible, began every evening to gain in his eyes a new degree of probability, till at length the delusion has gone to such an extrem-ity, that he now no more doubts of it than he does of his own existence. The first hint that I had of all this was his giving up wafers, and the old signet stamp with the initials of Corduroy & Co., and beginning to seal his letters with a crowned heart, and the

motto, "*tandem triumphans*," on the top of it, which the first two or
three times I took little notice of, thinking he had borrowed some
gentleman's seal who was accidentally in the shop to have his measure taken; but at last I understood what had occurred from another
quarter. There were several expressions in his letters about the
same time which I could not well understand. In one letter he told
me, that "whatever the world might say, he had no doubt he should
live to see the day when nobody would venture to question the
respectability of his house." I was afraid something had happened,
but meeting with a friend newly from Scotland, he assured me he
had never heard the firm called in question. He lost his only son
shortly after, and wrote me,—"I now look to my nephew to *carry on
our line.*" Now I had been bred to another trade, and knew nothing
about being a tailor, so I thought the good man had his intellects
affected by his affliction. But I now understand, that, by *his house*,
he meant the race of the Corduroys, and that by my *carrying on the
line*, he only expresses his wish that I may not be the last of them.

This phrenzy, for I can give it no other name, grew every day
more alarming. He began to brag to all his acquaintance what a
great family he was come of, and could scarcely take a customer's
measure for a pair of breeches without entertaining him with some
old-fashioned stories about the good Sir James Douglas, and Archibald Bell-the-Cat. He looked down on all his neighbours, although
they were come of as respectable burgesses of the town as himself.
He left the Antiburghers too, where his father and he had always
been elders, and took a pew in the Episcopal chapel, because he
had a notion Episcopacy was the genteeler religion. In short, he
became as proud as a peacock; and when he was made a baillie,
one would have thought, as his friends tell me, he scarcely knew
which hip to sit on. He had his arms taken out regularly in the
heralds' book, which cost him the matter of L. 10, and he had
them painted and glazed, and hung up in his back-shop and his
parlour. He made his daughters cut out fire-screens in the shape
of hearts, and made his wife a present of a tea-chest which
resembles a heart below, and has a crown for the lid. His common
reading has long been either in Mr Nisbett, before-mentioned, or
in some old papers from the session-clerk's office, which he has
great difficulty in decyphering; but if he can only meet with the
death or marriage of a Corduroy or a Douglas, that is quite enough
to make up for weeks of trouble. He once gave a dinner, I am
informed, to a large party of friends, on hearing it mentioned by a
lawyer on a circuit that three Corduroys were hanged at Jedburgh
for *stouthrieff* and *sorning*, (which I believe means, after all, only

robbery and sturdy begging,) in the year 1500. He is always, in this way, making what he calls *family discoveries*, though I believe this of the three thieves is the greatest. He has got a large book like a ledger, bound in red leather, with brass clasps, where he has copied the first leaf of his father's bible, and any thing he has picked up about people of his name, and this he calls *his history*. He keeps this book, and a few old papers, such as his grandmother's marriage-lines, and the like, in an old trunk, which he has built into the wall, and this he calls *his charter-chest*. Before he took to these fancies, he had built a very snug cottage about two miles from the town; but he has, since that time, had all the windows taken out, and new ones put in, with panes of glass cut in the shape of diamonds as if it were a church, not forgetting paintings of red hearts and royal crowns, of which there are at least a dozen, including the sky-lights. His fire-places are also made with a pointed arch at the top; and his fenders have battlements on them like the top of a castle. His parlour is stuck full of pictures of old gentlemen in wigs and coats-of-mail, and young ladies very indecent about the bosom, whom he calls his ancestors; but his apprentice told me he had himself heard him bidding for some of them at an auction. When he shews his visitors the real portrait which he has of his father, he always remarks that he was a wonderfully modest man, and *never spoke of his family;* "but," adds he, "he had no taste for research."

The whole neighbourhood consider him as one out of his mind on this head, and call him Count Corduroy, by way of derision; and I am much afraid that, if I stay much longer among them, they will christen me the Young Count. What makes me write you at present, is more particularly this, that I hear him talking about getting his *lands*, as he calls them, (although he has not above twenty acres altogether, including Craig-Corduroy cottage) erected into a barony. I have also heard him hinting that supporters would not stand him above L. 100. If he goes on at this rate, I do not see how any body will employ him, as every one already says he has got a bee in his bonnet, and might easily be cognosced. But as my uncle takes in the Sale-Room, I am in hopes you may either insert this letter, or at least some remarks of your own, which may put an end to his delusion, which will be a great obligation on,

Sir,
Your most obedient servant,
CHRISTOPHER CORDUROY, Jun.

We have not inserted this letter without some little hesitation, as we cannot foresee much good that is likely to happen from the dissolution of a dream which can make the dreamer so happy without doing the rest of the world any harm. We are not quite sure, moreover, but the hero of this tale may be entitled to more respect than his nephew seems inclined to allow him. In truth, such a person as he is, were he only to cultivate his talents for self-deception, might easily attain to as great a pitch of excellence in that department as either Abon Hassan or Don Quixote could ever boast of. By a wise application of his powers, he might consider himself as quite independent of external things; and having all the sources of his happiness within himself, might present to the world an excellent specimen of the stoical wise man—the "εν εαυτω τελειος και καταφρονητης των εξω" of Antoninus. After all, our readers will be disposed to believe with us, that there was more wisdom in the observations of old John of Gaunt than Bolingbroke was willing to allow, when he asked him with such an air of confidence—

——Oh! who can hold a fire in his hand
By thinking on the frosty Caucasus?
Or cloy the hungry edge of appetite
By bare imagination of a feast?
Or wallow naked in December snow,
By thinking on fantastic summer's heat?

Q. E.

THE SHORTER FICTION

From

BLACKWOOD'S EDINBURGH MAGAZINE

ALARMING INCREASE OF DEPRAVITY
AMONG ANIMALS

Ætas parentum, pejor avis, tulit
Nos nequiores, mox daturos
Progeniem vitiosiorem.

THE HACKNEYED lines of the satirist which we have selected for
our motto, contain a truth which, however melancholy, is so generally admitted, that, aiming at some novelty in our communications to
the public, we would have disdained even to quote or allude to
them, had the human species alone been concerned; but, on the
contrary, would have left lamentations over the gradual deterioration
of mankind to those "slipper'd pantaloons" whom time has spared
to bear unwearied testimony to the virtues of former times and the
degeneracy of the present. Accordingly, our present anecdotes will
neither be found to refer to the Parliamentary Reports upon
Mendicity,—nor to appeal to the learned magistrate, Mr Colquhoun's Essay on the Police of the Metropolis, who classes his
offenders with as much regularity as a botanist his specimens,—nor
to invoke the genius of Mr Owen, to devise an impracticable remedy
for an incurable disease. These are all matters with which the public
ear has been crammed even to satiety; and it was only upon
discovering that the ulcer was extending itself more widely than
even our worst fears had anticipated, that we thought of calling the
attention of the public to some very novel phenomena, from which it
appears, that the moral deterioration so generally lamented has not
confined itself within the bounds of humanity, but is fast extending
its influence to the lower orders of creation.

It is no longer the vile biped man alone, whose crimes against society, and depredations on the property of others, furnish food (in the absence of sieges, battles, and other more specious and magnificent exercises of violence) for the diurnal penman, and the peruser of his lucubrations; but our very dogs and horses infringe the eighth commandment, and commit felony beyond the benefit of clergy. There are two melancholy instances of depravity in the newspapers of this month, which we meant to have transferred to our Chronicle of Remarkable Events, but thought them far too important to be passed over without a commentary.

"*Shadwell Office.*—A man named Sargent, constable of St George's in the East, made a complaint before the sitting Magistrates against a horse for stealing hay. The constable said, that the horse came regularly every night to the coach-stands in St George's, and ate his bellyful, and would then gallop away. He defied the whole of the parish officers to apprehend him; for, if they attempted to go near him while he was eating, he would up with his heels and kick at them, or run at them, and if they did not go out of the way he would bite them: he therefore thought it best to state the case to the Magistrates.

"One of the Magistrates. 'Well, Mr Constable, if you should be annoyed again by this body in the execution of your duty, you may apprehend him, if you can, and bring him before us to answer your complaints.'"

"*Hatton Garden.—A Canine Robber.*—Mrs Knight and another lady gave information of being robbed by a dog in the following singular manner: She stated, that as she and her sister were returning about six o'clock in the preceding evening from St Pancras Church towards Battle Bridge, a hairy dog, resembling a drover's or shepherd's dog, unaccompanied by any person, jumped suddenly up from the road side, and laying hold of the ridicule she had in her hand with his teeth, forcibly snatched it from her, and crossing off the road, made his escape. Her ridicule contained a pound note, a sovereign, eighteen shillings in silver, a silver thimble, a pair of silver spectacles, and several other articles. The constable stated, that a dog answering the same description attacked a poor woman on Saturday near the Veterinary College, and robbed her of a bundle, containing two shirts, some handkerchiefs, and some other things, with which he ran away; and that the poor woman was so frightened, it had nearly cost her her life. There were several other charges made against the same dog, which is supposed to have been trained up to the business, and that his master must be at some place not far distant. The officers undertook to be on the alert to apprehend this depredator, or else to shoot him."

We repeat our lamentation. These are indeed melancholy instances of depravity in the lower orders! Here we find not only the dog, the natural protector of our property, commencing depredations upon it, but even the horse—the Houyhnhnm himself—totally degenerating from his natural innocence of character, and conducting himself like an absolute yahoo.

A stern moralist may indeed observe, that something of this kind might have been anticipated from the dog: his alliance with those nightly robbers, the fox and the wolf, prepared us for suspicion; and his loyalty to his chief, like that of an ancient Highlander or Borderer, has been always deemed consistent with a certain negligence of the strict rules of property. Gilbertfield, that "Imp of fame," as he was christened by Burns, has already acknowledged and apologised for a degree of laxity of morals in this particular. See the Last Dying Words of Bonny Heck, a famous Greyhound in the shire of Fife.

> Now Honesty was ay my Drift,
> An innocent and harmless Shift,
> A Kaill-pot-lid gently to lift,
> or Amry-Sneck.
> Shame fa the Chafts, dare call that Thift,
> quo' bonny *Heck*.

But whatever suspicions may have fallen on the dog, the conduct of the horse, until this unfortunate and public disclosure, had left his character untainted even by suspicion; nor could it possibly have been supposed that he could have wanted a halter for any other service than that of tying him to his stall. There might be, perhaps, here and there, a Highland pony (by the way, we had one of that kind ourselves), who could too well understand the mode of opening a country stable door, and pull the bobbin till the latch came up, with the intelligence of Red Riding-hood herself; nay, who had even become so well acquainted with the more complicated mechanism of the lock of the corn chest, that it was not found advisable to leave the key in it. But as late antiquaries of the Gothic race seem disposed to question the title of the Mountain Celt to the name of Man, we may well deny the title of his stump'd, shaggy, dwarfish Pony, to be called Horse. At any rate, these acts of petty larceny, on the part of the dog or horse, can never be compared with the acts of street robbery imputed to the ill-advised quadrupeds whose misconduct has given occasion to this article.

It frequently happens, however, that a glance at the annals of past ages diminishes our estimate of the atrocity of the present, and consoles those too nervous moralists who are shocked at the increased depravity of our own times. Without, therefore, attempting any plea for the *padding* attempts of the dog, or the acts of *stouthrief* and *sorning* committed by the horse in question, and that upon the pittance of hay belonging to a stand of hackney coachmen, in which he might therefore have been compared to a robber of the poors' box. Without, we repeat, having the least intention of advocating so frail a cause, we proceed to report a few facts which have come to our knowledge, and may serve to shew that, after all, such instances of felony are not without example in the animal kingdom. Indeed a proverb current in the border counties, which says, "some will hund their dog whare they dar'na gang themsel," seems to indicate, that although there were varieties of the canine species that might give themselves to discover and catch the encroaching thieves of a different tribe, yet there were others who assisted their masters in the same trade, and even excelled them in boldness and address; this perhaps may be elucidated in the sequel.

The first instance we shall refer to, occurred in the celebrated case of Murdieston and Millar, whose trial proved fatal to the bipeds accused, and (as has generally been averred) to their four-footed aider and abettor. Although we are uncertain, at this distance of time, whether it was Lord Braxfield or Monboddo, who was said to have passed sentence upon them; yet thus far we know to be the fact, that the late Lord Melville, while at the Scottish bar, was Advocate Depute upon the occasion.

Murdieston occupied a farm on the north bank of the Tweed, and nearly opposite the ancient baronial castle of Traquair; Millar, the other "Minion of the Moon," lived with him as his shepherd; and they laboured in their vocation of sheep-stealing for years, with unsuspected diligence and perseverance. While returning home with their stolen droves, they avoided, even in the night, the roads along the banks of the river, or those that descend to the valley through the adjoining glens. They chose rather to come along the ridge of mountains that separate the small river of Leithen from the Tweed. But even here there was sometimes danger, for the shepherds occasionally visit their flocks even before day; and often when Millar had driven his prey from a distance, and while he was yet miles from home, and the *weather-gleam* of the eastern hills began to be tinged with the brightening dawn, he has left them to the charge of his dog, and descended himself to the banks of the Leithen, off his way, that he might not be seen connected with their company. Yarrow, although between three and four miles from his master, would continue, with care and silence, to bring the sheep onward to the ground belonging to Murdieston's farm, where his master's appearance could be neither a matter of question nor surprise.

Adjoining to the thatched farm-house was one of those old square towers, or peel houses, whose picturesque ruins were then seen ornamenting the course of the river, as they had been placed alternately along the north and south bank, generally from three to six hundred yards from it—sometimes on the shin, and sometimes in the hollow, of a hill. In the vault of this tower, it was the practice of these men to conceal the sheep they had recently stolen; and while the rest of their people were absent on Sunday at the Church, they used to employ themselves in cancelling with their knives the earmarks, and impressing with a hot-iron a large O upon the face, that covered both sides of the animal's nose, for the purpose of obliterating the *brand* of the true owner. While his accomplices were so busied, Yarrow kept watch in the open air, and gave notice, without fail, by his barking, of the approach of those who were not of *the fancy*.

That he might vary the scene of his depredations, Millar had one night crossed the Tweed, and betaken himself to a wild farm among the mountains of Selkirkshire; and as the shepherds have wonderfully minute knowledge of localities, he found no difficulty in collecting part of a flock and bringing away what number he judged convenient. Sheep are very loth to descend a hill in the night time, and more so to cross a river. Millar, to keep as clear as possible of the haunts of men, on his return, brought his drove over the shoulder of Wallace's hill, opposite, and intended to swim them across a pool in the river Tweed. But his prey being taken from the most remote part of the farm, happened to be mostly old ewes (of all kinds of sheep the most stubborn in their propensities); and all the exertions of a very active man, intimately acquainted with the habits of the animals, and assisted by the most sagacious dog probably ever known, were found inadequate to overcome the reluctance of the sheep to take the river. Millar continued to exert himself until the dawn of the morning warned him that any further effort was inconsistent with his habitual caution. Still he was unwilling to relinquish his booty, since, could he only get the sheep across the river, he was within little more than a quarter of a mile from the old tower. He therefore left the future conduct of the enterprise, as he had often done before, to Yarrow—crossed the river himself, and went home, encouraging the dog by his voice, while he was yet not too distant, so as to risk being heard by some early riser. The trust-worthy dog paused not, nor slackened his exertions—the work was now all his own;—such had been his efforts, as he furiously and desperately drove in first one flank of the drove and then another, that two of the ewes were forced from the bank into the river, and were drowned, as they could not regain their situations for the pressure of their companions—but he was finally unsuccessful—for he, too, knew the danger of being seen in the broad light of the morning driving sheep "where sheep shou'd na be." The ewes were observed, in the course of the ensuing day, wending their weary way homeward, and half covered with a new keel, with which Millar had himself marked them, in a small sheep-fold, in a lonely place on his way. Millar himself was astonished at the stubbornness of the sheep, and the persevering energy of his dog. And he told the story to a respectable sheep-farmer in prison, while under sentence of death.

Murdieston and Millar suffered death, and Yarrow was generally supposed to have suffered the same fate. Nay, his dying speech was cried through the streets of Edinburgh, along with that of his master. But as we have heard of a person unexpectedly reprieved, who had the pleasure of purchasing his own last speech, it is certain that Yarrow had an opportunity to have done the same, if he had possessed such a taste, or means to indulge it. This celebrated dog was purchased by a sheep-farmer in the neighbourhood, but did not take kindly to honest courses, and his master having apparently no work of a different capacity, in which to engage him, he was remarked to show rather less sagacity than the ordinary shepherd's dog.

The case of Millar, although curious, is not singular. A young gentleman of fortune and fashion, lately residing as a visitor in Edinburgh, was the master of a beautiful and accomplished spaniel bitch, who, in her way, was as much an adept in irregular appropriation as Yarrow himself, and had in all probability been, like him, educated to steal for the benefit of her master. It was some time ere her new master, who had bought the animal from a person who dealt in selling dogs, became aware of this irregularity of morals, and he was astonished and teazed by the animal bringing him articles which she had picked up in an irregular manner. But when he perceived that the spaniel proceeded upon system, he used to amuse his friends by causing her to give proofs of her sagacity in the Spartan art of privately stealing, putting, of course, the shop-keepers where he meant she should exercise her faculty, on guard as to the issue.

The process was curious, and excites some surprise at the pains which must have been bestowed to qualify the animal for these practices. So soon as the master entered a shop, the dog seemed to avoid all appearance of recognizing or acknowledging any connexion with him, but lounged about with an indolent, disengaged, and independent sort of manner, as if she had come into the shop of her own accord. In the course of looking over some wares, her master indicated, by a touch on the parcel and a look towards the spaniel, that which he desired she should appropriate, and then left the shop. The dog, whose watchful eye caught the hint in an instant, instead of following her master out of the shop, continued to sit at the door, or lie by the fire, or watch the counter, until she observed the attention of the people of the shop withdrawn from the prize which she wished to secure. Whenever she saw an opportunity of doing so unobserved, she never failed to jump upon the counter with her fore feet, possess herself of the gloves, or whatever else had been pointed out to her, and escape from the shop to join her master. It is easy to conceive for what purposes this animal's sagacity had been thus perverted, but it would be difficult to form a probable guess at the particular method of training her to this mode of peculation.

We knew well a gentleman, in the profession of the law (to which his worth and honour rendered him an ornament), who used to give an account of an embarrassing accident which befell him on a journey to London, and which may serve as a corollary to our tale of the spaniel. In this gentleman's youth (probably between the 1750 and 1760), the journey betwixt Edinburgh and London was usually performed on horseback. The traveller might either ride post, or, if willing to travel more economically, he bought a horse, and sold him at the end of his journey. The gentleman of whom we speak, who was a good judge of horses as well as a good horseman, had chosen the latter mode of travelling, and had sold the horse on which he rode from Scotland, so soon as he arrived in London. With a view to his return, he went to Smithfield to purchase a horse the evening before he set out northwards. About dusk a handsome horse was offered to him at so cheap a rate, that he was led to suspect the animal to be unsound: as he could, however, discover no blemish, and as the seller, eager (for reasons well known to himself) to conclude a hasty bargain, readily abated even his first moderate demand, our traveller became the purchaser of a horse, in which his skill could discern no blemish, at a very cheap rate.

On the next morning he set out on his journey. His horse had excellent paces; and the first few miles, while the road was well frequented, our traveller spent in congratulating himself on his good fortune. On Finchley Common, and at a place where the road runs down one slight ascent and up another, the traveller met a clergyman driving a one-horse chaise. There was nobody within sight; and the horse, by his manœuvre, plainly intimated what had been the profession of his first master. Instead of passing the one-horse chaise, he laid his counter close up to it, and stopt it, having no doubt that his rider would take so fair an opportunity of exercising his vocation. The clergyman, under the same mistake, produced his purse unasked, and assured the inoffensive and surprised horseman, that it was unnecessary to draw his pistol. The traveller rallied his horse, with apologies to the venerable member of the Church whom he had unwittingly affrighted, and pursued his journey. The horse next made the same suspicious approach to a coach, from the windows of which a blunderbuss was levelled, with denunciations of death and destruction to our countryman, though *sackless*, as he expressed it, of all offence in deed or word. In a word—after his life had been once or twice endangered by the suspicions to which his horse's conduct gave rise, and his liberty as often threatened by peace-officers, who were disposed to apprehend him as the notorious highwayman who had formerly ridden the horse in question, he found himself obliged to part with the inauspicious animal for a mere trifle; and to purchase, at a pretty dear rate, a horse of less external figure and action, but of better moral habits.

Thus have we in some measure paralleled the remarkable circumstances which seemed at first so startling to credibility. We sincerely hope, however, that these symptoms of flagrant immorality will not extend themselves among the lower tribes of creation. We are now on our guard, and may suspect malice prepense in other instances. All remember the dog of Islington and his master.—

> The dog and man at first were friends;
> 　But when a pique began,
> The dog, to gain some private ends,
> 　Went mad and bit the man.

The case of a fall from a horse has been generally imputed to chance-medley; but if the modern Houyhnhnms so far degenerate from those of Captain Gulliver, may we not justly find a bill for murder on the same *species facti?* If these things are to proceed unchecked, we may hear of a cow picking a milkmaid's pockets, or of a horse stopping the mail-coach instead of stopping with it. We still hope, however, better things of the quadrupeds of this realm; and trust, that animals, which have hitherto in the article of theft been more sinned against than sinners, will not take generally to these practices, of which they have as yet only been the passive subjects.

Tweedside, 30th Sept.

PHANTASMAGORIA

TO THE VEILED CONDUCTOR OF BLACKWOOD'S
EDINBURGH MAGAZINE

SIR,

There are few things so much affected by the change of manners and circumstances, as the quality and the effect of evidence. Facts which our fathers were prepared to receive upon very slender and hearsay testimony, we are sometimes disposed to deny positively, even when fortified by all that the laws of evidence can do for them, by the confession of the perpetrator of wickedness, by the evidence of its victims, by the eye-sight and oath of impartial witnesses, and by all which could, in an ordinary case, "make faith," to use a phrase of the civilians, betwixt man and man. In the present day he would be hooted as an idiot, who would believe an old woman guilty of witchcraft, upon evidence, on the tenth part of which a Middlesex jury would find a man guilty of felony; and our ancestors would have pelted, as a Sadducee and an infidel, any one who, on the twentieth degree of testimony so rejected, would not have condemned the accused to pitched faggots and tarred barrels.

To accommodate those who love the golden mean in judgment, or are inclined, with Gines de Passamonte's ape, to pronounce the adventures in Montesinos's cave partly true and partly false, Dr Ferriar of Manchester has invented a new mode of judging evidence with respect to those supernatural matters, in which, without impeaching the truth of the narrator, or even the veracity of the eyes to whose evidence he appeals, you may ascribe his supposed facts to the effects of preconceived ideas acting upon faulty or diseased organs.

I have, Sir, unfortunately no means of making myself the head of any new class of believers or infidels upon these mysterious points; for it is evident, that narratives of this marvellous complexion must be either true or false, or partly true, partly fictitious; and each of these classes have already their leaders and patrons. As, however, you, Sir, are yourself a mystical being, and, in the opinion of some, a nonentity, you cannot fail to be interested in examples referring to the mystical, and to that which, being hard of belief, is sometimes rejected as incredible. You are not, perhaps, being yourself a reserved personage, entitled to expect ample communication on the part of your correspondents; yet thus much I am willing to announce to you, as the preface to the present and future correspondence.

My father, Sir Mickelmast Shadow, lived in a glen, into which the sun does not shine above ten times a year, though we have no reason to complain of want of moisture. He was wont to say, that he was descended from the celebrated Simon Shadow, whom the renowned Sir John Falstaff desired to have in his regiment, in respect he was like to be a cool soldier, and refreshing to sit under after a hot day's march. My father abridged his days, by venturing out into the meridian sun (an hour remarkable for cutting short our family) with the purpose of paying his respects to an eclipse, which a rascally almanack-maker falsely announced as being on the point of rendering our globe a visit. I succeeded to him, Sir, in his retired habits, and his taste for the uncertain, undefined, and mysterious. Warned by my poor father's untimely fate, I never venture into broad day-light; but should you, Sir, leave your bower at sun-rise or sun-set, like your prototype the veiled prophet of Moore, it is possible that you may meet and distinguish your correspondent by his tall slim figure, thin stilts of legs, and disproportioned feet. For I must inform you, in case of a disagreeable surprise, that my appearance reverses that of Michael Scott and the wizards of old, from whom the devil is said to have stolen the shadow; whereas, in my case, it would seem he had stolen the substance, and left the shade to walk the earth without it.

My education and reading have been as fantastic as my person; and from a kindred propensity to those stories which, like the farther end of the bridge in Mirza's vision, are concealed by shadows, clouds, and darkness, they have been turned towards the occult sciences and mystical points of study. My library is furnished with authors who treat of the divining rod, of the magical mirror, the weapon-salve, charms, lamens, sigils, christals, pentacles, talismans, and spells. My hereditary mansion, Castle Shadoway, has a tower, from which I can observe the stars (being something of an astrologer, like the valiant Guy Mannering) and a dungeon haunted by the restless ghost of a cooper, whilome confined there till his death by one of my ancestors, for having put too slight hoops on a barrel of March beer, by which the generous liquor was lost. This goblin shall hammer, dub-a-dub, scratch, rustle, and groan with any from the Hermitage Castle to Castle Girnigo, for an hundred pounds down, play or pay. Besides this, I pretend to be acquainted with all spirits that walk the earth, swim the wave, or wing the sky; goblins, night-mares, hags, vampires, break-necks, black men and green women, familiars, puck-hairies, Oberon, and all his moon-light dancers. The wandering Jew, the high-priest of the Rosy-cross, the Genius of Socrates, the dæmon of Mascon, the drummer of Tedworth, are all known to me, with their real character, and essence, and true history. Besides all these points of occult knowledge, my conversation has lain much among old spinsters and widows, who pardoned the disproportion between my club-feet and spindle-shanks, and my general resemblance to a skeleton hung in chains, in consideration of my conversational talents as an excellent listener. In this way, my mind, from youth upwards, has become stored with matter deep and perilous, to read or narrate which, with due effect, the hand of the clock should point to twelve, and the candles be long in the snuff.

The time now approaches, Sir, that I must expect, in the course of nature, to fade away into that unknown and obscure state in which, as there is no light, there can of course be no shadow. I am unwilling so much curious and excellent information should go with me to the darksome bourne. To your veiled and mysterious character, Sir, you are indebted, as I have already hinted, for the preference which I give to your work as the means of recording these marvels. You must not be apprehensive that I will overwhelm you with too many marvels at once, for I am aware, by experience, of the indigestion which arises after having, like Macbeth, "supp'd full with horrors." Farther, you may place absolute reliance upon the statements which I may give concerning my authorities. Trusting this offer may be acceptable, and that at a time when you are moving heaven and earth for furnishing instruction and amusement to your readers, you will not think the assistance of the inferior regions to be despised, I send you the first article of my treatise, which, with your permission, I entitle

PHANTASMAGORIA.

Come like SHADOWS—so depart.

No I

The incident which I am about to narrate, came to your present correspondent through the most appropriate channel for such information, by the narration, namely, of an old woman. I must however add, that though this old lady literally wore the black silk gown, small haunch-hoop, and triple ruffles, which form the apparel most proper to her denomination, yet in sense, spirit, wit, and intelligence, she greatly exceeded various individuals of her own class, who have been known to me, although their backs were clothed with purple robes or military uniforms, and their heads attired with cocked hats or three-tailed periwigs. I have not, in my own mind, the slightest doubt that she told the tale to me in the precise terms in which she received it from the person principally concerned. Whether it was to be believed in its full extent, as a supernatural visitation, she did not pretend to determine, but she strongly averred her conviction, that the lady to whom the event happened was a woman not easily to be imposed upon by her own imagination, however excited; and that the whole tone of her character, as well as the course of her life, exempted her from the slightest suspicion of an attempt to impose on others. Without farther preface, and without any effort at ornament or decoration, I proceed to my narrative, only premising, that though I suppress the name of the lady, out of respect to surviving relations, yet it is well known to me.

A lady, wife to a gentleman of respectable property on the borders of Argyleshire, was, about the middle of the last century, left a widow, with the management of an embarrassed estate and the care of an only son. The young gentleman approached that period of life when it was necessary that he should be sent into the world in some active professional line. The natural inclination of the youth, like most others of that age and country, was to enter into the army, a disposition which his mother saw with anxiety, as all the perils of the military profession were aggravated to her imagination by maternal tenderness, and a sense of her own desolate situation. A circumstance however occurred, which induced her to grant her consent to her son's embracing this course of life with less reluctance than it would otherwise have been given.

A Highland gentleman, named Campbell (we suppress his designation), and nearly related to Mrs ——, was about this time named to the command of one of the independent companies, levied for protecting the peace of the Highlands, and preventing the marauding parties in which the youth of the wilder clans were still occasionally exercised. These companies were called *Sidier-dhu*, i.e. black soldiers, to distinguish them from the *Sidier-roy*, or red soldiers, of the regular army; and hence, when embodied into a marching regiment (the well-known Forty-Second), the corps long retained, and still retains, the title of the Black Watch. At the period of the story the independent companies retained their original occupation, and were generally considered as only liable to do duty in their native country. Each of these corps consisted of about three hundred men, using the Highland garb and arms, and commanded by such gentlemen as the Brunswick government imagined they might repose confidence in. They were understood to engage only to serve in the Highlands, and no where else, and were looked upon rather as a kind of volunteer than as regular soldiers.

A service of this limited nature, which seemed to involve but little risk of actual danger, and which was to be exercised in his native country alone, was calculated to remove many of the objections which a widowed mother might be supposed to have against her only son entering into the army. She had also the highest reliance on the kindness and affection of her kinsman, Captain Campbell, who, while he offered to receive the young gentleman as a cadet into his independent company, gave her his solemn assurance to watch over him in every respect as his own son, and to prevent his being exposed to any unnecessary hazard until he should have attained the age and experience necessary for his own guidance. Mrs —— greatly reconciled to parting with her son, in consequence of these friendly assurances on the part of his future commander. It was arranged that the youth should join the company at a particular time; and in the mean while, Mrs ——, who was then residing at Edinburgh, made the necessary preparations for his proper equipment.

These had been nearly completed, when Mrs —— received a piece of melancholy intelligence, which again unsettled her resolution; and while it filled her with grief on account of her relation, awakened in the most cruel manner all the doubts and apprehensions which his promises had lulled to sleep. A body of Katerans, or freebooters, belonging, if I mistake not, to the country of Lochiel, had made a descent upon a neighbouring district of Argyleshire, and driven away a considerable *creagh*, or spoil of cattle. Captain Campbell, with such of his independent company as he could assemble upon a sudden alarm, set off in pursuit of the depredators, and after a fatiguing march came up with them. A slight skirmish took place, in course of which the cattle were recovered, but not before Captain Campbell had received a severe wound. It was not immediately, perhaps not necessarily, mortal, but was rendered so by want of shelter and surgical assistance, and the same account, which brought to Edinburgh an account of the skirmish, communicated to Mrs —— the death of her affectionate kinsman. To grief for his loss, she had now to add the painful recollection, that her son, if he pursued the line which had been resolved on, would be deprived of the aid, countenance, and advice, of the person to whose care, as to that of a father, she had resolved to confide him. And the very event, which was otherwise so much attended with grief and perplexity, served to shew that the service of the independent companies, however limited in extent, did not exempt those engaged in it from mortal peril. At the same time, there were many arguments against retracting her consent, or altering a plan in which so much progress had been already made; and she felt as if, on the one hand, she sacrificed her son's life, if she permitted him to join the corps; on the other, that his honour or spirit might be called in question by her obliging him to renounce the situation. These contending emotions threw her—a widow, with no one to advise her, and the mother of an only son whose fate depended upon her resolving wisely—into an agony of mind, which many readers may suppose will account satisfactorily for the following extraordinary apparition.

I need not remind my Edinburgh friends, that in ancient times their forefathers lived, as they do still in Paris, in *flats*, which had access by a common stair. The apartments occupied by Mrs —— were immediately above those of a family with whom she was intimate, and she was in the habit of drinking tea with them every evening. It was duskish, and she began to think that her agitation of mind had detained her beyond the hour at which she should have joined her friends, when, opening the door of her little parlour to leave her own lodging, she saw standing directly opposite to her in the passage, the exact resemblance of Captain Campbell, in his complete Highland dress, with belted plaid, dirk, pistols, pouch, and broadsword. Appalled at this vision, she started back, closed the door of the room, staggered backwards to a chair, and endeavoured to convince herself that the apparition she had seen was only the effect of a heated imagination. In this, being a woman of a strong mind, she partly succeeded, yet could not prevail upon herself again to open the door which seemed to divide her from the shade of her deceased relative, until she heard a tap on the floor beneath, which was the usual signal from her friendly neighbours to summon her to tea. On this she took courage, walked firmly to the door of the apartment, flung it open, and—again beheld the military spectre of the deceased officer of the Black Watch. He seemed to stand within a yard of her, and held his hand stretched out, not in a menacing manner, but as if to prevent her passing him. This was too much for human fortitude to endure, and she sunk down on the floor, with a noise which alarmed her friends below for her safety.

On their hastening up stairs, and entering Mrs ——'s lodging, they saw nothing extraordinary in the passage, but in the parlour found the lady in strong hysterics. She was recalled to herself with difficulty, but concealed the extraordinary cause of her indisposition. Her friends naturally imputed it to the late unpleasant intelligence from Argyleshire, and remained with her till a late hour, endeavouring to amuse and relieve her mind. The hour of rest however arrived, and there was a necessity, (which Mrs —— felt an alarming one,) that she should go to her solitary apartment. She had scarce set down the light which she held in her hand, and was in the act of composing her mind, ere addressing the Deity for protection during the perils of the night, when, turning her head, the vision she had seen in the passage was standing in the apartment. On this emergency she summoned up her courage, and addressing him by his name and surname, conjured him in the name of Heaven to tell her wherefore he thus haunted her. The apparition instantly answered, with a voice and manner in no respect differing from those proper to him while alive,—"Cousin, why did you not speak sooner,—my visit is but for your good,—your grief disturbs me in my grave,—and it is by permission of the Father of the fatherless and Husband of the widow, that I come to tell you not to be disheartened by my fate, but to pursue the line which, by my advice, you adopted for your son. He will find a protector more efficient, and as kind as I would have been; will rise high in the military profession, and live to close your eyes." With these words the figure representing Captain Campbell completely vanished.

Upon the point of her being decidedly awake and sensible, through her eyes and ears, of the presence and words of this apparition, Mrs —— declared herself perfectly convinced. She said, when minutely questioned by the lady who told me the story, that his general appearance differed in no respect from that which he presented when in full life and health, but that on the last occasion, while she fixed her eyes on the spectre in terror and anxiety, yet with a curiosity which argued her to be somewhat familiarized with his presence, she observed a speck or two of blood upon his breast-ruffle, and band, which he seemed to conceal with his hand when he observed her looking at him. He changed his attitude more than once, but slightly, and without altering his general position.

The fate of the young gentleman in future life seemed to correspond with the prophecy. He entered the army, rose to considerable rank, and died in peace and honour, long after he had closed the eyes of the good old lady who had determined, or at least professed to have determined, his destination in life upon this marvellous suggestion.

It would have been easy for a skilful narrator to give this tale more effect, by a slight transference or trifling exaggeration of the circumstances. But the author has determined in this and future communications to limit himself strictly to his authorities, and rests your humble servant,

SIMON SHADOW.

THE SHORTER FICTION

MY AUNT MARGARET'S MIRROR

BY THE AUTHOR OF WAVERLEY

> There are times
> When Fancy plays her gambols, in despite
> Even of our watchful senses, when in sooth
> Substance seems shadow, shadow substance seems,
> When the broad, palpable, and mark'd partition
> 'Twixt that which is and is not, seems dissolved,
> As if the mental eye gain'd power to gaze
> Beyond the limits of the existing world.
> Such hours of shadowy dreams I better love
> Than all the gross realities of life.
>
> ANONYMOUS

MY AUNT MARGARET was one of that respected sisterhood, upon whom devolve all the trouble and solicitude incidental to the possession of children, excepting only that which attends their entrance into the world. We were a large family, of very different dispositions and constitutions. Some were dull and peevish—they were sent to Aunt Margaret to be amused; some were rude, romping, and boisterous—they were sent to Aunt Margaret to be kept quiet, or rather, that their noise might be removed out of hearing; those who were indisposed were sent with the prospect of being nursed—those who were stubborn, with the hope of their being subdued by the kindness of Aunt Margaret's discipline; in short, she had all the various duties of a mother, without the credit and dignity of the maternal character. The busy scene of her various cares is now over—of the invalids and the robust, the kind and the rough, the peevish and pleased children who thronged her little

47

parlour from morning to night, not one now remains alive but myself; who, afflicted by early infirmity, was one of the most delicate of her nurselings, yet, nevertheless, have outlived them all.

It is still my custom, and shall be so while I have the use of my limbs, to visit my respected relation at least three times a week. Her abode is about half a mile from the suburbs of the town in which I reside; and is accessible, not only by the high road, from which it stands at some distance, but by means of a green-sward foot-path, leading through some pretty meadows. I have so little left to torment me in life, that it is one of my greatest vexations to know that several of these sequestered fields have been devoted as sites for building. In that which is nearest the town, wheel-barrows have been at work for several weeks in such numbers, that, I verily believe, its whole surface, to the depth of at least eighteen inches, was mounted in these monotrochs at the same moment, and in the act of being transported from one place to another. Huge triangular piles of planks are also reared in different parts of the devoted messuage; and a little group of trees, that still grace the eastern end, which rises in a gentle ascent, have just received warning to quit, expressed by a daub of white paint, and are to give place to a curious grove of chimneys.

It would, perhaps, hurt others in my situation to reflect that this little range of pasturage once belonged to my father (whose family was of some consideration in the world), and was sold by patches to remedy distresses in which he involved himself in an attempt by commercial adventure to redeem his diminished fortune. While the building scheme was in full operation, this circumstance was often pointed out to me by the class of friends who are anxious that no part of your misfortunes should escape your observation. "Such pasture ground!—lying at the very town's-end—in turnips and potatoes, the parks would bring £20 per acre, and if leased for building—O, it was a gold mine!—And all sold for an old song out of the ancient possessor's hands." My comforters cannot bring me to repine much on this subject. If I could be allowed to look back on the past without interruption, I could willingly give up the enjoyment of present income, and the hope of future profit, to those who have purchased what my father sold. I regret the alteration of the ground only because it destroys associations, and I would more willingly (I think) see the Earl's Closes in the hands of strangers, retaining their sylvan appearance, than know them for my own, if torn up by agriculture, or covered with buildings. Mine are the sensations of poor Logan:

> The horrid plough has razed the green
> Where yet a child I stray'd;
> The axe has fell'd the hawthorn screen,
> The school-boy's summer shade.

I hope, however, the threatened devastation will not be consummated in my day. Although the adventurous spirit of times short while since passed gave rise to the undertaking, I have been encouraged to think, that the subsequent changes have so far damped the spirit of speculation, that the rest of the woodland foot-path leading to Aunt Margaret's retreat will be left undisturbed for her time and mine. I am interested in this, for every step of the way, after I have passed through the green already mentioned, has for me something of early remembrance:—There is the stile at which I can recollect a cross child's maid upbraiding me with my infirmity, as she lifted me coarsely and carelessly over the flinty steps, which my brothers traversed with shout and bound. I remember the suppressed bitterness of the moment, and, conscious of my own inferiority, the feeling of envy with which I regarded the easy movements and elastic steps of my more happily formed brethren. Alas! these goodly barks have all perished on life's wide ocean, and only that which seemed so little sea-worthy, as the naval phrase goes, has reached the port when the tempest is over. Then there is the pool where, manoeuvring our little navy, constructed out of the broad water-flags, my elder brother fell in, and was scarce saved from the watery element, to die under Nelson's banner. There is the hazel copse, also, in which my brother Henry used to gather nuts; thinking little that he was to die in an Indian jungle in quest of rupees.

There is so much more of remembrance about the little walk, that,—as I stop, rest on my crutch-headed cane, and look round with that species of comparison between the thing I was and that which I now am,—it almost induces me to doubt my own identity; until I find myself in face of the honey-suckle porch of Aunt Margaret's dwelling, with its irregularity of front, and its odd projecting latticed windows; where the workmen seem to have made a study that no one of them should resemble another, in form, size, or in the old-fashioned stone entablature, and labels, which adorn them. This tenement, once the manor-house of Earl's Closes, we still retain a slight hold upon; for, in some family arrangements, it had been settled upon Aunt Margaret during the term of her life. Upon this frail tenure depends, in a great measure, the last shadow of the family of Bothwell of Earl's Closes, and their last slight connexion with their paternal inheritance. The only representative will then be an infirm old man, moving not unwillingly to the grave, which has devoured all that were dear to his affections.

When I have indulged such thoughts for a minute or two, I enter the mansion, which is said to have been the gatehouse only of the original building, and find one being on whom time seems to have made little impression; for the Aunt Margaret of to-day bears the same proportional age to the Aunt Margaret of my early youth, that the boy of ten years old does to the man of (by'r Lady!) some fifty-six years. The old lady's invariable costume has doubtless some share in confirming one in the opinion, that time has stood still with Aunt Margaret.

The brown or chocolate-coloured silk gown, with ruffles of the same stuff at the elbow, within which are others of Mechlin lace— the black silk gloves, or mitts, the white hair combed back upon a roll, and the cap of spotless cambric, which closes around the venerable countenance, as they were not the costume of 1780, so neither were they that of 1826; they are altogether a style peculiar to the individual Aunt Margaret. There she sits, as she sate thirty years since, with her wheel or the stocking, which she works by the fire in winter, and by the window in summer; or, perhaps, venturing as far as the porch in an unusually fine summer evening. Her frame, like some well-constructed piece of mechanics, still performs the operations for which it had seemed destined; going its round with an activity which is gradually diminished, yet indicating no probability that it will soon come to a period.

The solicitude and affection which had made Aunt Margaret the willing slave to the inflictions of a whole nursery have now for their object the health and comfort of one old and infirm man; the last remaining relative of her family, and the only one who can still find interest in the traditional stores which she hoards; as some miser hides the gold which he desires that no one should enjoy after his death.

My conversation with Aunt Margaret generally relates little either to the present or to the future: for the passing day we possess as much as we require, and we neither of us wish for more; and for that which is to follow we have on this side of the grave neither hopes, nor fears, nor anxiety. We therefore naturally look back to the past; and forget the present fallen fortunes and declined importance of our family, in recalling the hours when it was wealthy and prosperous.

With this slight introduction, the reader will know as much of Aunt Margaret and her nephew as is necessary to comprehend the following conversation and narrative.

Last week, when, late in a summer evening, I went to call on the old lady to whom my reader is now introduced, I was received by her with all her usual affection and benignity; while, at the same time, she seemed abstracted and disposed to silence. I asked her the reason. "They have been clearing out the old chapel," she said; "John Clayhudgeons having, it seems, discovered that the stuff within,—being, I suppose, the remains of our ancestors,— was excellent for top-dressing the meadows."

Here I started up with more alacrity than I have displayed for some years; but sate down while my aunt added, laying her hand upon my sleeve, "The chapel has been long considered as common ground, my dear, and used for a penfold, and what objection can we have to the man for employing what is his own, to his own profit? Besides, I did speak to him, and he very readily and civilly promised, that, if he found bones or monuments, they should be carefully respected and reinstated; and what more could I ask? So, the first stone they found bore the name of Margaret Bothwell, 1585, and I have caused it to be laid carefully aside, as I think it betokens death; and having served my namesake two hundred years, it has just been cast up in time to do me the same good turn. My house has been long put in order, as far as the small earthly concerns require it, but who shall say that their account with Heaven is sufficiently revised?"

"After what you have said, aunt," I replied, "perhaps I ought to take my hat and go away, and so I should, but that there is on this occasion a little alloy mingled with your devotion. To think of death at all times is a duty—to suppose it nearer from the finding an old gravestone is superstition; and you, with your strong useful common sense, which was so long the prop of a fallen family, are the last person whom I should have suspected of such weakness."

"Neither would I deserve your suspicions, kinsman," answered Aunt Margaret, "if we were speaking of any incident occurring in the actual business of human life. But for all this, I have a sense of superstition about me, which I do not wish to part with. It is a feeling which separates me from this age, and links me with that to which I am hastening; and even when it seems, as now, to lead me to the brink of the grave, and bids me gaze on it, I do not love that it should be dispelled. It soothes my imagination, without influencing my reason or conduct."

"I profess, my good lady," replied I, "that had any one but you made such a declaration, I should have thought it as capricious as that of the clergyman, who, without vindicating his false reading,

preferred, from habit's sake, his old Mumpsimus to the modern
Sumpsimus."

"Well," answered my aunt, "I must explain my inconsistency in
this particular, by comparing it to another. I am, as you know, a
piece of that old-fashioned thing called a Jacobite; but I am so in
sentiment and feeling only; for a more loyal subject never joined in
prayers for the health and wealth of George the Fourth, whom
God long preserve! But I dare say that kind-hearted Sovereign
would not deem that an old woman did him much injury, if she
leaned back in her arm-chair, just in such a twilight as this, and
thought of the high-mettled men, whose sense of duty called them
to arms against his grandfather; and how, in a cause which they
deemed that of their rightful prince and country—

> They fought till their hand to the broadsword was glued,
> They fought against fortune with hearts unsubdued.

Do not come at such a moment, when my head is full of plaids,
pibrochs, and claymores, and ask my reason to admit what, I am
afraid, it cannot deny,—I mean, that the public advantage peremp-
torily demanded that these things should cease to exist. I cannot,
indeed, refuse to allow the justice of your reasoning; but yet, being
convinced against my will, you will gain little by your motion. You
might as well read to an infatuated lover the catalogue of his mis-
tress's imperfections; for, when he has been compelled to listen to
the summary, you will only get for answer, that, 'he lo'es her a' the
better.'"

I was not sorry to have changed the gloomy train of Aunt Margaret's thoughts, and replied in the same tone, "Well, I can't help
being persuaded that our good King is the more sure of Mrs.
Bothwell's loyal affection, that he has the Stuart right of birth, as
well as the Act of Succession, in his favour."

"Perhaps my attachment, were its source of consequence, might
be found warmer for the union of the rights you mention," said
Aunt Margaret; "but, upon my word, it would be as sincere if the
King's right were founded only on the will of the nation, as declared
at the Revolution. I am none of your *jure divino* folks."

"And a Jacobite notwithstanding."

"And a Jacobite notwithstanding; or rather, I will give you leave
to call me one of the party, which, in Queen Anne's time, were
called *Whimsicals*; because they were sometimes operated upon by
feelings, sometimes by principle. After all, it is very hard that you
will not allow an old woman to be as inconsistent in her political
sentiments, as mankind in general show themselves in all the various
courses of life; since you cannot point out one of them, in which

the passions and prejudices of those who pursue it are not perpetually carrying us away from the path which our reason points out."

"True, aunt; but you are a wilful wanderer, who should be forced
back into the right path."

"Spare me, I entreat you," replied Aunt Margaret. "You remember the Gaelic song, though I dare say I mispronounce the words—

> Hatil mohatil, na dowski mi.
> I am asleep, do not waken me.

I tell you, kinsman, that the sort of waking dreams which my imagination spins out, in what your favourite Wordsworth calls 'moods
of my own mind,' are worth all the rest of my more active days.
Then, instead of looking forwards, as I did in youth, and forming
for myself fairy palaces, upon the verge of the grave, I turn my eyes
backward upon the days, and manners, of my better time; and the
sad, yet soothing recollections, come so close and interesting, that
I almost think it sacrilege to be wiser or more rational, or less
prejudiced, than those to whom I looked up in my younger years."

"I think I now understand what you mean," I answered, "and
can comprehend why you should occasionally prefer the twilight of
illusion to the steady light of reason."

"Where there is no task," she rejoined, "to be performed, we
may sit in the dark if we like it—if we go to work, we must ring for
candles."

"And amidst such shadowy and doubtful light," continued I,
"imagination frames her enchanted and enchanting visions, and
sometimes passes them upon the senses for reality."

"Yes," said Aunt Margaret, who is a well-read woman, "to those
who resemble the translator of Tasso,

> Prevailing poet, whose undoubting mind
> Believed the magic wonders which he sung.

It is not required for this purpose, that you should be sensible of
the painful horrors, which an actual belief in such prodigies inflicts
—such a belief, now-a-days, belongs only to fools and children. It
is not necessary, that your ears should tingle, and your complexion
change, like that of Theodore, at the approach of the spectral huntsman. All that is indispensable for the enjoyment of the milder feeling
of supernatural awe is, that you should be susceptible of the slight
shuddering which creeps over you, when you hear a tale of terror
—that well-vouched tale which the narrator, having first expressed
his general disbelief of all such legendary lore, selects and produces,
as having something in it which he has been always obliged to give
up as inexplicable. Another symptom is, a momentary hesitation to
look round you, when the interest of the narrative is at the highest;

and the third, a desire to avoid looking into a mirror, when you are alone, in your chamber, for the evening. I mean such are signs which indicate the crisis, when a female imagination is in due temperature to enjoy a ghost story. I do not pretend to describe those which express the same disposition in a gentleman."

"That last symptom, dear aunt, of shunning the mirror, seems likely to be a rare occurrence amongst the fair sex."

"You are a novice in toilette fashions, my dear cousin. All women consult the looking-glass with anxiety, before they go into company; but when they return home, the mirror has not the same charm. The die has been cast—the party has been successful or unsuccessful, in the impression which she desired to make. But, without going deeper into the mysteries of the dressing-table, I will tell you that I, myself, like many other honest folks, do not like to see the blank black front of a large mirror in a room dimly lighted, and where the reflection of the candle seems rather to lose itself in the deep obscurity of the glass, than to be reflected back again into the apartment. That space of inky darkness seems to be a field for Fancy to play her revels in. She may call up other features to meet us, instead of the reflection of our own; or, as in the spells of Hallowe'en, which we learned in childhood, some unknown form may be seen peeping over our shoulder. In short, when I am in a ghost-seeing humour, I make my hand-maiden draw the green curtains over the mirror, before I go into the room, so that she may have the first shock of the apparition, if there be any to be seen. But to tell you the truth, this dislike to look into a mirror in particular times and places has, I believe, its original foundation in a story, which came to me by tradition from my grandmother, who was a party concerned in the scene of which I will now tell you."

THE MIRROR

Chapter One

YOU ARE FOND (said my aunt) of sketches of the society which has passed away. I wish I could describe to you Sir Philip Forester, the 'Chartered Libertine' of Scottish good company, about the end of the last century. I never saw him, indeed, but my mother's traditions were full of his wit, gallantry, and dissipation. This gay knight flourished about the end of the 17th and beginning of the 18th century. He was the Sir Charles Easy and the Lovelace of his day and country: renowned for the number of duels he had fought, and the successful intrigues which he had carried on. The supremacy which he had attained in the fashionable world was absolute; and when we combine it with one or two anecdotes, for which, 'if laws were made for every degree,' he ought certainly to have been hanged, the popularity of such a person really serves to show, either, that the present times are much more decent, if not more virtuous, than they formerly were; or, that high breeding then was of more difficult attainment than that which is now so called; and, consequently, entitled the successful professor to a proportional degree of plenary indulgences and privileges. No beau of this day could have borne out so ugly a story as that of Pretty Peggy Grindstone, the miller's daughter at Sillermills—it had well nigh made work for the Lord Advocate. But it hurt Sir Philip Forester no more than the hail hurts the hearth-stone. He was as well received in society as ever, and dined with the Duke of A—— the day the poor girl was buried. She died of heart-break. But that has nothing to do with my story.

Now, you must listen to a single word upon kith, kin, and ally; I promise you I will not be prolix. But it is necessary to the authenticity of my legend, that you should know that Sir Philip Forester, with his handsome person, elegant accomplishments, and fashionable manners, married the younger Miss Falconer, of King's-Copland. The elder sister of this lady had previously become the wife of my grandfather, Sir Geoffrey Bothwell, and brought into our family a good fortune. Miss Jemima, or Miss Jemmie Falconer, as she was usually called, had also about ten thousand pounds sterling; then thought a very handsome portion indeed.

The two sisters were extremely different, though each had their admirers while they remained single. Lady Bothwell had some touch of the old King's-Copland blood about her. She was bold, though not to the degree of audacity; ambitious, and desirous to raise her house and family; and was, as has been said, a considerable spur to my grandfather, who was otherwise an indolent man; but whom, unless he has been slandered, his lady's influence involved in some political matters which had been more wisely let alone. She was a woman of high principle, however, and masculine good sense, as some of her letters testify, which are still in my wainscot cabinet.

Jemmie Falconer was the reverse of her sister in every respect. Her understanding did not reach above the ordinary pitch, if, indeed, she could be said to have attained it. Her beauty, while it lasted, consisted, in a great measure, of delicacy of complexion and regularity of features, without any peculiar force of expression. Even these charms faded under the sufferings attendant on an ill-sorted match. She was passionately attached to her husband, by whom she was treated with a callous, yet polite, indifference; which, to one whose heart was as tender as her judgment was weak, was more painful perhaps than absolute ill-usage. Sir Philip was a voluptuary, that is, a completely selfish egotist: whose disposition and character resembled the rapier he wore, polished, keen, and brilliant, but inflexible and unpitying. As he observed carefully all the usual forms towards his lady, he had the art to deprive her even of the compassion of the world; and useless and unavailing as that may be while actually possessed by the sufferer, it is, to a mind like Lady Forester's, most painful to know she has it not.

The tattle of society did its best to place the peccant husband above the suffering wife. Some called her a poor spiritless thing, and declared, that with a little of her sister's spirit, she might have brought to reason any Sir Philip whatsoever, were it the termagant Falconbridge himself. But the greater part of their acquaintance affected candour, and saw faults on both sides; though, in fact, there only existed the oppressor and the oppressed. The tone of such critics was—"To be sure, no one will justify Sir Philip Forester, but then we all know Sir Philip, and Jemmie Falconer might have known what she had to expect from the beginning.—What made her set her cap at Sir Philip?—He would never have looked at her if she had not thrown herself at his head, with her poor ten thousand pounds. I am sure, if it is money he wanted, she spoiled his market. I know where Sir Philip could have done much better. —And then, if she *would* have the man, could not she try to make him more comfortable at home, and have his friends oftener, and not plague him with the squalling children, and take care all was handsome and in good style about the house? I declare I think Sir Philip would have made a very domestic man, with a woman who knew how to manage him."

Now these fair critics, in raising their profound edifice of domestic felicity, did not recollect that the corner-stone was wanting; and that to receive good company with good cheer, the means of the banquet ought to have been furnished by Sir Philip; whose income (dilapidated as it was) was not equal to the display of the hospitality required, and at the same time to the supply of the good knight's *menus plaisirs*. So, in spite of all that was so sagely suggested by female friends, Sir Philip carried his good humour every where abroad, and left at home a solitary mansion, and a pining spouse.

At length, inconvenienced in his money affairs, and tired even of the short time which be spent in his own dull house, Sir Philip Forester determined to take a trip to the continent, in the capacity of a volunteer. It was then common for men of fashion to do so; and our knight perhaps was of opinion that a touch of the military character, just enough to exalt, but not render pedantic, his qualities as a *beau garçon*, was necessary to maintain possession of the elevated situation which he held in the ranks of fashion.

Sir Philip's resolution threw his wife into agonies of terror; by which the worthy baronet was so much annoyed, that, contrary to his wont, he took some trouble to soothe her apprehensions; and once more brought her to shed tears, in which sorrow was not altogether unmingled with pleasure. Lady Bothwell asked, as a favour, Sir Philip's permission to receive her sister and her family into her own house during his absence on the continent. Sir Philip readily assented to a proposition which saved expense, silenced the foolish people who might have talked of a deserted wife and family, and gratified Lady Bothwell; for whom he felt some respect, as for one who often spoke to him, always with freedom, and sometimes with severity, without being deterred either by his raillery, or the *prestige* of his reputation.

A day or two before Sir Philip's departure, Lady Bothwell took the liberty of asking him, in her sister's presence, the direct question, which his timid wife had often desired, but never ventured, to put to him.

"Pray, Sir Philip, what route do you take when you reach the continent?"

"I go from Leith to Helvoet by a packet with advices."

"That I comprehend perfectly," said Lady Bothwell drily; "but you do not mean to remain long at Helvoet, I presume, and I should like to know what is your next object?"

"You ask me, my dear lady," answered Sir Philip, "a question which I have not dared to ask myself. The answer depends on the fate of war. I shall, of course, go to head-quarters, wherever they may happen to be for the time; deliver my letters of introduction; learn as much of the noble art of war as may suffice a poor interloping amateur; and then take a glance at the sort of thing of which we read so much in the Gazette."

"And I trust, Sir Philip," said Lady Bothwell, "that you will remember that you are a husband and a father; and that though you think fit to indulge this military fancy, you will not let it hurry you into dangers which it is certainly unnecessary for any save professional persons to encounter."

"Lady Bothwell does me too much honour," replied the adventurous knight, "in regarding such a circumstance with the slightest interest. But to soothe your flattering anxiety, I trust your ladyship will recollect, that I cannot expose to hazard the venerable and paternal character which you so obligingly recommend to my protection, without putting in some peril an honest fellow, called Philip Forester, with whom I have kept company for thirty years, and with whom, though some folks consider him a coxcomb, I have not the least desire to part."

"Well, Sir Philip, you are the best judge of your own affairs; I have little right to interfere—you are not my husband."

"God forbid!"—said Sir Philip hastily; instantly adding, however, "God forbid that I should deprive my friend Sir Geoffrey of so inestimable a treasure."

"But you are my sister's husband," replied the lady; "and I suppose you are aware of her present distress of mind——"

"If hearing of nothing else from morning to night can make me aware of it," said Sir Philip, "I should know something of the matter."

"I do not pretend to reply to your wit, Sir Philip," answered Lady Bothwell; "but you must be sensible that all this distress is on account of apprehensions for your personal safety."

"In that case, I am surprised that Lady Bothwell, at least, should give herself so much trouble upon so insignificant a subject."

"My sister's interest may account for my being anxious to learn something of Sir Philip Forester's motions; about which otherwise, I know, he would not wish me to concern myself: I have a brother's safety too to be anxious for."

"You mean Captain Falconer, your brother by the mother's side: —What can he possibly have to do with our present agreeable conversation?"

"You have had words together, Sir Philip," said Lady Bothwell.

"Naturally; we are connexions," replied Sir Philip, "and as such have always had the usual intercourse."

"That is an evasion of the subject," answered the lady. "By words, I mean angry words, on the subject of your usage of your wife."

"If," replied Sir Philip Forester, "you suppose Captain Falconer simple enough to intrude his advice upon me, Lady Bothwell, in my domestic matters, you are indeed warranted in believing that I might possibly be so far displeased with the interference, as to request him to reserve his advice till it was asked."

"And being on these terms, you are going to join the very army in which my brother Falconer is now serving."

"No man knows the path of honour better than Captain Falconer," said Sir Philip. "An aspirant after fame, like me, cannot choose a better guide than his footsteps."

Lady Bothwell rose and went to the window, the tears gushing from her eyes.

"And this heartless raillery," she said, "is all the consideration that is to be given to our apprehensions of a quarrel which may bring on the most terrible consequences? Good God! of what can men's hearts be made, who can thus dally with the agony of others?" Sir Philip Forester was moved; he laid aside the mocking tone in which he had hitherto spoken.

"Dear Lady Bothwell," he said, taking her reluctant hand, "we are both wrong:—you are too deeply serious; I, perhaps, too little so. The dispute I had with Captain Falconer was of no earthly consequence. Had any thing occurred betwixt us that ought to have been settled *par voie du fait*, as we say in France, neither of us are persons that are likely to postpone such a meeting. Permit me to say, that, were it generally known that you or my Lady Forester are apprehensive of such a catastrophe, it might be the very means of bringing about what would not otherwise be likely to happen. I know your good sense, Lady Bothwell, and that you will understand me when I say, that really my affairs require my absence for some months;—this Jemima cannot understand; it is a perpetual recurrence of questions, why can you not do this, or that, or the third thing; and when you have proved to her that her expedients are totally ineffectual, you have just to begin the whole round again. Now, do you tell her, dear Lady Bothwell, that *you* are satisfied. She is, you must confess, one of those persons with whom authority goes farther than reasoning. Do but repose a little confidence in me, and you shall see how amply I will repay it."

Lady Bothwell shook her head, as one but half satisfied. "How difficult it is to extend confidence, when the basis on which it ought to rest has been so much shaken! But I will do my best to make Jemima easy; and farther, I can only say, that for keeping your present purpose I hold you responsible both to God and man."

"Do not fear that I will deceive you," said Sir Philip; "the safest conveyance to me will be through the general post-office, Helvoet-sluys, where I will take care to leave orders for forwarding my letters. As for Falconer, our only encounter will be over a bottle of Burgundy; so make yourself perfectly easy on his score."

Lady Bothwell could *not* make herself easy; yet she was sensible that her sister hurt her own cause by *taking on*, as the maid-servants call it, too vehemently; and by showing before every stranger, by manner, and sometimes by words also, a dissatisfaction with her husband's journey, that was sure to come to his ears, and equally certain to displease him. But there was no help for this domestic dissension, which ended only with the day of separation.

I am sorry I cannot tell, with precision, the year in which Sir Philip Forester went over to Flanders; but it was one of those in which the campaign opened with extraordinary fury; and many bloody, though indecisive, skirmishes were fought between the French on the one side, and the allies on the other. In all our modern improvements there are none, perhaps, greater than in the accuracy and speed with which intelligence is transmitted from any scene of action to those in this country whom it may concern. During Marlborough's campaigns, the sufferings of the many who had relations in, or along with, the army were greatly augmented by the suspense in which they were detained for weeks, after they had heard of bloody battles, in which, in all probability, those for whom their bosoms throbbed with anxiety had been personally engaged. Amongst those who were most agonized by this state of uncertainty was the, I had almost said deserted, wife of the gay Sir Philip Forester. A single letter had informed her of his arrival on the continent—no others were received. One notice occurred in the newspapers, in which Volunteer Sir Philip Forester was mentioned as having been intrusted with a dangerous reconnoissance, which he had executed with the greatest courage, dexterity, and intelligence, and received the thanks of the commanding officer. The sense of his having acquired distinction brought a momentary glow into the lady's pale cheek; but it was instantly lost in ashen whiteness at the recollection of his danger. After this they had no news whatever, neither from Sir Philip, nor even from their brother Falconer. The case of Lady Forester was not indeed different from that of hundreds in the same situation; but a feeble mind is necessarily an irritable one, and the suspense which some bear with constitutional indifference or philosophical resignation, and some with a disposition to believe and hope the best, was intolerable to Lady Forester, at once solitary and sensitive, low-spirited, and devoid of strength of mind, whether natural or acquired.

Chapter Two

As she received no further news of Sir Philip, whether directly or indirectly, his unfortunate lady began now to feel a sort of consolation, even in those careless habits which had so often given her pain. "He is so thoughtless," she repeated a hundred times a day to her sister, "he never writes when things are going on smoothly; it is his way: had any thing happened he would have informed us."

Lady Bothwell listened to her sister without attempting to console her. Probably she might be of opinion, that even the worst intelligence which could be received from Flanders might not be without some touch of consolation; and that the Dowager Lady Forester, if so she was doomed to be called, might have a source of happiness unknown to the wife of the gayest and finest gentleman in Scotland. This conviction became stronger as they learned from inquiries made at head-quarters, that Sir Philip was no longer with the army; though whether he had been taken or slain in some of those skirmishes which were perpetually occurring, and in which he loved to distinguish himself, or whether he had, for some unknown reason or capricious change of mind, voluntarily left the service, none of his countrymen in the camp of the allies could form even a conjecture. Meantime his creditors at home became clamorous, entered into possession of his property, and threatened his person, should he be rash enough to return to Scotland. These additional disadvantages aggravated Lady Bothwell's displeasure against the fugitive husband; while her sister saw nothing in any of them, save what tended to increase her grief for the absence of him whom her imagination now represented,—as it had before marriage,—gallant, gay, and affectionate.

About this period there appeared in Edinburgh a man of singular appearance and pretensions. He was commonly called the Paduan Doctor, from having received his education at that famous university. He was supposed to possess some rare receipts in medicine, with which, it was affirmed, he had wrought remarkable cures. But though, on the one hand, the physicians of Edinburgh termed him an empiric, there were many persons, and among them some of the clergy, who, while they admitted the truth of the cures and the force of his remedies, alleged that Doctor Baptista Damiotti made use of charms and unlawful arts in order to obtain success in his practice. The resorting to him was even solemnly preached against, as a seeking of health from idols, and a trusting to the help which was to come from Egypt. But the protection which the Paduan doctor received from some friends of interest and consequence enabled him to set these imputations at defiance, and to assume, even in the city of Edinburgh, famed as it was for abhorrence of witches and necromancers, the dangerous character of an expounder of futurity. It was at length rumoured, that, for a certain gratification, which of course was not an inconsiderable one, Doctor Baptista Damiotti could tell the fate of the absent, and even show his visitors the personal form of their absent friends, and the action in which they were engaged at the moment. This rumour came to the ears of Lady Forester, who had reached that pitch of mental agony in which the sufferer will do any thing, or endure any thing, that suspense may be converted into certainty.

Gentle and timid in most cases, her state of mind made her equally obstinate and reckless, and it was with no small surprise and alarm that her sister, Lady Bothwell, heard her express a resolution to visit this man of art, and learn from him the fate of her husband. Lady Bothwell remonstrated on the improbability that such pretensions as those of this foreigner could be founded in any thing but imposture.

"I care not," said the deserted wife, "what degree of ridicule I may incur: if there be any one chance out of a hundred that I may obtain some certainty of my husband's fate, I would not miss that chance for whatever else the world can offer me."

Lady Bothwell next urged the unlawfulness of resorting to such sources of forbidden knowledge.

"Sister," replied the sufferer, "he who is dying of thirst cannot refrain from drinking even poisoned water. She who suffers under suspense must seek information, even were the powers which offer it unhallowed and infernal. I go to learn my fate alone; and this very evening will I know it: the sun that rises to-morrow shall find me, if not more happy, at least more resigned."

"Sister," said Lady Bothwell, "if you are determined upon this wild step, you shall not go alone. If this man be an impostor, you may be too much agitated by your feelings to detect his villany. If, which I cannot believe, there be any truth in what he pretends, you shall not be exposed alone to a communication of so extraordinary a nature. I will go with you, if indeed you determine to go. But yet re-consider your project, and renounce inquiries which cannot be prosecuted without guilt, and perhaps without danger."

Lady Forester threw herself into her sister's arms, and, clasping her to her bosom, thanked her a hundred times for the offer of her company; while she declined with a melancholy gesture the friendly advice with which it was accompanied.

When the hour of twilight arrived,—which was the period when the Paduan doctor was understood to receive the visits of those who came to consult with him,—the two ladies left their apartments in the Canongate of Edinburgh, having their dress arranged like that of women of an inferior description, and their plaids disposed around their faces as they were worn by the same class; for, in those days of aristocracy, the quality of the wearer was generally indicated by the manner in which her plaid was disposed, as well as by the fineness of its texture. It was Lady Bothwell who had suggested this species of disguise, partly to avoid observation as they should go to the conjuror's house, and partly in order to make trial of his penetration by appearing before him in a feigned character. Lady Forester's servant, of tried fidelity, had been employed by her to propitiate the doctor by a suitable fee, and a story intimating that a soldier's wife desired to know the fate of her husband; a subject upon which, in all probability, the sage was very frequently consulted.

To the last moment, when the palace clock struck eight, Lady Bothwell earnestly watched her sister, in hopes that she might retreat from her rash undertaking; but as mildness, and even timidity, is capable at times of vehement and fixed purposes, she found Lady Forester resolutely unmoved and determined when the moment of departure arrived. Ill satisfied with the expedition, but determined not to leave her sister at such a crisis, Lady Bothwell accompanied Lady Forester through more than one obscure street and lane, the servant walking before, and acting as their guide. At length he suddenly turned into a narrow court, and knocked at an arched door, which seemed to belong to a building of some antiquity. It opened, though no one appeared to act as porter; and the servant stepping aside from the entrance, motioned the ladies to enter. They had no sooner done so, than it shut, and excluded their guide. The two ladies found themselves in a small vestibule, illuminated by a dim lamp, and having, when the door was closed, no communication with the external light or air. The door of an inner apartment, partly open, was at the further side of the vestibule.

"We must not hesitate now, Jemima," said Lady Bothwell, and walked forwards into the inner room, where, surrounded by books, maps, philosophical utensils, and other implements of peculiar shape and appearance, they found the man of art.

There was nothing very peculiar in the Italian's appearance. He had the dark complexion and marked features of his country, seemed about fifty years old, and was handsomely, but plainly, dressed in a full suit of black clothes, which was then the universal costume of the medical profession. Large wax-lights, in silver sconces, illuminated the apartment, which was reasonably furnished. He rose as the ladies entered; and, notwithstanding the inferiority of their dress, received them with the marked respect due to their quality, and which foreigners are usually punctilious in rendering to those to whom such honours are due.

Lady Bothwell endeavoured to maintain her proposed incognito; and as the doctor ushered them to the upper end of the room, made a motion declining his courtesy, as unfitted for their condition.

"We are poor people, sir," she said; "only my sister's distress has brought us to consult your worship whether——"

He smiled as he interrupted her—"I am aware, madam, of your sister's distress, and its cause; I am aware, also, that I am honoured with a visit from two ladies of the highest consideration—Lady Bothwell and Lady Forester. If I could not distinguish them from the class of society which their present dress would indicate, there would be small possibility of my being able to gratify them by giving the information which they came to seek."

"I can easily understand," said Lady Bothwell——

"Pardon my boldness to interrupt you, mi-lady," cried the Italian; "your ladyship was about to say, that you could easily understand that I had got possession of your names by means of your domestic. But in thinking so, you do injustice to the fidelity of your servant, and I may add, to the skill of one who is also not less your humble servant—Baptista Damiotti."

"I have no intention to do either, sir," said Lady Bothwell, maintaining a tone of composure, though somewhat surprised, "but the situation is something new to me. If you know who we are, you also know, sir, what brought us here."

"Curiosity to know the fate of a Scottish gentleman of rank, now, or lately, upon the continent," answered the seer; "his name is Il Cavaliero Philippo Forester; a gentleman who has the honour to be husband to this lady, and, with your ladyship's permission for using plain language, the misfortune not to value as it deserves that inestimable advantage."

Lady Forester sighed deeply, and Lady Bothwell replied—

"Since you know our object without our telling it, the only question that remains is, whether you have the power to relieve my sister's anxiety."

"I have, madam," answered the Paduan scholar; "but there is still a previous inquiry. Have you the courage to behold with your own eyes what the Cavaliero Philippo Forester is now doing? or will you take it on my report?"

"That question my sister must answer for herself," said Lady Bothwell.

"With my own eyes will I endure to see whatever you have power to show me," said Lady Forester, with the same determined spirit which had stimulated her since her resolution was taken upon this subject.

"There may be danger in it."

"If gold can compensate the risk," said Lady Forester, taking out her purse.

"I do not such things for the purpose of gain," answered the foreigner. "I dare not turn my art to such a purpose. If I take the gold of the wealthy, it is but to bestow it on the poor; nor do I ever accept more than the sum I have already received from your servant. Put up your purse, madam; an adept needs not your gold."

Lady Bothwell, considering this rejection of her sister's offer as a mere trick of an empiric, to induce her to press a larger sum upon him, and willing that the scene should be commenced and ended, offered some gold in turn, observing that it was only to enlarge the sphere of his charity.

"Let Lady Bothwell enlarge the sphere of her own charity," said the Paduan, "not merely in giving of alms, in which I know she is not deficient, but in judging the character of others; and let her oblige Baptista Damiotti by believing him honest till she shall discover him to be a knave. Do not be surprised, madam, if I speak in answer to your thoughts rather than your expressions, and tell me once more whether you have courage to look on what I am prepared to show?"

"I own, sir," said Lady Bothwell, "that your words strike me with some sense of fear; but whatever my sister desires to witness I will not shrink from witnessing along with her."

"Nay, the danger only consists in the risk of your resolution failing you. The sight can only last for the space of seven minutes; and should you interrupt the vision by speaking a single word, not only would the charm be broken, but some danger might result to the spectators. But if you can remain steadily silent for the seven minutes, your curiosity will be gratified without the slightest risk; and for this I will engage my honour."

Internally Lady Bothwell thought the security was but an indifferent one; but she suppressed the suspicion, as if she had believed that the adept, whose dark features wore a half-formed smile, could in reality read even her most secret reflections. A solemn pause then ensued, until Lady Forester gathered courage enough to reply to the physician, as he termed himself, that she would abide with firmness and silence the sight which he had promised to exhibit to them. Upon this, he made them a low obeisance, and saying he went to prepare matters to meet their wish, left the apartment. The two sisters, hand in hand, as if seeking by that close union to divert any danger which might threaten them, sat down on two seats in immediate contact with each other: Jemima seeking support in the manly and habitual courage of Lady Bothwell; and she, on the other hand, more agitated than she had expected, endeavouring to fortify herself by the desperate resolution which circumstances had forced her sister to assume. The one perhaps said to herself, that her sister never feared any thing; and the other might reflect, that what so feeble minded a woman as Jemima did not fear, could not properly be a subject of apprehension to a person of firmness and resolution like her own.

In a few moments the thoughts of both were diverted from their own situation, by a strain of music so singularly sweet and solemn, that, while it seemed calculated to avert or dispel any feeling unconnected with its harmony, increased, at the same time, the solemn excitation which the preceding interview was calculated to produce. The music was that of some instrument with which they were unacquainted; but circumstances afterwards led my ancestress to believe that it was that of the harmonica, which she heard at a much later period in life.

When these heaven-born sounds had ceased, a door opened in the upper end of the apartment, and they saw Damiotti, standing at the head of two or three steps, sign to them to advance. His dress was so different from that which he had worn a few minutes before, that they could hardly recognise him; and the deadly paleness of his countenance, and a certain stern rigidity of muscles, like that of one whose mind is made up to some strange and daring action, had totally changed the somewhat sarcastic expression with which he had previously regarded them both, and particularly Lady Bothwell. He was barefooted, excepting a species of sandals in the antique fashion; his legs were naked beneath the knee; above them he wore hose, and a doublet of dark crimson silk close to his body; and over that a flowing loose robe, something resembling a surplice, of snow-white linen; his throat and neck were uncovered, and his long, straight, black hair was carefully combed down at full length.

As the ladies approached at his bidding, he showed no gesture of that ceremonious courtesy of which he had been formerly lavish. On the contrary, he made the signal of advance with an air of command; and when, arm in arm, and with insecure steps, the sisters approached the spot where he stood, it was with a warning frown that he pressed his finger to his lips, as if reiterating his condition of absolute silence, while, stalking before them, he led the way into the next apartment.

This was a large room, hung with black, as if for a funeral. At the upper end was a table, or rather a species of altar, covered with the same lugubrious colour, on which lay divers objects resembling the usual implements of sorcery. These objects were not indeed visible as they advanced into the apartment; for the light which displayed them, being only that of two expiring lamps, was extremely faint.—The master—to use the Italian phrase for persons of this description—approached the upper end of the room, with a genuflexion like that of a catholic to the crucifix, and at the same time crossed himself. The ladies followed in silence, and arm in arm. Two or three low broad steps led to a platform in front of the altar, or what resembled such. Here the sage took his stand, and placed the ladies beside him, once more earnestly repeating by signs his injunctions of silence. The Italian then, extending his bare arm from under his linen vestment, pointed with his forefinger to five large flambeaux, or torches, placed on each side of the altar. They took fire successively at the approach of his hand, or rather of his finger, and spread a strong light through the room. By this the visitors could discern that, on the seeming altar, were disposed two naked swords laid crosswise; a large open book, which they conceived to be a copy of the Holy Scriptures, but in a language to them unknown; and beside this mysterious volume was placed a human skull. But what struck the sisters most was a very tall and broad mirror, which occupied all the space behind the altar, and, illumined by the lighted torches, reflected the mysterious articles which were laid upon it.

The master then placed himself between the two ladies, and, pointing to the mirror, took each by the hand, but without speaking a syllable. They gazed intently on the polished and sable space to which he had directed their attention. Suddenly the surface assumed a new and singular appearance. It no longer simply reflected the objects placed before it, but, as if it had self-contained scenery of its own, objects began to appear within it, at first in a disorderly, indistinct, and miscellaneous manner, like form arranging itself out of chaos; at length, in distinct and defined shape and symmetry. It was thus that, after some shifting of light and darkness over the face of the wonderful glass, a long perspective of arches and columns began to arrange itself on its sides, and a vaulted roof on the upper part of it; till, after many oscillations, the whole vision gained a fixed and stationary appearance, representing the interior of a foreign church. The pillars were stately, and hung with scutcheons; the arches were lofty and magnificent; the floor was lettered with funeral inscriptions. But there were no separate shrines, no images, no display of chalice or crucifix on the altar. It was, therefore, a Protestant church upon the continent. A clergyman dressed in the Geneva gown and band stood by the communion-table, and, with the Bible opened before him, and his clerk awaiting in the back ground, seemed prepared to perform some service of the church to which he belonged.

At length, there entered the middle aisle of the building a numerous party, which appeared to be a bridal one, as a lady and gentleman walked first, hand in hand, followed by a large concourse of persons of both sexes, gaily, nay richly, attired. The bride, whose features they could distinctly see, seemed not more than sixteen years old, and extremely beautiful. The bridegroom, for some seconds, moved rather with his shoulder towards them, and his face averted; but his elegance of form and step struck the sisters at once with the same apprehension. As he turned his face suddenly, it was frightfully realised, and they saw, in the gay bridegroom before them, Sir Philip Forester. His wife uttered an imperfect exclamation, at the sound of which the whole scene stirred and seemed to separate.

"I could compare it to nothing," said Lady Bothwell while recounting the wonderful tale, "but to the dispersion of the reflection offered by a deep and calm pool, when a stone is suddenly cast into it, and the shadows become dissipated and broken." The master pressed both the ladies' hands severely, as if to remind them of their promise, and of the danger which they incurred. The exclamation died away on Lady Forester's tongue, without attaining perfect utterance, and the scene in the glass, after the fluctuation of a minute, again resumed to the eye its former appearance of a real scene, existing within the mirror, as if represented in a picture, save that the figures were moveable instead of being stationary.

The representation of Sir Philip Forester, now distinctly visible in form and feature, was seen to lead on towards the clergyman that beautiful girl, who advanced at once with diffidence and with a species of affectionate pride. In the meantime, and just as the clergyman had arranged the bridal company before him, and seemed about to commence the service, another group of persons, of whom two or three were officers, entered the church. They moved, at first, forward, as though they came to witness the bridal ceremony, but suddenly one of the officers, whose back was towards the spectators, detached himself from his companions, and rushed hastily towards the marriage party; when the whole of them turned towards him, as if attracted by some exclamation which had accompanied his advance. Suddenly the intruder drew his sword; the bridegroom unsheathed his own, and made towards him; swords were also drawn by other individuals, both of the marriage party, and of those who had last entered. They fell into a sort of confusion, the clergyman, and some elder and graver persons, labouring apparently to keep the peace, while the hotter spirits on both sides brandished their weapons. But now, the period of the brief space during which the soothsayer, as he pretended, was permitted to exhibit his art, was arrived. The fumes again mixed together, and dissolved gradually from observation; the vaults and columns of the church rolled asunder, and disappeared; and the front of the mirror reflected nothing save the blazing torches, and the melancholy apparatus placed on the altar or table before it.

The doctor led the ladies, who greatly required his support, into the apartment from whence they came; where wine, essences, and other means of restoring suspended animation, had been provided during his absence. He motioned them to chairs, which they occupied in silence; Lady Forester, in particular, wringing her hands, and casting her eyes up to heaven, but without speaking a word, as if the spell had been still before her eyes.

"And what we have seen is even now acting?" said Lady Bothwell, collecting herself with difficulty.

"That," answered Baptista Damiotti, "I cannot justly, or with certainty, say. But it is either now acting, or has been acted, during a short space before this. It is the last remarkable transaction in which the Cavalier Forester has been engaged."

Lady Bothwell then expressed anxiety concerning her sister, whose altered countenance, and apparent unconsciousness of what passed around her, excited her apprehensions how it might be possible to convey her home.

"I have prepared for that," answered the adept; "I have directed the servant to bring your equipage as near to this place as the narrowness of the street will permit. Fear not for your sister; but give her, when you return home, this composing draught, and she will be better to-morrow morning. Few," he added, in a melancholy tone, "leave this house as well in health as they entered it. Such being the consequence of seeking knowledge by mysterious means, I leave you to judge the condition of those who have the power of gratifying such irregular curiosity. Farewell, and forget not the potion."

"I will give her nothing that comes from you," said Lady Bothwell; "I have seen enough of your art already. Perhaps you would poison us both to conceal your own necromancy. But we are persons who want neither the means of making our wrongs known, nor the assistance of friends to right them."

"You have had no wrongs from me, madam," said the adept. "You sought one who is little grateful for such honour. He seeks no one, and only gives responses to those who invite and call upon him. After all, you have but learned a little sooner the evil which you must still be doomed to endure. I hear your servant's step at the door, and will detain your ladyship and Lady Forester no longer. The next packet from the continent will explain what you have already partly witnessed. Let it not, if I may advise, pass too suddenly into your sister's hands."

So saying, he bid Lady Bothwell good night. She went, lighted by the adept, to the vestibule, where he hastily threw a black cloak over his singular dress, and opening the door, entrusted his visitors to the care of the servant. It was with difficulty that Lady Bothwell sustained her sister to the carriage, though it was only twenty steps distant. When they arrived at home, Lady Forester required medical assistance. The physician of the family attended, and shook his head on feeling her pulse.

"Here has been," he said, "a violent and sudden shock on the nerves. I must know how it has happened."

Lady Bothwell admitted they had visited the conjuror, and that Lady Forester had received some bad news respecting her husband, Sir Philip.

"That rascally quack would make my fortune were he to stay in Edinburgh," said the graduate; "this is the seventh nervous case I have heard of his making for me, and all by effect of terror." He next examined the composing draught which Lady Bothwell had unconsciously brought in her hand, tasted it, and pronounced it very germain to the matter, and what would save an application to the apothecary. He then paused, and looking at Lady Bothwell very significantly, at length added, "I suppose I must not ask your ladyship any thing about this Italian warlock's proceedings?"

"Indeed, doctor," answered Lady Bothwell, "I consider what passed as confidential; and though the man may be a rogue, yet, as we were fools enough to consult him, we should, I think, be honest enough to keep his counsel."

"*May* be a knave—come," said the doctor, "I am glad to hear your ladyship allows such a possibility in any thing that comes from Italy."

"What comes from Italy may be as good as what comes from Hanover, doctor. But you and I will remain good friends, and that it may be so, we will say nothing of whig and tory."

"Not I," said the doctor, receiving his fee, and taking his hat; "a Carolus serves my purpose as well as a Willielmus. But I should like to know why old Lady Saint Ringan's, and all that set, go about wasting their decayed lungs in puffing this foreign fellow."

"Ay—you had best set him down a Jesuit, as Scrub says." On these terms they parted.

The poor patient—whose nerves, from an extraordinary state of tension, had at length become relaxed in as extraordinary a degree —continued to struggle with a sort of imbecility, the growth of superstitious terror, when the shocking tidings were brought from Holland, which fulfilled even her worst expectations.

They were sent by the celebrated Earl of Stair, and contained the melancholy event of a duel betwixt Sir Philip Forester, and his wife's half-brother, Captain Falconer, of the Scotch-Dutch, as they were then called, in which the latter had been killed. The cause of quarrel rendered the incident still more shocking. It seemed that Sir Philip had left the army suddenly, in consequence of being unable to pay a very considerable sum, which he had lost to another volunteer at play. He had changed his name, and taken up his residence at Rotterdam, where he had insinuated himself into the good graces of an ancient and rich burgomaster, and by his handsome person and graceful manners captivated the affections of his only child, a very young person of great beauty, and the heiress of much wealth. Delighted with the specious attractions of his proposed son-in-law, the wealthy merchant—whose idea of the British character was too high to admit of his taking any precaution to acquire evidence of his condition and circumstances—gave his consent to the marriage. It was about to be celebrated in the principal church of the city, when it was interrupted by a singular occurrence.

Captain Falconer having been detached to Rotterdam to bring up a part of the brigade of Scottish auxiliaries, who were in quarters there, a person of consideration in the town, to whom he had been formerly known, proposed to him for amusement to go to the high church, to see a countryman of his own married to the daughter of a wealthy burgomaster. Captain Falconer went accordingly, accompanied by his Dutch acquaintance, with a party of his friends, and two or three officers of the Scotch brigade. His astonishment may be conceived when he saw his own brother-in-law, a married man, on the point of leading to the altar the innocent and beautiful creature, upon whom he was about to practise a base and unmanly deceit. He proclaimed his villany on the spot, and the marriage was interrupted of course. But against the opinion of more thinking men, who considered Sir Philip Forester as having thrown himself out of the rank of men of honour, Captain Falconer admitted him to the privileges of such, accepted a challenge from him, and in the rencounter received a mortal wound. Such are the ways of Heaven, mysterious in our eyes. Lady Forester never recovered the shock of this dismal intelligence.

"And did this tragedy," said I, "take place exactly at the time when the scene in the mirror was exhibited?"

"It is hard to be obliged to maim one's story," answered my aunt; "but to speak the truth, it happened some days sooner than the apparition was exhibited."

"And so there remained a possibility," said I, "that by some secret and speedy communication the artist might have received early intelligence of that incident."

"The incredulous pretended so," replied my aunt.

"What became of the adept?" demanded I.

"Why, a warrant came down shortly afterwards to arrest him for high-treason, as an agent of the Chevalier St. George; and Lady Bothwell recollecting the hints which had escaped the doctor, an ardent friend of the Protestant succession, did then call to remembrance, that this man was chiefly *proné* among the ancient matrons of her own political persuasion. It certainly seemed probable that intelligence from the continent, which could easily have been transmitted by an active and powerful agent, might have enabled him to prepare such a scene of phantasmagoria as she had herself witnessed. Yet there were so many difficulties in assigning a natural explanation, that, to the day of her death, she remained in great doubt on the subject, and much disposed to cut the Gordian knot by admitting the existence of supernatural agency."

"But, my dear aunt," said I, "what became of the man of skill?"

"Oh, he was too good a fortune-teller not to be able to foresee that his own destiny would be tragical if he waited the arrival of the man with the silver greyhound upon his sleeve. He made, as we say, a moonlight flitting, and was nowhere to be seen or heard of. Some noise there was about papers or letters found in the house, but it died away, and Doctor Baptista Damiotti was soon as little talked of as Galen or Hippocrates."

"And Sir Philip Forester," said I, "did he too vanish for ever from the public scene?"

"No," replied my kind informer. "He was heard of once more, and it was upon a remarkable occasion. It is said that we Scots, when there was such a nation in existence, have, among our full peck of virtues, one or two little barleycorns of vice. In particular, it is alleged that we rarely forgive, and never forget, any injuries received; that we used to make an idol of our resentment, as poor Lady Constance did of her grief; and are addicted, as Burns says, to 'Nursing our wrath to keep it warm.' Lady Bothwell was not without this feeling; and, I believe, nothing whatever, scarce the restoration of the Stuart line, could have happened so delicious to her feelings as an opportunity of being revenged on Sir Philip Forester for the deep and double injury which had deprived her of a sister and of a brother. But nothing of him was heard or known till many a year had passed away."

At length—it was on a Fastern's E'en (Shrovetide) assembly, at which the whole fashion of Edinburgh attended, full and frequent, and when Lady Bothwell had a seat amongst the lady patronesses, that one of the attendants on the company whispered into her ear, that a gentleman wished to speak with her in private.

"In private? and in an assembly-room?—he must be mad—tell him to call upon me to-morrow morning."

"I said so, my lady," answered the man, "but he desired me to give you this paper."

She undid the billet, which was curiously folded and sealed. It only bore the words, "*On business of life and death*," written in a hand which she had never seen before. Suddenly it occurred to her that it might concern the safety of some of her political friends; she therefore followed the messenger to a small apartment where the refreshments were prepared, and from which the general company was excluded. She found an old man, who at her approach rose up and bowed profoundly. His appearance indicated a broken constitution, and his dress, though sedulously rendered conforming to the etiquette of a ball-room, was worn and tarnished, and hung in folds about his emaciated person. Lady Bothwell was about to feel for her purse, expecting to get rid of the supplicant at the expense of a little money, but some fear of a mistake arrested her purpose. She therefore gave the man leisure to explain himself.

"I have the honour to speak with the Lady Bothwell?"

"I am Lady Bothwell; allow me to say that this is no time or place for long explanations.—What are your commands with me?"

"Your ladyship," said the old man, "had once a sister."

"True; whom I loved as my own soul."

"And a brother."

"The bravest, the kindest, the most affectionate," said Lady Bothwell.

"Both these beloved relatives you lost by the fault of an unfortunate man," continued the stranger.

"By the crime of an unnatural, bloody-minded murderer," said the lady.

"I am answered," replied the old man, bowing, as if to withdraw.

"Stop, sir, I command you," said Lady Bothwell.— "Who are you, that, at such a place and time, come to recal these horrible recollections? I insist upon knowing."

"I am one who means Lady Bothwell no injury; but, on the contrary, to offer her the means of doing a deed of Christian charity which the world would wonder at, and which Heaven would reward; but I find her in no temper for such a sacrifice as I was prepared to ask."

"Speak out, sir; what is your meaning?" said Lady Bothwell.

"The wretch that has wronged you so deeply," rejoined the stranger, "is now on his deathbed. His days have been days of misery, his nights have been sleepless hours of anguish—yet he cannot die without your forgiveness. His life has been an unremitting penance—yet he dares not part from his burthen while your curses load his soul."

"Tell him," said Lady Bothwell sternly, "to ask pardon of that Being whom he has so greatly offended; not of an erring mortal like himself. What could my forgiveness avail him?"

"Much," answered the old man. "It will be an earnest of that which he may then venture to ask from his Creator, lady, and from yours. Remember, Lady Bothwell, you too have a deathbed to look forward to; your soul may, all human souls must, feel the awe of facing the judgment-seat, with the wounds of an untented conscience, raw, and rankling—what thought would it be then that should whisper, 'I have given no mercy, how then shall I ask it?'"

"Man, whosoever thou mayst be," replied Lady Bothwell, "urge me not so cruelly. It would be but blasphemous hypocrisy to utter with my lips the words which every throb of my heart protests against. They would open the earth and give to light the wasted form of my sister—the bloody form of my murdered brother.—Forgive him?—Never, never!"

"Great God!" cried the old man, holding up his hands; "is it thus the worms which thou hast called out of dust obey the commands of their Maker? Farewell, proud and unforgiving woman. Exult that thou hast added to a death in want and pain the agonies of religious despair; but never again mock Heaven by petitioning for the pardon which thou hast refused to grant."

He was turning from her.

"Stop," she exclaimed; "I will try; yes, I will try to pardon him."

"Gracious lady," said the old man, "you will relieve the overburdened soul which dare not sever itself from its sinful companion of earth without being at peace with you. What do I know—your forgiveness may perhaps preserve for penitence the dregs of a wretched life."

"Ha!" said the lady, as a sudden light broke on her, "it is the villain himself." And grasping Sir Philip Forester, for it was he, and no other, by the collar, she raised a cry of "Murder, murder! seize the murderer!"

At an exclamation so singular, in such a place, the company thronged into the apartment, but Sir Philip Forester was no longer there. He had forcibly extricated himself from Lady Bothwell's hold, and had run out of the apartment which opened on the landing-place of the stair. There seemed no escape in that direction, for there were several persons coming up the steps, and others descending. But the unfortunate man was desperate. He threw himself over the balustrade, and alighted safely in the lobby, though a leap of fifteen feet at least, then dashed into the street, and was lost in darkness. Some of the Bothwell family made pursuit, and had they come up with the fugitive they might have perhaps slain him; for in those days men's blood ran warm in their veins. But the police did not interfere; the matter most criminal having happened long since, and in a foreign land. Indeed it was always thought that this extraordinary scene originated in a hypocritical experiment, by which Sir Philip desired to ascertain whether he might return to his native country in safety from the resentment of a family which he had injured so deeply. As the result fell out so contrary to his wishes, he is believed to have returned to the continent, and there died in exile. So closed the tale of the MYSTERIOUS MIRROR.

THE TAPESTRIED CHAMBER,

OR

THE LADY IN THE SACQUE

BY THE AUTHOR OF WAVERLEY

THE FOLLOWING narrative is given from the pen, so far as memory permits, in the same character in which it was presented to the author's ear; nor has he claim to further praise, or to be more deeply censured, than in proportion to the good or bad judgment which he has employed in selecting his materials, as he has studiously avoided any attempt at ornament which might interfere with the simplicity of the tale.

At the same time it must be admitted, that the particular class of stories which turns on the marvellous, possesses a stronger influence when told, than when committed to print. The volume taken up at noonday, though rehearsing the same incidents, conveys a much more feeble impression, than is achieved by the voice of the speaker on a circle of fire-side auditors, who hang upon the narrative as the narrator details the minute incidents which serve to give it authenticity, and lowers his voice with an affectation of mystery while he approaches the fearful and wonderful part. It was with such advantages that the present writer heard the following events related, more than twenty years since, by the celebrated Miss Seward, of Lichfield, who, to her numerous accomplishments, added, in a remarkable degree, the power of narrative in private conversation. In its present form the tale must necessarily lose all the interest which was attached to it, by the flexible voice and intelligent features of the gifted narrator. Yet still, read aloud, to an undoubting audience by the doubtful light of the closing evening, or, in silence, by a decaying taper, and amidst the solitude of a half-lighted apartment, it may redeem its character as a good ghost-story. Miss Seward always affirmed that she had derived her information from an authentic source, although she suppressed the names of the two persons chiefly concerned. I will not avail myself of any particulars I may have since secured concerning the details of the locality, but suffer them to rest under the same general description in which they were first related to me; and, for the same reason, I will not add to, or diminish the narrative, by any circumstance, whether more or less material, but simply rehearse, as I heard it, a story of supernatural terror.

About the end of the American war, when the officers of Lord Cornwallis's army, which surrendered at Yorktown, and others, who had been made prisoners during the impolitic and ill-fated controversy, were returning to their own country, to relate their adventures, and repose themselves, after their fatigues; there was amongst them a general officer, to whom Miss Seward gave the name of Browne, but merely, as I understood, to save the inconvenience of introducing a nameless agent in the narrative. He was an officer of merit, as well as a gentleman of high consideration for family and attainments.

Some business had carried General Browne upon a tour through the western counties, when, in the conclusion of a morning stage, he found himself in the vicinity of a small country town, which presented a scene of uncommon beauty, and of a character peculiarly English.

The little town, with its stately old church, whose tower bore testimony to the devotion of ages long past, lay amidst pastures and corn-fields of small extent, but bounded and divided with hedge-row timber of great age and size. There were few marks of modern improvement. The environs of the place intimated neither the solitude of decay, nor the bustle of novelty; the houses were old, but in good repair; and the beautiful little river murmured freely on its way to the left of the town, neither restrained by a dam, nor bordered by a towing-path.

Upon a gentle eminence, nearly a mile to the southward of the town, were seen, amongst many venerable oaks and tangled thickets, the turrets of a castle, as old as the wars of York and Lancaster, but which seemed to have received important alterations during the age of Elizabeth and her successor. It had not been a place of great size; but whatever accommodation it formerly afforded, was, it must be supposed, still to be obtained within its walls; at least, such was the inference which General Browne drew from observing the smoke arise merrily from several of the ancient wreathed and carved chimney-stalks. The wall of the park ran alongside of the highway for two or three hundred yards; and through the different points by which the eye found glimpses into the woodland scenery, it seemed to be well stocked. Other points of view opened in succession; now a full one, of the front of the old castle, and now a side glimpse at its particolour towers; the former rich in all the bizarrerie of the Elizabethan school, while the simple and solid strength of other parts of the building seemed to show that they had been raised more for defence than ostentation.

Delighted with the partial glimpses which he obtained of the castle through the woods and glades by which this ancient feudal fortress was surrounded, our military traveller was determined to inquire whether it might not deserve a nearer view, and whether it contained family pictures or other objects of curiosity worthy of a stranger's visit; when, leaving the vicinity of the park, he rolled through a clean and well-paved street, and stopped at the door of a well-frequented inn.

Before ordering horses to proceed on his journey, General Browne made inquiries concerning the proprietor of the chateau which had so attracted his admiration; and was equally surprised and pleased at hearing in reply a nobleman named, whom we shall call Lord Woodville. How fortunate! Much of Browne's early recollections both at school, and at college, had been connected with young Woodville, whom, by a few questions, he soon ascertained to be the same with the owner of this fair domain. He had been raised to the peerage by the decease of his father a few months before, and, as the general learned from the landlord, the term of mourning being ended, was now taking possession of his paternal estate, in the jovial season of merry autumn, accompanied by a select party of friends to enjoy the sports of a country famous for game.

This was delightful news to our traveller. Frank Woodville had been Richard Browne's fag at Eton, and his chosen intimate at Christ Church; their pleasures and their tasks had been the same; and the honest soldier's heart warmed to find his early friend in possession of so delightful a residence, and of an estate, as the landlord assured him with a nod and a wink, fully adequate to maintain and add to his dignity. Nothing was more natural than that the traveller should suspend a journey, which there was nothing to render hurried, to pay a visit to an old friend under such agreeable circumstances.

The fresh horses, therefore, had only the brief task of conveying the general's travelling carriage to Woodville Castle. A porter admitted them at a modern gothic lodge, built in that style to correspond with the castle itself, and at the same time rang a bell to give warning of the approach of visitors. Apparently the sound of the bell had suspended the separation of the company, bent on the various amusements of the morning; for, on entering the court of the chateau, several young men were lounging about in their sporting dresses, looking at, and criticising, the dogs which the keepers held in readiness to attend their pastime. As General Browne alighted, the young lord came to the gate of the hall, and for an instant gazed, as at a stranger, upon the countenance of his friend, on which war, with its fatigues and its wounds, had made a great alteration. But the uncertainty lasted no longer than till the visitor had spoken, and the hearty greeting which followed was such as can only be exchanged betwixt those, who have passed together the merry days of careless boyhood or early youth.

"If I could have formed a wish, my dear Browne," said Lord Woodville, "it would have been to have you here, of all men, upon this occasion, which my friends are good enough to hold as a sort of holiday. Do not think you have been unwatched during the years you have been absent from us. I have traced you through your dangers, your triumphs, your misfortunes, and was delighted to see that, whether in victory or defeat, the name of my old friend was always distinguished with applause."

The general made a suitable reply, and congratulated his friend on his new dignities, and the possession of a place and domain so beautiful.

"Nay, you have seen nothing of it as yet," said Lord Woodville, "and I trust you do not mean to leave us till you are better acquainted with it. It is true, I confess, that my present party is pretty large, and the old house, like other places of the kind, does not possess so much accommodation as the extent of the outward walls appears to promise. But we can give you a comfortable old-fashioned room, and I venture to suppose that your campaigns have taught you to be glad of worse quarters."

The general shrugged his shoulders, and laughed. "I presume," he said, "the worst apartment in your chateau is considerably superior to the old tobacco-cask, in which I was fain to take up my night's lodging when I was in the Bush, as the Virginians call it, with the light corps. There I lay, like Diogenes himself, so delighted with my covering from the element, that I made a vain attempt to have it rolled on to my next quarters; but my commander for the time would give way to no such luxurious provision, and I took farewell of my beloved cask with tears in my eyes."

"Well, then, since you do not fear your quarters," said Lord Woodville, "you will stay with me a week at least. Of guns, dogs, fishing-rods, flies, and means of sport by sea and land, we have enough and to spare: you cannot pitch on an amusement but we will find the means of pursuing it. But if you prefer the gun and pointers, I will go with you myself, and see whether you have mended your shooting since you have been amongst the Indians of the back settlements."

The general gladly accepted his friendly host's proposal in all its points. After a morning of manly exercise, the company met at dinner, where it was the delight of Lord Woodville to conduce to the display of the high properties of his recovered friend, so as to recommend him to his guests, most of whom were persons of distinction. He led General Browne to speak of the scenes he had witnessed; and as every word marked alike the brave officer and the sensible man, who retained possession of his cool judgment under the most imminent dangers, the company looked upon the soldier with general respect, as on one who had proved himself possessed of an uncommon portion of personal courage; that attribute of all others, of which every body desires to be thought possessed.

The day at Woodville Castle ended as usual in such mansions. The hospitality stopped within the limits of good order: music, in which the young lord was a proficient, succeeded to the circulation of the bottle: cards and billiards, for those who preferred such amusements, were in readiness: but the exercise of the morning required early hours, and not long after eleven o'clock the guests began to retire to their several apartments.

The young lord himself conducted his friend, General Browne, to the chamber destined for him, which answered the description he had given of it, being comfortable, but old-fashioned. The bed was of the massive form used in the end of the seventeenth century, and the curtains of faded silk, heavily trimmed with tarnished gold. But then the sheets, pillows, and blankets looked delightful to the campaigner, when he thought of his "mansion, the cask." There was an air of gloom in the tapestry hangings, which, with their worn-out graces, curtained the walls of the little chamber, and gently undulated as the autumnal breeze found its way through the ancient lattice-window, which pattered and whistled as the air gained entrance. The toilette, too, with its mirror, turbaned, after the manner of the beginning of the century, with a coiffure of murrey-coloured silk, and its hundred strange-shaped boxes, providing for arrangements which had been obsolete for more than fifty years, had an antique, and in so far a melancholy, aspect. But nothing could blaze more brightly and cheerfully than the two large wax candles; or if aught could rival them, it was the flaming bickering faggots in the chimney, that sent at once their gleam and their warmth, through the snug apartment; which, notwithstanding the general antiquity of its appearance, was not wanting in the least convenience, that modern habits rendered either necessary or desirable.

"This is an old-fashioned sleeping apartment, general," said the young lord, "but I hope you find nothing that makes you envy your old tobacco-cask."

"I am not particular respecting my lodgings," replied the general; "yet were I to make any choice, I would prefer this chamber by many degrees, to the gayer and more modern rooms of your family mansion. Believe me, that when I unite its modern air of comfort with its venerable antiquity, and recollect that it is your lordship's property, I shall feel in better quarters here, than if I were in the best hotel London could afford."

"I trust—I have no doubt—that you will find yourself as comfortable as I wish you, my dear general," said the young nobleman; and once more bidding his guest good night, he shook him by the hand, and withdrew.

The general once more looked round him, and internally congratulating himself on his return to peaceful life, the comforts of which were endeared by the recollection of the hardships and dangers he had lately sustained, undressed himself, and prepared for a luxurious night's rest.

Here, contrary to the custom of this species of tale, we leave the general in possession of his apartment until the next morning.

The company assembled for breakfast at an early hour, but without the appearance of General Browne, who seemed the guest that Lord Woodville was desirous of honouring above all whom his hospitality had assembled around him. He more than once expressed surprise at the general's absence, and at length sent a servant to make inquiry after him. The man brought back information that General Browne had been walking abroad since an early hour of the morning, in defiance of the weather, which was misty and ungenial.

"The custom of a soldier,"—said the young nobleman to his friends; "many of them acquire habitual vigilance, and cannot sleep after the early hour at which their duty usually commands them to be alert."

Yet the explanation which Lord Woodville then offered to the company seemed hardly satisfactory to his own mind, and it was in a fit of silence and abstraction that he awaited the return of the general. It took place near an hour after the breakfast bell had rung. He looked fatigued and feverish. His hair, the powdering and arrangement of which was at this time one of the most important occupations of a man's whole day, and marked his fashion as much as, in the present time, the tying of a cravat, or the want of one, was dishevelled, uncurled, void of powder, and dank with dew. His clothes were huddled on with a careless negligence, remarkable in a military man, whose real or supposed duties are usually held to include some attention to the toilette; and his looks were haggard and ghastly in a peculiar degree.

"So you have stolen a march upon us this morning, my dear general," said Lord Woodville; "or you have not found your bed so much to your mind as I had hoped and you seemed to expect. How did you rest last night?"

"Oh, excellently well! remarkably well! never better in my life" —said General Browne rapidly, and yet with an air of embarrassment which was obvious to his friend. He then hastily swallowed a cup of tea, and, neglecting or refusing whatever else was offered, seemed to fall into a fit of abstraction.

"You will take the gun to-day, general?" said his friend and host, but had to repeat the question twice ere he received the abrupt answer, "No, my lord; I am sorry I cannot have the honour of spending another day with your lordship: my post horses are ordered, and will be here directly."

All who were present showed surprise, and Lord Woodville immediately replied, "Post horses, my good friend! what can you possibly want with them, when you promised to stay with me quietly for at least a week?"

"I believe," said the general, obviously much embarrassed, "that I might, in the pleasure of my first meeting with your lordship, have said something about stopping here a few days; but I have since found it altogether impossible."

"That is very extraordinary," answered the young nobleman. "You seemed quite disengaged yesterday, and you cannot have had a summons to-day; for our post has not come up from the town, and therefore you cannot have received any letters."

General Browne, without giving any further explanation, muttered something of indispensable business, and insisted on the absolute necessity of his departure in a manner which silenced all opposition on the part of his host, who saw that his resolution was taken, and forbore all further importunity.

"At least, however," he said, "permit me, my dear Browne, since go you will or must, to show you the view from the terrace, which the mist, that is now rising, will soon display."

He threw open a sash-window, and stepped down upon the terrace as he spoke. The general followed him mechanically, but seemed little to attend to what his host was saying, as, looking across an extended and rich prospect, he pointed out the different objects worthy of observation. Thus they moved on till Lord Woodville had attained his purpose of drawing his guest entirely apart from the rest of the company, when, turning round upon him with an air of great solemnity, he addressed him thus:

"Richard Browne, my old and very dear friend, we are now alone. Let me conjure you to answer me upon the word of a friend, and the honour of a soldier. How did you in reality rest during last night?"

"Most wretchedly indeed, my lord," answered the general, in the same tone of solemnity;—" so miserably, that I would not run the risk of such a second night, not only for all the lands belonging to this castle, but for all the country which I see from this elevated point of view."

"This is most extraordinary,"—said the young lord, as if speaking to himself—"then there must be something in the reports concerning that apartment." Again turning to the general, he said, "For God's sake, my dear friend, be candid with me, and let me know the disagreeable particulars which have befallen you under a roof where, with consent of the owner, you should have met nothing save comfort."

The general seemed distressed by this appeal, and paused a moment before he replied. "My dear lord," he at length said, "what happened to me last night is of a nature so peculiar and so unpleasant, that I could hardly bring myself to detail it even to your lordship, were it not that, independent of my wish to gratify any request of yours, I think that sincerity on my part may lead to some explanation about a circumstance equally painful and mysterious. To others, the communication I am about to make, might place me in the light of a weak-minded, superstitious fool, who suffered his own imagination to delude and bewilder him; but you have known me in childhood and youth, and will not suspect me of having adopted in manhood, the feelings and frailties from which my early years were free." Here he paused, and his friend replied:

"Do not doubt my perfect confidence in the truth of your communication, however strange it may be; I know your firmness of disposition too well, to suspect you could be made the object of imposition, and am aware that your honour and your friendship will equally deter you from exaggerating whatever you may have witnessed."

"Well then," said the general, "I will proceed with my story as well as I can, relying upon your candour; and yet distinctly feeling that I would rather face a battery than recall to my mind the odious recollections of last night."

He paused a second time, and then perceiving that Lord Woodville remained silent and in an attitude of attention, he commenced, though not without obvious reluctance, the history of his night adventures in the Tapestried Chamber.

"I undressed and went to bed, so soon as your lordship left me yesterday evening; but the wood in the chimney, which nearly fronted my bed, blazed brightly and cheerfully, and, aided by a hundred exciting recollections of my childhood and youth, which had been recalled by the unexpected pleasure of meeting your lordship, prevented me from falling immediately asleep. I ought, however, to say, that these reflections were all of a pleasant and agreeable kind, grounded on a sense of having for a time exchanged the labour, fatigues, and dangers of my profession, for the enjoyments of a peaceful life, and the reunion of those friendly and affectionate ties, which I had torn asunder at the rude summons of war.

"While such pleasing reflections were stealing over my mind, and gradually lulling me to slumber, I was suddenly aroused by a sound like that of the rustling of a silken gown, and the tapping of a pair of high-heeled shoes, as if a woman were walking in the apartment. Ere I could draw the curtain to see what the matter was, the figure of a little woman passed between the bed and the fire. The back of this form was turned to me, and I could observe, from the shoulders and neck, it was that of an old woman, whose dress was an old-fashioned gown, which, I think, ladies call a sacque; that is, a sort of robe completely loose in the body, but gathered into broad plaits upon the neck and shoulders, which fall down to the ground, and terminate in a species of train.

"I thought the intrusion singular enough, but never harboured for a moment the idea that what I saw was any thing more than the mortal form of some old woman about the establishment, who had a fancy to dress like her grandmother, and who, having perhaps (as your lordship mentioned that you were rather straitened for room) been dislodged from her chamber for my accommodation, had forgotten the circumstance, and returned by habit, to her old haunt. Under this persuasion I moved myself in bed and coughed a little, to make the intruder sensible of my being in possession of the premises.—She turned slowly round—But, gracious heaven! my lord, what a countenance did she display to me! There was no longer any question what she was, or any thought of her being a living being. Upon a face which wore the fixed features of a corpse were imprinted the traces of the vilest and most hideous passions which had animated her while she lived. The body of some atrocious criminal seemed to have been given up from the grave, and the soul restored from the penal fire, in order to form, for a space, an union with the ancient accomplice of its guilt. I started up in bed, and sat upright, supporting myself on my palms, as I gazed on this horrible spectre. The hag made, as it seemed, a single and swift stride to the bed where I lay, and squatted herself down upon it, in precisely the same attitude which I had assumed in the extremity of my terror, advancing her diabolical countenance within half a yard of mine, with a grin which seemed to intimate the malice and the derision of an incarnate fiend."——

Here General Browne stopped—and wiped from his brow the cold perspiration with which the recollection of his horrible vision had covered it—"My lord," he said, "I am no coward. I have been in all the mortal dangers incidental to my profession, and I may truly boast, that no man ever saw Richard Browne dishonour the sword he wears; but in these horrible circumstances, under the eyes, and, as it seemed, almost in the grasp of an incarnation of an evil spirit, all firmness forsook me, all manhood melted from me like wax in the furnace, and I felt my hair individually bristle—I felt the current of my life-blood arrested, and I sank back in a swoon, as very a victim to panic terror as ever was a village girl, or a child of ten years old—How long I lay in this condition I cannot pretend to guess.

"But I was roused by the castle clock striking one, so loud that it seemed as if it were in the very room. It was some time before I dared open my eyes, lest they should again encounter the horrible spectacle. When, however, I summoned courage to look up, she was no longer visible. My first idea was to pull my bell, wake the servants, and remove to a garret or a hay-loft, to be ensured against a second visitation. Nay, I will confess the truth, that my resolution was altered, not by the shame of exposing myself, but by the fear that, as the bell-cord hung by the chimney, I might, in making my way to it, be again crossed by the fiendish hag, who, I figured to myself, might be still lurking about some corner of the apartment.

"I will not pretend to describe what hot and cold fever-fits tormented me for the rest of the night, through broken sleep, weary vigils, and that dubious state which forms the neutral ground between them—An hundred terrible objects appeared to haunt me; but there was the great difference betwixt the vision which I have described, and those which followed, that I knew the last to be deceptions of my own fancy and over-excited nerves.

"Day at last appeared, and I rose from my bed ill in health, and humiliated in mind. I was ashamed of myself as a man and a soldier, and still more so, at feeling my own extreme desire to escape from the haunted apartment, which, however, conquered all other considerations; so that, huddling on my clothes with the most careless haste, I made my escape from your lordship's mansion, to seek in the open air some relief to my nervous system, shaken as it was by this horrible rencounter with a visitant, for such I must believe her, from the other world. Your lordship has now heard the cause of my discomposure, and of my sudden desire to leave your hospitable castle. In other places I trust we may often meet; but God protect me from ever spending a second night under that roof!"

Strange as the general's tale was, he spoke with such a deep air of conviction, that it cut short all the usual commentaries which are made on such stories. Lord Woodville never once asked him if he was sure he did not dream of the apparition, nor suggested any of the possibilities by which it is fashionable to explain apparitions into vagaries of the fancy, or deceptions of the optic nerves. On the contrary, he seemed deeply impressed with the truth and reality of what he had heard; and, after a considerable pause, regretted, with much appearance of sincerity, that his early friend should in his house have suffered so severely.

"I am the more sorry for your pain, my dear Browne," he continued, "that it is the unhappy, though most unexpected, result of an experiment of my own. You must know, that for my father and grandfather's time, at least, the apartment which was assigned to you last night, had been shut on account of reports that it was disturbed by supernatural sights and noises. When I came, a few weeks since, into possession of the estate, I thought the accommodation, which the castle afforded for my friends, was not extensive enough to permit the inhabitants of the invisible world to retain possession of a comfortable sleeping apartment. I therefore caused the Tapestried Chamber, as we call it, to be opened; and, without destroying its air of antiquity, I had such new articles of furniture placed in it as became the more modern times. Yet as the opinion that the room was haunted very strongly prevailed among the domestics, and was also known in the neighbourhood and to many of my friends, I feared some prejudice might be entertained by the first occupant of the Tapestried Chamber, which might tend to revive the evil report which it had laboured under, and so disappoint my purpose of rendering it an useful part of the house. I must confess, my dear Browne, that your arrival yesterday, agreeable to me for a thousand reasons besides, seemed the most favourable opportunity of removing the unpleasant rumours which attached to the room, since your courage was indubitable, and your mind free of any pre-occupation on the subject. I could not, therefore, have chosen a more fitting subject for my experiment."

"Upon my life," said General Browne, somewhat testily, "I am infinitely obliged to your lordship—very particularly indebted indeed. I am likely to remember for some time the consequences of the experiment, as your lordship is pleased to call it."

"Nay, now you are unjust, my dear friend," said Lord Woodville. "You have only to reflect for a single moment, in order to be convinced that I could not augur the possibility of the pain to which you have been so unhappily exposed. I was yesterday morning a complete sceptic on the subject of supernatural appearances. Nay, I am sure that had I told you what was said about that room, those very reports would have induced you, by your own choice, to select it for your accommodation. It was my misfortune, perhaps my error, but really cannot be termed my fault, that you have been afflicted so strangely."

"Strangely indeed!" said the general, resuming his good temper; "and I acknowledge that I have no right to be offended with your lordship for treating me like what I used to think myself—a man of some firmness and courage.—But I see my post horses are arrived, and I must not detain your lordship from your amusement."

"Nay, my old friend," said Lord Woodville, "since you cannot stay with us another day, which, indeed, I can no longer urge, give me at least half an hour more. You used to love pictures, and I have a gallery of portraits, some of them by Vandyke, representing ancestry to whom this property and castle formerly belonged. I think that several of them will strike you as possessing merit."

General Browne accepted the invitation, though somewhat unwillingly. It was evident he was not to breathe freely or at ease, till he left Woodville Castle far behind him. He could not refuse his friend's invitation, however; and the less so, that he was a little ashamed of the peevishness which he had displayed towards his well-meaning entertainer.

The general, therefore, followed Lord Woodville through several rooms, into a long gallery hung with pictures, which the latter pointed out to his guest, telling the names, and giving some account of the personages whose portraits presented themselves in progression. General Browne was but little interested in the details which these accounts conveyed to him. They were, indeed, of the kind which are usually found in an old family gallery. Here, was a Cavalier who had ruined the estate in the royal cause; there, a fine lady who had reinstated it by contracting a match with a wealthy Roundhead. There, hung a gallant who had been in danger for corresponding with the exiled court at Saint Germain's; here, one who had taken arms for William at the Revolution; and there, a third that had thrown his weight alternately into the scale of Whig and Tory.

While Lord Woodville was cramming these words into his guest's ear, "against the stomach of his sense," they gained the middle of the gallery, when he beheld General Browne suddenly start, and assume an attitude of the utmost surprise, not unmixed with fear, as his eyes were caught and suddenly riveted by a portrait of an old lady in a sacque, the fashionable dress of the end of the seventeenth century.

"There she is—" he exclaimed, "there she is, in form and features, though far inferior in demoniac expression, of the accursed hag who visited me last night."

"If that be the case," said the young nobleman, "there can remain no longer any doubt of the horrible reality of your apparition. That is the picture of a wretched ancestress of mine, of whose crimes a black and fearful catalogue is recorded in a family history in my charter-chest. The recital of them would be too horrible: it is enough to say, that in yon fatal apartment incest, and unnatural murder, were committed. I will restore it to the solitude to which the better judgment of those who preceded me had consigned it; and never shall any one, so long as I can prevent it, be exposed to a repetition of the supernatural horrors which could shake such courage as yours."

Thus the friends, who had met with such glee, parted in a very different mood; Lord Woodville to command the tapestried chamber to be unmantled, and the door built up; and General Browne to seek in some less beautiful country, and with some less dignified friend, forgetfulness of the painful night which he had passed in Woodville Castle.

DEATH OF THE LAIRD'S JOCK

TO THE EDITOR OF THE KEEPSAKE

YOU HAVE asked me, sir, to point out a subject for the pencil, and I feel the difficulty of complying with your request; although I am not certainly unaccustomed to literary composition, or a total stranger to the stores of history and tradition, which afford the best topics for the painter's art. But although *sicut pictura poesis* is an ancient and undisputed axiom—although poetry and painting both address themselves to the same object of exciting the human imagination, by presenting to it pleasing or sublime images of ideal scenes; yet the one conveying itself through the ears to the understanding, and the other applying itself only to the eyes, the subjects which are best suited to the bard or tale-teller are often totally unfit for painting, where the artist must present in a single glance all that his art has power to tell us. The artist can neither recapitulate the past nor intimate the future. The single *now* is all which he can present; and hence, unquestionably, many subjects which delight us in poetry or in narrative, whether real or fictitious, cannot with advantage be transferred to the canvas.

Being in some degree aware of these difficulties, though doubtless unacquainted both with their extent, and the means by which they may be modified or surmounted, I have, nevertheless, ventured to draw up the following traditional narrative as a story in which, when the general details are known, the interest is so much concentrated in one strong moment of agonizing passion, that it can be understood, and sympathized with, at a single glance. I therefore presume that it may be acceptable as a hint to some one among the numerous artists, who have of late years distinguished themselves as rearing up and supporting the British school.

Enough has been said and sung about

> The well contested ground,
> The warlike Borderland—

to render the habits of the tribes who inhabited them before the union of the Crowns familiar to most of your readers. The rougher and sterner features of their character were softened by their attachment to the fine arts, from which has arisen the saying that, on the frontiers, every dale had its battle, and every river its song. A rude species of chivalry was in constant use, and single combats were practised as the amusement of the few intervals of truce which suspended the exercise of war. The inveteracy of this custom may be inferred from the following incident.

Bernard Gilpin, the Apostle of the North, the first who undertook to preach the protestant doctrines to the Border dalesmen, was surprised, on entering one of their churches, to see a gauntlet or mail-glove hanging above the altar. Upon inquiring the meaning of a symbol so indecorous being displayed in that sacred place, he was informed by the clerk that the glove was that of a famous swordsman, who hung it there as an emblem of a general challenge and gage of battle, to any who should dare to take the fatal token down. "Reach it to me," said the reverend churchman. The clerk and sexton equally declined the perilous office, and the good Bernard Gilpin was obliged to remove the glove with his own hands, desiring those who were present to inform the champion that he, and no other, had possessed himself of the gage of defiance. But the champion was as much ashamed to face Bernard Gilpin as the officials of the church had been to displace his pledge of combat.

The date of the following story is about the latter years of Queen Elizabeth's reign; and the events took place in Liddesdale, a hilly and pastoral district of Roxburghshire, which, on a part of its boundary, is divided from England only by a small river.

During the good old times of *rugging and riving* (that is, tugging and tearing), under which term the disorderly doings of the warlike age are affectionately remembered, this valley was chiefly inhabited by the sept or clan of the Armstrongs. The chief of this warlike race was the Laird of Mangerton. At the period of which I speak, the estate of Mangerton, with the power and dignity of chief, was possessed by John Armstrong, a man of great size, strength, and courage. While his father was alive, he was distinguished from others of his clan who bore the same name, by the epithet of the *Laird's Jock*, that is to say, the Laird's son Jock or Jack. This name he distinguished by so many bold and desperate achievements, that he retained it even after his father's death, and is mentioned under it both in authentic records and in tradition. Some of his feats are recorded in the Minstrelsy of the Scottish Border, and others mentioned in contemporary chronicles.

At the species of singular combat which we have described the Laird's Jock was unrivalled, and no champion of Cumberland, Westmoreland, or Northumberland could endure the sway of the huge two-handed sword which he wielded, and which few others could even lift. This "awful sword," as the common people term it, was as dear to him as Durindana or Fushberta to their respective masters, and was near as formidable to his enemies as those renowned falchions proved to the foes of Christendom. The weapon had been bequeathed to him by a celebrated English outlaw named Hobbie Noble, who, having committed some deed for which he was in danger from justice, fled to Liddesdale, and became a follower, or rather a brother-in-arms, to the renowned Laird's Jock; till venturing into England with a small escort, a faithless guide, and with a light single-handed sword instead of his ponderous one, Hobbie Noble, attacked by superior numbers, was made prisoner and executed. At his death he bequeathed the highly prized sword to the Laird's Jock, in whose castle he had left it.

With this weapon, and by means of his own strength and address, the Laird's Jock maintained the reputation of the best swordsman on the border-side, and defeated or slew many who ventured to dispute with him the formidable title.

But years pass on with the strong and the brave as with the feeble and the timid. In process of time, the Laird's Jock grew incapable of wielding his weapons, and finally of all active exertion, even of the most ordinary kind. The disabled champion became at length totally bed-ridden, and entirely dependent for his comfort on the pious duties of an only daughter, his perpetual attendant and companion.

Besides this dutiful child, the Laird's Jock had an only son, upon whom devolved the perilous task of leading the clan to battle, and maintaining the warlike renown of his native country, which was now disputed by the English upon many occasions. The young Armstrong was active, brave, and strong, and brought home from dangerous adventures many tokens of decided success. Still the ancient chief conceived, as it would seem, that his son was scarce yet entitled by age and experience to be intrusted with the two-handed sword, by the use of which he had himself been so dreadfully distinguished.

At length, an English champion, one of the name of Foster (if I rightly recollect), had the audacity to send a challenge to the best swordsman in Liddesdale; and young Armstrong, burning for chivalrous distinction, accepted the challenge.

The heart of the disabled old man swelled with joy, when he heard that the challenge was passed and accepted, and the meeting fixed at a neutral spot, used as the place of rencontre upon such occasions, and which he himself had distinguished by several victories. He exulted so much in the conquest which he anticipated, that, to nerve his son to still bolder exertions, he conferred upon him, as champion of his clan and province, the celebrated weapon which he had hitherto retained in his own custody.

This was not all. When the day of combat arrived, the Laird's Jock, in spite of his daughter's affectionate remonstrances, determined, though he had not left his bed for two years, to be a personal witness of the duel. His will was still a law to his people, who bore him on their shoulders, wrapt in plaids and blankets, to the spot where the combat was to take place, and seated him on a fragment of rock, which is still called the Laird's Jock's stone. There he remained with eyes fixed on the lists or barrier, within which the champions were about to meet. His daughter, having done all she could for his accommodation, stood motionless beside him, divided between anxiety for his health, and for the event of the combat to her beloved brother. Ere yet the fight began, the old men gazed on their chief, now seen for the first time after several years, and sadly compared his altered features and wasted frame, with the paragon of strength and manly beauty which they had once remembered. The young gazed on his large form and powerful make, as upon some antediluvian giant who had survived the destruction of the deluge.

But the sound of the trumpets on both sides recalled the attention of every one to the lists, surrounded as they were by numbers of both nations, eager to witness the event of the day. The combatants met in the lists. It is needless to describe the struggle: the Scottish champion fell. Foster, placing his foot on his antagonist, seized on the redoubted sword, so precious in the eyes of its aged owner, and brandished it over his head as a trophy of his conquest. The English shouted in triumph. But the despairing cry of the aged champion, who saw his country dishonoured, and his sword, long the terror of their race, in possession of an Englishman, was heard high above the acclamations of victory. He seemed, for an instant, animated by all his wonted power; for he started from the rock on which he sate, and while the garments with which he had been invested fell from his wasted frame, and showed the ruins of his strength, he tossed his arms wildly to heaven, and uttered a cry of indignation, horror, and despair, which, tradition says, was heard to a preternatural distance, and resembled the cry of a dying lion more than a human sound.

His friends received him in their arms as he sank utterly exhausted by the effort, and bore him back to his castle in mute sorrow; while his daughter at once wept for her brother, and endeavoured to mitigate and soothe the despair of her father. But this was impossible; the old man's only tie to life was rent rudely asunder, and his heart had broken with it. The death of his son had no part in his sorrow: if he thought of him at all, it was as the degenerate boy, through whom the honour of his country and clan had been lost, and he died in the course of three days, never even mentioning his name, but pouring out unintermitted lamentations for the loss of his noble sword.

I conceive, that the moment when the disabled chief was roused into a last exertion by the agony of the moment is favourable to the object of a painter. He might obtain the full advantage of contrasting the form of the rugged old man, in the extremity of furious despair, with the softness and beauty of the female form. The fatal field might be thrown into perspective, so as to give full effect to these two principal figures, and with the single explanation, that the piece represented a soldier beholding his son slain, and the honour of his country lost, the picture would be sufficiently intelligible at the first glance. If it was thought necessary to show more clearly the nature of the conflict, it might be indicated by the pennon of Saint George being displayed at one end of the lists, and that of Saint Andrew at the other.

I remain, sir,
Your obedient servant,
THE AUTHOR OF WAVERLEY.

A HIGHLAND ANECDOTE

BY SIR WALTER SCOTT, BART.

TO THE EDITOR OF THE KEEPSAKE

THE SAME course of reflection which led me to transmit to you the account of the death of an ancient borderer*, induces me to add the particulars of a singular incident, affording a point which seems highly qualified to be illustrated by the pencil. It was suggested by the spirited engraving of the Gored Huntsman, which adorned the first number of your work, and perhaps bears too close a resemblance to the character of that print to admit of your choosing it as a subject for another. Of this you are the only competent judge.

The story is an old but not an ancient one: the actor and sufferer was not a very aged man, when I heard the anecdote in my early youth. Duncan, for so I shall call him, had been engaged in the affair of 1746, with others of his clan; and was supposed by many to have been an accomplice, if not the principal actor in a certain tragic affair, which made much noise a good many years after the rebellion. I am content with indicating this, in order to give some idea of the man's character, which was bold, fierce, and enterprising. Traces of this natural disposition still remained on Duncan's rugged features, and in his keen grey eye. But the limbs, like those of the aged borderer in my former tale, had become unable to serve the purposes and obey the dictates of his inclination. On the one side of his body he retained the proportions and firmness of an active mountaineer; on the other, he was a disabled cripple, scarce able to limp along the streets. The cause which reduced him to this state of infirmity was singular.

Twenty years or more before I knew Duncan, he assisted his brothers in farming a large grazing† in the Highlands, comprehending an extensive range of mountain and forest land, morass, lake, and precipice. It chanced that a sheep or goat was missed from the flock, and Duncan, not satisfied with despatching his shepherds in one direction, went himself in quest of the fugitive in another.

In the course of his researches, he was induced to ascend a small and narrow path, leading to the top of a high precipice. Dan-

---

* "The Death of the Laird's Jock," published in the "Keepsake" for 1829.—ED.
† A pastoral farm.

gerous as it was at first, the road became doubly so as he advanced. It was not much more than two feet broad, so rugged and difficult, and, at the same time, so terrible, that it would have been impracticable to any but the light step and steady brain of a Highlander. The precipice on the right hand rose like a wall, and on the left, sunk to a depth which it was giddy to look down upon, but Duncan passed cheerfully on, now whistling the Gathering of his Clan, now taking heed to his footsteps, when the difficulties of the path peculiarly required caution.

In this manner, he had more than half ascended the precipice, when in mid way, and it might almost be said, in middle air, he encountered a buck of the red-deer species coming down the cliff by the same path in an opposite direction. If Duncan had had a gun no rencontre could have been more agreeable, but as he had not this advantage over the denizen of the wilderness, the meeting was in the highest degree unwelcome. Neither party had the power of retreating, for the stag had not room to turn himself in the narrow path, and if Duncan had turned his back to go down, he knew enough of the creature's habits to be certain that he would rush upon him while engaged in the difficulties of the retreat. They stood therefore perfectly still, and looked at each other in mutual embarrassment for some space.

At length the deer, which was of the largest size, began to lower his formidable antlers, as they do when they are brought to bay, and are preparing to rush upon hound and huntsman. Duncan saw the danger of a conflict in which he must probably come by the worst, and as a last resource, stretched himself on the little ledge of rock, which he occupied, and thus awaited the resolution which the deer should take, not making the least motion for fear of alarming the wild and suspicious animal. They remained in this posture for three or four hours, in the midst of a rock which would have suited the pencil of Salvator, and which afforded barely room enough for the man and the stag, opposed to each other in this extraordinary manner.

At length the buck seemed to take the resolution of passing over the obstacle which lay in his path, and with this purpose approached towards Duncan very slowly, and with excessive caution. When he came close to the Highlander he stooped his head down as if to examine him more closely, when the devil, or the untameable love of sport, peculiar to his country, began to overcome Duncan's fears. Seeing the animal proceed so gently, he totally forgot not only the dangers of his position, but the implicit compact which certainly might have been inferred from the circumstances of the situation.

With one hand Duncan seized the deer's horn, whilst with the other he drew his dirk. But in the same instant the buck bounded over the precipice, carrying the Highlander along with him. They went sheer down upwards of a hundred feet, and were found the next morning on the spot where they fell. Fortune, who does not always regard retributive justice in her dispensations, ordered that the deer should fall undermost and be killed on the spot, while Duncan escaped with life, but with the fracture of a leg, an arm, and three ribs. In this state he was found lying on the carcass of the deer, and the injuries which he had received rendered him for the remainder of his life the cripple I have described. I never could approve of Duncan's conduct towards the deer in a moral point of view (although, as Dangle says, he was my friend), but the temptation of a hart of grease, offering, as it were, his throat to the knife, would have subdued the virtue of almost any deer-stalker. Whether the anecdote is worth recording, or deserving of illustration, remains for your consideration. I have given you the story exactly as I recollect it.

ESSAY ON THE TEXT

1. 'THE INFERNO OF ALTISIDORA': genesis, composition, the later editions, the present text, notes 2. 'CHRISTOPHER CORDUROY' (108): genesis, composition, the later editions, the present text, notes 3. THE *BLACKWOOD'S* STORIES (116): genesis, composition, the later editions, the present text, notes 4. THE *KEEPSAKE* STORIES (143): genesis, composition, the later editions, the present text, notes.

The following conventions are used in transcriptions from Scott's manuscript and proofs: deletions are enclosed ⟨thus⟩ and insertions ↑thus↓; superscript letters are lowered without comment. The same conventions are used as appropriate for indicating variants between the printed editions. All manuscripts referred to are in the National Library of Scotland unless otherwise indicated.

1. 'THE INFERNO OF ALTISIDORA'

GENESIS

The year 1810 was important in Scott's development as a writer of prose fiction although this was not immediately apparent in the wider world. In May he completed *The Lady of the Lake* and at some stage he appears to have worked on the 'Memoirs' which were later to form the opening of Lockhart's *Life*.[1] On 15 September, James Ballantyne, Scott's friend and his partner in the printing business James Ballantyne and Co., wrote about some early chapters of *Waverley* that had evidently been sent to him for comment. Then in October Scott completed what was to be his first published work of fiction.

Ballantyne expressed his general approval of *Waverley*: 'What you have sent of Waverley has amused me very much', he wrote, but suggested that the sample was too short for him to be sure: 'you have sent too little to enable me to form a decided opinion'. Having offered some criticism of the account of Waverley's education, he nevertheless ended with encouragement to continue: 'Should you go on? My opinion is—clearly, *certainly*. I have no doubt of success, though it is impossible to guess how much.'[2] Lockhart, believing that the first part of the novel was written in 1805 and that this letter refers to 'the time when Scott *first* resumed his long-forgotten MS. of his Waverley', concludes that 'the novel appears to have been forthwith laid aside again'.[3] However P. D. Garside disputes this version of events and concludes in his EEWN edition of *Waverley* that according to 'the most recent researches it was probably begun in 1808 (not 1805 as traditional accounts have argued), continued in 1810, and completed in 1813–14'.[4] Garside further argues that Ballantyne's comments on the sample sent to him suggest that it may well have comprised only the first four chapters of the novel and that one of his criticisms 'could well have helped trigger Scott's opening remarks in Chapter 5'.[5] It would appear then that Scott, rather than abandoning the novel for several years after receiving Ballantyne's criticisms, responded by writing more chapters. It is not clear how many—certainly he did not finish the novel at this stage but it seems likely he wrote at least Chapters 5 to 7 of the first volume, and may have completed Chapter 11, taking the novel into the Highland scenes in continuance of his interest in the Highlands in *The Lady of the Lake*.[6] Whatever writing of *Waverley* he did would probably have begun in late September. In an earlier essay Garside notes his 'underlying sense' that *The Lady of the Lake* (concluded May 1810), the later sections of the 'Memoirs', and Chapters 5–7 of *Waverley* form 'part of the same creative process'.[7] It would seem that this same creative streak continued and produced what was to be his first completed and published piece of fiction, 'The Inferno of Altisidora'. On 23 October 1810, shortly after he had been working on *Waverley*, he wrote to James Ballantyne from his Border home, Ashestiel:

> I send you a wild sort of an introduction to a set of imitations in which I have made some progress for the Register. But I want your opinion on the plan and preliminary vision. Not having a Don Quixote here I cannot prefix the motto, but you will find the passage towards the end of the 4th vol: where Altesidore gives an account of her pretended death and of what she saw in the Infernal Regions. I will make considerable improvements if you like the general idea. You may take Counsellor Erskine into your deliberations. I think the imitations will consist of Crabbe, Southey, W. Scott, Wordsworth, Moore and perhaps a ghost story for Lewis. I should be ambitious of trying Campbell, but his peculiarity consists so much in the matter and so little in the manner that (to his huge praise be it said) I rather think I cannot touch him, understand I have no idea of parody but of serious anticipation if I can accomplish it—The subject of Crabbe is "The Poacher" a character in his line but which he has never touched.[8]

In due course Scott's 'wild sort of an introduction' appeared in the *Edinburgh Annual Register* for 1809 (published in August 1811) immediately after another piece of his, an essay 'On the Present State of Periodical Criticism'. 'The Inferno of Altisidora' was printed above the obviously fictional name Caleb Quotem and with the equally fictional date of April 1. And it preceded three poems by Scott: 'The Poacher' (imitating Crabbe), a song (imitating Moore), and 'The

Vision of Triermain' (Scott imitating himself), later revised as the opening of *The Bridal of Triermain*. In this way he provided part of his planned series of imitations.

Scott had admired Crabbe's work which he described as possessing 'great vigour and force of painting' but dealing with subjects which were 'low', 'coarse', and 'disgusting', a formula which he follows in his imitation.[9] He also had mixed feelings about Moore, admiring and condemning his 'prurient genius'.[10] Both had distinctive styles and his interest was clearly sufficient to prompt him to imitate them. For his self-imitation he turned to the familiar metre and subject matter of poems like *The Lay of the Last Minstrel*. However this time he moved to the other side of the Border, to an area of Cumberland with which he had become familiar during his courtship of Charlotte Carpenter in Gilsland in 1797. Only 10 km from Gilsland was Lanercost Priory which Scott was likely to have visited and where a Roland de Vaux of Triermain was buried. In his *History of the County of Cumberland* (1794), probably known to Scott although there is no copy in the Abbotsford Library, William Hutchinson, quoting an earlier manuscript source, records four lines of verse from a brass or inscription in the parish church of Lanercost, beginning 'Sir ROWLAND VAUX, that sometime was the Lord of Triermaine,/ Is dead, his body clad in lead, and ligs law under this stane'.[11] However Scott was anticipated in the literary use of the name by Coleridge who introduced Lord Roland de Vaux of Tryermaine as a character in Part 2 of 'Christabel', written in 1800. Unfortunately for Coleridge 'Christabel' was not published until 1816, well after the appearance of Scott's poem, and Coleridge prefaced it with a defence against the charge of plagiarism which could now be plausibly ascribed to it. Looking only at the published dates one would assume that Coleridge borrowed from Scott both the innovative metre Scott had used in *The Lay of the Last Minstrel* and subsequent poems and a character's name. In fact the boot was on the other foot: Scott had known the poem by heart since at least 1801 either having heard it recited or having read a manuscript copy.[12] Nevertheless, even if Scott knew the poem, and thus the reference to Roland de Vaux of Triermain, he may have felt justified in using the name. Arthur H. Nethercot has demonstrated that Coleridge took it (and others in his poem) from Hutchinson. Scott may well have done the same,[13] but it seems likely that he knew it quite independently of Coleridge's poem and, in using it, was merely (in an anonymous poem that was nevertheless intended to be recognised by some readers as his) asserting his ownership of the poetic territory of the late medieval and early modern Borders. In any case the name seems to have conjured up a whole world for him which he embodied in his new fragment of poetry.

Scott's involvement with the *Edinburgh Annual Register* derived in part from his uncomfortable relationship with Archibald Constable and from dissatisfaction with the Whig bias of the *Edinburgh Review*.[14] On 18 March 1807, A. G. Hunter, who was visiting London, wrote to tell his partner Constable that William Davies (of the publishing firm Cadell and Davies) had suggested to him the idea of an Edinburgh equivalent of the successful London *Annual Register*. Constable, replying on 22 March, showed some interest in the notion: 'The plan . . . so far as I have yet considered it, I confess is not unpromising'.[15] Meanwhile Hunter mentioned the idea 'in strict confidence' to Scott who was also at the time in London, and reported to Constable that 'I am happy to say that he approves most highly of our plan, and says that if a proper editor and conductor be got it will do famously, and that it can be sub-divided among all the proper and right folks'. At the same time he went on to tell his partner that Scott 'has a scheme of an antiquarian repository, along with young Rose, Ellis, Canning, etc., and he says that one of these works will assist the other, and go hand in hand'.[16] However by the following year Scott's relationship with Constable had soured and he pre-empted any possibility of Constable taking up Cadell's suggestion by himself playing a major role in the establishment of the *Edinburgh Annual Register*. Unlike Constable's Whig-inclined *Edinburgh Review*, the new journal was intended to take a Tory line or, as Scott puts it in a letter to George Ellis of 18 November 1808, to be '*valde* [vigorously] anti-Foxite'.[17] The *Register* when it finally appeared in 1810 came in two main parts, a history of the year (written initially by Southey and in later years by others including Scott and Lockhart), and a literary and historical miscellany containing, *inter alia*, original poetry. Thus the *Edinburgh Annual Register* now incorporated within it the other idea of an antiquarian miscellany, which Scott had originally suggested to Hunter might 'go hand in hand' with it, along with a further element, the publication of recent poetry. Scott had earlier entertained this idea of a miscellany in writing to Southey with a proposal for a periodical to be called the *British Librarian*, when he suggested that 'smaller tracts which have an interest independent of their scarcity or antiquity ought to be reprinted at length',[18] as the *Edinburgh Annual Register* was in fact to do.

    Although Scott told Ellis that the journal was to be 'conducted under the auspices of James Ballantyne', adding 'I cannot help him, of course, very far, but I will certainly lend him a lift as an adviser', he seems to have taken on the effective editorship of the literary section. As Kenneth Curry, editor of Scott's uncollected essays in the *Register*, notes, 'his disclaimer of active assistance and management is belied by the numerous and continual references to the *Register* both during its planning stages and its early years as he sought contributions and recommended the annual to his correspondents'.[19] From his friends and associates Scott was able to add such material as John

Wilson's *The Magic Mirror* (in the third issue), Hogg's *Poetic Mirror* (in the seventh issue), and shorter works by Hogg, Southey, Joanna Baillie, R. P. Gillies, and C. K. Sharpe. At the early stage of his involvement with the *Register*, Scott was himself a major contributor, mostly of poetry and essays. His own contributions to the literary section of the *Register* include, amongst many other items, his 'Biographical Memoir of John Leyden, M.D.' in the issue for 1811.[20] Typically, the volume in which 'The Inferno of Altisidora' appeared also included two essays by Scott ('Cursory Remarks upon the French Order of Battle, Particularly in the Campaigns of Buonaparte', and 'On the Present State of Periodical Criticism'), a reprint of his poem *The Vision of Don Roderick* as well an epitaph for Anna Seward.[21] His one digression into prose fiction was 'The Inferno of Altisidora', and it is evidence of Scott's deep involvement in the *Edinburgh Annual Register* at this stage that he chose to use it as the place in which to publish his first completed piece of prose fiction.

THE COMPOSITION OF THE INFERNO OF ALTISIDORA

If, as Garside suggests, *The Lady of the Lake*, the 'Memoirs', and parts of *Waverley* 'form part of the same creative process', the essay 'On the Present State of Periodical Criticism' and 'The Inferno of Altisidora' also have their own creative unity. Just as the 'Memoirs' deal with Scott's own education which he then goes on to satirise gently in *Waverley*, so the essay deals in vigorous but relatively straightforward discursive prose with matters which Scott develops into the satiric fantasy of 'The Inferno': the party spirit infecting contemporary criticism of literature, the role and character of Francis Jeffrey, Richard Cumberland's experiment in the *London Review* with using named reviewers rather than the anonymous reviewers normal at the time and, lastly, the alleged inconsistency of the *Edinburgh Review*'s critical criteria. The last of these provides a good example of how the two texts treat the same topic. In the essay Scott notes Jeffrey's criticism of the minute detail in *Marmion* in the same issue as he praised similarly minute detail in Crabbe's *Poems* and presents it as evidence of Jeffrey's critical inconsistency.[22] In 'The Inferno of Altisidora' he goes somewhat further in suggesting that Jeffrey was capable of dealing in an inconsistent way with, not two books, but even the same book, by describing how the figure who represents Jeffrey in the game played in the inferno 'often shewed his dexterity by striking the same volume alternately in different directions, leaving the gaping crowd totally at a loss whether it was his intention to strike it over the lists, or to shiver it to atoms' (9.35–38). In similar fashion relatively minor details are carried over from one text to the next. In the essay Scott claims that 'What we now think of Winstanly, who declared that Milton's fame had become "extinguished and stunk, because he reviled our sovereign lord king Charles," will be the opinion of future times concerning all critics, whether Whig or Tory, Pittite or Foxite, who shall make their literary decisions truckle to party politics'.[23] In 'The Inferno' he makes the same point through the comment of Tempus on his saving of Southey's blank verse poem *Madoc* from oblivion: '"Since I saved," answered he, "a poem in the same measure, the work of an old blind man, out of the hands of some gay courtiers, I have hardly made a more valuable acquisition"' (8.21–24). The essay's explicitly named Winstanly (as representative of the court party) and Milton become the fiction's less explicit but still recognisable 'gay courtiers' and 'blind old man'. There is, in short, so much overlap between the two that it is reasonable to conclude that the essay and the fantasy, though so different in their literary form, both arise from one single phase of creative activity.

While we have no record of which was written first, it is altogether more likely that the direct approach of the essay came first and that the writing of it generated the idea of the more imaginative treatment of 'The Inferno'. In a year in which fiction was very much on his mind and when he had been working on what was later to appear as his first novel, Scott's active involvement in the *Edinburgh Annual Register* had led him almost by accident, it would seem, into his first completed piece of prose fiction, and the first to be published. It is interesting in this context to remember how *Waverley* begins with a chapter in which Scott rehearses the various kinds of fiction suggested by different titles before deciding on his own style of fiction. Thus discursive prose leads to the fictive, and although it serves as a fanciful introduction to the imitations of Crabbe, Moore and Scott, the satiric vision that constitutes 'The Inferno of Altisidora' is a literary work in its own right.

While 'On the Present State of Periodical Criticism' and 'The Inferno of Altisidora' are so closely related in theme that they might be considered as one creative impulse, they also show a relation to other works on which Scott was working at this time. For instance, the scene in Chapter 6 of *Waverley* (a part of the novel very likely written in 1810) where the 'bibliopolist' laments to Mr Pembroke the poor rewards enjoyed by writers and the limits to what booksellers can do for them —'Ah, Caleb! Caleb! Well, it was a shame to let poor Caleb starve, and so many fat rectors and squires among us. I gave him a dinner once a-week; but, Lord love you, what's once a-week, when a man does not know where to go the other six days?'[24]—provides a slightly satirical counterpart to Scott's defence in the 'Essay on Periodical Criticism' of the actions of the bookseller or 'bibliopolist' (Scott uses the same term here) in his dealings with writers where he argues that the blame for poor returns to writers does not lie with the bookseller.[25] Another instance is suggested by Curry's comment that one model for 'The Inferno' may have been Swift's *Battle of the Books*.[26] Although the two works are very different they do share the general notion of books being involved in a conflict or contest. Swift was, indeed, very much on Scott's mind in 1810: through the year he worked on his edition of Swift's works although in the latter part his work was more interrupted, perhaps as much as anything by his fiction-writing although he offers his correspondents other reasons for the disruption.[27]

The letter to James Ballantyne of 23 October makes it clear that Scott had written 'The Inferno' by that date although this may have been an early sketch since he promises Ballantyne to 'make considerable improvements if you like the general idea'. On the other hand the letter seems to imply that of the imitations only that of Crabbe had so far been written. Whether Scott went on soon after to write the others or whether he wrote them later, he certainly completed them some time before the publication of the volume on 1 August 1811.

THE LATER EDITIONS

'The Inferno of Altisidora' itself was not reprinted in Scott's lifetime.[28] By contrast the attached poems were frequently reprinted. The imitations of Moore and Crabbe were reprinted much as they stood in the *Edinburgh Annual Register* but 'The Vision of Triermain' was considerably expanded: it forms only the first 133 lines of the first canto of *The Bridal of Triermain*, a poem in three cantos with an Introduction and Conclusion. The early editions of the poem (in which Scott's authorship was not acknowledged) include a short Preface which tells us little about why and when Scott came to expand the 'Vision' into the *Bridal*:

> In the Edinburgh Annual Register for the year 1809, three Fragments were inserted, written in imitation of Living Poets. It must have been apparent, that by these prolusions, nothing burlesque, or disrespectful to the authors was intended, but that they were offered to the public as serious, though certainly very imperfect, imitations of that style of composition by which each of the writers is supposed to be distinguished. As these exercises attracted a greater degree of attention than the author anticipated, he has been induced to complete one of them, and present it as a separate publication.[29]

Writing to Joanna Baillie on 4 August 1811 just after the publication of the volume, Scott pretends to preserve his anonymity:

> There is an article by a Mocking Bird (not in caricature but in serious sadness) who gives a good imitation of Crabbe, an indifferent one of Moor and one of me which begins very well indeed but falls off (as I think) grievously. Ballantyne says if the article

is approved he expects for next year a scene in imitation of Miss Baillie and also a ditty in the manner of Southey. The author lies conceald as yet.[30]

It is not clear when he began to expand the original lines but Scott refers to a 'Mocking Bird' in this letter and mentions the same bird in the verse Introduction to *The Bridal of Triermain* (not part of the material printed in the *Edinburgh Annual Register*), which rather suggests that he began work on the Introduction about this time. The first reference to *The Bridal of Triermain* in Grierson's edition of Scott's letters is not until 1 November 1812 when Scott writes to James Ballantyne of his determination to publish *Rokeby* by Christmas '& Triermain as soon after as may be'.[31] *The Bridal of Triermain* was duly published with John Ballantyne and Co. as publisher on 9 March 1813.[32] No author's name appears on the title page which gives the poem's full title as *The Bridal of Triermain, or The Vale of St John*. Second, third, and fourth editions followed within the year (the fourth edition, dated 1814, appeared on 23 December 1813). By the fourth edition, which was published by Longman, John Ballantyne and Co. had ceased to act as a publisher. A fifth edition appeared in 1817, published by Longman and Constable. In February 1819, another 'fourth' edition appeared in a combined edition with *Harold the Dauntless*. This was the first time that *The Bridal of Triermain* appeared with the author's name on the title page, and by admitting his authorship of *The Bridal of Triermain* Scott had also acknowledged 'The Inferno of Altisidora'.

Scott's own explanation of the reasons for his anonymity is to be found in his introduction to *The Lord of the Isles* in the Magnum edition of his *Poetical Works*:

> being much urged by my intimate friend, now unhappily no more, William Erskine, (a Scottish judge, by the title of Lord Kinedder,) I agreed to write the little romantic tale called the "Bridal of Triermain;" but it was on the condition, that he should make no serious effort to disown the composition, if report should lay it at his door. As he was more than suspected of a taste for poetry, and as I took care, in several places, to mix something which might resemble (as far as was in my power) my friend's feeling and manner, the train easily caught, and two large editions were sold. A third being called for, Lord Kinedder became unwilling to aid any longer a deception which was going farther than he expected or desired, and the real author's name was given.[33]

After this there were no separate editions of the poem in Britain during Scott's lifetime but its authorship continued to be acknowledged by its being included in collections of his poetry, firstly in a collection published on 13 March 1820, in *Miscellaneous Poems*, and finally in the seven editions of the *Poetical Works* before its inclusion after his death in the Magnum *Poetical Works* of 1833–34.

Because the poems, after their first appearance in the *Edinburgh Annual Register*, were always printed without the introductory dream allegory, some adjustments were required. In the first edition of *The Bridal of Triermain* (the first occasion on which the lines from the *Edinburgh Annual Register* were reprinted) and in subsequent editions of that poem, the headings 'Fragment First', 'Fragment Second' and 'Fragment Third' were removed, as was the footnote at the end of the song claiming that 'The rest was illegible, the fragment being torn across by a racket stroke' (16.36). However even in other parts of the text Scott introduced some minor revisions. Thus 'Round Glaramara's distant head' (18.3) becomes 'Round Skiddaw's dim and distant head', presumably to correct the topography, with a consequent change of 'dimly gleam'd' (18.4) to 'faintly gleam'd' in the following line. Similarly 'nether earth' (19.29) changes to 'middle earth' possibly because 'nether earth' might be interpreted as referring to hell, a contextually inappropriate meaning. Most other changes are very minor such as the capitalisation of 'stranger' (12.26) and the grammatical correction of 'breathes' (19.36) to 'breathe'.

THE PRESENT TEXT

The current edition is based on the text in the *Edinburgh Annual Register*, in the copy held by the National Library of Scotland. The *Edinburgh Annual Register* is, for the prose introduction, the only available text. For the poems, numerous other editions which appeared in Scott's lifetime are available, some showing signs of his revising hand. However as none of these revisions belong to the original period of composition they have not been included in this edition, which aims to reflect Scott's initial period of active engagement with the text: the composition in manuscript and the printing of the text in the *Edinburgh Annual Register* which followed soon afterwards. In the absence of manuscript material, all changes to the *Register* text are editorial. These involve emendations to the Spanish of the motto (such as 'nuevo' in place of 'nuero'), as well as several changes of punctuation and the correction of obvious errors (for example, 'Tiermain' is replaced by 'Triermain' at 17.5). In accordance with Scott's usual practice, we have inserted the number 'I' before the first stanza of 'The Vision of Triermain'.

NOTES

1 For a discussion of the dating of the 'Memoirs' see *Scott on Himself*, ed. David Hewitt (Edinburgh, 1981), xxiv–xxv.
2 MS 3879, f. 189r. Lockhart reproduced the part of the letter relating to *Waverley*; see J. G. Lockhart, *Memoirs of the Life of Sir Walter Scott*,

Bart., 7 vols (Edinburgh, 1837–38), 2.329–31.
3 *Life*, 2.329, 331.
4 See his Essay on the Text, *Waverley*, EEWN 1, 367.
5 Essay on the Text, *Waverley*, EEWN 1, 376–77. Garside had earlier suggested, with examples including an allusion to Swift, that 'Several elements in chapter v . . . have the ring of Scott's literary position late in 1810' ('Dating *Waverley*'s Early Chapters', *The Bibliotheck*, 13 (1986), 75).
6 See Essay on the Text, *Waverley*, EEWN 1, 379.
7 Garside, 'Dating *Waverley*'s Early Chapters', 79 (note 34).
8 *The Letters of Sir Walter Scott*, ed. H. J. C. Grierson and others, 12 vols (London, 1932–37), 1.412. Lockhart, perhaps correctly, emends 'anticipation' to 'imitation'; see *Life*, 2.352.
9 *Letters*, 2.149.
10 *Letters*, 1.265.
11 William Hutchinson, *The History of the County of Cumberland*, 2 vols (Carlisle, 1794), 1.55.
12 For a discussion of how Scott came to know 'Christabel' and his indebtedness to it see John Sutherland, *The Life of Walter Scott: A Critical Biography* (Oxford, 1995), 100–02.
13 See Arthur H. Nethercot, *The Road to Tryermaine: A Study of the History, Background, and Purposes of Coleridge's "Christabel"* (New York, 1962), 167–75.
14 A full account of the establishment of the *Edinburgh Annual Register* can be found in *Sir Walter Scott's Edinburgh Annual Register*, ed. Kenneth Curry (Knoxville, 1977), to which we are indebted.
15 Thomas Constable, *Archibald Constable and his Literary Correspondents*, 3 vols (Edinburgh, 1873), 1.111, 117.
16 Constable, 1.119.
17 *Letters*, 2.129.
18 *Letters*, 2.195: Scott to Robert Southey, 4 May 1809.
19 *Letters*, 2.129; Curry, 7.
20 'Biographical Memoir of John Leyden, M.D.', *Edinburgh Annual Register for 1811*, 4 (2), xli–lxviii.
21 See *EAR for 1809*, 2 (2), 526–41, 556–81, 601–35, 643–44. Scott acknowledged authorship of the Bonaparte essay and the epitaph but not of the essay on periodical criticism. Curry, however, presents a strong case for his authorship of the last which Southey also believed to be by Scott; see Curry, 132–34.
22 'On the Present State of Periodical Criticism', *EAR for 1809*, 2 (2), 571.
23 'On the Present State of Periodical Criticism', *EAR for 1809*, 2 (2), 576.
24 *Waverley*, EEWN 1, 31.21–25.
25 'On the Present State of Periodical Criticism', *EAR for 1809*, 2 (2), 558. The similarity of subject matter adds to the likelihood that this chapter was written in 1810. The name Caleb also suggestively overlaps with the name of the supposed author of 'The Inferno of Altisidora'.
26 Curry, 119.

27 See *Letters*, 2.305, 323, 385–86.
28 It was first reprinted by Curry, but without the poems which it was designed to introduce, in Curry, 119–32.
29 *The Bridal of Triermain; or, The Vale of St John*, 1st edn (Edinburgh, 1813), vii–viii.
30 *Letters*, 2.525–26.
31 *Letters*, 3.165. For the dating see James C. Corson, *Notes and Index to Sir Herbert Grierson's Edition of the Letters of Sir Walter Scott* (Oxford, 1979), 87–88.
32 *Edinburgh Evening Courant*, 8 March 1813, [1].
33 *The Poetical Works of Sir Walter Scott, Bart.*, [ed. J. G. Lockhart], 12 vols (Edinburgh, 1833–34), 10.8–9. This was written in April 1830 and Scott's memory was at fault: there were 5 editions of the poem without an author's name before the appearance of the combined edition with *Harold the Dauntless* in which Scott's name is given.

2. 'CHRISTOPHER CORDUROY'

GENESIS

In 1809 Scott, in a bid to escape his dependence on Archibald Constable as a publisher, set up a rival publishing house which, despite bearing the name of John Ballantyne and Co., was owned half by Scott and half by the Ballantyne brothers, John and James. John Ballantyne was appointed as manager, although Scott as the major shareholder had a large say in the running of the business, and premises were set up in Edinburgh at 4 Hanover Street. Although it did well initially with *The Lady of the Lake* (1810), the publishing venture was not a great success and Scott was, within a few years, obliged to return to Constable, who in 1817 was finally manoeuvred into buying up the remaining stock and thus, as Lockhart puts it, 'at one sweep cleared the Augean stable in Hanover Street of unsaleable rubbish to the amount of L.5270!'.[1] In the meantime John Ballantyne had reincarnated himself as a highly successful auctioneer, selling goods on commission, as well as items he had bought up himself, and operating out of the same Hanover Street premises.

On 4 January 1817 there appeared the first issue of a journal called *The Sale-Room*, published by John Ballantyne from his auction rooms in Hanover Street, and printed by James Ballantyne and Co., a business managed by Ballantyne but now fully owned by Scott after he purchased Ballantyne's half-share in 1815. Modelled on such works as Henry Mackenzie's *Lounger* and *Mirror*, *The Sale-Room* is a collection of miscellaneous writings, essays, sketches, reviews, poems, short stories and letters from fictitious correspondents on a wide variety of topics by a number of different authors. Lockhart attributes this new enterprise to John Ballantyne's continuing desire to be a publisher, but Lockhart had his own axe to grind in trying to shift the blame for the failure of the publishing house onto John and it is quite possible that the idea was Scott's own.

Certainly Scott had already demonstrated in 'The Inferno of Altisidora' that he could write in the requisite style: he was an enthusiastic supporter of the new journal from the beginning and contributed strongly to the initial issues. Having promised in an undated letter to John Ballantyne, written presumably at the end of 1816, 'When I come back I will have a sketch of No I to show you',[2] he writes to John on 26 December, 'I have herewith returnd to James No: I & will be answerable for No II & III' while also suggesting that he can engage 'a classical scholar of uncommon genius' in the enterprise.[3] The fact that Scott himself was engaging others in writing for the journal suggests he was taking a leading hand in its editing. In a later undated letter he writes, 'I return on friday & bring No. 1. 2. & 3. Look early out for a light [?tight] No. 4'.[4] However what Scott thought at this stage would be No. 4 may well have ended up as No. 5, 'The Search After Happiness', a poem which is the only work of his from *The Sale-Room* which he publicly acknowledged other than the Fare-well Address for the actor John Philip Kemble which appears above his name in the fourteenth issue. Writing to his friend Morritt on 30 January he confessed that 'For amusement and to help a little publica-tion that is going on here I have spun a doggrel tale calld the Search after Happiness of which I shall send a copy if it is of a frank-able size',[5] while to John Ballantyne he had described it as 'a slip-shod tale in verse'.[6] Somewhat later, on 3 May, he promised 'another on the refitting of Old plays for the modern stage when I come to town',[7] and an article on the reworking of Massinger's *City Madam* duly appears in the eighteenth and nineteenth issues.

These references in the letters tally with a copy of a note by the bookseller James Stillie found inside the front cover of the copy of *The Sale-Room* in the Bernard C. Lloyd Collection at the University of Aberdeen.[8] It and its accompanying ascription read as follows:

Articles in this Volume
By Sir Walter Scott
Pages   1 to 6   ^x9 to 14
     17 to 22   33 to 39
    °43 to 45   137 to 144
     145 to 148
	This is a copy of a note by the late
	Mr. James Stillie, bookseller,
	written in the cover of a copy of
	'The Sale-Room' which I bought
	at Dowell's in December 1900
	                         S.I.N.

Two of these ^{xo} articles have appeared in my Library Manual with cuts—both Annexed But none appeared in his works except one 33–37.^{xx}	^xVicissitudes of Peter Grievance (not correctly reprinted) pp. 9–140 °Aspirations of Christopher Corduroy pp 43–45 ^{xx}Poem 'The Search after Happiness' see poems 1837. vol XI. p. 352.
Article 64 By Henry MacKenzie author of Man of Feeling	The Sale-Room was edited by John Ballantyne

As already noted, much of what the note claims is corroborated by Scott's own letters. It is, however, more specific than Scott's letters. The pages cited cover all of the first issue (1–6; 7–8 are blank), Doctor Dunder and Peter Grievance in the second issue (9–14), the encounter of Peter Grievance with Andrew Pismire in the third issue (17–22), 'The Search after Happiness' in the fifth issue (33–39), and the essay on refitting of old plays which begins in the eighteenth issue (137–44) and continues (although the note does not acknow-ledge this) in the nineteenth issue (145–48). Interestingly the pages cited exclude the series 'Fifteen Days in Paris' which begins in the second issue (15–16) and occupies the whole of the fourth issue (25–32). This supports our assumption above that Scott's reference to a 'light' or 'tight' fourth issue refers to what became the fifth issue, 'The Search after Happiness'. More interestingly still the note ascribes a further piece to Scott which is not mentioned in the letters, the story of Christopher Corduroy in the sixth issue (43–45).

James Stillie, to whom this note is attributed, was an Edinburgh bookseller of both new and, later, secondhand books who also operated a circulating library. He died in 1893 in his eighties.[9] We have been able to trace only two issues of the *Stillie's Library Manual* mentioned in the note. The earlier of the two, dated 1884 and described as 'Second Series', contains an edited reprint of the story of Peter Grievance from the second number of *The Sale-Room*. A notice on the title page informs the reader that 'Mr Stillie being frequently asked to explain his connection with Sir Walter Scott, begs respectfully to state, that in early life he was apprenticed to John Ballantyne & Co., Booksellers—of which Sir Walter was the partner'; a further note records that the 'short Sketches appearing in this and previous Catalogue, were written for a short-lived periodical in 1817, published by John Ballantyne & Co.'. Below is an illustration of a man seated at a table in a room with Gothic features and with the Douglas coat of arms on the wall over the motto 'Tandem triumphans' and various pieces of heart-shaped furniture. Clearly this illustration was originally produced for the story of Christopher Corduroy which was evidently printed in the first series of Stillie's *Manual* since the works advertised at the end of this second series include the 'Library Annotated Catalogue, Including Sir Walter Scott's Humorous Sketch of the Aspirations of Christopher Corderoy, *with Etchings*, 6d.'. The *Manual* provides details of books Stillie has on sale including a set of the *Edinburgh Annual Register* described as 'John Ballantyne's (the publisher) copy, with many portraits and caricatures, also a page in autograph of Sir Walter Scott'.[10] The second issue we have traced is a special one entitled *Stillie's Memorial Manual*; it is undated but the list includes an 1890 publication.[11] It contains the article on *The City Madam* (printed on pages 137 to 144 of *The Sale-Room* and mentioned in Stillie's note).

Late in his life in 1892 Stillie was involved in a scandal. In 1890 doubts were raised about the genuineness of manuscripts he had sold and in late 1892 a series of articles in the *Edinburgh Evening Dispatch* exposed various supposedly genuine manuscripts of Burns and others (including some he had sold) as forgeries.[12] Before the controversy reached the papers Stillie told a reporter of the *Dispatch* that he had been the 'message boy' at John Ballantyne and Co. and was 'Often at Abbotsford, and always welcome, as he carried the money to Sir W.'.[13] In a letter to Walter Waithman Caddel printed in the *Dispatch*, he further claimed that 'Having been an apprentice of a firm in which Sir Walter Scott was a partner, and had his continued friendship for upwards of fifty years, and copied many of his manuscripts, I should, therefore, know his handwriting more than anyone else.' When Caddel challenged him on the grounds that he would have to be 107 to have known Scott for 50 years, Stillie responded, 'My connection with Sir Walter Scott was on or before 1816'.[14] A note in his name on 'Burns and Scott's Manuscripts' at the end of the *Memorial Manual* also claims that he was an apprentice to John Ballantyne and Co. in 1818.[15]

Some of his claims (for example, that he was a friend of Scott for 'upwards of 50 years') are clearly exaggerated but there is no special reason to doubt that he was associated with the publisher of *The Sale-Room* at, or close to, the time it was published.[16] His association with forgeries might also call his testimony into question although it is very possible that he was himself misled. Nevertheless, even though Stillie would have been only ten in 1817 when *The Sale-Room* was published, the fact that his ascriptions agree with the evidence of Scott's letters (apart from 'Christopher Corduroy' on which the surviving letters are silent) suggests he had accurate information about the authorship of *The Sale-Room*. Furthermore Stillie's ascription is perhaps supported by a rather cryptic notice 'To Correspondents' at the end of the issue in which 'Christopher Corduroy' appears. The notice begins '*We request the continuance of Christopher Corduroy's correspondence. Nobody, but himself, can be aware of the* full extent *of the debt we owe him*'.[17] If the debt referred to is a debt to *The Sale-Room* then the allusion could only be to Scott who had supplied so much of the material to this point.

In this edition we have accepted Stillie's ascription of Christopher Corduroy's letter to Scott. Not only its style but also its content support this: for all that Scott was himself rebuilding Abbotsford in partly medieval style, the satirical portrayal of the elder Christopher's gothicising of his cottage comes very naturally from a writer who was later to describe the creation of Castle Treddles in *Chronicles of the Canongate* with similarly satirical intent, though fully conscious, no doubt, of the parallels with his own life. We have therefore included it in this collection of his stories.

However while we have accepted the ascription of the letter to Scott, it was very early on ascribed to Lockhart. In the pirated Glasgow edition derived from James Hogg's recollections of Scott there are a number of footnotes not found in the American edition on which it is based.[18] One of these claims that 'It is a circumstance not generally known, that a communication to this publication [*The Sale-Room*] signed Christopher Corduroy, was the first thing that attracted Scott's notice to Lockhart, of whom he previously knew nothing'.[19] An assertion of this kind by Hogg, one of the original contributors to *The*

Sale-Room, would carry some authority but, as Jill Rubenstein points out, 'The footnotes are clearly not Hogg's'.[20] They not only mock him but also include comments on the Duke of Buccleuch which Hogg would never have countenanced. Lacking the authority of Hogg or any other source with credible claims to knowledge, their reliability must be called into question. In addition, the notice to correspondents in *The Sale-Room* which we have already cited could not possibly apply to Lockhart. It is however just conceivable that there is a small kernel of truth in the ascription to Lockhart: the surrounding material, which comments on the letter, includes three quotations in Greek. Scott claimed to have little knowledge of Greek, and on at least one occasion, although much later in life, in 1830, asked Lockhart, a good Greek scholar, to inscribe two Greek words into his own manuscript,[21] but as only a year before he had asked William Erskine to supply a Greek quotation it is inherently more likely that it was Erskine he asked for help on this occasion.[22]

Scott seems, then, to have begun *The Sale-Room* with enthusiasm, contributing strongly to the early issues. After this comes an apparent gap which may have something to do with the beginning of a three-year period in which Scott suffered intense pain from gallstones. There were particularly agonising attacks on 28 February and 4 March. Evidently he was well enough to write his article on *The City Madam* in May but whether or not he contributed during the gap or after this article is unclear.[23] His apparent waning of interest after the earlier issues might in part be explained by his concern with his new novel, *Rob Roy*, which is first mentioned in late April and for which a contract was agreed on 5 May. Scott had finished work on his previous novel in November 1816 and his period of most intense work on *The Sale-Room* thus fell between the two novels.[24]

The last issue, numbered 28, appeared on 12 July. By the time that *The Sale-Room* came to an end Scott had made a very substantial contribution to it with sketches, essays and poetry and he seems to have been overall the biggest contributor. He was also able to attract contributions from other authors. James Hogg contributed a letter signed 'Z' in which the letter-writer meets Charlie Dinmont of the Water-Cleuch (Hogg's complimentary counterpart to Scott's own Dandie Dinmont from *Guy Mannering*) as well as a poem entitled 'The Gipsies'.[25] The classical scholar James Bailey wrote an article on translations of Greek comedy[26] and James Ballantyne seems to have provided an essay on Kemble's retirement from the stage.[27] As we have seen, according to James Stillie's note another contributor was Henry Mackenzie with a letter on door-knocking signed Thomas Tranquil in the ninth issue which is certainly very much in Mackenzie's *Mirror* and *Lounger* style.[28]

THE COMPOSITION OF 'CHRISTOPHER CORDUROY'

If the dates on the various issues are to be trusted, Scott wrote, as usual, at speed: he sent the copy for the first issue on 26 December 1816 and it appeared on 4 January 1817. However there is the strong possibility that the issues were given standard dates a week apart which may not always accurately reflect the actual date of publication.[29] Be that as it may, it is likely that there was only a short gap between composition and publication and although Scott apparently corrected proofs it is unlikely he had much time to undertake extensive revision.[30] Certainly his early contributions were made in the midst of an active writing life. For instance in a letter, undated but plausibly assigned to 6 January by Corson, Scott writes 'I will send the Saleroom as soon as possible but I must complete my review of Lord Byron'; this refers to a substantial review of two works by Byron which occupied thirty-six pages in the *Quarterly Review* and which he completed on 10 January.[31]

THE LATER EDITIONS

There were no later editions of *The Sale-Room* in Scott's lifetime. As already noted, James Stillie reprinted parts of *The Sale-Room* in his *Manual*. For copyright reasons this would not have been possible during Scott's lifetime and Stillie's *Manual* did not appear until the 1880s and 1890s. Stillie had a personal and particular interest which led him to publish parts of *The Sale-Room* but beyond that there seems to have been little interest in a work which the influential Lockhart had condemned as 'a dull and hopeless concern'.[32] In the earlier twentieth century, Robert Cochrane and W. Forbes Gray assigned this sketch, one of the best in *The Sale-Room*, to Scott on stylistic grounds with Gray including short extracts from it in his article but otherwise it does not seem to have received any attention.[33]

THE PRESENT TEXT

Although Stillie by his page numbers ascribes only the actual story of Christopher Corduroy to Scott and not the prefatory and concluding comments we have included introduction, letter and conclusion as they represent a unified whole.[34] In the absence of a manuscript and of later editions from Scott's lifetime this edition is based entirely on the printed text of *The Sale-Room*, in the specific copy held by the National Library of Scotland, the only emendations being the correction of some obvious errors including minor errors in the Greek. However in the light of the general uncertainties about diacritics among Scott and his contemporaries, diacritics have not been inserted in the text, but do appear in the relevant explanatory notes.

NOTES

1 *Life*, 4.110. Lockhart's account simplifies a fraught negotiation that continued throughout the autumn of 1817: see Essay on the Text, *The Heart of Mid-Lothian*, ed. David Hewitt and Alison Lumsden, EEWN 6, 475–80.
2 MS 863, f. 97r.
3 *Letters*, 1.513.
4 *Letters*, 1.507.
5 *Letters*, 4.383.
6 MS 863, f. 209r: Scott to John Ballantyne, undated.
7 *Letters*, 1.515.
8 University of Aberdeen, Special Collections and Archives, WS M62.
9 Stillie died on 8 August 1893, and his death certificate gives his age at the time of death as 86. Stillie himself claims to have reached the age of 88 and he alludes to his Ayrshire birth (*Stillie's Memorial Manual* (Edinburgh, n.d.), Supplement, [4]; the only copy to have been found is in Edinburgh University Library, Corson C.S.60). The only baptismal record in the Scottish Old Parish Records which could apply to him is that of a James Stillie baptised on 10 May 1807 in Old Cumnock in Ayrshire.
10 *Stillie's Library Manual* (Edinburgh, 1884), 26. The only copy to have been found is in Internationaal Instituut voor Sociale Geschedenis, Amsterdam.
11 *Stillie's Memorial Manual*, Supplement, [1].
12 *Edinburgh Evening Dispatch*, 22 November–16 December 1892.
13 *Edinburgh Evening Dispatch*, 29 November 1892, 2.
14 *Edinburgh Evening Dispatch*, 2 December 1892, 2.
15 *Stillie's Memorial Manual*, Supplement, [4].
16 Stillie clearly had access to in-house information and material: the NLS holds proofsheets of some pages from Volume 5 of Scott's *Life of Napoleon Buonaparte* which bear a note above his name claiming that they are 'Authenticated by, having been given him while in the employment of the Ballantynes' (MS 496, f. 1r).
17 *The Sale-Room*, 48.
18 See James Hogg, *The Domestic Manners and Private Life of Sir Walter Scott* (Glasgow, 1834). The American edition is entitled *Familiar Anecdotes of Sir Walter Scott* (New York, 1834).
19 Hogg, *Domestic Manners*, 98.
20 James Hogg, *Anecdotes of Scott*, ed. Jill Rubenstein (Edinburgh, 1999), xxviii.
21 *Life*, 1.129–30.
22 *Letters*, 4.148.
23 The ambiguous wording of his announcement to John Ballantyne of his *City Madam* article might be taken to mean that he had very recently contributed to *The Sale-Room*: 'I am glad you like the Saleroom I will give you another on the refitting of Old plays for the modern stage when I come to town' (*Letters*, 1.515). Alternatively he could have already sent the *City Madam* article and this could represent a promise, evidently not fulfilled, to provide another on the same subject.

24 For the early history of *Rob Roy* see *Rob Roy*, ed. David Hewitt, EEWN 5, 345–49.

25 See Gillian Hughes, 'James Hogg's Contributions to *The Sale-Room*', *The Bibliotheck*, 23 (1998), 64–68.

26 *Letters*, 4.357–58; see also MS 1583, ff. 1–3, consisting of copies made by James Bailey of letters to him from Scott and John Ballantyne regarding various matters, including his contributions to *The Sale-Room*: in a note (f. 3r) Bailey records that he contributed no. 16.

27 See *Letters*, 4.162n.

28 In Stillie's note, quoted above, 'Article 64' seems to refer to the Thomas Tranquil letter which begins on *The Sale-Room*, 64.

29 Scott's letter promising 'another on the refitting of Old plays for the modern stage' is dated simply 'Saturday'. But it is postmarked 4 May, which means it was written on Saturday 3 May 1817. If the promise does refer to the *City Madam* essay, then the issue which includes the essay could not have appeared on its official date of 3 May.

30 That Scott received proofs is clear from his undated note to John Ballantyne regarding 'The Search After Happiness': 'I enclose your letter & the proof . . . I will try to give you a slip-shod tale in verse for your next No as soon as I can write it' (MS 863, f. 209r).

31 *Letters*, 1.527. Scott's review of *Childe Harold's Pilgrimage*, Canto 3, and *The Prisoner of Chillon* appeared in Number 31 of the *Quarterly Review* which is dated October 1816 but was actually published in February 1817.

32 *Life*, 4.41.

33 Robert Cochrane, 'A Forgotten Skit of Sir Walter's', *Sir Walter Scott Quarterly*, 1 (1927), 74–76; W. Forbes Gray, 'Some Forgotten Writings of Walter Scott', *Quarterly Review*, 255 (1930), 116–32.

34 Presumably Stillie reprinted only the letter and his page numbers refer only to the part he reprinted. We have here referred to the whole article as 'Christopher Corduroy' for convenience; it bears no distinct title in *The Sale-Room*.

3. THE *BLACKWOOD'S* STORIES

GENESIS

The story of Scott's fictional writing for *Blackwood's Edinburgh Magazine* is also the story of his close relationship with William Laidlaw, his factor and amanuensis. Initiated by Laidlaw's involvement with *Minstrelsy of the Scottish Border* the relationship began to develop in 1817 into true literary collaboration. This was the result of two very different events. In April, William Blackwood established a Tory magazine, initially named *The Edinburgh Monthly Magazine*, to counter the Whig *Edinburgh Review*, edited by Francis Jeffrey and published by Constable; and in May, in the wake of two farming failures, Laidlaw moved at Scott's invitation to the farm of Kaeside on the Abbotsford estate.

In establishing his magazine, to be edited by Thomas Pringle and James Cleghorn, Blackwood was naturally eager to involve Scott, who had recently entrusted him with the publication of the first series of *Tales of My Landlord.*[1] Scott provided some articles for the fledgling magazine, the most noteworthy being a series on the Scottish gypsies written with a degree of collaboration from Pringle. At this stage, Scott's contributions comprised non-fiction only. Meanwhile, Laidlaw had taken up residence at Kaeside, and Scott set about finding for him 'some literary labour . . . that will make ends meet'.[2] The first such employment involved the *Edinburgh Annual Register*, for which Scott himself was writing the historical section at this time. In June, Scott sent Laidlaw an advance of £25 'for the Chronicle part of the Register', promising him a similar amount later and suggesting that he should 'look out for two or three good original articles; and, if you would read and take pains to abridge one or two curious books of travels, I would send out the volumes'.[3] As Scott knew, however, there was little scope for Laidlaw's considerable talents in this type of work, nor was the remuneration sufficient. Scott had already approached Constable with the suggestion that he employ Laidlaw, 'a man of most uncommon genius'.[4] This proposal had fallen on deaf ears. There was, however, still Blackwood.

As it happened, Blackwood was particularly keen to remain in Scott's good graces at this time. When the first few numbers of his magazine proved disappointingly dull, he gave his editors notice that he would dispense with their services at the end of their six-month agreement; they immediately began negotiations with Constable and were appointed editors of his *Edinburgh Magazine* from October.[5] Blackwood meanwhile had moved swiftly. He had secured the services of John Wilson and John Gibson Lockhart, both of whom had strongly supported the *Monthly Magazine*, as editors of his periodical, now retitled *Blackwood's Edinburgh Magazine*.[6] When the first number appeared in October it included a 'Notice from the Editor' which flagged an innovative and adventurous work planned as 'a Depository of Miscellaneous Information and Discussion'.[7]

With the move of Pringle and Cleghorn to Constable, and the reinvention of William Blackwood's magazine, Scott found himself solicited by both sides. In a letter of 9 September, Pringle, who was already helping with Constable's magazine, applied to Scott for a contribution for the third number, which he was well aware would coincide with the launch of Blackwood's rebadged periodical.[8] Blackwood, in forwarding the concluding number of the *Edinburgh Monthly Magazine* to Scott, humbly requested his 'support and countenance', assuring him that 'Any thing from you whether in prose or verse wd be perfectly invaluable to me at present' and offering him payment, however 'disproportionate' to the value of his contribution.[9] He added, almost as an afterthought, an offer to employ 'a Mr Laidlaw' frequently mentioned 'in very high terms' by James Hogg, and in whom, according to Hogg, Scott took an interest, to provide 'communications on Rural affairs' and 'articles connected with Agriculture' in return for regular remuneration.[10]

Scott, who was primarily occupied with *Rob Roy* at the time,[11] replied on 21 September pledging his support, but reserving the right to contribute to Constable's magazine.[12] While waiving 'pecuniary recompense' for the 'broken hints detached fragments & so forth' which he might occasionally furnish he made it clear that his reward would lie in Laidlaw's regular employment. If his friend, 'a man of a singularly original & powerful mind acquainted with science well skilld in literature and an excellent agriculturist', were entrusted with supplying 'agricultural or literary articles', and in return receive 'at least' £120 a year, Scott himself would provide his 'best advice & frequent assistance'.[13] He tempted Blackwood with the conditional promise of regular antiquarian articles from Laidlaw and himself and a glimpse of material already to hand, such as 'an excellent essay on converting high & overploughd lands into grass' which Laidlaw had originally written for Scott's own use and 'a curious letter of the well known Chevalier Ramsay . . . on the state political and œconomical of France about 60 years since'. He might find, too, some other 'quodlibets' for his 'starting number'.[14] Thus although Blackwood's offer to employ Laidlaw is sometimes viewed as a master-stroke of the publisher's,[15] as it no doubt was by Blackwood himself, the truth of the matter appears to be that in attempting to use Laidlaw as bait Blackwood was himself, as Edgar Johnson puts it, 'hooked by the great fish he was trying to catch'.[16]

Shortly afterwards, on 23 September, Laidlaw wrote to Blackwood accepting a six-month trial period on the magazine.[17] He expects Blackwood to furnish him with a regular supply of London papers to aid him in compiling the 'Register'[18] and he already has some 'original communications' in view, including the agricultural essay which Scott had recommended to Blackwood.[19] He is careful to remind Blackwood that everything he writes will 'have the honour of passing thro Mr. Scotts hands'.[20] And so the stage was set for regular contributions, especially of antiquarian and agricultural interest, from Scott and Laidlaw. When the first number of *Blackwood's Edinburgh Magazine* burst upon Edinburgh on 20 October, however, it included only one contribution from Abbotsford, and that was very different in nature from the articles foreshadowed by Scott. Well suited to the tone of the new periodical, 'Alarming Increase of Depravity Among Animals', written from 'Tweedside', was considered by Lockhart 'certainly one of the best pieces of grave burlesque since Swift'.[21] And although Lockhart was justified in attributing it to Scott, it was the product of collaboration between Scott and Laidlaw.

However, no fewer than three articles in the first *Blackwood's* caused a general furore as well as specific lawsuits and threats of legal action. Alongside Wilson's inflammatory 'Observations on Coleridge's Biographia Literaria', and Lockhart's attack on Leigh Hunt in 'On the Cockney School of Poetry. No. I', there appeared a piece of local satire, 'Translation from an Ancient Chaldee Manuscript'.[22] The idea of James Hogg, who wrote the first part, the 'Chaldee Manuscript' was completed by Lockhart and Wilson during a riotous evening in which Blackwood himself participated. An allegorical account, couched in biblical language, of the events surrounding the establishment of Blackwood's two magazines, its identifiable and sometimes cruel portraits of Edinburgh personalities ensured that the number sold out immediately.

If Blackwood had courted Scott for the *Edinburgh Monthly Magazine* and subsequently for *Blackwood's*, he was now desperate to retain him. As Lockhart and Wilson realised, Scott was their only hope. Writing separately but in similar terms, both urged Blackwood to enlist Scott's support. 'If Scott is secured . . . all is and must be well', and 'With whatever Scott says, agree', wrote Wilson,[23] while Lockhart expanded upon the theme, recommending that Blackwood ask Scott '1st, To write a paper in No. 2. 2nd, To speak against the exclusion of your Magazine . . . in a Faculty meeting. 3rd, Not to say any ill of you, your Magazine, or virtually of the Chaldee MS. itself. Upon him everything depends, for in any Faculty meeting, where literature is concerned, who can stand against Maugraby?'.[24] Blackwood's concern at Scott's possible reaction to the 'Chaldee Manuscript' had led to a pre-emptive move. In a letter to Scott of 20 October acknowledging receipt of the proofs of 'Alarming Increase', and prior to sending the magazine, he expresses his overwhelming gratitude for his assistance, mentioning Laidlaw[25] and hoping that Scott will 'on the whole' enjoy the October number which he considers 'likely to make some noise'.[26] He then refers specifically to the 'Chaldee MS.', attempting to absolve himself of any responsibility for its inclusion by hiding behind his alleged 'Editor', who 'took his own way' and with whom he 'cannot interfere'.[27] The 'Chaldee Manuscript' did indeed displease Scott, but not on his own account. Although it amused him, he was upset by the treatment of some of his friends, as Blackwood correctly anticipated. Heartened by Laidlaw's view that 'I never saw any no. of a magazine so interesting',[28] Blackwood implored him to intercede with Scott, alleging the editor's last minute inclusion of the article despite Blackwood's own decision to the contrary, and claiming 'No one can regret more than I do that this article appeared'.[29] Laidlaw's response was to show Blackwood's letter to Scott, who then wrote to the publisher[30] acknowledging his displeasure, but affirming that unless there was further trouble his concern for Laidlaw would ensure his continued support.[31]

Scott and Blackwood met briefly the following week, an encounter which Scott described in a letter to Charles Kirkpatrick Sharpe, one of the victims of the 'Chaldee Manuscript'. He explains the reason for his continued involvement with the magazine as 'The having Laidlaw in tow with his helpless family', and affirms Blackwood's promise 'to republish the work omitting the offensive article & offering an apology to the parties aggrieved with a solemn engagement that no personalities should disgrace the work in future'.[32] It was therefore largely through Scott's agency that the 'Chaldee Manuscript' aftermath was minimised and that a mightily relieved Blackwood could look forward to further articles from Abbotsford. The 'Chaldee' may nevertheless have had an effect on the nature and regularity of Scott and Laidlaw's contributions, although, as discussed below, other factors were to come into play. Just prior to the publication of the number on 20 October, the two men had drawn up plans for a series of articles for *Blackwood's*. Writing to Blackwood on 18 October, Scott no doubt cheered him with the news that Laidlaw projected 'a series of letters under the signature of Magrauby' to be revised and corrected by Scott. Scott himself might possibly write at some length for the series, but if so Blackwood was not to divulge the extent of his involvement, and Scott would 'reserve the right of printing such myself, should I ever think it proper'.[33] 'Maugraby' we have already seen applied to Scott himself by Lockhart when he urged Blackwood to 'secure' Scott after the 'Chaldee' affair. The name of a powerful magician in the continuation of the *Arabian Nights*, Maugraby was perhaps a nickname which had accrued to Scott, who had been designated 'The Great Magician' by John Wilson as early as 1814.[34] Its use suggests that

Scott rather than Laidlaw was the prime mover in this case. After the furore of the October number, Blackwood was understandably eager for the first letter of the series, telling Laidlaw on 29 October 'how very anxious' he was 'to see your articles', and hinting, 'I hope Maugraby is ready'.[35] Maugraby was *not* ready and, as a series at least, never was. The November number of *Blackwood's* included nothing from either Scott or Laidlaw except the latter's 'Scottish Chronicle' and 'Agricultural Report' in the 'Register'. In late November or early December Laidlaw informed Blackwood that Scott's ill health 'has prevented him from finishing Magrabie's letter & I cannot speak to him again about it—altho I expect he will yet have it in time'.[36]

What exactly was the 'Magrabie's letter' which lay unfinished on Scott's desk? There are two possibilities: Laidlaw's 'Sagacity of a Shepherd's Dog' which appeared in January 1818,[37] and Scott's 'Phantasmagoria', which was included in the May number.[38] Much hinges on what Laidlaw means by 'finishing'. If he is referring to revision or even to the writing of a conclusion, 'Sagacity' is the obvious candidate; if to a story of Scott's which is as yet incomplete, 'Phantasmagoria' is the more likely, as its composition was indeed interrupted, with most of the ghost story and the first few lines of the introduction written and then laid aside.[39] Although it is tempting to link 'Phantasmagoria' and the Maugraby series to Scott's earlier plan, formed as far back as 1812, to collaborate with Charles Kirkpatrick Sharpe on 'a selection of the most striking and absurd stories of apparitions witchcraft demonology & so forth' which would include 'any of those mystical tales of tradition which we may be able yet to recover or may have stored in our memory',[40] the timescale involved seems to indicate that it was more likely 'Sagacity of a Shepherd's Dog' which was to have been the first of the projected series. Although Laidlaw clearly expects Scott is on the mend and that the letter will still be ready in time for the December number, issued on 20 December, Scott was struggling to finish *Rob Roy*, his illness having delayed submission of the final copy until 23 December.[41] In the event, another month would elapse before the appearance of 'Sagacity', which is in the form of a letter to the editor, as was proposed for the Maugraby series. However, this is not significant, as this was true of many contributions to *Blackwood's*. Intriguingly, it is signed 'M', and this is not an editorial addition; it occurs in the manuscript in Laidlaw's hand.[42] If this piece had been intended to open the planned series, perhaps a series title was to have given the full name 'Maugraby'; or perhaps the 'M' represents the last vestige of the idea. For it is at this time that the name 'Maugraby' as well as mention of a series disappears from the correspondence. Certainly, Laidlaw had recently been feeling disenchanted with his employment on the magazine. Delays in receiving essential publications had led him to contemplate resigning from the chronicle part of the 'Register';[43] and Blackwood's about-face on the inclusion of agricultural articles had left him anxious concerning his own ability to produce the literary pieces required in their stead.[44] His reservations may have combined with Scott's engagement with his new novel, *The Heart of Mid-Lothian*,[45] to doom the Maugraby series.

Now in the same manuscript as the fragments of 'Alarming Increase' held by the National Library of Scotland, 'Sagacity of a Shepherd's Dog' forms a contrasting pendant to the story of Millar and Yarrow as it relates the true story of Nimble, a sheepdog who, at a single command from her master, a participant in a Cameronian service on the hillside opposite, rounded up the scattered ewes at milking-time on her own. The manuscript demonstrates a very different form of collaboration between Scott and Laidlaw from 'Alarming Increase'. It is in Laidlaw's hand with editorial changes by Scott, who occasionally glosses a Scots term or rephrases to achieve a more literary tone. His additions do not generally extend beyond a few words, but two are of some significance. The first involves the parallel between the human and ovine flocks, which is surprisingly underplayed by Laidlaw, but which Scott intensifies by adding, 'The preachers undertake these pilgrimages to look after the few sheep in the wilderness'. His longest addition is the concluding paragraph in which the sermon and the sagacity of the sheepdog have an equal share in the conversation of the congregation as it returns home.[46] Thus despite Scott's additions, 'Sagacity' remains very much Laidlaw's own work, and the praise which it drew from both Scott and Blackwood buoyed him considerably.[47]

The February number of *Blackwood's* contained from Abbotsford only Scott's 'Battle of Sempach', a literal translation of a Swiss ballad which he had first read in 1810.[48] The March number, however, boasted two non-fiction articles by Scott—a review of Mary Shelley's *Frankenstein* and a short piece concerning the origin of the inhabitants of Buckhaven in Fife.[49] It included also, from 'Tweedside', a short story entitled 'Narrative of a Fatal Event', a first-person account purportedly written to alleviate the narrator's remorse at allowing a friend to drown through his own fear of the 'dead-grip'.[50] This intriguing tale of guilt and superstition has been attributed to Scott.[51] It is, however, not by Scott, but by the newly confident Laidlaw.

The manuscript of 'Fatal Event' has not been traced, but documentary evidence convincingly establishes its authorship. Writing to Scott on 2 March 1818, Laidlaw reports on oxen, seed-oats, and his latest literary attempt, 'an odd kind of article for the Magazine' which has its source in 'a story that a highland lad told of letting his companion drown beside him while they were bathing on the shore opposite Jura'; he is delaying sending it to Scott as it is 'very rough yet' and he is unhappy with the ending.[52] Scott responds immediately to his friend's hesitant tone, assuring him on 4 March, 'I will be glad to see your article for the Maga—use is every thing in composition'.[53] Although we do not have the manuscript of 'Fatal Event', this exchange shows that Laidlaw intended to polish the article himself before submitting it to Scott; Scott's revisions were expected to be editorial only. Other evidence points the same way. We may be confident that Laidlaw was responsible for the extensive scientific and specifically botanical detail, which is important to the plot; he was not simply, as we have seen, 'acquainted with science' but Scott was to praise him also as 'a great botanist'.[54] The story's hallucinatory atmosphere, too, is almost certainly the creation of Laidlaw, whose memory of the Highland tale appears to have been sparked by a similarly dreamlike story in the previous month's *Blackwood's*, Wilson's 'Remarkable Preservation from Death at Sea',[55] which Laidlaw had praised to Blackwood on 27 February as 'a piece of the deepest interest I ever read'.[56] All the available evidence, then, suggests that, as with 'Sagacity', Scott made only minor changes to 'Narrative of a Fatal Event', and that the story should be attributed to Laidlaw.[57] However, Laidlaw did not persist with this genre of story, and his next contribution to *Blackwood's*, 'Effect of Farm Overseers on the Morals of Farm Servants',[58] is little more than an 'agricultural' essay barely disguised by the use of a fictional narrator and dialogue form.

Perhaps the appearance of 'Fatal Event' prompted Scott to write his second fictional piece for *Blackwood's*. Like Laidlaw's story it both involves Highland people and came to the writer through a person closely concerned—although in Scott's case it was at one further remove. On 24 April he informed William Blackwood that he had just seen Laidlaw, and 'I intend to give him for you a very curious and authentic ghost-legend which I had *from the lady to whom the lady who saw the spirit told the story*'.[59] This story, 'Phantasmagoria', was, as already mentioned, composed in two stages, but Scott's wording here suggests that he had either not begun to write it or that it was as yet unfinished.

'Phantasmagoria' was ready for the May number of *Blackwood's*, and Blackwood must have been both surprised and delighted when it actually arrived. For the supernatural story which Scott had promised was prefaced by a lengthy and whimsical letter over the name of the story's putative narrator, one Simon Shadow. Thus through his association with Laidlaw, and possibly through Laidlaw's own 'Narrative of a Fatal Event', Scott had been led to draw on that fund of orally derived material which he had previously employed in written form only within the larger framework of the novels.[60] For the moment, however, the possibilities presented by this new departure were not further exploited. Although 'Phantasmagoria' was mooted as the first of a series, further instalments failed to materialise.[61] It was another six months before a contribution from Scott appeared in *Blackwood's*, and when it did it was not fiction but a review.[62]

By this time there had been a change in the ownership of the magazine. From August 1818 the title page included the name of the London publisher John Murray, previously Blackwood's agent, who had just bought a half-share of *Blackwood's*.[63] Murray now furnished some articles from London, and this must have relieved the pressure on William Blackwood; certainly there is no evidence of his requesting contributions from Abbotsford during this period. Murray, however, was immediately faced with the prospect of lawsuits and even found himself the addressee of a pamphlet urging him 'to renounce this infamous magazine'.[64] By late January 1819, there were beginning to be consequences for Laidlaw, and therefore ultimately for Scott himself. As he reports to Laidlaw on 28 January, 'I have not neglected your magazine matters—But there is a pause there which I do not quite understand but fear it bodes no good to the contributors Wilson seems much discontented with Blackwood & Bd. & Murray are by the ears again. But they have promised to look after what is due to you'.[65] Shortly afterwards, Scott is resigned to the ending of their arrangement with Blackwood, telling Laidlaw 'I am afraid you will make no more of Blackwood . . . The whole concern is broke up betwixt Murray & him & he is off post haste to London to try what he can do to solder matters'.[66] Blackwood's efforts were in vain. From the March number, 'John Murray' gave way to 'T. Cadell and W. Davies' on the title page.

Despite the poor prospect of further payment from Blackwood, one more article of Laidlaw's, 'Narrative Illustrating the Pastoral Life', appeared in the March number.[67] Signed with rare openness by 'W. L.', this story returns to the Highland setting of 'Narrative of a Fatal Event', whose title it perhaps deliberately recalls. However, it falls far short of the standard set by 'Fatal Event' and there is every indication that Scott had little involvement with it. If Murray's withdrawal from the magazine had indirectly led Blackwood to include Laidlaw's story, it predictably also prompted an attempt to meet with Scott. By now, however, Scott had had enough. Writing to James Ballantyne from his sickbed on 1 April, he asked him to postpone Blackwood's proposed visit, adding, 'I can hardly personally undertake any thing which can be essentially useful to him having so much work before me . . . Yet I am convinced I could put him on good plans if they were not to end in *my stars* and *goodness me* when benefit was expected to any but himself'.[68]

Scott and Laidlaw's involvement with *Blackwood's* was effectively at an end.[69] With the termination of Laidlaw's employment Scott had no reason to contribute regularly, and the novels were now his primary interest and occupation. However, although the opportunities of the early days had not all been fulfilled, the arrangement had borne fruit. Through his collaboration with Laidlaw, Scott had been drawn into providing two short fictional pieces, 'Alarming Increase of Depravity Among Animals' and 'Phantasmagoria', both suited in their different ways to the theatre of *Blackwood's*. 'Phantasmagoria', in particular, constituted a significant step in Scott's development as a short story writer. The idea of fictionalising stories heard from relatives and friends would be available to him in the grim days after the crash when financial considerations demanded a work other than a novel.[70] The legacy of Scott's association with William Laidlaw and *Blackwood's* is to be seen in *Chronicles of the Canongate* and the *Keepsake* stories.

THE COMPOSITION OF THE *BLACKWOOD*'S STORIES

'Alarming Increase of Depravity Among Animals'. As articles in *Blackwood's* were generally anonymous we have to call upon both manuscript and external evidence in assigning the authorship of 'Alarming Increase'. In this case attribution to Scott is supported by Lockhart's testimony,[71] by the nature of the surviving manuscript fragments, and by the Swiftian ring of the opening remarks and various connecting passages which is uncharacteristic of Laidlaw's known writings.

There is no manuscript of the complete story, but there are four fragments which belong to different stages of the composition. Two are in the National Library of Scotland (NLS), and consist of early versions of the 'thieving spaniel' episode (in Scott's hand),[72] and of the Murdieston and Millar tale (in Laidlaw's hand).[73] A further two fragments are to be found in the Fales Library, New York University, one containing the description of the mischievous propensities of Highland ponies, and the other an elaborated version of the 'thieving spaniel'.[74] These fragments provide both material and textual evidence from which a conjectural account of the composition of the article can be developed.

First stage of composition. It is probable that in its earliest form the article consisted of the summary of the newspaper material with its two examples of animal depravity, plus two examples from the past, which, as the tale-teller says, diminish 'our estimate of the atrocity of the present' (31.43). These would have to be stories of a horse and a dog to parallel the newspaper reports, and thus the anecdotes of the thieving spaniel and the highwayman's horse are probably integral to the article as first drafted.

The immediate inspiration for 'Alarming Increase' is stated to be 'two melancholy instances of depravity in the newspapers of this month, which we meant to have transferred to our Chronicle of Remarkable Events' (30.7–9), but which were thought 'far too important to be passed over without a commentary' (30.9–10). This tongue-in-cheek reference to the intended destination of the items suggests that Laidlaw may have noticed them in the newspapers forwarded by Blackwood[75] and brought them to Scott's attention. The two instances of animal larceny which inspired 'Alarming Increase' were reported in the London newspapers between 6 and 14 September. The story of the hay-stealing horse appeared in the *Morning Chronicle* of 6 September, while the canine robber featured in the same paper on 11 September, and in both the *Examiner* and the *Observer* on 14 September.[76] Given the reference to Robert Owen in 'Alarming Increase' (29.24), it is noteworthy that, in the very month in which Scott was writing, Robert Owen held a second public meeting on his plans for reforming society to improve the lot of the poor, and backed it up with a letter to the public in the *Morning Chronicle* of 10 September.[77] This letter was critiqued on 14 September in the issue of the *Examiner* which carried the report of the canine robber.[78] Of these newspapers, the *Morning Chronicle* is Scott's most likely source. Its account of the canine theft is extremely close to the text in 'Alarming Increase', differing almost solely in accidentals;[79] while the account of the thieving horse in 'Alarming Increase' varies only slightly from the *Morning Chronicle* report and in ways which adjust it to the context of the article.[80] In the light of the date at the end of the published article, '*30th Sept.*' (37.3), and of the writer's statement that the reports appeared in 'the newspapers of this month' (30.8), it is likely that a draft was completed by the end of September.

The one surviving manuscript fragment pertaining to this first stage in the composition is the story of the 'thieving spaniel' in the NLS, which, in comparison to both the corresponding Fales fragment and the published version of the article, is undeveloped; for example, where in the manuscript the gentleman bought 'a beautiful spaniel & possessd him for some time before he discoverd that he possessd the Lacedemonian property of privately stealing' (f. 7r), the corresponding passage in the printed text (34.27–41) is nearly five times longer. The spaniel story is on a strip of paper about one-third the size of the other leaves, and although it has been joined to other pieces of paper to create a full-sized leaf it has the characteristics of what Scott called a 'paper apart'. When Scott wished to add to a narrative he had already sent for copying and printing, he would send a 'p.a.' with the extra material. Since the story as it appears here is very brief, it is unlikely that this document was intended for submission to the publisher, but it is possible that at first Scott had been casting around for a story to show that the dogs of the past were just as depraved as those of the present, and drafted it only when he had remembered a suitable case.

Second stage of composition. From internal evidence it appears that the original draft cannot have included the Murdieston and Millar material. Firstly, the NLS manuscript of the 'thieving spaniel' alludes to them in passing, and gives no hint that they are to be treated in greater detail later: 'The celebrated sheep-stealers Murdieson & Miller were assisted in their depredations by a dog traind for the purpose who performd his part with great sagacity and poor *Yarrow* sufferd along with the human culprits' (f. 7r). Secondly, the remark within the published text that the story of the highwayman's horse 'may serve as a corollary to our tale of the spaniel' (35.23–24) suggests that it immediately followed the spaniel story. Thus the surviving manuscript version of the Murdieston and Millar story in the NLS constitutes a second compositional stage.

The manuscript is in Laidlaw's hand with some corrections and additions possibly made later. It consists of two folios numbered '1' and '2' (now MS 3937, ff. 8–9, the foliation used here). The first of these leaves contains the general information about the thieves' *modus operandi* which corresponds to, but is not identical with, the printed text's 'Murdieston occupied . . . those who were not *of the fancy*' (32.26–33.18). The bottom half of f. 8v is empty. The second leaf tells the story of Yarrow's failed attempt to drive the sheep across the Tweed. This account begins 'Murdistone & Millar——↑That he might vary the scene of his depradations↓ Millar had crossed the Tweed' (f. 9r). The use of a title suggests that the anecdote was written before the more general information on the first leaf, despite the order in which the folios are now numbered. This is corroborated by the insertion of 'That he might vary the scene of his depradations', which is clearly intended to link the anecdote to the preliminary material on the preceding leaf.

The text of the anecdote as it appears on the second leaf suggests that Laidlaw was not writing a finished piece for publication but rather providing a draft for Scott to use in writing up the story himself. After the title 'Murdistone & Millar' (f. 9r) the text continues on the same line after a dash, and the following lines show every indication of haste, almost of carelessness. There is considerable verbal repetition: 'all the art of a very artfull & active man' (f. 9r); 'Millar⟨s⟩ him self was astonished at the stubborn ness of the sheep & the astonishing & persevering energy of his dog' (f. 9v). And Laidlaw has even left two blank spaces in which the appropriate verbs may be supplied: 'The trust⟨y⟩ worthy dog [SPACE] not nor [SPACE]' (f. 9r).

It seems, then, that Laidlaw, in conversation with Scott, or even upon reading Scott's original draft, may have remarked that he was privy to a little-known episode involving Yarrow, and related it to him; certainly as a member of a sheep-farming family he was more likely than Scott to hear a story originally told by Millar 'to a respectable sheep-farmer in prison, while under sentence of death' (34.13–14). Scott may then have asked Laidlaw first to write the story down, and then, on seeing Laidlaw's notes, to provide him with more detail. Laidlaw has made many emendations and additions to his own manuscript, several of which are interlinear and lengthy, and the text which these passages are designed to replace has not been deleted, as though they represent alternatives rather than corrections. Perhaps at the same time Scott requested the more general picture of the sheep-stealers' methods for insertion before the anecdote itself. The handwriting of Laidlaw's introduction shows a little more care, the style is more polished, and there are fewer emendations, as though Laidlaw were now writing a piece for publication, rather than furnishing material for Scott's use.

On about 8 October Scott wrote to Blackwood, enclosing 'an article which we must see in proof as clubbing our information we had but just time to have it copied over'.[81] It is probable that 'clubbing our information' refers to Scott's bringing together his own first draft, and Laidlaw's Murdieston and Millar material. At the same time the comment about having 'just time to have it copied over', and the request for proofs, point to the third and fourth stages of composition.

Third stage: the Fales fragments. These fragments, both of which are in Scott's hand, include the short depiction of the mischievous propensities of Highland ponies, and a version of the 'thieving spaniel'. The 'Highland pony' text occupies the top half of a leaf, numbered '3' by Scott. Beginning 'here and there a highland poney', it ends with 'has given occasion to this article', that is, the final words of the paragraph as published at 31.41. The 'thieving spaniel' occupies a leaf numbered '4' by Scott.

Both come later in the compositional process than the NLS version of the 'thieving spaniel', and could well have been written at the same time as Scott was combining Laidlaw's material with his own original draft. For instance the 'thieving spaniel' is a more developed version than that held by the NLS. Scott has changed some details (for example, the animal is now a bitch—although the pronouns applied to it are inconsistent). There are stylistic changes too, such as the replacement of 'Lacedemonian property'[82] with 'Spartan art' (f. 4r). As the 'thieving spaniel' in the Fales manuscript begins with a reference to Murdieston and Millar ('The case of Murdieson and Millar though curious is not ⟨quit⟩ singular'), it is clear that, unlike the NLS version, it was preceded by the Murdieston and Millar material which had therefore, as in the printed text, displaced the spaniel story as the first anecdote.[83]

There is clearly no room in this document for the rest of the text to have been inscribed on it, but as the 'Highland pony' fragment bears traces of Laidlaw's handwriting which seem to remain from instructions to a copyist, possibly Laidlaw himself, it would seem that these materials are part of a collection of documents which were due to be 'copied over', to use Scott's phrase in his letter of around 8 October.[84]

This deduction is supported by endorsements on both leaves by Mrs Robert Carruthers of Druin when she gave them to acquaintances in the 1880s. Mrs Carruthers was Anne Ballantyne Laidlaw, a daughter of William Laidlaw's. She had married Robert Carruthers,[85] the son of the Dr Robert Carruthers who compiled the account of Laidlaw's relationship with Scott which became 'Abbotsford Notanda', appended to the third edition of Robert Chambers's *Life of Sir Walter Scott*.[86] Thus these leaves had been retained by Laidlaw, and passed to his heirs. They did not form part of the clean copy sent to Blackwood, which was probably prepared by Laidlaw himself, and which is not known to be extant.

Fourth stage: proofs. It is probably significant that despite the approaching publication date of 20 October it was six days before the proofs of 'Alarming Increase' were returned to Blackwood.[87] When they failed to arrive as expected, there was panic on both sides, because Laidlaw, as he informed Blackwood on 20 October, had sent them under cover of William Kerr but with only Blackwood's name on the package.[88] In the same letter Laidlaw reveals that the proofs were of 'Essay on the Depravity &c corrected and enlarged'.

Numerous variations can be seen in the printed text of the 'Highland pony' and the 'thieving spaniel' when compared to the Fales manuscript. On the whole these are minor and could have been made in the preparation of the final copy, or in proof, or even post-proof; indeed some may have been made at one stage, some at the others. In the case of the 'thieving spaniel' fragment, the only substantive changes involve the opening phrase, where 'The case of Murdieson and Millar' has been changed to 'The case of Millar' (34.27), one example of transposition, and the alteration or replacement of two or three isolated words (for example, 'although' (34.27) for 'though'). Variations between the 'Highland pony' fragment and the *Blackwood's* text almost always involve accidentals, such as the addition of commas and capitalisation (e.g. 'Mountain', 'Man', 'Pony', 'Horse' at 31.36–38). Substantive changes include the replacement of words or phrases (for example, 'in' (31.35) for 'within', and 'has given' (31.41) for 'gave'), one addition (in *Blackwood's* the quadrupeds have become 'ill-advised' at 31.40) and the deletion of a whole clause ('can never be compared' at 31.39 replaces 'could never—such at least was our first impression be compared'). But although such changes would seem to imply careful scrutiny of the text, the Fales manuscript's confusion of masculine, feminine and neuter pronouns in relation to the spaniel remains in the printed text.

Given the evidence adduced so far, it is the Murdieston and Millar story which is most likely to have been enlarged, with the 'Highland pony' and the 'thieving spaniel' excluded by the state of the Fales text.[89] Comparison of the manuscript and the published version of

Murdieston and Millar indicates that there was substantial rewriting. No doubt much of this happened in 'clubbing' their information, but it is certain that there was extensive revision in proof. It was normal practice for Scott to revise in proof, but his demand that he be sent proofs must indicate his belief that alterations were inevitable given the state of the manuscript supplied to Blackwood. Laidlaw, too, writing to Blackwood on 9 October, emphasises the necessity for proofs, and assures the publisher that 'altho sending proofs may put you to a little additional expence, *yet you will find it worth it all*' (Laidlaw's emphasis).[90] Laidlaw's claim that the proofs will benefit Blackwood are typical of his veiled references to Scott in correspondence with the publisher,[91] and almost certainly point to the revisions being Scott's.

Indeed Laidlaw's general account of Murdieston and Millar's activities has been expanded by one-third in the published version, and the material arranged in a more logical sequence. In the manuscript, for example, the description of the thieves' homeward routes follows the passage on their use of the peel-tower for re-marking the stolen sheep, but this is reversed in *Blackwood's*. A comparison of Laidlaw's opening lines with the *Blackwood's* text illustrates the types of detailed changes made throughout, and leaves little doubt that they are Scott's. The manuscript reads

> Murdiston possessed a small Farm called Ormiston on the North Bank of the Tweed a little above ↑ the antient Baronial ↓ Traquair and Millar his coadjutor lived with him as his herd. (f. 8r)

In the printed version (see 32.26–30), amongst other changes, the inaccurate 'possessed' has become 'occupied' (32.26; Murdieston was a tenant of the Earl of Traquair), 'coadjutor' has been replaced by the literary 'Minion of the Moon' (32.28), and a summary of the sheep-stealers' activities, in Scott's characteristic tone, has been supplied.

Further changes to the manuscript are equally suggestive. Laidlaw's 'when ⟨th⟩ he had driven his prey from a distance and the day threatened to dawn upon him' (f. 8v) has been replaced by the more picturesque 'when Millar had driven his prey from a distance, and while he was yet miles from home, and the *weather-gleam* of the eastern hills began to be tinged with the brightening dawn' (32.37–39). His factual description of 'the old square towers' (f. 8r) along the Tweed is similarly embellished in the printed text (33.4–9), which also adds a long sentence detailing Yarrow's behaviour after Millar's departure, as well as a depiction of the dog at his post outside the peel-tower (33.16–18).

The story of Yarrow and the old ewes has been subjected to fewer changes in structure and wording, although it is less carefully prepared than Laidlaw's general introduction. Even so, there is radical rewriting, occasionally involving loss of meaning, at several points: 'he found no dificulty in collecting as many as he dirst ⟨venture⟩ think of disposing of of a flock of ewes' (f. 9r) becomes in *Blackwood's* 'he found no difficulty in collecting part of a flock and bringing away what number he judged convenient' (33.22–25). This alteration may constitute a stylistic improvement but it disguises Laidlaw's reference to the sale of the stolen sheep and thus is part of a noticeable change in emphasis between the draft and the published text. In Laidlaw's account, the behaviour of the sheep is as prominent as the heroic efforts of the dog; their reluctance to cross the river, for example, is explained by their affection for their home pasture (f. 9r). In the printed text the primary focus is on Yarrow and his relationship with Millar: not only is the reader kept ignorant of the outcome of the dog's exertions for as long as possible, but his weighty responsibilities are stressed by the addition 'the work was now all his own' (33.43–34.1); and where in the manuscript Millar's delegation of the work to Yarrow and his own departure from the scene are briefly treated (f. 9r), the *Blackwood's* text has Millar 'encouraging the dog by his voice, while he was yet not too distant, so as to risk being heard by some early riser' (33.41–42).

Significantly, in *Blackwood's* Yarrow has earned a reprieve, not just from the authorities but also from Scott; no longer does he suffer 'along with the human culprits' as in the earlier version. Scott, it appears, has acquired new information, probably from Laidlaw, and this would explain the presence of semi-contradictory statements in the published version, which begins with the claim that the 'trial proved fatal to the bipeds accused, and (as has generally been averred), to their four-footed aider and abettor' (32.19–21), but ends with Yarrow surviving to work for a neighbouring farmer.

It is also likely at this stage that Scott wrote the introductory paragraph to the story, which does not appear in the manuscript and concerns the trial and the legal people involved. The concluding reference to the fate of the three accomplices, similarly absent from Laidlaw's draft, is also probably Scott's, for although he appears to have drawn on Laidlaw's knowledge of Yarrow's second career, its tone is consonant with the opening section of the article as a whole, written, as we believe, by Scott, and uncharacteristic of Laidlaw's other writing. It is consonant too with the accounts of the Highland pony and the thieving spaniel which are definitely Scott's.

Laidlaw's warning that the proofs had been 'corrected and enlarged' must indicate his awareness that Blackwood would encounter problems as a result. And indeed, when Blackwood, in a letter to Scott of the same date, 20 October, confirmed the arrival of the parcel, he emphasised the labour required to have the article corrected in time:

> I am sorry I should have given you so much trouble about the missing packet which at last, as I wrote Mr Laidlaw, made it's

appearance on Thursday night. It was therefore still in time and by making considerable exertions we got the whole of the sheets nearly ready for press on Saturday night, and I hope to be able to send you a complete copy by this day's post.[92]

Laidlaw's anxiety of 20 October was therefore needless. Not only had the proofs reached Blackwood, but despite the 'exertions' which they occasioned a copy of the October number, featuring 'Alarming Increase of Depravity Among Animals', would arrive at Abbotsford that very day.

Thus manuscript fragments and documentary evidence allow us to reconstruct the history of the composition of 'Alarming Increase'. Drawing inspiration from the chance occurrence of two amusing instances of animal larceny reported in the newspapers of September 1817 (to which he may have been alerted by William Laidlaw), Scott saw the potential both of seeing them as part of an alarming trend and of countering such a view with similar anecdotes from the past. After preparing a rough draft of stories known to him, he encouraged Laidlaw to expand on the exploits of Murdieston and Millar. At a later stage, as well as further developing his own draft he polished Laidlaw's contribution, embellishing it with more literary turns of phrase and placing the emphasis firmly upon the dog Yarrow (whereas for the sheep-farmer Laidlaw the plight of the sheep had equal importance). Thus 'Alarming Increase' is in many ways typical of Scott's writing as a whole. He did not write down perfect, completed works at one sitting; his art was incremental. Revision and expansion, often through knowledge garnered from others, transform the original story. In the case of 'Alarming Increase of Depravity Among Animals' the result is a hugely entertaining narrative, full of sociological and historical insight. To quote again the words of Lockhart, it is indeed 'one of the best pieces of grave burlesque since Swift'.

Changes in the second edition. As detailed in the section on Genesis above,[93] at Scott's insistence William Blackwood reprinted the October number of his magazine, which included 'Alarming Increase of Depravity Among Animals', omitting the notorious 'Chaldee Manuscript'. The text of Scott's contribution in this reprint (consulted in the copy held in the Baillieu Library of the University of Melbourne) has clearly been reset. In the process some changes have been made, including 'bellyfull' for 'bellyful' (30.15) but 'Kail-pot-lid' for 'Kaill-pot-lid' (31.20); several obvious errors have been corrected: at 35.24, for example, 'gentlemen's' has been emended to 'gentleman's', and at 32.7 the '-ing' of 'having' has been supplied.

'Phantasmagoria'. The only certain dates in the history of the composition of 'Phantasmagoria' are 24 April 1818, when Scott promised the story to Blackwood,[94] and 20 May 1818, when it appeared in print. While these dates give no indication of when the story was written, the introductory letter exploits the image of the 'Veiled Conductor' frequently applied to the shadowy editor of *Blackwood's* after his appearance as the 'man with the veil' in the 'Chaldee Manuscript',[95] and therefore cannot be earlier than October 1817. This date, as we shall see, would probably hold for at least the second part of the story proper. However, whenever the article was begun, and whatever stages of composition followed, it is most likely that it was brought to its present state only just before being sent to Blackwood for publication.

The manuscript of 'Phantasmagoria'. Evidence from the manuscript, which has survived in its entirety,[96] does provide some clues to the composition process. The manuscript comprises seven folios, of which the introductory letter occupies three (ff. 7–9) and the story four (ff. 10–13). The first page of the letter is written on stiff yellow paper and differs in colour and size from the next two pages, which are identical in colour (blue-grey) and dimensions.[97] The story proper is written on four pages of stiff yellow paper which is larger than that employed for the opening page of the letter. As P. D. Garside has shown, paper size is a more significant factor in determining composition history than are watermarks.[98] In the case of 'Phantasmagoria' the differences in the paper employed would seem to suggest different periods of composition for letter and story, with the added possibility that the letter itself was written in two stages.

At first the manuscript text seems to confirm a two-stage process of composition. The last page of the introductory letter, f. 9, is written in a thick black pen right to the end, whereas f. 10, the first page of the story, is in a fine, lighter pen. It therefore seems safe to say that ff. 9 and 10 were written on separate occasions. The letter ends three-quarters of the way down f. 9 with the story's title and epigraph, and the catchwords 'The incident', which are centred on the page. Scott's usual practice was to fill the page with text, and the catchword would normally appear in the bottom right-hand corner; a new chapter or section just followed on, and he never began a new chapter or section on a new page unless the preceding page was full. That there is room on f. 9 for eight or nine lines more indicates that what followed on f. 9 had already been written. In other words the story was written, or at least begun, first.

However, close examination of the manuscript text points to a rather more complex process. The manuscript of the letter reveals that the introductory material was not initially cast as a letter. The title 'Phantasmagoria / No. I' is written at the top of the page in a light fine pen, but has been deleted and 'Sir.' written next to it at the left hand margin above the text, in a fine but slightly darker pen. The text of the letter continues in the first pen for just over three lines, ending mid-sentence on 'testimony'. It then changes to a darker, thicker pen and less careful hand. The hand remains the same to the end of the letter, although there is a change of pen three-quarters of the way down f. 8, no doubt because the writing had become so thick as to mar legibility. The new pen continues until the end of the letter and the catchwords 'The incident'. On the top right of f. 7, beginning a line above the title, and in a very thick and dark pen, is written 'For the Veild ⟨Editor⟩ ↑Conductor↓ of ⟨the⟩ ↑Blackwoods↓ / Edinh Magazine' ('Blackwoods' is cramped at the end of the line, suggesting that only this word has been added). Although this might indicate that Scott originally intended the article either for Constable's *Edinburgh Magazine* (the former *Scots Magazine*, now under the editorship of Pringle and Cleghorn) or else for the first incarnation of William Blackwood's magazine, the *Edinburgh Monthly Magazine*, his reference to the 'Veild ⟨Editor⟩' would suit only *Blackwood's Edinburgh Magazine*.

The story proper begins on f. 10r, and the first line is indented at the margin, suggesting that Scott always intended an introduction of some sort. It begins in a light fine pen which could well be the first pen of the introductory letter. This continues for a page and three-quarters, ending with 'advice' (at 42.42). Not only does a darker pen then take over and continue to the end of the story, but the line is differently angled and the script less rounded. It is clear that Scott read and revised the initial pages when he wrote the concluding section, as he added the explanatory passage concerning the size and conditions of service of the Independent Companies in a pen similar to that used after 'advice' (40.39–40).

It follows that the story, despite being written on matching paper, was produced at two sittings. But how does it relate to the composition of the preceding letter? The opening words of the story, 'The incident which I am about to narrate came to your present correspondent', seem to indicate that Scott always meant the work for periodical publication; they also demand the existence of preceding material (as does the marginal indent), probably in the form of a direct address to the editor. Taking this with the details presented above, one possible account of the history of composition would run as follows: Scott initially began a story which he called 'Phantasmagoria. No. I' but after writing the opening lines concerning the receipt of evidence felt that this subject merited more elaboration than would fit easily into a story. He therefore decided on a prefatory letter to the editor, and it was possibly at this early stage that he deleted the title and added 'Sir'. He then took a new sheet (again of yellow paper, but of a different size) and began the story proper, leaving the letter for another day. He did not complete the story at one sitting. When he resumed writing, he added 'For the Veild Conductor' etc. at the top of the introductory letter (although the title may have been deleted

and/or 'Sir' added at this time). When he first notified William Blackwood of the impending contribution he was perhaps involved in this
process, although it is possible that he had not yet begun it at all.
Unless more documentary evidence comes to light we cannot be more
specific about the composition of Scott's final fictional piece for *Blackwood's*.

Changes in the manuscript. As Scott wrote he changed and corrected
his manuscript. Twice he wrote 'lift' where he meant to write 'lived'
and immediately corrected it before continuing his sentence (at 39.3
and 43.16) and once he replaced 'that' with the grammatically correct
'these' (at 44.23). He can also be seen restructuring his sentences as
he writes, for instance in the following passage: '⟨she was perfectly
in⟩ the whole tone of her character as well as the course of her life
exempted her from the slightest suspicion of an attempt to impose on
others' (at 41.12–14) where he presumably started to write something
like 'she was perfectly incapable of lying' but then decided on a more
elaborate construction. Similarly the deletion of 'perish' and its replacement by 'go with me to the darksome bourne' (at 40.16–17) is
both more elaborate and more dramatic. Other changes are the result
of later revision, whether more precise expression as in 'few occasions'
becoming 'little risque' (at 42.7, where a different pen is used to
make the change) or additional information as in the long passage on the
Independent Companies added on the verso of the previous folio
at 41.43–42.5.

Changes between manuscript and printed text. The process of revision
continued with the move from manuscript to printed text although it
is not clear that Scott played any part in these changes. The *Blackwood's*
text corrects several mistakes (for example changing 'humane fortitude' to 'human fortitude' at 43.39), avoids the repetition of 'death'
within two lines by changing the second occurrence to 'loss' (42.40),
modernises the spelling of the manuscript's 'hystericks' (at 43.43)
and 'risque' (at 42.7), clarifies the idea by replacing 'offerd' with 'so
rejected' (38.18) and provides a more logical sequence of tenses by
changing 'did' to 'does' (39.4). However it also introduces a number
of mistakes, including the wrong preposition in 'sunk down in the
floor' (43.39; MS 'on') and a misreading of 'curious' as 'current'
(40.16). Of two significant changes to proper names, one corrects
Scott's mistake in once referring to Captain 'Cameron' rather than
'Campbell' (42.35) and the other misinterprets Simon Shadow's
father's name as 'Michaelmas' (39.3) where the name Scott seems to
have given him is 'Mickelmast', apparently a reference to his long,
thin body.

THE LATER EDITIONS

'Alarming Increase of Depravity Among Animals'. Apart from its inclusion in the reprint of the October number of *Blackwood's*, 'Alarming Increase of Depravity Among Animals' was not reprinted during Scott's lifetime, and was not included in the Magnum edition of his collected works.

'Phantasmagoria'. This story was not reprinted in any of the standard editions of Scott's works within his lifetime but did appear in *Literary Gems*, an anthology of short pieces by a number of authors, in 1826, where it is described as 'Said to have been Written by the Author of Waverley, &c'.[99] Three years later in 1829 the story was reprinted in a collection published by Galignani in Paris entitled *Tales and Essays*. The text of 'Phantasmagoria' in this second collection derives from *Literary Gems*: almost every punctuation change introduced by *Literary Gems* is carried over into *Tales and Essays* and the Advertisement explains that 'the publishers have gleaned the materials of the present volume from various miscellaneous publications of a recent date'. In each collection the text has been slightly revised, mostly in punctuation although both change 'thus much' to 'this much' (at 38.43) and modernise the spelling of 'shew' to 'show' (at 43.2). In addition, where *Blackwood's* had created a problem by adding a comma before 'greatly reconciled' (42.17) (having failed to recognise the obsolete meaning of *reconciled* as 'became reconciled'), *Tales and Essays* rectifies the absence of a verb form suitable to this new punctuation by adding 'being' before 'greatly'. There is no evidence that Scott was associated with either text; nevertheless, they do include some corrections of obvious errors which have been adopted in this edition. The story was not included in the Magnum edition of Scott's collected works.

THE PRESENT TEXT

'Alarming Increase of Depravity Among Animals'. The present text is based on the first edition of the *Blackwood's* text and specifically on the copy held by the Barr Smith Library of the University of Adelaide. As there is no complete manuscript extant, and those fragments which survive did not form part of the final draft, most changes are based on the second edition of *Blackwood's* or are editorial. We have however accepted the authority of the Fales manuscript in one instance and changed 'home' to 'him' (34.36), as it is clear that the spaniel does not carry the purloined articles as far as her master's house. Editorial changes include 'acts' (32.3) for 'arts' (evidently a misreading of the manuscript) as 'acts' rather than 'arts' may be said to be 'committed' (32.4); we have also completed the change of the spaniel's sex (partly effected by Scott in the Fales manuscript) by regularising the pronouns relating to her (at 34.30, 34.32, 34.33, 34.36, 35.5 and 35.9). We have followed the second printing in correcting obvious errors, changing 'gentlemen's' to 'gentleman's' (35.24), for example, and supplying the final syllable of 'having' (32.7).

'Phantasmagoria'. The present text is based on the original *Blackwood's* text and specifically on the copy held by the Barr Smith Library of the University of Adelaide. Variations from the manuscript have been accepted when they are a clear improvement of the intelligibility or style of a kind that Scott himself might have made or might have authorised others to make. Thus we have accepted, amongst others, the change from 'mystical' to 'supernatural' (38.24), of 'did' to 'does' (39.4), and of 'death' to 'loss' (42.40). On the other hand we have restored a number of readings from the manuscript where it has clearly been misinterpreted, such as the case discussed above of 'curious' (40.16) misread as 'current' and others such as 'widowd' (at 42.9) misread as 'beloved'. Almost always a misreading weakens the effect of Scott's prose; thus when Scott describes the worries of a 'widowd mother' at the prospect of her only son joining the army, her widowhood helps explain her anxiety but that she is 'beloved' is simply irrelevant. Similarly Scott's use of Mickelmast as the first name for the elder Shadow continues a joke whereas the *Blackwood's* reading 'Michaelmas' is merely puzzling. We also abide by Scott's clear manuscript preference for 'narratives' and 'narrative' (38.31 and 41.15—16) and 'relative' (43.32) as nouns where *Blackwood's* fussily adopts 'narration' and 'relation'. Thus, even within the compass of this short text, it is possible by returning to the manuscript to restore the sharpness of some of Scott's writing where it has been lost in the process of printing.

NOTES

1 See *The Black Dwarf*, ed. P. D. Garside, EEWN 4a, 125–27. In the event, Blackwood's association with the Waverley Novels was limited to the first four editions of *Tales of My Landlord*.

2 *Letters*, 4.428: Scott to Laidlaw, 5 April 1817.

3 *Letters*, 4.465: Scott to Laidlaw, 16 June 1817.

4 *Letters*, 4.353: Scott to Constable, January 1817.

5 Constable's *Scots Magazine* was retitled *The Edinburgh Magazine* from August 1817.

6 Although the September number of the *Edinburgh Monthly Magazine* announced its discontinuation without mentioning a successor, the title page provided with it for the volume as a whole bore the new name.

7 *Blackwood's Edinburgh Magazine*, 2 (October 1817), 2. Henceforward *BEM*.

8 MS 3888, ff. 150r–51r.

9 MS 3888, f. 189r–v.

10 MS 3888, f. 189v. This letter (which is undated but endorsed by Scott 'Mr Blackwood Sept'), together with further negotiations concerning Laidlaw's employment on the magazine, demonstrates Lockhart's error in stating that Laidlaw had conducted the Chronicle during the magazine's first incarnation (see *Life*, 4.64). The earliest extant evidence of James Hogg's intercession on Laidlaw's behalf is a letter of 25 September 1817 in which he recommends him as 'an universal theorist and versed in the [TEAR] science of tillage cropping &c' who could give *Blackwood's* 'a pastoral and agricultural turn', allowing it to rival Constable's *Farmer's Magazine* (*The Collected Letters of James Hogg*, ed. Gillian Hughes, 3 vols (Edinburgh, 2004–08), 1.303). However, Laidlaw had already accepted Blackwood's proposal.

11 See *Rob Roy*, EEWN 5, 353–56.

12 MS 4937, f. 71r.

13 MS 4937, ff. 71v–72r.

14 MS 4937, f. 72r.

15 For Margaret Oliphant, 'That the big fish swallowed this fine bait as sweetly as could be desired is clear': Margaret Oliphant, *Annals of a Publishing House: William Blackwood and His Sons*, 3rd edn, 2 vols (Edinburgh, 1897), 1.146.

16 Edgar Johnson, *Sir Walter Scott: The Great Unknown*, 2 vols (London, 1970), 1.613.

17 MS 4002, f. 165r; unfortunately Blackwood's letter to Laidlaw offering him employment does not appear to be extant.

18 MS 4002, f. 166r. In the *Edinburgh Monthly Magazine* the 'Register' had usually comprised 'Foreign Intelligence', 'Proceedings of Parliament', 'British Chronicle', 'Appointments, Promotions, &c', 'Commercial Report', 'Agricultural Report', 'Meteorological Report' and 'Births, Marriages, and Deaths'. It was only in Laidlaw's first 'Register' that most of the usual sections were retained—although the notable omission is the 'Agricultural Report' which Laidlaw provided only every second month. By November, the first two sections were replaced by the 'Scottish Chronicle', which itself disappeared after June 1818.

19 MS 4002, f. 165v. Laidlaw's agricultural essay, although foreshadowed in the 'Notice from the Editor' prefixed to the first number of the revamped magazine as 'Letter to Walter Scott, Esq. from Mr William Laidlaw, on an interesting Agricultural Subject', was destined never to appear in *Blackwood's*.

20 MS 4002, f. 166r.

21 See Lockhart's letter of 21 February 1818 to the Welsh clergyman David Williams, in 'John Gibson Lockhart and "Blackwood's Magazine"', *London Scotsman*, 9 May 1868, 434.

22 *BEM*, 2 (October 1817), 3–18; 38–41; 89–96.

23 Oliphant, 1.140–41.

24 Oliphant, 1.144. For James Hogg's desperate requests to Blackwood and Laidlaw not to divulge his own role, see his letters of 28 October 1817 (*Collected Letters of James Hogg*, 1.307, 308).

25 MS 3888, f. 201r.

26 MS 3888, f. 201v.

27   MS 3888, ff. 201v–202r.

28   MS 4002, f. 173r: Laidlaw to Blackwood, 24 October 1817.

29   MS 3888, f. 217r: Blackwood to Laidlaw, 29 October 1817.

30   *Letters*, 5.6–7.

31   James Hogg was still warning Blackwood as late as 5 January 1818 that 'If Scott see the least symptoms of your neglect of Laidlaw I find he is off at a tangent at once and it is not only what the *want* of his support would injure your work but what his name would effect in your opponnent's—policy is requisite even with the greatest heros' (*Collected Letters of James Hogg*, 1.323).

32   *Letters*, 5.208. Grierson's date of '5 Nov [1818]' is corrected to '[1817]' in *Letters*, 12.489.

33   *Letters*, 5.5.

34   See Wilson's poem 'The Magic Mirror' in the *Edinburgh Annual Register for 1810*, 3 (2), cvii–cxiv.

35   MS 3888, f. 218r.

36   MS 4003, f. 127r. He adds that 'As you were thinking Hoggs paper on smearing would do for the agricultural article in next no. I have not pressed Mr S. to search again for mine', no doubt referring here to the article lauded by Scott during his initial negotiations with Blackwood. This comment is particularly useful, revealing as it does that 'agricultural' articles were not to have been included in the Maugraby series. It also helps us to date this letter to late November or early December, as Laidlaw laments the rejection of Hogg's paper in a letter to Blackwood with the postmark '10 DEC' and the contents clearly suggest December 1817 (MS 4002, f. 178r). Hogg had signalled his essay 'on the Smearing of Sheep as it affects the qualities of the wool and the flock' to Blackwood in a letter of 19 October 1817 (*Collected Letters of James Hogg*, 1.305). As Gillian Hughes points out, a 'letter from Hogg to the Editor on sheep-smearing was subsequently published in the *Dumfries and Galloway Courier* of 21 September 1824' (*Collected Letters of James Hogg*, 1.306).

37   *BEM*, 2 (January 1818), 417–21.

38   *BEM*, 3 (May 1818), 211–15.

39   For a detailed discussion of the manuscript, see 132–34.

40   *Letters*, 3.144–45: Scott to Charles Kirkpatrick Sharpe, 6 June [6 July? 1812].

41   *Rob Roy*, EEWN 5, 353–56. Scott had indeed improved enough to furnish an article for the December number—the antiquarian 'Pecuniary Distress of James VI' (*BEM*, 2 (December 1817), 312–15) which, consisting almost entirely of quotations, would have cost him little effort. In January he produced another article, reverting to a favourite theme with 'On the Gypsies of Hesse-Darmstadt in Germany' (*BEM*, 2 (January 1818), 409–14), writing once again from 'Tweedside'; this article is not Maugraby, as Laidlaw is clearly referring to a new article when he tells Blackwood on 5 January, 'I have got a very interesting article upon the German gypsies from Mr. Scott' (MS 4003, ff. 113v–114r).

42   MS 3937, f. 6r. The manuscript of 'Sagacity' occupies ff. 1–6.

43   The Bancroft Library, University of California, Berkeley, BANC MSS

92/487z: Scott to Laidlaw, 10 December [1817]; MS 4003, f. 113r:
Laidlaw to Blackwood, 5 January 1818.

44 MS 4002, f. 178r.

45 *The Heart of Mid-Lothian*, EEWN 6, 484–87.

46 MS 3937, ff. IV, 6r; *BEM*, 2 (January 1818), 417, 421.

47 Edinburgh University Library, MS La. III. 584, f. 102v: Laidlaw to
Scott. (This letter is undated but as it mentions the approaching search
for the Regalia it must predate 4 February, when the 'discovery' was
made.) MS 4003, f. 115v: Laidlaw to Blackwood, 24 January 1818.

48 *BEM*, 2 (February 1818), 530–32. See *Letters*, 2.399: Scott to Margaret
Clephane, 27 October 1810.

49 'Remarks on *Frankenstein, or the Modern Prometheus; A Novel*', *BEM*, 2
(March 1818), 613–20, and 'Buckhaven', *BEM*, 2 (March 1818),
626–27.

50 *BEM*, 2 (March 1818), 630–35.

51 Following A. Wood ('A *Causerie*—Sir Walter Scott and "Maga"', *BEM*,
232 (July 1932), 5), Alan Lang Strout ascribes the story to Scott on
the basis of 'Tweedside': *A Bibliography of Articles in "Blackwood's Magazine" Volumes I through XVIII, 1817—1825*, Library Bulletin no. 5,
Texas Technological College (Lubbock, Texas, 1959), 37. This
ascription is continued in a typed contributors' list among the Blackwood Papers held by the National Library of Scotland, 'List of
Contributions to *Blackwood's Magazine*, 1817–70' (MS 4893) which
incorporates material from an earlier list apparently compiled in
Blackwoods' offices (but covering only 1821–1870) as well as later
research especially that of Strout. The story is similarly attributed in
Tales of Terror from 'Black-wood's Magazine', ed. Robert Morrison and
Chris Baldick (Oxford, 1995), where it is reprinted on 9–17. William
Blackwood himself kept a list (unfortunately now lost) of the contri-
butions of some of his individual supporters during the early period of
Blackwood's, but as he combined Scott's and Laidlaw's contributions
under 'Laidlaw' it is of no help in deciding between Scott and Laidlaw
as author; for this see Alan Lang Strout, 'The Authorship of Articles in
Blackwood's Magazine, Numbers xvii–xxiv (August 1818–March 1819)',
The Library, 5th series, 11 (1956), 187, 199.

52 EUL, MS La. III. 584, f. 111r.

53 MS 969, f. 18v.

54 *Letters*, 5.235: Scott to Lord Montagu, 27 November 1818.

55 *BEM*, 2 (February 1818), 490–94.

56 MS 4003, f. 119r.

57 Lockhart may very well be including this piece among Laidlaw's com-
positions when he refers to 'one or more articles on the subject of
Scottish superstitions' with which he believed Scott 'assisted' Laidlaw
(*Life*, 4.65).

58 *BEM*, 3 (April 1818), 83–87.

59 MS 3925, f. 168v (Scott to Blackwood, with no addressee or year, but
included amongst a small collection of letters to various members of
the Blackwood family).

60 A few anecdotes appear in Scott's letters, where they usually represent

an extension of the oral story-telling for which he was renowned rather
than an attempt at fictionalisation in the literary sense.

61   Perhaps Scott remembered, or became aware of, a series entitled 'The
Phantasmagoria' which had appeared in the *European Magazine* as early
as 1803, the year after M. Philipstal first staged the exhibition of optical
illusions for which he coined the name. See *European Magazine*, 43
(March 1803), 186–88; 43 (April 1803), 270–72; and 44 (August
1803), 102–04.

62   'Remarks on General Gourgaud's Account of the Campaign of 1815',
BEM, 4 (November 1818), 220–28.

63   Samuel Smiles, *A Publisher and His Friends: Memoir and Correspondence
of the Late John Murray*, 2 vols (London, 1891), 1.480. For a full account
of the partnership from the opposing viewpoints see Smiles, 1.480–96,
and Oliphant, 1.159–73.

64   Smiles, 1.491.

65   MS 969, f. 27v.

66   MS 23126, f. 8r–v. Grierson dates the letter 'February? 1819' (*Letters*,
5.300). According to the NLS transcript at MS 23126, ff. 10–12, this
letter is docketed 1818 by Laidlaw (see f. 10r). However the '1818' on
f. 9v does not seem to be in Laidlaw's hand: the '8's are not formed in
Laidlaw's characteristic way, and it was his usual practice to add Scott's
name as well (see for example MS 23126, ff. 3v, 14r, and 27r). Scott's
comments regarding the breakdown of the arrangement with Murray
point to February 1819, as does his intention to return to Abbotsford
'on or about the 12 March' (f. 8v), as he tells Morritt on 5 March 'I go
to the country on the 12' (*Letters*, 5.318).

67   *BEM*, 4 (March 1819), 663–66. Laidlaw had perhaps submitted the
piece somewhat earlier; at the time of 'Effect of Farm Overseers on the
Morals of Farm Servants', he had told Blackwood of 'two or three
things in hand' which were awaiting Scott's 'little touch' (MS 4003, f.
121r: Laidlaw to Scott, 3 April 1818).

68   MS 5317, f. 57r.

69   Scott would, it is true, supply Blackwood with reviews of Galt's *The
Omen* in 1826 (*BEM*, 20 (July 1826), 52–59) and of Lord Pitsligo's
Thoughts Concerning Man's Condition and Duties in This Life as late as
1829 (*BEM*, 25 (May 1829), 593–600), but these were isolated examples.

70   See the section on the Genesis of the *Keepsake* stories below, 143–45.

71   See above, 118, and note 21.

72   MS 3937, f. 7r.

73   MS 3937, ff. 8–9.

74   Fales Manuscript Collection, Box 153, Folder 24, Fales Library, New
York University (the 'Highland pony' fragment), and Box 153, Folder
31 (the 'thieving spaniel'). The two fragments which originally formed
part of the same manuscript (hereafter 'the Fales manuscript') were
numbered '3' and '4' by Scott; this foliation is used here.

75   As explained above, 118, Blackwood supplied newspapers for Laidlaw's
use in compiling the chronicle.

76   See the *Morning Chronicle*, 6 September 1817, [3], and 11 September

1817, [3]; *Examiner*, 14 September 1817, 592; *Observer*, 14 September 1817, [unnumbered].

77 *Morning Chronicle*, 10 September 1817, [2].

78 *Examiner*, 14 September 1817, 577–78.

79 It seems to have been the direct source of the text in the *Observer*. The *Examiner* calls the dog a 'thief' rather than a 'robber' and alters the ending from 'to apprehend this depredator, or else to shoot him' to 'to apprehend the canine thief; or as he is an outlaw, to shoot him', a version which surely would have attracted Scott had he seen it.

80 It names the magistrates concerned and ends with the general comment 'This novel case caused no little diversion'.

81 MS 4937, f. 79r. This letter is undated, but dovetails perfectly with Laidlaw's letter to Blackwood of 9 October (MS 4002, ff. 167–68). Grierson's '1818–19' (*Letters*, 5.180) appears to be incorrect.

82 MS 3937, f. 7r.

83 The compositor may have fallen victim to eyeslip, as the sentence begins in the printed text 'The case of Millar, although curious, is not singular' (34.27). Alternatively, this could represent a correction intended to reflect the true content of the anecdote.

84 MS 4937, f. 79r.

85 In 1857 at the age of 30 Anne Laidlaw had married Robert Carruthers, a printer and publisher from Inverness. The marriage took place in Contin, Ross, where the Laidlaws had been living with William's brother James and his family, and where Laidlaw himself had died twelve years earlier. Mr and Mrs Carruthers then moved to Inverness, and the 1881 census shows them living in Drummond Terrace, Druin.

86 Robert Carruthers, 'Abbotsford Notanda': appendix to Robert Chambers, *Life of Sir Walter Scott*, 3rd edn (Edinburgh and London, 1871), 111–96.

87 MS 4002, ff.169–70: Laidlaw to Blackwood, 15 October 1817.

88 MS 4002, f. 171r.

89 The evidence of the Fales 'Highland pony' fragment suggests that the paragraph introducing the anecdotes may have been lengthened at some stage. It is difficult to say whether the long opening section has suffered alteration. Although we can deduce from Scott's foliation that it occupied two folios, the printed text would occupy closer to three, but without the newspaper reports it would occupy only two.

90 MS 4002, f. 168r.

91 See for example Laidlaw's comment to Blackwood on 24 January 1818: 'I was no little flattered by your approbation of J. Hoy & his Dog for I have learned from the *highest authority* that there are few better judges' (MS 4003, f. 115v).

92 MS 3888, f. 201r.

93 See 119.

94 MS 3925, f. 168v.

95 *BEM*, 2 (October 1817), 92.

96 MS 4940, ff. 7–13, foliated ff. [ ]–7 by Scott. In the following discussion the NLS foliation is used.

97 A detailed description of the MS runs thus: f. 7: 25.2×19.8cm.; no wm; stiff yellow paper; f. 8 and f. 9 represent one sheet cut in two:

f. 8: 31.5×18.2 to 19.3 cm.; wm: heraldic shield with crest; thin blue-grey paper; f. 9: dimensions and paper type as f. 8; wm: VALLEY-FIELD 1816; ff. 10–13 represent two sheets cut in two: f. 10: 32.9×20.5 cm.; wm: seated female figure in oval frame—stiff yellow paper; f. 11: dimensions as f. 10; wm: VALLEYFIELD 1813 or 1815; f. 12 : as f. 10; f. 13 as f. 11.

98   See Garside, 'Dating *Waverley*'s Early Chapters', 69–71.

99   *Literary Gems: In Two Parts* (Edinburgh, 1826), 293–306. No editor is named but the Preface is signed 'J. S.'. Given James Stillie's knowledge of obscure pieces written by Scott it is tempting to identify him as 'J. S.' but the tone of the preface may be too self-assured for Stillie who was still only in his late teens in 1826. For details of James Stillie's involvement with the Ballantyne Press and Scott, see the Essay on the Text of 'Christopher Corduroy', 109–11.

4. THE *KEEPSAKE* STORIES

GENESIS

In *The Keepsake for 1829*, an annual volume published for the Christmas market of 1828, there appeared, alongside works by Coleridge, the two Shelleys, Wordsworth and others, three stories ('My Aunt Margaret's Mirror', 'The Tapestried Chamber', 'Death of the Laird's Jock') and a short essay ('Description of the Engraving Entitled a Scene at Abbotsford') by Walter Scott. The following year's *Keepsake* included Scott's drama 'The House of Aspen' and two years later *The Keepsake for 1832* contained his short piece 'A Highland Anecdote'. The negotiations which led to the appearance of these items in *The Keepsake* had begun early in the year, but the origins of at least 'My Aunt Margaret's Mirror' lay earlier, perhaps as early as 1826, and certainly as early as an ultimately unfulfilled plan of 1827 to produce a second series of *Chronicles of the Canongate* consisting like the first of a collection of short stories. On the other hand, 'Death of the Laird's Jock' and 'A Highland Anecdote' were both explicitly written for *The Keepsake*.

Chronicles of the Canongate, unique amongst Scott's fiction in being originally published as two volumes rather than the normal three (or sometimes four), was deliberately brought out in that format for legal reasons, as Claire Lamont has demonstrated in her 'Essay on the Text' in the Edinburgh Edition of the novel.[1] In the aftermath of the financial collapse which had engulfed both Scott and his publisher Constable, there was a danger that the creditors of Archibald Constable and Co., represented by the papermaker Cowan, would lay claim to the proceeds of any work in the standard three-volume novel format on the grounds that Scott had contracted to write a novel for Constable. The two-volume format was a way of avoiding such a claim. But while there were good legal reasons for this unfamiliar format, it was only natural that James Ballantyne, as Scott's long-standing literary adviser and printer, and Robert Cadell, formerly Constable's partner but now establishing himself as Scott's new publisher, would feel some nervousness about the reception of this new work on the part of an audience which had grown accustomed to the appearance of regular three-volume novels by the Author of Waverley. Thus on 21 August 1826 Cadell wrote to Scott concerning his latest thoughts on *Chronicles of the Canongate*, recording that

> Mr Ballantyne and I have had a good deal of conversation on the subject and at first, with his usual sagacity and deep interest in the Authors Works he suggested three volumes in place of two
> —to this the alleged claims of Mr Cowan seemed an objection—

I am quite clear therefore that the plan of two volumes should be adhered to—from the quarter alluded to there can be no claim for *two* volumes.[2]

Cadell appears to accept the two-volume format here and even suggests to Scott 'perhaps you could give two more volumes of Chrystal in the Spring'. As a result Scott was led to write to John Gibson (his own lawyer and one of the Trustees of James Ballantyne and Co. who were administering Scott's financial affairs after the collapse of that firm, in which he was once again partner with Ballantyne) suggesting that 'It would be easy to carry on the "Canongate Chronicles" to two volumes more'. Nevertheless the hankering after a three-volume work continued, possibly because of the long delay in Scott's resuming work on the *Chronicles* while he completed his life of Napoleon. Consequently after another 'long conversation' with Ballantyne, Cadell wrote nearly a year later on 2 August 1827 to Scott that he had 'no hesitation in stating that a three volume Novel would be well received' after Scott had finished the *Chronicles* and *Tales of a Grandfather*.[3] He particularly urged the idea of a continuation of *Quentin Durward* but added that 'After a New Quentin—a second series of the Chronicles might follow if the good public like the first two volumes'.[4] The proviso about public approval, slipped in at this point and perhaps little heeded by Scott, would come back later.

For all this, only three weeks later on 24 August, when writing to tell Scott that the *Chronicles* could be published by the first or second week of September, but that he intends to hold it till the last week of October as 'it will not be consistent with Bookselling prudence to adventure it at this dull season', Cadell is still regretting that there is not a third volume—Scott could easily produce one and still do a new three-volume novel as well to be concluded 'in March April or May'.[5] Even though he wrote the next day to say that he had met Gibson who had reiterated the arguments for a two-volume work,[6] his suggestion of further *Chronicles* had struck a chord with Scott, who wrote back to him two days later that

> Your plan would have been an excellent one for I have as many small pieces as I think would make one or even two volumes of the Chronicles. Should it be thought advisable they may be printed as Second Series of the Chronicles & place such an interval betwixt them and the first series as would make them inaccessible to the Cormorant Cowan.[7]

Cadell took the hint and the next day wrote about the possibility of following *Chronicles of the Canongate* with another two-volume work, leading Scott not only to reply the following day 'I . . . am glad you like the idea of two volumes of the Chronicle[s]'[8] but also to mention the idea to Gibson a little later.[9] Thus the yearning for a three-volume work finally bore an unforeseen fruit in a definite plan to follow the original series of *Chronicles of the Canongate* with a two-volume continuation. On 16 September 1827 Scott recorded in his journal that 'The Ladies went to church. I God forgive me finishd the *Chronicles*' (meaning the first series of *Chronicles of the Canongate*).[10] A month later, when he had nearly finished *Tales of a Grandfather*, he was eager to resume his writing of short stories, telling Cadell on 19 October, 'We must now think of the Continuation of the Chronicles as I am ready to go on directly and have no wish to lose [time]';[11] a week later he reported 'I will begin the Chronicles immediately'.[12] Yet in spite of this he did not begin. The fallout of his financial failure continued and a certain Mr Abud was pursuing him for debt. On 2 November he was even 'ruminating upon the difference and comparative merits of the Isle of Man and of the Abbey [of Holyrood]' as sanctuaries for debtors. No wonder then that he goes on to record 'I have finishd my *Tales* and have now nothing literary in hand. It would be an evil time to begin any thing'.[13] Finally on 7 November we find him writing that he has 'Commenced a review, that is an Essay on Ornamental Gardening for the *Quarterly*. But I stuck fast for want of books. As I did not wish to leave the mind leisure to recoil I immediately began the 2d Series of the *Chronicles of Canongate*, the first having been well approved', although, with some inconsistency, he also reports the following day:

> I staid at home and began the third volume of *Chronicles* or rather the 1st volume of the Second Series. This I pursued with little intermission from morning till night yet only finishd nine pages. Like the machinery of a steam engine the imagination does not work freely when first set upon a new task.[14]

At last the long contemplated continuation of the *Chronicles*, destined ultimately to provide material for *The Keepsake*, was under way.

Over the next week or so Scott wrote on, but with difficulty. On 12 November he lamented that 'On these last two days I have written only three pages. But not from inaptitude or incapacity to labour. It is odd enough—I think it difficult to place me in a situation of danger or disagreeable circumstances purely personal which would shake my powers of mind yet they sink under mere lowness of spirit as this journal bears evidence in too many passages'.[15] His depression arose not only from his worries about Abud but also from having recently made several visits to Lady Jane Stuart, mother of his first love, Williamina, visits which aroused painful memories. Meanwhile Cadell was urging him on: 'I hope your No 2 is now ready, you really should lose no time, folk here are gaping for it'.[16] (The reference to 'No 2' is ambiguous: it probably means copy for the second series but could conceivably refer specifically to a second story if Scott had already sent one story to the press.) It is only on 22 November, after turning aside to work on the essay on ornamental gardening, that he finally notes that he has 'Sent copy of 2 Series of *Chronicles of Canongate* to Ballantyne'.[17] After this, while correcting proofs of the story, he finished work on the review essay, sending it off on 25 November to Lockhart in London[18] but unfortunately bundling up four leaves of his story in the packet.[19] After waiting for the appearance of the missing pages he finally decided to return to writing without them and was able to record on 3 December, 'Finishd my tale of the Mirror'.[20] The next day the conclusion, added to the missing leaves now returned from London, was sent to Ballantyne. It is clear then that Scott had been working on the story which eventually appeared as 'My Aunt Margaret's Mirror'. By now the threat from Abud had receded and Scott was in a more cheerful mood and relieved that 'In less than a month we are enabled to turn chase on my persecutors who seem in a fair way of losing their recourse on us' and contemplating the subject for his next story: 'I feel a little puzzled about the character and stile of the next tale. The world has had so much of chivalry. Yet scarce a good sum yet'.[21] The entry for the next day makes clear that the story he had in mind was the one that, in the event, provided the plot of *The Fair Maid of Perth*: 'I did a good deal in the way of preparing my new tale and resolved to make some thing out of the story of Harry Wynd. The North Inch of Perth would be no bad name and it may be possible to take a difference betwixt the old highlander and him of modern date.'[22] Once again there is some ambiguity here: the word 'preparing' could refer to research into the story or it could possibly mean writing an introductory section such as is found with all the stories of the first series of the *Chronicles*. At this stage Scott evidently saw this as just one of a set of tales in the second series of the *Chronicles*; he could perhaps foresee that it could be as long as 'The Surgeon's Daughter' which fills the whole second volume of the first series but he could not have had its final three-volume length in mind at this stage. This was soon to change, but for the moment the entries for the next few days in the journal simply record his progress, slow at first then quicker, on the new tale. He also records his correction of proofs which, after 8 December when he sends proofs of his essay to Lockhart, can only be of the earlier sections of the new series.

All seemed to be going well but on 11 December he had a shock in the form of 'a letter from Caddel of an unpleasant tenor'. He goes on to explain:

> It seems Mr. Cadell is dissatisfied with the moderate success of the 1st Series of *Chronicles* and disapproving of about half the volume already written of the second Series obviously ruing his engagement. I have replied that I was not fool enough to suppose that my favour with the public could last for ever and was neither

shockd nor alarmd to find that it had ceased now as cease it must one day soon. It might be inconvenient for me in some respects but I would be quite contented to resign the bargain rather than that more loss should be incurd. I saw, I told them, no other receipt than lying lea for a little while taking a fallow-break to reli[e]ve my Imagination which may be esteemd nearly cropd out.[23]

The next day, having thought again, he suggests that he cannot afford to give up writing at the moment

and that is the only reason why I do not give up literary labour, but at least I will not push the losing game of novel writing. I will take back the sheets now objected to but it cannot be expected that I am to write upon return. I cannot but think that a little thought will open some plan of composition which may promise novelty at the least.[24]

Ballantyne and Cadell's objections had clearly rattled him and he even began to look for an explanation in recent events: 'After all may there not be in this failure to please some reliques of the very unfavourable matters in which I have been engaged of late, the threat of imprisonment, the resolution to become Insolvent?' However, he concluded that this was not the problem but rather the lack of new material. To Ballantyne, in a letter of the same day, 12 December, significantly headed 'private', he complains, 'I wish I had known of the bad success of the Chronicles 1st. Series a little sooner as I would have certainly postponed this series and tried something else'. As yet he is uncertain how to proceed and he ends the letter by saying 'What next may be resolved on is not easy to say. I can always shift for one but I am afraid the presses must suffer by an inter-regnum and I see no chance of other remedy'.[25] Scott should perhaps not have taken the strictures of Cadell and Ballantyne so much to heart. They both clearly hankered for a new three-volume novel yet here was Scott busily embarked on a two-volume collection of stories. The only way to divert him back to his traditional form was to object to the material he was writing; if that was their aim they were successful.

This next stage opens some six weeks later with a short prelude. On 19 January 1828 Scott records in his journal:

I have an invitation from Messrs. Saunders and Ottley, Booksellers, offering me from £1500 to £2000 annually to conduct a Journal but I am their humble servant. I am too indolent to stand to that sort of work. And I must reserve the undisturbd use of my leisure and possess my soul in quiet. A large income is not my object. I must clear my debts and that is to be done by writing things of which I can retain the property. Made my excuses accordingly.[26]

By an odd coincidence this was followed the next day by a similar offer, similarly declined but with more significant consequences. The story is best told in Scott's own words:

> After Court hours I had a visit from Mr. Charles Heath the
> engraver accompanied by a son of Reynolds the dramatist. His
> object was to engage me to take charge as Editor of a yearly
> publication calld the *Keepsake*, of which the plates are beyond
> comparaison beautiful. But the Letterpress indifferent enough.
> He proposed £800 a year if I would become Editor, and £400 if
> I would contribute from 70 to 100 pages. I declined both but
> told him I might give him some trifling thing or other and askd
> the young men to breakfast the next day. . . . Each novel of three
> volumes brings £4000 and I remain proprietor of the mine when
> the first ore is cropd out. This promises a good harvest from
> what we have experienced. Now to become a stipendiary Editor
> of a Newsyear gift book is not to be thought of, nor could I
> agree to work for any quantity of supply to such a publication.
> Even the pecuniary view is not flattering though these gentlemen
> meant it should be so. But one hundred of their close printed
> pages, for which they offer £400, is not nearly equal to one volume
> of a novel for which I get £1300 and have the reversion of the
> copyright. No—I may give them a trifle for nothing or sell them
> an article for a round price but no permanent engagement will I
> make.[27]

Charles Heath was the owner of *The Keepsake* and Frederic Mansel
Reynolds was, as things turned out, soon to become its editor. The
next day Scott had 'the young gentlemen'[28] to breakfast and repeated
his determination not to accept their offer. However he was already
having second thoughts about contributing material for the annual:

> However I have since thought there are these rejected parts of
> the *Chronicles* which Cadell and Ballantyne criticized so severely
> which might well enough make up a trifle of this kind and settle
> the few accompts which, will I nill I, have crept in upon this new
> year, so I have kept the treaty open. If I give them one hundred
> pages I should expect £500.[29]

The next day, having 'my two youths again to breakfast', Scott remained cautious in his promises: 'I did not say more about my determination save that I would help them if I could make it convenient'.
But he adds that 'The Chief Commissioner', his friend Sir William
Adam, 'has agreed to let Heath have his pretty picture of "A Study at
Abbotsford" by Edwin Landseer', in which Scott's favourite dog Maida
appears.[30] This is, of course, the picture whose description Scott supplied for *The Keepsake*, but it is not clear whether it was now or later
that Scott was asked, or offered, to write it.

Scott's impression of Reynolds was not particularly favourable: 'The
youth Reynolds is what one would suppose his father's son to be,
smart and forward and knows the world I suppose'. He was later to
characterise him as a 'conceited vulgar Cockney' and 'that impudent

lad Reynolds'.[31] Nevertheless, after having proceeded with the story of Harry Wynd, now the subject of a whole novel, he wrote to Reynolds on 18 February to offer him the rejected stories as recorded in his journal: 'methinks I will let them have the Tales which Jem Ballantyne and Cadell quarrelld with—I have askd £500 for them, pretty well that. I suppose they will be fools enough to give it me.'[32] In his letter to Reynolds he speaks of 'one or two stories for they might be either blended to gether or kept separate', and thus it seems that he may still have been thinking of using a framing device to present them as a single whole. He does not want to surrender his copyright and proposes that Heath be allowed to print the stories only in *The Keepsake* 'while the author after a reasonable period time suppose three years should have leave to printed them if he pleased in a collected form with works of the same kind but not separately'.[33] However the address he used was not quite accurate, giving Reynolds the opportunity to reply in a tone just short of insolent: 'unfortunately, I have not sufficient wealth to merit the distinction of giving my name to a street; and the Square most contiguous to my residence, is *Fitzroy*, not *Soho*.'[34] He also informs Scott that 'I have felt a pleasure in receiving, what you have rejected; I allude to the Editorship of The Keepsake', and assures him, 'we have already secured Southey, Wordsworth, and Coleridge (and since writing this Moore, & Luthell) and are now, in treaty with Rogers, and Campbell. I mention this to shew you, that even *you* need not fear that your contributions shall be disgraced by their companions',[35] a casual and scarcely respectful reference to some of the greatest writers of the time which can only have fortified Scott's impression of his impudence. In response to Scott's query Reynolds expresses a preference for Scott's contribution to be presented as two separate tales, and in this, as we have seen, he had his way.[36]

Reynolds next discusses the question of illustrations, a key component of *The Keepsake*: 'you may conceive that Mr Heath would be delighted to have your Tale, or Tales, illustrated, if you thought they would be finished in time; or, even if in your answer, you would be kind enough to give a sketch of any scene, or scenes, you conceived most suitable for illustration, Mr Heath would employ one of our first painters immediately.'[37] His obvious intention here was to move quickly to commissioning illustrations of the material already under discussion and, if there was to be any delay in Scott sending the stories, to get him to propose particular scenes from the tales immediately so that the illustrations could be commissioned even before the stories were received. Scott, however, either misunderstood Reynolds's intentions or chose to appear to do so, and he wrote back with suggestions of two other stories as he recorded in his journal on 11 March: 'I sent Reynolds a sketch of two Scottish stories for subjects of art for his *Keepsake*. The death of the Laird's jock the one, the other the adventure of Duncan Stuart with the stag.'[38] The letter to Reynolds has survived in printed form and begins 'Two stories struck me as being susceptible of pictural illustration; I will mention the outline of each, and you may consider whether they would suit an artist or not. If they should be thought fit for the pencil, I will give you a detailed account of them, yet without attempting much ornament'. With regard to the story of 'A Highland Anecdote' Scott expresses some reservations about whether it was too close to a story in an earlier *Keepsake*: 'I do not know whether the resemblance of this subject to that of the huntsman will be an objection, or whether the difference of costume and situation will rather make the one a pendant for the other'.[39] As the introductory comments to 'A Highland Anecdote' make clear, the story referred to is 'The Gored Huntsman' which had appeared anonymously in the first issue of *The Keepsake* and was illustrated with an engraving of a huntsman with a stag hanging over him and attacking him with its antlers.[40] The remainder of the letter provides a synoptic account of the stories which would become 'Death of the Laird's Jock' and 'A Highland Anecdote'.[41]

From all of this it is clear that Lockhart was wrong in stating that 'Death of the Laird's Jock' was one of the stories rejected by Ballantyne and Cadell.[42] Both 'Death of the Laird's Jock' and 'A Highland Anecdote' were specifically written up for *The Keepsake* as being suitable for illustration and they were written at the same time since they appear in the one manuscript with 'A Highland Anecdote' following directly after 'Death of the Laird's Jock' on the same page.[43]

Scott was no stranger to writing connected to pictures. Indeed he had already, in 1821, suggested this same story to the painter Benjamin Haydon as a possible subject for his art.[44] Similarly in a letter of 1811 to Thomas Eagles he had proposed the events in 'the old ballad called the Raid of the Reidswire' as 'a fine subject for a Border painting'.[45] In March 1827 he had been asked by his old friend Adam Fergusson on behalf of Robert Balmanno to write a letter describing David Wilkie's painting of a scene at Abbotsford. This letter was then published by Balmanno later in the year along with an engraving of the painting. Moreover he was also supplying Reynolds with a description of the Landseer picture. Now the process was to be reversed and, instead of describing an existing picture, Scott was to describe scenes which could then be painted and engraved.[46]

This was not quite the end of Scott's dealings with Reynolds and Heath. He had agreed to supply one hundred pages for *The Keepsake* but the four items printed in *The Keepsake for 1829* amounted to only seventy-five pages of print and 'A Highland Anecdote' was not long enough to make up the difference. Consequently it was only after further irritating letters from Reynolds and Heath and a decision on his part to give them his early drama *The House of Aspen* that he was finally able to bring his troublesome relations with them to an end. Nevertheless, even if dealing with the two 'young gentlemen' had brought its share of annoyance, it had provided Scott with an opportunity to publish material rejected by Ballantyne and Cadell and further spurred him on to write up other stories.

THE COMPOSITION OF THE *KEEPSAKE* STORIES

Many of the details of the composition of these stories have been covered in the preceding section and some dates are known with certainty. Nevertheless some issues remain unclear. In particular, while we know that a version of 'My Aunt Margaret's Mirror' was written before the original plan of a second set of short stories was abandoned, we cannot be certain exactly what other material had been completed.

Cadell, according to Scott, disapproved of 'about half the volume already written' and Scott agreed to 'take back the sheets now objected to'.[47] But exactly what parts in particular did Cadell object to? Unfortunately Cadell's letter to Scott in which he expressed his and Ballantyne's concern is no longer extant. A few months later Scott refers to 'the Tales which Jem Ballantyne and Cadell quarrelld with'[48] and three years later, in December 1830, when James Ballantyne has expressed reservations about the early sections of *Count Robert of Paris*, Cadell writes to Scott on Ballantyne's behalf telling Scott that 'the case is wholly different, as I allege to him, from the two short Tales of the Second Chronicles of the Canongate where we saw the whole. Now we only see but a very small portion'.[49]

It would appear, then, that Ballantyne and Cadell had objected to two stories. Yet we cannot entirely rely on this. Scott might after all be referring to a story which he had projected for the *Chronicles* but not actually written and it is very clear that Cadell's memory was not always accurate. For instance, his memory failed him when he wrote to Scott in August 1831 about including the *Keepsake* stories in the collected edition of the Waverley Novels and remarked that 'the Magic Mirror—The Tapestried Chamber &c were all originally, as you well know, Chronicles of the Canongate';[50] while the record shows, as we shall see, that this is accurate as regards 'My Aunt Margaret's Mirror', it is demonstrably inaccurate with regard to 'Death of the Laird's Jock' (Cadell's '&c' here can only refer to 'Death of the Laird's Jock') since there is no doubt that the latter story was specifically written for *The Keepsake*, as we have seen.

If Cadell was wrong about 'Death of the Laird's Jock' could he also be wrong about 'The Tapestried Chamber'? Two things suggest that he may have been. Firstly, the existing manuscript of 'The Tapestried Chamber' begins in a way that indicates it too was written specifically for *The Keepsake*.[51] In the manuscript the story opens with an epigraph, 'The moving accident is not my trade', and continues 'In other words considering these narratives as rather materials to supply or direct the attention of the artists the author has avoided interweaving them with labourd description imagined dialogue or additional incident'.[52] These introductory words confirm that the extant manuscript was prepared for *The Keepsake*, which prided itself on illustrating the stories it included. This sentence and the epigraph were omitted from the printed text (presumably to avoid repeated reference in Scott's contributions to the fact that they were produced as subjects for illustration) so that the evidence that the story was written for *The Keepsake* was lost.[53] Secondly, 'The Tapestried Chamber', unlike all the other texts in both series of *Chronicles of the Canongate*, does not have an introductory chapter in the voice of Chrystal Croftangry. Taking these two things together, there must be some doubt whether 'The Tapestried Chamber' was part of the material originally written for the second series of *Chronicles of the Canongate*. However it is possible that Scott, without having actually written it, may have intended to write a story on this subject for the second series before the idea of using short stories was given up, or alternatively that he wrote an earlier draft of which the manuscript does not survive and then redrafted it for *The Keepsake*.

Thus the only material which can be definitely identified as being part of the originally conceived second series of *Chronicles of the Canongate* and then used in *The Keepsake* is 'My Aunt Margaret's Mirror'. However it may well be that at least part of the rejected material was not a story but rather prefatory material. On 15 December Scott's journal reads, 'Workd in the morning on the sheets which are to be cancelld and on the Tale of *Saint Valentine's Eve*' and two days later, 'Sent off the beginning of the Chronicles to Ballantyne. I hate cancels; they are a double labour'.[54] This is likely to refer to the four sheets that had been put in type by 8 November and appears to involve something more than the simple excision of one story. The implication seems to be that Scott had both cut and substantially revised parts of the beginning of the *Chronicles* as first written. The reduced and revised material is very likely to have been part of the first of the two chapters, both headed 'Chapter I', with which the first edition of the second series of *Chronicles of the Canongate* begins. Certainly this introductory chapter comes to a rather hurried conclusion rather than pursuing to its end the leisurely pace characteristic of Chrystal Croftangry's lucubrations in the first series. We cannot now determine whether this omitted material included an earlier version of the prefatory material to 'My Aunt Margaret's Mirror' as it now stands but we should certainly not reject the possibility.

Where does all of this leave us? There remains an uncertainty about when 'The Tapestried Chamber' was written. It is clear that 'the Tale of the Mysterious Mirror', a version of 'My Aunt Margaret's

Mirror', was written as part of the second series of *Chronicles of the Canongate* and that both 'Death of the Laird's Jock' and 'A Highland Anecdote' were written specifically for *The Keepsake*. It is also clear that Scott had a couple of tales in mind for Reynolds and Heath from the beginning. One would have been what became 'My Aunt Margaret's Mirror'; the other presumably was 'The Tapestried Chamber' but whether it also was already written is unclear. If it was, Scott rewrote it from the beginning for *The Keepsake*.

'My Aunt Margaret's Mirror'. We know that Scott finished his 'tale of the Mirror' as originally conceived for the second series of *Chronicles of the Canongate* on 3 December 1827, but when did he begin it? What did he mean, when he first suggested the idea of a second series on 26 August, by saying 'I have as many small pieces as I think would make one or even two volumes of the Chronicles'?[55] Were these pieces already written or were they merely ideas for pieces? Since we find no references to him revising existing material for the second series of the *Chronicles*, we might conclude that they were at this stage only ideas. However there is a possibility that Scott did already have at least part of one story to hand. In the introductory part of 'My Aunt Margaret's Mirror', the narrator writes as if the present year is 1826 (50.17). While it is possible that Scott, writing in 1827, chose to use the previous year's date, it is also possible that at least the introduction was indeed written in 1826. One thing in particular suggests that it may have been. The narrator of the introduction is not Scott—the details of his life do not agree with Scott's— but there are strong similarities with Scott's life: childhood lameness, a sibling nearly drowned (Scott's sister Anne in reality, the narrator's brother in the introduction) and an elder brother in the navy (Scott's brother Robert, corresponding to an unnamed brother in the fiction). Furthermore Aunt Margaret appears to be a conflation of his great-aunt Margaret Swinton and his aunt Janet Scott whose small house near the churchyard in Kelso may very well have inspired the fictional Aunt Margaret's house.[56] Now all of these would have been in his mind in 1826 since in that same year he was revising and expanding the autobiographical memoir he had started in 1808. Indeed amongst the material added in 1826 was the story of his sister's narrow escape from drowning.[57] We have seen earlier in relation to 'The Inferno of Altisidora' that Scott's interests in one piece of writing may be carried over into another of the same period and this may have been what happened here. Indeed, it is notable that a form of the quotation put into Aunt Margaret's mouth—'They fought till their hand to the broadsword was glued,/ They fought against fortune with hearts unsubdued' (52.14–15)—is used by Scott in the second 'Letter on the Proposed Change of Currency' by 'Malachi Malagrowther', originally published in the *Edinburgh Weekly Journal*, 1 March 1826.[58] One obvious possibility was that Scott wrote the introductory section in 1826 intending it to be part of the first series of the *Chronicles*. However, there is no allusion in his letters or journal to him working on any stories other than those finally included in the first *Chronicles*. Moreover the narrator, at least as we have him now, is clearly not Chrystal Croftangry; for one thing he lives in a small country town, not in Edinburgh.

Another intriguing possibility is that the story was originally intended for *Blackwood's Edinburgh Magazine*. On 5 July 1826 William Blackwood wrote to Scott about producing two issues of the magazine in the one month and asked for his help: 'Being anxious therefore to make both as interesting as possible I hope you will pardon me for saying that if you have leisure to give me any aid, however brief the article might be, you would add much to former favours.'[59] On 21 July Scott wrote in his journal, 'I wrote nothing to-day but part of a trifle for Blackwood'.[60] There is no record of any Scott contribution to *Blackwood's* at or around this time other than a review of *The Omen* by John Galt, which appeared in the July 1826 issue.[61] As he had received payment for this on 23 June it cannot be the trifle mentioned on 21 July. Thus the possibility remains open that Scott originally intended the story for *Blackwood's* and that it was begun in July 1826. Moreover towards the end of the introductory section the narrator's age is given as fifty-six and in 1826 Scott was in his fifty-sixth year. Taking into account the narrator's other similarities to Scott this provides a further argument that this part was written in 1826. If so, perhaps he wrote only the strongly autobiographical introduction at that stage; certainly he cannot have completed it then since, as we have seen, he was still writing the story in November and December of 1827.

Further information about the composition of 'My Aunt Margaret's Mirror' emerges in April and May 1828 when Scott was in London where he was able to work directly with Reynolds in preparing his text for publication. On 13 April he notes in his journal: 'Amused myself by converting the Tale of the Mysterious Mirror into "Aunt Margaret's Mirror", designd for Heath's What dye call it. Cadell will not like this but I cannot afford to have my goods thrown back upon my hands.'[62] The term 'converting' is intriguingly open. It could mean (1) that Scott merely revised some of the wording and changed the title, or (2) that he made more substantial revisions which more closely associated the mirror with Aunt Margaret, including perhaps adding the section on her own mirror at the end of the introductory material which then links to the mirror in the tale, or (3) that he actually wrote all the introductory section at this point introducing a previously absent Aunt Margaret as narrator of the actual story (although this is not compatible with our earlier suggestion that the introductory section may have been written at the time he was revising his memoir in 1826). Unfortunately, in the absence of a known surviving manuscript of the story, we cannot know what changes Scott made. However, there is some reason to believe that at least one feature of the introduction may have been added at this point: the memorable moment when Aunt Margaret tells the narrator that recently in clearing out the old family chapel a tombstone was unearthed bearing her name closely recalls an event which had happened to a visitor to Abbotsford at Melrose Abbey on 25 March 1828, when Mrs Charles Kerr similarly found a gravestone with her own name on it.[63] It is highly likely that Scott incorporated this recent event into the story as he revised it.

'The Tapestried Chamber', 'Death of the Laird's Jock' and 'A Highland Anecdote'. We do not know exactly when Scott wrote these stories but we can fairly confidently assume that the last two were written some time after Scott provided Reynolds with a brief summary of their content on 11 March 1828. On 19 April, while Scott was still in London, Reynolds called about 'the drawing of the Laird's Jock', causing Scott to comment that 'he is assiduous and attentive but a little forward'.[64] This might mean that Scott had now written the full version of 'Death of the Laird's Jock' but Reynolds could have had a drawing prepared from the original synoptic account. On 25 April, according to his journal, Scott 'Put all the "Mirror" in proof and corrected it. This is the contribution (part of it) to Mr. Reynolds' and Heath's *Keepsake*.'[65] 'All' must mean all that he had so far revised since the following day he wrote to Reynolds, 'I return the Sheets and add the rest of the Copy of the Tale which does not run out so far as I thought. I can easily go on either with the second Tale or the description of M[r] Landseers picture which ever is most required'.[66] The 'second Tale' is evidently 'The Tapestried Chamber' since this description is not likely to refer to 'Death of the Laird's Jock' which Scott always linked with 'A Highland Anecdote'. Scott seems to have either written it or rewritten it at this point presumably before leaving London on 26 May. He also supplied 'A Scene at Abbotsford', and 'Death of the Laird's Jock' and 'A Highland Anecdote' (if they had not already been supplied) but Reynolds held back the last of these for later use.

The Manuscripts. As already noted, no manuscript of 'My Aunt Margaret's Mirror' is known to be extant, but the manuscripts of the other three tales survive. That of 'The Tapestried Chamber' is now located in the British Library (Add. MS 33267). Scott has foliated the leaves of the manuscript 2–10, with the first leaf of text unnumbered. Pencilled library foliation numbers these folios 3–11.[67]

The single continuous manuscript containing 'Death of the Laird's Jock' and 'A Highland Anecdote' is in the Sterling Library, University of London (MS SL V 27). It is foliated 1–6 and begins with 'Death of the Laird's Jock'; 'A Highland Anecdote' starts at a point two thirds of the way down f. 4r.[68] Both manuscripts are closely written with approximately fifty lines of handwriting to the page. In the manuscript of 'The Tapestried Chamber' the paragraphing is sometimes indicated by a new indented line and sometimes by placing the letters 'NL' within the line either at the immediate time of writing or as a later insertion. On the other hand the paragraphing of 'Death of the Laird's Jock' and 'A Highland Anecdote' is nearly always indicated with a new indented line and only twice by the insertion of 'NL'. Scott's earlier practice had been to rely heavily on the use of 'NL' or even, between paragraphs of dialogue, simply a dash; perhaps this greater use of the conventional print layout of indented new lines reflects his consciousness that he is preparing material for an unfamiliar printer rather than the one who had handled all his novels, James Ballantyne. Scott follows his normal practice of inserting new material either, if it is short, in the margin or, for longer material, on the verso of the previous folio.

Changes within the Manuscript. Although Scott wrote fluently and produced a generally tidy manuscript he did make changes as he went along. In many cases he changed his mind in the very act of first composition and crossed out his original words and continued on the same line. In such cases we can often see his ideas evolving as he writes. For instance, when the manuscript reads at 91.8–9 'Hobbie Noble ⟨lost⟩ attackd by superior numbers ⟨lost at once his⟩ was made prisoner and executed' it would seem that Scott intended at first to write something like 'Hobbie Noble lost at once his liberty and his life', began to do so with the word 'lost', then decided that he needed to add an extra detail, then began again to write according to his original idea, and finally decided to abandon the formula and to adopt another form of wording altogether (perhaps because he realised that loss of life did not take place at the same time as loss of liberty). Likewise when the manuscript reads at 93.9 '⟨The combat or rather the field⟩ The fatal field' we can see him first trying to identify his actual subject by a clarification ('or rather the field') and then realising it is best to begin again with the true subject. Sometimes he appears to have decided his language was too informal as when he changed 'chum' to 'chosen intimate' at 78.23 or that his idiom was incorrect, for example in 'he did not dream ⟨the app⟩ of the apparition' at 86.13. In 'A Highland Anecdote' he was dealing with his central character's possible involvement in a notorious murder[69] and was being careful about seeming to implicate him too deeply. He achieved this by introducing a qualification so that the manuscript reads he 'was supposed ⟨to have been⟩ by many to have been an accomplice if not the principal actor in a certain tragic affair' (at 94.16–18) with the implication that not everyone believed in Duncan's involvement in the murder. Other changes are puzzling. Why did he change the location of the 'The Tapestried Chamber' from the 'midland counties' to the 'western' ones at 77.12? Did this bring him closer to the location identified by his source, Anna Seward, or was it a further fictionalisation? Or did he simply decide that, because he had heard the story from Seward in Lichfield, the original location was probably in the west midlands? It is impossible to tell.[70]

Insertions in the margin or on the verso of the previous leaf may have been made at much the same time or when Scott read his manuscript over before resuming writing or before sending it off to the publisher. Where these could be seen as addressing a problem that might not be immediately obvious at the time of writing later intervention may be more likely. For instance in the following passage at 86.39–41 the insertion, which appears on the previous verso, might have been made to avoid any implication that Lord Woodville was only interested in his friend's arrival because it gave him a chance to test the supernatural associations of the tapestried chamber: 'your arrival yesterday ↑ agreeable to me for a thousand reasons besides ↓ seemd the most favourable opportunity'. (In inserting these words, however, Scott caused a repetition with the word 'disagreeable' two lines further on; the problem was resolved in the printed text by changing the adjective to 'unpleasant'). Other longer insertions include the following at 81.38–42: 'His hair the powdering and arrangement of which was at this time one of the most important occupations of a man's whole day ↑ and marked his fashion as much as in the present day the tying of a cravat or the want of one, ↓ was dishevelld uncurld void of powder and dank with dew.' Here, we might surmise, he is anxious to offer another reason beyond mere vanity for the time spent on this activity.

Changes between Manuscript and Printed Text. Since the manuscript apparently does not survive, we cannot, in the case of 'My Aunt Margaret's Mirror', determine whether the *Keepsake* text was also set up directly from the manuscript or, as is very possible, from proofs originally prepared for the second series of *Chronicles of the Canongate* and then amended by Scott for their new location. (If Reynolds never had the manuscript this would explain why he apparently preserved only the manuscripts of the other three tales). By contrast the very visible presence of inky fingerprints on the surviving manuscript of 'The Tapestried Chamber' and less distinct marks on the manuscript of 'Death of the Laird's Jock' and 'A Highland Anecdote' suggests that the printed text of *The Keepsake* was set up directly from Scott's manuscript. Some minor changes to the manuscript Scott had submitted were however made before it reached the printer. In 'A Highland Anecdote' Reynolds inserted after the title the words 'By Sir Walter Scott Bart./ To the Editor/ of the Keepsake', a change dictated by the separate publication of this story. He is also probably responsible for scoring through the words 'Subjects for a painter' which follow the title of 'Death of the Laird's Jock' since they are appropriate to Scott's purpose but not needed in the printed text.

The compositors were generally accurate when working with Scott's handwriting but they did introduce some obvious mistakes; thus Duncan's 'rugged features' in 'A Highland Anecdote' (94.21–22) appear rather tamely, and inappropriately, as his 'very good features' in *The Keepsake*, a mistake which undoubtedly arose from the splitting of the word 'rugged' at the end of the line in the manuscript. Similarly, the general answers 'hastily' in the *Keepsake* version of 'The Tapestried Chamber' rather than, in the more pertinent language of the manuscript, 'testily' (87.2), and at 89.7 'topics for the painters art' in the manuscript of 'Death of the Laird's Jock' becomes 'copies for the painter's art' in *The Keepsake*. At the same time the *Keepsake* version corrects a number of obvious mistakes in Scott's manuscript. These changes include the substitution of the correct word where Scott has clearly used the wrong word as in the change of 'tell-teller' to 'tale-teller' (89.13), 'call calld Woodville' to 'call Lord Woodville' (78.12), and of 'few' to 'view' (82.36); the rectification of omissions as in the change of 'in a remarkable' to 'in a remarkable degree' (76.24); and the correction of grammar as in the change of 'was' to 'were' in 'The rougher and sterner features of their character were softened' (89.34–35). Most of these corrections were probably effected by the intermediaries; so, too, very likely, were the frequent substitutions of new words to avoid repetitions, for example the replacement of the manuscript's 'victory' by 'conquest' (92.25) because of the use of 'victory' four lines later (92.29). The intermediaries were also no doubt responsible for the regularisation of the punctuation, including the addition of numerous commas (a punctuation mark rarely found in Scott's manuscripts) and the regularisation of his capitalisation (as in the use of lower case 'champion' (92.27) rather than the inappropriate 'Champion'). Sometimes, however, these corrections seem to be at odds with Scott's intentions: the decapitalisation of Scott's reference to Bernard Gilpin as 'the Apostle of the North' to 'apostle of the north' (at 90.3) fails to recognise this as an honorific designation of this early preacher of Protestantism in the north of England. Some changes are puzzling: why is 'as Dangle says' changed to 'as the man in the play said' in 'A Highland Anecdote' (at 96.13)? A reference to Dangle in Sheridan's *The Critic* is clearly intended but Scott's 'a' often looks like a 'u' and 'Dangle' in the manuscript looks like 'Dungle'. Possibly the compositors failed to recognise the name and substituted something inappropriate, prompting Scott at proof stage to fall back on a favourite tag.

THE LATER EDITIONS

There is only one other edition of the *Keepsake* stories with which Scott had any involvement. This was what Scott and his associates called the 'Magnum' edition of the collected Waverley Novels issued in forty-eight monthly volumes between June 1829 and May 1833, although Scott died before the appearance on 1 October 1832 of Volume 41 containing 'My Aunt Margaret's Mirror', 'The Tapestried Chamber' and 'Death of the Laird's Jock'. The original plans for the Magnum had envisaged forty volumes covering the novels from *Waverley* to *Woodstock* but, attractively priced at five shillings (£0.25) a volume, it had proved to be enormously popular, so much so that a reissue of the whole edition had begun in January 1831. Given its huge sales there was every reason to continue it beyond *Woodstock* and the only question was how many volumes it would eventually comprise. On 3 June 1830 Cadell, visiting Scott, raised the question of the ultimate length of the Magnum suggesting that it should be forty-eight or fifty volumes, not forty-seven as this would 'sound ill'. According to Cadell, Scott 'seemed to like this'[71] and on 20 December Scott's journal notes that Cadell has proposed 'assembling all my detachd works of fiction [and] Articles in annuals so that the whole, supposing I write as is proposed Six new volumes, will run the Collection to fifty when it is time to close it'.[72] The original agreement with Charles Heath had allowed Scott to reprint his contributions to *The Keepsake* after three years and, since these three stories had appeared in *The Keepsake for 1829* which was published in 1828, they were now available to be reprinted and could be pressed into service as part of the attempt to make up the forty-eight volumes.

Cadell continued to push the idea of an even number of volumes and he records 'a most interesting conversation whether or not Sir Walter should write any more Novels after Count Robert—his own wish is not to write any more—altho Laidlaw as an amanuensis gave him great relief, still he felt the Fiction a strain—I repeated on this occasion as I had said before that I was by no means convinced that 48 Vols of the Novels might not be as productive as 50 in the long run'.[73] The question of how much more Scott should write stayed very much on Cadell's mind as he worried about Scott's declining mental and physical state: on 2 June he and Lockhart 'had a long Confab about Sir Walter Count Robert &c. we agreed on every point and both see that the less Sir Walter writes after this, so much the better—indeed it would be better if he were to write no more Novels'.[74] All the same Scott persisted with his writing and on 7 July Cadell, again visiting Abbotsford, 'made out a memorandum of the Volumes of the Novels to follow Woodstock and thought with Castle Dangerous & what appeared in the Annuals including also the glossary about 50 Volumes might be made up'.[75] This memorandum survives and on it the 'Annual tales' are placed in Volume 50 along with the Glossary and with a proposed 'L'Envoy' to the novels in Volume 49. Cadell's anxiety about Scott's power to fulfil this had not, however, been allayed and on 9 August he talked with Laidlaw 'who told me that the morning after I came Sir Walter could not get on with Castle Dangerous his ideas got confused—& he has since then laid it aside—of the Tales of a Grandfather (French) Second Series —there is about two Volumes done—and as to Count Robert he has not touched it since I condemned the Third Volume—so that here are three unfinished works—Mr Laidlaw and I are quite agreed that it would be a most fortunate circumstance if he were not to work any more'.[76]

Despite this Cadell continued to hope for fifty volumes and in a letter to Scott of 30 August he submits to Scott 'two views for the Conclusion of the Magnum in which I require your aid & counsel'. Both plans involved fifty volumes. In the first 'The Magic Mirror &c' along with other material would make up Volumes 49 and 50. But there was a problem: 'Under this arrangement the 41st Vol: would, even if the two Drovers were carried to 48 & 49 be unusually thick, but above all we would have difficulty with this arrangement of filling up more than Vol 49'. Needless to say the ever-resourceful publisher had a solution to propose and it was one that drastically affected the future presentation of the *Keepsake* stories:

> When considering this it struck me that the Magic Mirror— The Tapestried Chamber &c were all originally, as you well know, Chronicles of the Canongate, and that as a good and sage bookseller I might throw them in along with "The Highland"—"The two Drovers" & The Surgeon's Daughter and eke out the whole to 2 vols forming Vols 41 & 42, and thus save giving a thick Volume—gain a Volume in our calculations, and avoid upmaking at the close—The three Tales of the First Chronicles will make of the Magnum size

	540 pages
The pieces in the Keepsake (which is sent with this) will make	70 —
The Appendix will make	30 —
	640

This is rather of the shortest for two volumes—it would be most important if you could aid us with some additions or notes—50 Pages would do.[77] As it turned out the final disposition of the Magnum in forty-eight volumes took 'The Surgeon's Daughter' out of Volume 41 and transported it to the final volume, thus leaving all the short fictions ('The Two Drovers', 'The Highland Widow' and the *Keepsake* stories of 1829) in one volume, along with Chrystal Croftangry's lengthy introduction to *Chronicles of the Canongate*. 'My Aunt Margaret's Mirror' and 'The Tapestried Chamber' were thus, by 'this piece of bookselling legerdemain' as Cadell called it,[78] returned to their original intended association with the *Chronicles* but at the price of excluding one of the key elements of the original *Chronicles* and of including a text, 'Death of the Laird's Jock', which had never before been part of them. This physical association of the *Keepsake* stories with the *Chronicles* has remained in most subsequent editions of the Waverley Novels[79] while the displacement of the title *Chronicles of the Canongate: Second Series* in favour of *The Fair Maid of Perth* has obscured the original connection of 'the story of Harry Wynd' with the *Chronicles*.

In preparing the Magnum edition Cadell's normal practice was to provide Scott with an interleaved copy of the text so that he could make corrections and add shorter notes on the blank pages—longer additions were written on separate pages. Usually this was one of the collected editions of groups of the novels but no such collected edition had as yet been published for *Chronicles of the Canongate* and instead Cadell provided an interleaved copy of one of the separate editions of the text.[80] Scott worked through the novels chronologically and had reached the First Series of the *Chronicles* by early August 1831. On 9 August he showed Cadell the introduction to the First Series[81] and sent it the next day, as he wrote to Cadell:

> I send you 1st vol Chronicles of the Canongate which may go to the press with the General Preface to which you promised to add an Appendix consisting of the account of what passd at the meeting for the Theatrical fund Another introduction specially belonging to the tale of the Highland widow to come in at page 146 so that the whole may proceed without interruption.[82]

Thus Cadell, when he proposed the inclusion of the *Keepsake* stories in a *Chronicles* volume of the Magnum, could tell Scott that 'all that is called for in the Introduction to the Chronicles which I already have, is the allusion to the Magic Mirror &c which can be done on the proof'.[83] However Scott, having embarked on the practice of providing individual introductions to the stories in the case of 'The Highland Widow', chose to continue this with the three *Keepsake* stories, as we shall see. The interleaved volumes of the First Series were quickly followed by those of the Second Series two days later leading Scott to remark: 'Anne of Geierstein comes next together with Aunt Margarets mirror I will thank you to see what other small pieces fall into my last volume for I am not sure that without your assistance I can remember them all'.[84] Six days later a more specific plaint reveals the reason for Scott's vagueness: 'I fear I have lost or mislaid the Keepsake or laid it by so well that I have forgot where I put it. I have vol which has the house of Aspen but not that with my Aunt Margarets mirror & other little trifles I should like to have a list of the whole which you think should be included in the Magnum'.[85] Thus prompted Cadell replied that 'The *Magic Mirror* I think had with it *The Tapestried Chamber* in the Keepsake of 1829—I am not aware of any other, what may be termed "*Work of Fiction*"'[86] and enclosed a copy of *The Keepsake for 1829* with his letter regarding the placement of the *Keepsake* stories. Evidently, and not without some justification, Cadell did not consider 'Death of the Laird's Jock' as a 'work of fiction' but this judgment must have been overturned since it was, as we know, to find a place in the Magnum.

It is not clear whether the copy sent by Cadell was interleaved as it does not seem to have survived; if it was, Scott made very little use of it to amend the text: the changes between *The Keepsake* and the Magnum are minor and mostly consist of variations to punctuation, including the addition of commas and hyphens and capitalisation, and spelling. Most of the added capitals are of no real significance (for example, 'the general' becomes 'the General' throughout 'The Tapestried Chamber'), but some carry more weight (for example, the capitalisation of 'revolution' (at 88.1) makes it absolutely clear that Scott is referring to the Glorious Revolution and the change of 'round-head' to 'Roundhead' (at 87.41–42) confirms that Scott is referring specifically to a supporter of Cromwell). Spelling changes (such as the substitution of 'haggard' (at 82.2) for the unusual 'haggered' and of 'toilet' for 'toilette' (at 54.8, 80.31 and 82.2) are also minor. There are just a few substantive changes: the use of 'thus' (81.34) rather than 'then' better fits the sequence of events and the Magnum undoubtedly restores the original sense with the substitution of 'parks' (at 48.31), meaning 'fields', for 'packs', thus correcting a mistake which may have arisen because the English compositor of *The Keepsake* did not understand the Scottish meaning of the word. All of these changes could have been made either by Scott or by his intermediaries but the significant revision of 'several victories' to 'numerous victories' (at 91.39–40) suggests authorial intervention. Be that as it may, Scott clearly did not spend much time on revision, and, only a couple of days after receiving the volume from Cadell, he sent him the 'introductions of the Keepsaksale'.[87] A mere three weeks later on 23 September he left Scotland for England and was soon on his way to Malta in an ultimately unsuccessful attempt to restore his physical and mental health. Once he left Britain he was no longer able to correct proofs and oversee the transformation of his manuscript into print; this responsibility fell to Lockhart who was not afraid to cut and redraft work which he considered badly written or inappropriate. The manuscripts of two of the *Keepsake* introductions survive, those for 'Death of the Laird's Jock' and 'The Tapestried Chamber'.[88] It is remarkable that Scott had been able to find time and energy for even these brief pieces but they do not seem to have found much favour with Lockhart: that for 'Death of the Laird's Jock' was never used, being simply replaced by a note saying no introduction was necessary, while the very brief introduction to 'The Tapestried Chamber' was substantially recast and reworked. Scott's valiant attempt to keep up the production of material for the Magnum had received pretty short shrift.

THE PRESENT TEXT

The text of the present edition is based on that in the two volumes of *The Keepsake* in which the stories occur, and specifically the copies of *The Keepsake for 1829* (for 'My Aunt Margaret's Mirror', 'The Tapestried Chamber', and 'Death of the Laird's Jock') and *The Keepsake for 1832* (for 'A Highland Anecdote') held in the Bernard C. Lloyd Walter Scott Collection in Aberdeen University Library. It aims to reflect the results of Scott's original engagement with the composition of the text rather than later revisions for the Magnum. Nevertheless a few readings have been adopted from the Magnum, but only where they clearly correct mistakes (as in 'parks' (48.31) for 'packs' where we have no manuscript witness to Scott's original wording) or where the Magnum's more emphatic punctuation and capitalisation clarifies the original meaning (e.g. 'Revolution' at 88.1). In keeping with the policy of reflecting Scott's original act of composition, later changes which alter the meaning of the text have not been adopted. This applies to the change mentioned above from 'several' to 'numerous' (at 91.39); this may well result from Scott's intervention, but the Magnum correction took place some time after the original period of composition. On the other hand, collation with the manuscripts of 'The Tapestried Chamber', 'Death of the Laird's Jock' and 'A Highland Anecdote' has allowed us to introduce a substantial number of superior readings; for instance, General Browne now imagines his visitor has 'returned by habit' (84.33) as in the manuscript rather than 'returned by twelve', and responds to his host 'testily' (87.2) rather than 'hastily', the 'stores of history and tradition' provide 'topics' (89.6–7) instead of 'copies' for the painter, and Duncan's features appear 'rugged' (94.21), not 'very good'. As in other texts, what appears as sloppy writing in the printed text becomes much tighter if we follow the manuscript: thus the printed text's unilluminating description of the towers of a castle as 'particular' gives way to the much more specific and contextually meaningful 'particolour' (77.39) of the manuscript and Duncan and the stag drop 'sheer down' (96.4) the precipice instead of 'thus down'. Following the manuscript also allows us to restore Scott's description of exactly how the famous sword was passed from Hobbie Noble to the Laird's Jock (at 91.9–10).[89] Careful attention to the manuscript punctuation is also rewarding. For instance, adoption of the manuscript readings allows us to retain the dashes through which Scott expresses the general's agitated response to the apparition in the tapestried chamber (at 85.8–11). Although the number of changes is quite small, the text altogether emerges as tighter and more effective.

NOTES

1   *Chronicles of the Canongate*, ed. Claire Lamont, EEWN 20, 289–93.
2   MS 794, f. 28v.
3   MS 3904, f. 216r.
4   MS 3904, f. 216v.
5   MS 3904, ff. 237r–v.
6   MS 3904, f. 242v.
7   *Letters*, 10.272.
8   *Letters*, 10.274.
9   *Letters*, 10.275: Scott to Cadell, 10 September 1827.
10   *The Journal of Sir Walter Scott*, ed. W. E. K. Anderson (Oxford, 1972), 352.
11   *Letters*, 10.291.
12   *Letters*, 10.294.
13   *Journal*, 371–72.
14   *Journal*, 375.
15   *Journal*, 378.
16   MS 794, f. 230r: Cadell to Scott, 16 November 1827.
17   *Journal*, 383. By 28 November Cadell was able to record in his diary that 4 sheets of the second series were in type; see MS 21043, ff. 50v–51r.
18   *Journal*, 384.
19   *Journal*, 385.
20   *Journal*, 388.
21   *Journal*, 389.
22   *Journal*, 389–90.
23   *Journal*, 393.
24   *Journal*, 394.
25   *Letters*, 10.329–30.
26   *Journal*, 420–21.
27   *Journal*, 421.
28   Heath, born in 1785, was not young; Reynolds's date of birth is unknown.
29   *Journal*, 421–22.
30   *Journal*, 422.
31   *Journal*, 525, 545.
32   *Journal*, 429.
33   Letter to F. M. Reynolds, 18 February 1828, Berg Collection, New York Public Library, f. 1r. (The letter is attached to Volume 1 of a copy

of the first edition of *Guy Mannering*.) In telling Reynolds that he had 'intended to have used' the stories 'in concluding the second series of the Tales of the Canongate' but that he could not do so 'because the story which precedes them has drawn to great length' (f. 1r), Scott not only distorted the truth but also avoided revealing the real reason why they were not being included in the second series of the *Chronicles*.

34   MS 3906, f. 103r.

35   MS 3906, f. 104r.

36   Another possibility is that in his letter Scott was referring to the introduction and tale proper of 'My Aunt Margaret's Mirror' which could without much difficulty have been separated into two stories.

37   MS 3906, f. 104v.

38   *Journal*, 442.

39   This letter was printed in the *Athenæum* for 1835, 55–56, but the original has not been traced. The *Athenæum* does not identify the recipient but this is clearly the letter to Reynolds which Scott mentions in his journal.

40   'The Gored Huntsman', in *The Keepsake for 1828*, 21–32; the engraving faces 31.

41   The relevant section is quoted in the Historical Note, 208–09, 212–13.

42   *Life*, 7.88.

43   Sterling Library, University of London, MS SL V 27.

44   *Letters*, 6.332–33: Scott to Benjamin Haydon, 7 January 1821.

45   *Letters*, 12.413: Scott to Thomas Eagles, 8 December 1811.

46   For the original letter to Fergusson, dated 27 March 1827, see *Letters*, 10.166–70. The first version to be published appeared under the title *Letter from Sir Walter Scott to Sir Adam Ferguson, Descriptive of a Picture Painted by David Wilkie, Esq. R.A., Exhibited at the Royal Academy, 1818* without any date of publication or publisher given, although the letter as printed is now dated 2 August 1827, having been revised by Scott.

47   *Journal*, 393, 394.

48   *Journal*, 429.

49   MS 3915, f. 142r.

50   MS 3919, f. 77r.

51   The MS of 'The Tapestried Chamber' is held by the British Library (BL, Add. MS 33267); it is described in detail below.

52   BL, Add. MS 33267, f. 2r.

53   Scott's rather over-insistent emphasis that the stories are not important in themselves but only as providing a stimulus for the illustrators may have arisen from some feeling that Heath in particular valued the illustrations more highly than the writing. Later, commenting on a letter from Heath, Scott was to remark on a more explicit statement of such an attitude: 'There was one funny part of it in which he assured me that the success of the new Edition of the waverley novels depended entirely on the excellence of the illustrations' (*Journal*, 525).

54   *Journal*, 396–97.

55   *Letters*, 10.272.

56   Scott's old friend Mrs Anne Murray Keith (1736–1818) may also have contributed to the character of Aunt Margaret; for details see Historical Note, 187–88.

57 See *Scott on Himself*, 9, where this is marked as an 1826 addition. The lines by Logan quoted by Scott in this story provide another link with his writing in 1826; he quotes them in his journal on 4 April 1826 (*Journal*, 125).

58 *The Prose Works of Sir Walter Scott, Bart.*, 28 vols (Edinburgh, 1834–36), 21.325.

59 MS 3903, ff. 53v–54r.

60 *Journal*, 176.

61 *BEM*, 20 (July 1826), 52–59.

62 *Journal*, 457.

63 This incident is recorded in Thiébault, 'Trois jours passés à Abbotsford'; see MS 921, f. 114r. Scott refers to the Kerrs' visit in his journal entries for 24 and 25 March (*Journal*, 447).

64 *Journal*, 461.

65 *Journal*, 463.

66 BL, Add. MS 27925, f. 113r.

67 The leaves, the edges of which have been trimmed and gilded at the time of binding, are now 18.7×30.6 cm. These leaves were created by cutting larger sheets in two so that the leaves with even numbers in Scott's foliation have a watermark of the British royal coat of arms on a shield surmounted by a crown and the odd-numbered sheets have '1827/ CC & Co'.

68 The leaves of this manuscript are in their present bound state 20.2×32.2 cm. As with the manuscript of 'The Tapestried Chamber', these were created by cutting in two a larger sheet. The odd-numbered leaves have a Britannia seated in an oval frame surmounted by a crown as a watermark while the even-numbered leaves are watermarked 'FELLOWS/ 1825'. The manuscript was sold at Sotheby's on 21 June 1937 as Lot 32 in the Duke of Newcastle's sale. The two manuscripts would originally have been in the possession of Reynolds and, either when he owned them or later, they were bound in similar bindings each with a decorative handwritten title page using similar wording and layout; the handwriting in the case of 'Death of the Laird's Jock' and 'A Highland Anecdote' appears to be less careful than that used for the title-page of 'The Tapestried Chamber', and it may be in a different hand.

69 See Historical Note, 212–14.

70 For further details see Historical Note, 196.

71 MS 21043, f. 77r.

72 *Journal*, 613.

73 MS 21043, ff. 94v.

74 MS 21043, f. 98v.

75 MS 21043, f. 101r.

76 MS 21043, f. 110r.

77 MS 3919, ff. 77r–v. Cadell seems to suggest that 'Death of the Laird's Jock' was also originally intended for *Chronicles of the Canongate* but, as we have seen, the chronology and the nature of the manuscript suggest his memory was inaccurate.

78 MS 3919, f. 77v.

79 For example in the Border Edition (1894) the introductory chapters,

'The Highland Widow' and 'The Two Drovers' are followed by 'My Aunt Margaret's Mirror', 'The Tapestried Chamber' and 'Death of the Laird's Jock' in one volume, with 'The Surgeon's Daughter' in another volume with *Count Robert of Paris*.

80 The interleaved copy of the first volume has not been traced but for Volume 2 Cadell used a copy of the first edition of 1827; this volume is now in the Widener Collection at Harvard (Houghton Library, HEW 9.10.3).

81 MS 21043, f. 109v.

82 MS 15980, f. 146r.

83 MS 3919, ff. 77v–78r.

84 MS 15980, f. 150r.

85 MS 15980, f. 152r.

86 MS 3919, f. 41r.

87 MS 15980, f. 162r.

88 MS 911, ff. 270–71. The introductions appear to have been dictated by Scott, as the manuscripts are not in his hand.

89 The sentence was probably omitted because it partly repeats another sentence a few lines before; however, it contains extra and significant information.

EMENDATION LIST

The base-texts used for the stories in this edition of Scott's shorter
fiction are as follows: for 'The Inferno of Altisidora' a copy of the
Edinburgh Annual Register for 1809 in the National Library of Scotland; for 'Christopher Corduroy' a copy of *The Sale-Room* also in the
National Library of Scotland; for 'Alarming Increase of Depravity
Among Animals' and 'Phantasmagoria' copies of *Blackwood's Edinburgh
Magazine*, Volumes 2 and 3, in the Barr Smith Library, University of
Adelaide; for 'My Aunt Margaret's Mirror', 'The Tapestried Chamber', and 'Death of the Laird's Jock' a copy of *The Keepsake for 1829*,
and for 'A Highland Anecdote' a copy of *The Keepsake for 1832*, both
in the Bernard C. Lloyd Walter Scott Collection in Aberdeen University Library. All emendations to these base-texts, whether verbal,
orthographic, or punctuational, are listed below, with the exception of
certain general categories of emendation described in the next paragraph, and of those errors which result from accidents of printing
such as a letter dropping out, provided always that evidence for the
'correct' reading has been found in at least one copy of the first editions
of these texts.

Inverted commas are sometimes found in the first edition for displayed verse quotations, sometimes not; the present text has standardised the inconsistent practices of the base-texts by eliminating such
inverted commas, except when they occur at the beginning or end of
direct speech. The typographic presentation of story and chapter headings, mottoes, poetry, and of the opening words of stories and chapters
has been standardised. Ambiguous end-of-line hyphens in the base-
text have been interpreted in accordance with the following authorities
(in descending order of priority): predominant first-edition usage;
second printings (when available); MS (when available).

Each entry in the list below is keyed to the text by page and line
number; the reference is followed by the new, EEWN reading, then
in brackets the reason for the emendation, and after the slash the
base-text reading that has been replaced. Occasionally, some explanation of the editorial thinking behind an emendation is required, and
this is provided in a brief note.

There is relevant manuscript material for 'Alarming Increase of
Depravity Among Animals', and extant manuscripts for 'Phantasmagoria', 'The Tapestried Chamber', 'Death of the Laird's Jock', and
'A Highland Anecdote'; some emendations recover readings from
these manuscripts which had been lost through misreading or misunderstanding, and these are indicated by the simple explanation '(MS)'.
The spelling and punctuation of some emendations from the manuscript have been normalised in accordance with the prevailing conven-

tions of the base-text, and although as far as possible emendations have been fitted into the existing base-text punctuation, occasionally it has been necessary to provide emendations with a base-text style of punctuation. Where the manuscript reading adopted by the EEWN has required editorial intervention to normalise spelling or punctuation, the exact manuscript reading is given in the form: '(MS actual reading)'. Where the new reading has required editorial interpretation of the manuscript, e.g. when interpreting a homophone, the explanation is given in the form '(MS derived: actual reading)'.

When faced with apparent errors the editors have consulted second printings of the stories to see how they overcame problems. The editors have adopted some readings from the second printing of 'Alarming Increase of Depravity Among Animals' in the second volume of *Blackwood's Edinburgh Magazine* as reprinted without the 'Chaldee Manuscript'; these are designated as 'BEM2'. They have also adopted one reading which appears in some copies of *The Keepsake for 1829* (designated Ed1b). Readings for 'Phantasmagoria' from *Literary Gems* or *Tales and Essays* are indicated by 'LG' and 'TE'. And readings for stories from *The Keepsake for 1829* as republished in the Magnum are indicated by '(Magnum)'. However there are still obvious errors which no one attended to in the past, and these emendations are indicated by 'Editorial'.

1.7 *Á* (Editorial) / *A*
On 23 October 1810 Scott wrote to James Ballantyne: 'Not having a Don Quixote here I cannot prefix the motto, but you will find the passage towards the end of the 4th vol' (*Letters*, 1.412). However, the passage is quoted incorrectly and changes to the Spanish motto have been made in conformity with the text in *El ingenioso hidalgo Don Quixote de la Mancha*, ed. Real Academia Española, 2 vols (Madrid, 1780); *CLA*, 242.
1.7 *nuevo flamante* (Editorial) / *nuero, flamante*
1.7 *encuadernado, le* (Editorial) / *enguardernado le*
1.8 *sacáron* (Editorial) / *sacaron*
1.8 *esparciéron* (Editorial) / *esparcieron*
1.8 *las hojas* (Editorial) / *los hojas*
1.9 viii, cap. (Editorial) / viii. cap.
3.21 losers." "That's (Editorial) / losers. "That's
6.34 *cæteris* (Editorial) / *cœteris*
8.25 affability.— (Editorial) / affability."—
10.24 *Party*; (Editorial) / *Party;*
10.31 *Hollands*; (Editorial) / *Hollands;*
17.2 TRIERMAIN [new line] I [new line] Where (Editorial) / TRIERMAIN [new line] Where
17.5 Triermain (Editorial) / Tiermain
18.17 brow, [new line] (Editorial) / brow [new line]
21.7 Εως, οτω αιει θελει (Editorial) / Εως τω αιει θελειν
21.21 αυτοποιητον (Editorial) / αυτο ωοιητον
24.28 Cœur-du-roy (Editorial) / Cœur-du roy
25.1 *triumphans*," (Editorial) / *triumphans*"
27.20 cloy (Editorial) / clog
Shakespeare's word is 'cloy' (*Richard II*, 1.3.296); Scott's terminal

'y' could be confused with a 'g'.

32.3	acts (Editorial) / arts
32.7	having the (BEM2) / hav-[eol] the
34.24	which to (BEM2) / which, to
34.30	who, in her (Editorial) / which, in its
34.32	her (Editorial) / his
34.33	her (Editorial) / his
34.36	him (MS) / home
34.36	she (Editorial) / he
35.5	her (Editorial) / his
35.9	her (Editorial) / his
35.24	gentleman's (BEM2) / gentlemen's
36.1	runs (Editorial) / run
36.12	unwittingly (Editorial) / unwillingly

'Unwittingly' makes better sense, and it is characteristic of Scott to leave his 't's uncrossed.

38.19	to pitched faggots (MS pitchd) / to faggots
38.19	tarred (MS tarrd) / tarr'd
38.21	Gines de Passamonte's (Editorial) / Giles Passamonte's
38.22	Montesinos's (Editorial) / Montosinos's
38.31	narratives (MS) / narrations
39.3	Mickelmast (MS) / Michaelmas
39.30	divining rod, of (TE divining-rod, of) / divining rod of
39.36	too (MS) / two
39.40	down, play (Editorial) / down play
39.43	puck-hairies (MS) / puck-harries
40.2	Genius (MS) / genius
40.4	Besides all these (MS) / Besides these
40.10	perilous, to (TE) / perilous to
40.10	narrate which, with (TE) / narrate, which with
40.12	be long in (MS) / be in
40.16	curious (MS) / current
40.31	SHADOWS (MS) / shadows
41.15	narrative (MS) / narration
41.39	Forty-Second (MS) / forty-second
42.5	volunteer (MS) / volunteers
42.9	widowed (MS widowd) / beloved
42.17	Mrs —— greatly (MS Mrs. —— greatly) / Mrs ——, greatly
42.19	commander. It (MS commander It) / commander; it
42.27	Katerans (MS) / Katerns
43.9	question by (LG, TE) / question, by
43.16	had (MS) / have
43.26	broadsword (MS) / broad sword
43.32	relative (MS) / relation
43.39	on (MS) / in
43.42	passage, but (LG, TE) / passage; but
44.22	figure representing (MS) / figure, representing
44.23	Campbell completely (MS) / Campbell, completely
44.29	on (MS) / in
44.32	breast-ruffle (MS breast:[eol]rufle) / breast, ruffle
47.26	hearing; (Editorial) / hearing:
47.29	discipline; (Magnum) / discipline:
48.31	parks (Magnum) / packs
48.39	Earl's Closes (Magnum) / Earls' Closes
55.31	audacity; (Editorial) / audacity:

58.26 Captain (Editorial) / Major
       In the first cluster of references to Lady Forester's brother he is
       termed 'Major', but in the second cluster (at 71.7, 23, 28, and 37)
       he is 'Captain', and this seems to be how Scott finally viewed him.
58.34 Captain (Editorial) / Major
58.41 Captain (Editorial) / Major
59.11 Captain (Editorial) / Major
64.2   whether——" (Magnum whether"——) / whether—"
66.3   feeble minded a (Editorial) / feeble a minded
66.28 linen; (Editorial) / linen:
70.37 fee, (Magnum) / fee;
70.37 hat; (Magnum) / hat
76.34 secured (MS securd) / received
76.34 details of the locality (Editorial) / localities of the detail
77.6   Seward (MS S—) / S.
       Scott names his source as 'Miss Seward' at 76.21–22 and 'S—' is
       clearly an abbreviation which should have been expanded in the
       printed text.
77.39 particolour (MS) / particular
78.14 soon (MS) / now
79.1   which war, with (ms) / which, war with
82.2   haggard (MS) / haggered
83.12 extraordinary,"—said (MS extraordinary"—said) / extraordinary,"
       said
83.13 himself—"then (MS himself—then) / himself; "then
83.33 may be; I know (Editorial) / may be," replied Lord Woodville; "I
       know
       MS and *Keepsake* introduce Lord Woodville's words with 'his friend
       replied' and then redundantly interrupt it with 'replied Lord Wood-
       ville'.
84.33 habit (MS) / twelve
84.36 round—But (MS) / round, but
85.6   terror (MS) / horror
85.8   fiend."—— [new paragraph] (MS) / fiend." [new paragraph]
85.9   stopped—and (MS stopd—and) / stopped, and
85.11 it—"My (MS) / it. [new paragraph] "My
85.17 bristle—I felt the (MS) / bristle. The
85.18 arrested (MS) / ceased to flow
85.20 old—How (MS) / old. How
85.36 them—An (MS) / them. An
86.13 nor (MS) / or
86.14 apparitions into (MS) / apparitions,—wild
86.15 deceptions (MS) / deception
87.2   testily (MS) / hastily
87.39 Cavalier (MS) / cavalier
87.41 Roundhead (Magnum) / round-head
88.1   Revolution (Magnum) / revolution
88.2   Whig and Tory (MS) / whig and tory
88.10 is—" he (MS) / is!" he
88.11 though far inferior (MS) / though inferior
88.11 expression, of the (MS expression of the) / expression to, the
88.25 tapestried (Ed1b) / tapstried
89.7   topics (MS) / copies
89.32 Borderland (MS) / border-land
89.34 the Crowns (MS) / England and Scotland

90.3   Apostle (MS) / apostle
90.3   North (MS) / north
90.24   chiefly inhabited (MS) / principally cultivated
91.5   brother-in-arms, to (Magnum) / brother-in-arms to
91.7   one (MS derived: won) / brand
91.9   executed. At his death he bequeathed the highly prized sword to the
        Laird's Jock, in whose castle he had left it. [new paragraph] With
        (MS executed. At his death he bequeathed the highly prized to the
        Lairds Jock in whose castle he had left it. ↑NL↓ With) / executed.
        With
92.4   people, who (Magnum) / people; who
92.7   Laird's Jock's stone (Editorial) / Laird Jock's stone
94.21   rugged (MS) / very good
95.5   right hand rose (MS right hang rose) / right, rose
95.11   mid way (MS) / midway
96.4   sheer (MS) / thus
96.13   as Dangle says (MS) / as the man in the play said

END-OF-LINE HYPHENS

All end-of-line hyphens in the present text are soft unless included in the list below. The hyphens listed are hard and should be retained when quoting.

3.13	tennis-balls	67.40	communion-table
3.38	low-browed	76.30	ghost-story
4.36	bare-faced	77.18	hedge-row
11.26	liberal-minded	80.32	murrey-coloured
24.32	Register-office	87.41	Round-head
44.32	breast-ruffle	91.29	two-handed

HISTORICAL NOTE

'THE INFERNO OF ALTISIDORA'

Historical Background. Scott's own essay 'On the Present State of Periodical Criticism', published in the same volume of the *Edinburgh Annual Register*, provides a good deal of the historical background necessary to understanding 'The Inferno of Altisidora'. In it he traces the rise of the *Edinburgh Review*, first published in October 1802 by Constable, and argues that its arrival changed the whole nature of periodical criticism. He describes the situation before the appearance of the *Edinburgh Review* as one where 'the leading English reviews, though originally established by men of letters, had gradually fallen under the dominion of the publishing bookseller' so that 'the reviewer, like a fee'd barrister, sacrificed his own feelings and judgement to the interest of the bookseller his employer'.[1] The *Edinburgh Review*, with its highly paid editor Francis Jeffrey, achieved a much greater dignity and independence, in which even works issued by its publisher, Constable, were subject to severe criticism. As Scott remarks, 'The style was bold, caustic, decided, and intolerant. To mark as far as possible the new principles of their criticism, the adventurers hung out the bloody flag in their title-page, and by the appropriate motto (*Judex damnatur si nocens absolvitur*) intimated their intention to discard the courteous rules and indulgent civility, under the restraint of which their contemporaries had been hitherto content to wage their drowsy warfare'.[2] Scott's admiration of Jeffrey comes through clearly in his praise of his mind as 'remarkable for prompt arrangement of the knowledge he possessed', 'distinguished for the clear, perspicuous statement of argument or theory', and 'unequalled for the ready and acute felicity of brilliant illustration', but he regretted a 'tone of general severity' in much of the *Review*'s writing. It is this climate of fearless and often savage criticism that is reflected in the violent actions of the players in the tennis match in 'The Inferno of Altisidora' in which Jeffrey appears as the 'wee reekit devil' who, 'possessed of uncommon activity and accuracy of aim, . . . far surpassed all his competitors' (9.34–35).

In keeping with the politics of its publisher and its editor, the *Edinburgh Review* was aligned with the Whig party in politics. Scott, and others, objected to the Whig bias of many contributions and the setting up of the *Edinburgh Annual Register* was in part a response to this. However, although in its chronicle of contemporary events it was able to adopt a strongly Tory line, begun by the Tory Southey and continued by later writers, the *Edinburgh Annual Register* did not have a reviews section and could not therefore combat the *Edinburgh Review* on its own territory. This problem was, however, addressed by the establishment of the *Quarterly Review* in February 1809 under the editorship of William Gifford, whose role in 'The Inferno of Altisidora' is that of the 'dæmon' who is 'indisputably the second-best' in the tennis game (10.15). While Scott was now able to 'rejoice in an opportunity of hearing both sides of a political question ably stated and supported, by persons whose powers and opportunities of information are so far beyond those by whom such points are usually disputed in periodical publications',[3] he deplored the fact that, as with the *Edinburgh Review*, the *Quarterly* was inclined to let political allegiance colour its judgment of literary works: 'These obvious partialities, by which the author's political creed is made the gage of his literary proficiency, we censure alike in both cases.'[4] In 'The Inferno of Altisidora' this condemnation of politically biased judgment is allegorised in the narrator's observation that 'the rivalry between these two leaders was attended with some acts of violence, especially after either of them had taken a cordial out of a small dram-bottle, to which they occasionally applied. These flasks . . . contained an alcohol called *Spirit of Party*' (10.20–24).

Reviews in journals were then anonymous, although Jeffrey's authorship of certain articles in the *Edinburgh* was widely known. Scott's essay makes special mention of one exception to this general anonymity, Richard Cumberland's *London Review*, 'instituted . . . with the professed purpose that each piece of criticism should bear in front the name of the party by whom it was composed'.[5] In the life of Cumberland he wrote for Ballantyne's Novelist's Library, Scott describes him as a 'learned and ingenious, but rather eccentric person'[6] and in the essay he finds 'something generous and spirited in the conception of this plan' but defends the practice of anonymous reviews even though he admits that the 'different manner and style of the principal contributors to the Edinburgh Review, for example, are easily detected, . . . like the champions of old, who, though sheathed in armour, were known by their bearings and cognizances'.[7] Adopting a very similar image in 'The Inferno of Altisidora', Scott describes how the players 'all wore vizards' although they were 'not complete disguises' (4.29–30). According to Scott in the essay, 'The difficulty . . . of enlisting individuals to fight with their visors up, may have hastened the conclusion of Mr Cumberland's unsuccessful attempt to establish a review upon his new plan',[8] while in the 'Inferno' Cumberland appears without a vizard: 'I did, indeed, remark one old gentleman, and, 'twas said, he had been a notable man in his day, who made a match to be played bare-faced; but whether, like Entellus of old, he had become stiff and unwieldy, or whether he was ill-seconded by his few and awkward partners, so it was, that he was soon obliged to give up the game' (4.34–39).

Sources. Scott's knowledge of the literary scene of his own time is his primary source of information for what is, after all, a portrayal of contemporary life although allegorised as a descent into an inferno.

Scott had a longstanding interest in Cervantes, who provided the central image of the tennis match for the allegory. His letters contain numerous mentions of *Don Quixote* and frequent references in his other works attest to his interest in 'the immortal work of Cervantes', as he calls it in the 'Essay on Romance'.⁹ That he should find inspiration for his fantasy in the pages of Cervantes is not at all surprising. As for imitation of other authors, this was not the first occasion on which Scott tried his hand. For instance, for *Minstrelsy of the Scottish Border*, published in 1802, he composed a new third part to 'Thomas the Rhymer',¹⁰ and his edition of *Sir Tristrem* of 1804 contained a 'Conclusion', acknowledged in the introduction as 'attempted by the Editor' but described in its heading more indirectly as 'abridged from the French metrical romance, in the style of Tomas of Erceldoune'.¹¹ As for the authors he imitated in the 'Inferno', George Crabbe was a longtime favourite of Scott's; he is quoted in Scott's letters and journal and he visited Scott in Edinburgh in 1822. Crabbe also figures prominently as a source of chapter mottoes in the novels. Writing to Crabbe Scott praises the 'clearness and accuracy of your painting whether natural or moral' but to Charles Kirkpatrick Sharpe he writes, rather less diplomatically, that Crabbe 'has, I think, great vigour and force of painting; but his choice of subjects is so low, so coarse, and so disgusting, that he reminds me of the dexterity of Pallet [a character in Smollett's *Peregrine Pickle*], who painted that which is as good for a sow as a pancake, in such a lively manner as so set a whole pigstye in an uproar'.¹² This characterisation of Crabbe is reflected in Scott's imitation, a picture of low life in the form of a portrait of a poacher (and murderer) living in a squalid hovel in the New Forest in constant fear of being apprehended and hanged. Thomas Moore is also a poet Scott admired and quoted and one who later visited him (in this case in 1825 at Abbotsford). During this visit Scott declared, *'Now, my dear Moore, we are friends for life'*,¹³ although he felt that there were many points of difference between them: 'Moore a scholar—I none —He a musician and artist—I without knowlege of a note—He a democrat—I an aristocrat—with many other points of difference besides his being an Irishman, I a Scotchman, and both tolerably national.'¹⁴ Despite expressing some concern about the moral effects of 'the sonnets which a prurient genius like Master Little [Moore] sings *virginibus puerisque*', he enjoyed hearing his daughters' singing master, Terence Magrath, sing Moore's songs.¹⁵ Indeed, it was the songs, such as those which had appeared a few years before in Moore's *Irish Melodies* of 1807, that he chose as the subject of his imitation. Although Scott did not again write an imitation of Moore he did pay him the compliment of parodying some lines from 'The Minstrel Boy' in his journal.¹⁶

Kenneth Curry suggests that the 'Inferno' owes a debt to Henry Mackenzie in *The Mirror* and *The Lounger*.¹⁷ Certainly there is much in the form (a letter to the editor), persona (an older man, sympathetically presented but opening himself to a little gentle ridicule) and stance (the viewpoint of a man of experience, a little worldly-wise but still responding to his feelings) that recalls Mackenzie in his two periodicals. It is interesting to see how Scott's adoption of the persona of an elderly gentleman with literary pretensions living in somewhat straitened circumstances in this first of his short fictions foreshadows the creation of Chrystal Croftangry as the last of his short story narrators in *Chronicles of the Canongate*. It is also interesting that this early piece of prose fiction, while it does relate a story, is primarily satirical and takes the form of a fanciful allegory, both features of the eighteenth-century essayists of whom Mackenzie is the prime Scottish example. Somewhat later, in 1814 when he resumed work on *Waverley* and came to write the last chapter, entitled 'A Postscript, which should have been a Preface', he dedicated it to 'Our Scottish Addison, Henry Mackenzie'.[18] By drawing attention to Mackenzie's similarities to Addison, Scott was particularly pointing to Mackenzie's role not as a novelist but as an essayist. Whether he had this particular focus when he was working on *Waverley* in 1810 cannot be known but Mackenzie was certainly in his mind in that year: in the section of his 'Memoirs' written about this time he mentions Mackenzie 'whom in later years I became entitled to call my friend' as an early favourite in his reading.[19]

While *The Bridal of Triermain* in its fully developed form encompassed three timeframes, the present, the historical medieval past, and the legendary world of King Arthur, the part published as 'The Vision of Triermain' deals only with the second of these, the historical Middle Ages centring around Sir Roland de Vaux of Triermain Castle. There were several historical figures of this name and place. Ranulph de Vaux granted the fief of Triermain within his barony of Gilsland to his son Roland in the 1190s. It was held by Roland's descendants, many also called Roland, until the male line died out in the reign of Edward IV.[20] Scott probably did not intend that his story should be attached to any particular Roland de Vaux as the exact date of the setting of the poem is unclear. Only a portion of one wall of Triermain Castle in Cumberland now stands but in Scott's time there were more extensive and suggestive remains.[21]

'CHRISTOPHER CORDUROY'

Historical Background. Like 'The Inferno of Altisidora', and unlike the other stories in this volume, this story is manifestly fictional in origin rather than being based on an historical event and furthermore is set in Scott's own time. While there is thus no need to discuss the sources or historical accuracy of the story there are aspects of it which relate to the broader historical context. The elder Christopher Corduroy's obsession with his supposed descent from the house of Douglas reflects the immense importance of that family in Scottish history, particularly in the Middle Ages. One instance of the importance of the family is that Sir James Douglas (1286–1330) was entrusted with carrying the heart of Robert the Bruce to the Holy Land. Although Douglas died in the unsuccessful attempt to fulfil this mission, the Douglas coat of arms displays a crowned heart in commemoration of this event. In asserting that his family name derives from *cœur du roi* ('the king's heart'), rather than accepting that the name was 'bestowed on some of [his] forefathers on account of their being instrumental in

introducing the use of that particular kind of stuff in the neighbourhood' (24.22–25), Christopher Corduroy stakes a claim to be a
Douglas. The issue of Douglas descent had become a matter of some
notoriety after the death of the Duke of Douglas in 1761. The Duke's
nephew, Archibald, born to his sister Lady Jane when she was fifty-
one, was accepted as his heir but this was disputed by the Duke of
Hamilton who claimed to be the true heir and alleged that Archibald's
claim to be Lady Jane's son was spurious. The case attracted enormous
attention in Scotland and eventually ended up in the House of Lords
where the decision was in favour of Archibald. Claims of true or
spurious descent from the house of Douglas had thus achieved great
prominence not very long before Scott wrote this story. However
Archibald Douglas's second wife, Lady Frances Scott, is described by
Lockhart as one of Scott's 'dearest friends through life'[22] and Scott
stayed at their home. Furthermore Douglas's daughter Jane married
Lord Montagu with whom Scott had strong connections. All this
makes it highly unlikely that Scott was in any way calling Archibald
Douglas's birth into question. Rather the ridiculous nature of Christo-
pher Corduroy's pretensions highlights the comparative strength of
Archibald Douglas's claims.

The Gothic Revival in architecture, begun in the mid eighteenth
century and pursued with increasing seriousness in the nineteenth,
underlies Christopher Corduroy's embellishment of his cottage with
Gothic details. The year 1817, during which 'Christopher Corduroy'
appeared, marked the first stage of a major remodelling of Scott's
house, Abbotsford, and over subsequent years he included Gothic
features in the interior, most notably in the hall. However he had
little time for what he later called 'the gingerbread tast[e] of Modern
Gothicizers'[23] and, as John Frew notes, 'the intention [behind the
design of the house] was clear. It aimed at a degree of historical
authenticity that would immediately distinguish Abbotsford from the
non-specific medievalism that had characterised the great majority of
country-house experiments produced in an earlier phase of the Gothic
Revival'.[24] The concern with the pretentiousness of modern exponents
of the Gothic continues in Scott's writing and surfaces again in his
description of Castle Treddles in *Chronicles of the Canongate*.

'ALARMING INCREASE OF DEPRAVITY AMONG ANIMALS'

Historical Background. Apart from the examples of animal larceny
taken from the newspapers, the narrator of 'Alarming Increase of
Depravity Among Animals' details four similar instances of which he
claims to have personal knowledge. The anecdotes of the Highland
pony, the thieving spaniel, and the highwayman's horse have not been
traced, and their status is uncertain: despite the narrator's claim, they
may well represent the further fictionalisation of anecdotes heard from
others or read in a newspaper or magazine.[25] The case of Murdieston
and Millar, however, was indeed 'celebrated' (32.18). Murdieston's
standing as a tenant-farmer, the scale of his and Millar's operations,

and the penalty which they risked and ultimately paid, quite apart from the exceptional abilities of Yarrow, ensured widespread and continuing interest, and accounts of their activities and trial feature not only in contemporary newspapers but in gazetteers, works on animal intelligence, legal commentaries, and shire histories.

For Scott, as a lawyer, it was probably details of the trial itself and the defendants' subsequent attempt to appeal to the House of Lords, rather than the sheep-stealers' methods, with which he was most familiar; in fact, as we have seen, the fragment of the 'thieving spaniel' held by the National Library of Scotland contains only a passing allusion to their story[26] and it was William Laidlaw who drafted the material relating to them for the article. Significantly, Laidlaw's manuscript does not include the introductory paragraph mentioning Lords Monboddo and Braxfield, and also Lord Melville, and these legal details would almost certainly have been supplied by Scott.

It is clear from the manuscript fragments held by the National Library of Scotland, in Laidlaw's hand, that the material relating to the sheep-stealers' *modus operandi* was written after the composition of the specific anecdote concerning Yarrow and the ewes, to which it serves as background.[27] This anecdote was probably of interest to Scott precisely because it did not form part of the common knowledge of Murdieston and Millar's activities, having been told by Millar 'to a respectable sheep-farmer' (34.13) while he was awaiting execution. The details of how the story came to Laidlaw are not known, but it is possible that the sheep-farmer who visited Millar in prison was Laidlaw's own father James Laidlaw, whose farm Blackhouse stood in one of the areas plundered by the sheep-stealers—in fact it adjoined the farm of Newby which was tenanted by William Gibson, the farmer who began the process which brought Murdieston and Millar to justice.[28] Whether or not it was Laidlaw's father who heard the story from Millar, it would almost certainly have been through Laidlaw's sheep-farming contacts, and very likely in his father's house or at a neighbouring farm, that it reached him.

The account of Murdieston and Millar's depredations and eventual fate given in 'Alarming Increase' agrees broadly with the versions in other sources, but these are also useful in providing further details. It seems that Alexander Murdieston[29] was born at Wintermuir, in the parish of Drummelzier, perhaps as early as 1727,[30] and he remained there until moving to Ormiston at Whitsun 1770.[31] He was 'connected with many of the best storefarming families in the county'[32] and had seemingly conducted himself well in Drummelzier: a character reference to this effect, signed by the minister of Drummelzier, was readily accepted in court.[33] At Ormiston Murdieston was a tenant of the Earl of Traquair, paying an annual rent in excess of £200,[34] a large sum which was apparently higher than that offered by his neighbours.[35] It was not long before he began to plunder the surrounding flocks through the agency of his shepherd John Millar and Millar's dog Yarrow. His underlying motives are obscure, and not generally speculated upon, but just two years after Murdieston and Millar's execution, the cartographer John Armstrong wrote of 'that notorious *Wolf* in human shape, Murdieson; who, with his guilty colleague, Millar, purloined the property of many, to satisfy an innate thirst for malicious avarice'.[36] Sir William Chambers, who purchased Glen Ormiston (the 'improved' Ormiston estate) in 1849, and who was himself the grandson of William Gibson, calls Murdieston 'a young man of disorderly habits',[37] perhaps implying vices such as gambling which would require more funds than sheep-farming alone could provide.

The range and extent of Murdieston and Millar's operations were extraordinary, and successful, with hardly a farm left untouched for miles around.[38] However, a chance observation led to their detection. William Gibson, concerned by a steady diminution of his flocks which he considered greater than could be accounted for by natural attrition, had been suspecting his own shepherds of 'unfair dealing'.[39] In July 1772, one of the oldest and most experienced of these, James Hyslop, noticed a black-faced ewe, previously missing, suckling her lamb as before. The ewe's face bore an additional, superimposed brand, which Hyslop recognised as that of Murdieston, whom he had previously known at Drummelzier.[40] Furthermore, shepherds on various farms had seen the ewe journeying home from the direction of Ormiston.[41] Having obtained a warrant from the Sheriff of Peebles, Gibson, accompanied by several other farmers and a sheriff's officer, searched Ormiston[42] on 9 July; the culprits offered no resistance, Murdieston retiring inside his house and Millar sitting some distance away.[43] Twelve sheep from Newby with altered marks were discovered, along with other stolen sheep,[44] numbering in all 'no fewer than thirty-three score of sheep belonging to various individuals'.[45] Murdieston and Millar were taken to Peebles that night, and the following morning were committed to prison,[46] the prison being 'the vault in the steeple, which being very insecure, needs to be guarded night and day'.[47]

Investigations into Murdieston and Millar's activities took some time, as the authorities attempted to trace all of the missing sheep, most of which had been disposed of by Millar at markets and fairs. Eventually, on Friday 8 January 1773, the two men, now in the Edinburgh Tolbooth, were brought to trial before the High Court of Justiciary on charges of stealing sheep, or receiving them and offering them for sale knowing them to be stolen. In light of Scott's claims that Monboddo, Braxfield and Melville were involved in various roles, it is important to note who the judges and advocates actually were. The Lords of Justiciary who heard the case were the Lord Justice Clerk (Thomas Miller of Barskimming), and Lords Auchinleck, Pitfour, Coalston, Kennet, and Kames.[48] The prosecution comprised the Lord Advocate, James Montgomery, with the Solicitor General, Henry Dundas (later Lord Melville), as well as a third advocate, Cosmo Gordon. Appearing for Murdieston were Alexander Lockhart, with Robert McQueen (later Lord Braxfield) who Scott incorrectly suggests was possibly the sentencing judge (see 32.22), as well as Robert Blair, Alexander Stevenson and Andrew Crosbie. Millar was defended by David Rae, John McLaurin and Alexander Wight.[49]

The trial opened at 8 a.m. on 8 January with the prosecution producing James Hyslop and a string of further witnesses—aggrieved
farmers and their shepherds, and those unlucky enough to have bought
sheep from Millar.[50] After twenty witnesses and twenty-four hours
without a break, the Lord Advocate decided not to address nine further
charges of theft specified in the indictment,[51] and the defence introduced its own witnesses, three farmers who had inspected the stolen
sheep at the request of the Sheriff of Peebles. These made varying
claims regarding the brands on the sheep and generalised statements
concerning the straying tendency of sheep and the possibility that a
bleeding ear could well result from 'the Itch' rather than from the
defacing of an earmark.[52] Their testimony ended at about 5 p.m. on
Saturday 9 January, when the Lord Advocate summed up for the
Crown, and Crosbie and Rae for Murdieston and Millar respectively.[53]

Between eleven o'clock and midnight, the jury was 'inclosed', and
ordered to return its verdict at noon on Monday 11 January.[54] They
were dismissed at five o'clock the next morning, Sunday 10 January,
presumably because they had reached their verdict, which was duly
delivered on the following day. Murdieston and Millar were found
guilty 'by a Great plurality of voices' of various charges in the Indictment.[55] The defence counsel immediately objected, and on 25 January
the Court heard their objections,[56] which hinged mainly upon the
verdict's being reached on a Sunday, and on its relating only to some
of the charges brought in the indictment, a result of the Lord Advocate's decision not to produce witnesses on all of the charges.[57] These
objections were overturned by the Court on 15 February, when both
of the accused were sentenced to be hanged in the Grassmarket of
Edinburgh on 24 March.[58] Murdieston and Millar then appealed to
the House of Lords on the same grounds; however a committee of
the House of Lords found their appeal 'incompetent',[59] thus establishing a precedent: appeals from the High Court of Justiciary could not
be made to the House of Lords.[60]

Murdieston and Millar's fate was now sealed. While we have no
record of Murdieston's conduct in the Tolbooth while awaiting execution, we know that Millar told at least one sheep-farmer of Yarrow's
exploit at the ford, and that on 20 March he prayed in the presence
of onlookers, including James Boswell, the biographer of Johnson.[61]
Four days later, on Wednesday 24 March 1773, he and Murdieston
were hanged, along with a housebreaker named John Watson; it was
reported that 'They all showed signs of penitence, and behaved as
became persons in their unhappy situation'.[62] As for Yarrow, he is
absent from the court records, unless appearing obliquely in the testimony of Adam Sibbald, a witness for the prosecution, who claimed it
'practicable for a single Man with a good Dog to separate and carry
off a small parcell of Ten or twelve sheep from a large flock'.[63] While
we have found no evidence to corroborate the information given in
'Alarming Increase' it is probable that Yarrow did indeed live to pursue
a second, although less brilliant, career.

'PHANTASMAGORIA'

Versions of the Story. In addition to the *Blackwood's* version of
Scott's ghost story, there exists another version, in Scott's own name,
which forms part of a note to 'Wandering Willie's Tale' in the Magnum
edition of *Redgauntlet*. This version, together with Scott's letter to
William Blackwood describing his forthcoming contribution as 'a very
curious and authentic ghost-legend which I had from the lady to whom
the lady who saw the spirit told the story',[64] indicates that the 'Phantasmagoria' story was founded upon an account which Scott had himself
heard and which he was happy to present to others as having been
attached to real people. In terms of the historical basis of the story,
the printed version of the *Redgauntlet* note provides some additional,
and occasionally conflicting, details, and is worth quoting:

> the belief was general throughout Scotland, that the excessive
> lamentation over the loss of friends disturbed the repose of the
> dead, and broke even the rest of the grave. There are several
> instances of this in tradition, but one struck me particularly, as I
> heard it from the lips of one who professed receiving it from
> those of a ghost-seer. This was a Highland lady, named Mrs
> C—— of B——, who probably believed firmly in the truth of
> an apparition, which seems to have originated in the weakness of
> her nerves and strength of her imagination. She had been lately
> left a widow by her husband, with the office of guardian to their
> only child. The young man added to the difficulties of his charge
> by an extreme propensity for a military life, which his mother
> was unwilling to give way to, while she found it impossible to
> repress it. About this time the Independent Companies, formed
> for the preservation of the peace of the Highlands, were in the
> course of being levied; and as a gentleman named Cameron,
> nearly connected with Mrs C——, commanded one of those com-
> panies, she was at length persuaded to compromise the matter
> with her son, by permitting him to enter this company in the
> capacity of a cadet; thus gratifying his love of a military life with-
> out the dangers of foreign service, to which no one then thought
> these troops were at all liable to be exposed, while even their
> active service at home was not likely to be attended with much
> danger. She readily obtained a promise from her relative that he
> would be particular in his attention to her son, and therefore
> concluded she had accommodated matters between her son's
> wishes and his safety in a way sufficiently attentive to both. She
> set off to Edinburgh to get what was awanting for his outfit, and
> shortly afterwards received melancholy news from the Highlands.
> The Independent Company into which her son was to enter had
> a skirmish with a party of catherans engaged in some act of spoil,
> and her friend the Captain being wounded, and out of the reach
> of medical assistance, died in consequence. This news was a
> thunderbolt to the poor mother, who was at once deprived of her
> kinsman's advice and assistance, and instructed by his fate of the

unexpected danger to which her son's new calling exposed him. She remained also in great sorrow for her relative, whom she loved with sisterly affection. These conflicting causes of anxiety, together with her uncertainty whether to continue or change her son's destination, were terminated in the following manner:—

The house in which Mrs C—— resided in the old town of Edinburgh, was a flat or story of a land, accessible, as was then universal, by a common stair. The family who occupied the story beneath were her acquaintances, and she was in the habit of drinking tea with them every evening. It was accordingly about six o'clock, when, recovering herself from a deep fit of anxious reflection, she was about to leave the parlour in which she sat in order to attend this engagement. The door through which she was to pass opened, as was very common in Edinburgh, into a dark passage. In this passage, and within a yard of her when she opened the door, stood the apparition of her kinsman, the deceased officer, in his full tartans, and wearing his bonnet. Terrified at what she saw, or thought she saw, she closed the door hastily, and, sinking on her knees by a chair, prayed to be delivered from the horrors of the vision. She remained in that posture till her friends below tapped on the floor to intimate that tea was ready. Recalled to herself by the signal, she arose, and, on opening the apartment door, again was confronted by the visionary Highlander, whose bloody brow bore token, on this second appearance, to the death he had died. Unable to endure this repetition of her terrors, Mrs C—— sunk on the floor in a swoon. Her friends below, startled with the noise, came up stairs, and, alarmed at the situation in which they found her, insisted on her going to bed and taking some medicine, in order to compose what they took for a nervous attack. They had no sooner left her in quiet, than the apparition of the soldier was once more visible in the apartment. This time she took courage and said, "In the name of God, Donald, why do you haunt one who respected and loved you when living?" To which he answered readily, in Gaelic, "Cousin, why did you not speak sooner? My rest is disturbed by your unnecessary lamentation—your tears scald me in my shroud. I come to tell you that my untimely death ought to make no difference in your views for your son; God will raise patrons to supply my place, and he will live to the fulness of years, and die honoured and at peace." The lady of course followed her kinsman's advice; and as she was accounted a person of strict veracity, we may conclude the first apparition an illusion of the fancy, the final one a lively dream suggested by the other two.[65]

The manuscript of this note, as it appears in the Interleaved Set of the Waverley Novels, differs in some respects from the printed version, and it too needs to be taken into account when we are considering the historical background to the story.[66]

Historical Background. The evidence suggests that Scott believed that a historical incident lay behind his story in its various versions. Although there are discrepancies between these versions it is possible, by comparing them, to form an idea of the story heard by Scott from 'the lady to whom the lady who saw the spirit told the story'.

In all of Scott's retellings, the captain in question commanded one of the Independent Companies which came to be embodied as the Royal Highland Regiment, or 'Black Watch'. Although independent companies were established in Scotland at various periods between 1603 and 1760,[67] Scott's story refers specifically to those established in 1725 at the recommendation of General Wade. These companies, which became known as 'An Freiceadan Dubh' or 'the Black Watch' at least as early as 1735,[68] were formed to deal solely with Highland affairs, taking charge of security by enforcing the disarming act (the 1725 act which authorised searching for and confiscating weapons), and dealing with a resurgence in cattle-stealing among the clans. The captain of Scott's story commands one of these companies, and in fact has done since its inception, for although the reference in 'Phantasmagoria' to the timing of his appointment is ambiguous in that his command could have postdated the levying of the companies (he was 'about this time named to the command of one of the Independent Companies, levied for protecting the peace of the Highlands, and preventing the marauding parties': 41.32–35), the note in *Redgauntlet* makes it clear both that the captain was one of the original commanders and that the events described must have occurred during the period when the companies were first being formed.

In 'Phantasmagoria' the captain is a Campbell (although at f.11r in the manuscript he is once termed 'Captain Cameron'); the one instance of the name in the printed version of the *Redgauntlet* note designates him a Cameron, but this represents an addition to the manuscript of the note, which omits his name altogether. That the captain was a Cameron is virtually impossible, as the Camerons were among the disaffected clans, and not at all 'such gentlemen as the Brunswick government imagined they might repose confidence in' (42.1–3). It is much more likely that if Camerons were involved it was as the marauders; Scott implies this in 'Phantasmagoria' by saying that they belonged 'if I mistake not, to the country of Lochiel' (42.28), and in fact the manuscript of the *Redgauntlet* note names them as 'the Camerons', rather than the 'catherans' of the printed version.[69] It is thus probable that at the time of 'Phantasmagoria' Scott believed the captain to have been a Campbell. Further, the *Redgauntlet* note has the widow address the apparition as 'Donald'.[70] It is unclear whether this constitutes his Christian name or simply the common nickname for a Highlandman—although the latter might be unusual in the mouth of a Highland woman, especially when speaking to a close relative.[71] From all of this it seems that Scott believed the protagonist to have been a Campbell, and just possibly a Donald Campbell.

Of the six companies raised in 1725, only the three 'large' companies were led by captains; the three 'small' companies were commanded by lieutenants, with commissions as captain-lieutenant.[72] There is no

Donald Campbell in the lists of commanders, but it is notable that three of the six are indeed Campbells: Sir Duncan Campbell of Lochnell, who commanded one of the large companies, and Colin Campbell of Skipness and John Campbell of Carrick, who both commanded small companies.[73] None of these men died at the period or in the circumstances described in 'Phantasmagoria'. They remained in command after the augmentation of 1727, as shown by an official list of 1731,[74] and at least until 1739 when the decision to create the regiment was made. Lochnell left in 1739, captained an Independent Company at Culloden in 1746 (according to family records), was Member of Parliament for Argyleshire from 1747–54, and died in 1765;[75] Colin Campbell of Skipness gained a full captaincy in the regiment, fought at Culloden, and died in 1756;[76] John Campbell of Carrick served in the embodied regiment with the rank of captain, dying at Fontenoy in 1745.[77]

The earliest surviving record of the more junior officers of these particular Independent Companies appears to be the list of 1731, which does not cover the first and second recruitment periods.[78] Some Campbells do appear in this list as junior officers: the second lieutenant of Lovat's Company was Dugald Campbell of Craignish, but he later became a captain in the 'Black Watch' Regiment, retiring in 1745; Lochnell's Company had a Colin Campbell as first lieutenant, and there was a Lieutenant Duncan Campbell in Carrick's Company.[79] The Colin Campbell in Lochnell's Company was very likely one of the two men of that name who, as we shall see, led a company in the embodied regiment. Duncan Campbell does not appear among the regimental officers, and we have been unable to trace him further. However no mention of an incident similar to the one described in 'Phantasmagoria' is to be found in relation to the Independent Companies of 1725 in the histories of those companies, in histories of the 'Black Watch' Regiment, or in contemporary newspapers (although the relevant holdings are admittedly often scanty).

As mentioned above, however, independent companies were raised at various periods in the seventeenth and eighteenth centuries, and in some ways those formed in the mid-eighteenth century might seem a firmer possibility than those of 1725. 'Simon Shadow' initially places the events of the story 'about the middle of the last century' (41.19), and the period between, say, 1740 and 1760, would possibly better suit the timeframe needed for Scott himself to have learned of the events from an old lady who had heard them from the widow herself, whilst it would allow time for her son to have pursued a brilliant career in the army and to have died 'in peace and honour, long after he had closed the eyes of the good old lady' (44.38–39). During this period, two groups of independent companies were raised, firstly in 1745–46 to supplement the regular forces during the Jacobite rebellion and then in 1760–61 during the Seven Years' War (1756–63).[80] The first group was clearly recruited for the kind of dangerous work which the widow of Scott's tale was anxious to avoid for her son; the second was intended for overseas service from the beginning. Thus neither group would seem to qualify, as the low risk and the condition of home service are fundamental to the story. There were also two 'fencible' regiments formed during the Seven Years' War, the Argyll Fencibles and the Sutherland Fencibles, the former being led by Lt-Col. Dougall Campbell of Balliemore ('Colonel Jack') and boasting twenty Campbell officers. However although these regiments were not required to leave Britain, they were treated like regular regiments and played a defensive role only; they were not engaged in the suppression of lawlessness in the Highlands which again is an integral aspect of the incidents which Scott describes.[81]

There is however a further possibility which would both bring the date forward to this later period and allow the involvement of the Independent Companies which formed the 'Black Watch' Regiment. When in 1739 the decision was taken to regiment the six existing Independent Companies, four additional companies were raised to bring the regiment to full strength. This regiment was originally intended for home service only; indeed the troops famously mutinied in 1743 when it was rumoured that they were to be sent to the West Indies.[82] A list of the officers of the ten companies compiled by Andrew Ross 'from the "Commission Books" in the Public Record Office, London, supplemented by original family papers and the information contained in Stewart of Garth's original list' includes three new captains named Campbell: the two Colin Campbells (Colin Campbell, younger of Monzie, and Colin Campbell of Balliemore) and Dougal Campbell of Craignish.[83] According to Stewart of Garth's own list, these three captains all retired, the first in 1743, the second at an unspecified date, and the third in 1745. Of the lesser officers, only two Campbells are unaccounted for, and both of these are ensigns. However, it is notable that whilst nine of the captains were commissioned in October or November 1839, one, John Monro of Newmore, was not appointed until May 1740, a circumstance explained by Ross as follows: 'Captain Monro was nominated in succession to one of the former captains, whose name is unfortunately left blank.'[84] By 'former captains' Ross appears to be referring to those captains of the Independent Companies, namely Lovat and Lochnell, who did not continue on into the embodied regiment. It remains possible, however, that Monro was replacing a newly appointed captain who had left his company a few months into his command. There is thus a faint chance that the original captain was Scott's Captain Campbell, killed in a skirmish while his company was still recruiting. However ultimately we have been unable to corroborate Scott's story as it stands.

Like her kinsman, the widowed mother has eluded identification. Scott does not name her in 'Phantasmagoria', allegedly on the grounds of 'respect to surviving relations' (41.17), but he does call her 'Mrs C—— of B——' in the *Redgauntlet* note,[85] and in 'Phantasmagoria' she is the widow of 'a gentleman of respectable property on the borders of Argyleshire' (41.18–19). As a relative of Captain Campbell, she may very well have been born a Campbell herself, but whom had she married? Not even an educated guess is possible.

'Simon Shadow' remarks that tales of 'marvellous complexion' must be 'either true or false, or partly true, partly fictitious' (38.31–32). 'Phantasmagoria' appears to belong to the latter group. Although very likely based upon a historical incident, that incident is lost to the historical record. By the time that Scott heard the story it had no doubt taken on the characteristics of traditional tales, a process which he himself furthered in setting down the story as 'Phantasmagoria'.

Informants and Sources. Although Scott's informant remains anonymous in all versions of the story, his depiction of her appearance and superior qualities in 'Phantasmagoria' may furnish some clues to her identity:

> ... though this old lady literally wore the black silk gown, small haunch-hoop, and triple ruffles, which form the apparel most proper to her denomination, yet in sense, spirit, wit, and intelligence, she greatly exceeded various individuals of her own class, who have been known to me, although their backs were clothed with purple robes or military uniforms, and their heads attired with cocked hats or three-tailed periwigs. (40.36–41.5)

The composition history of the article, which suggests that the 'Simon Shadow' introduction postdates the story proper,[86] may indicate that Scott's informant was indeed a well-born woman whom he knew intimately and for whom he had a high regard; one who wore the appropriate costume for her age and class, and one who was deceased by the time 'Phantasmagoria' appeared. Two women who were very dear to him and valuable in supplying him with material inevitably spring to mind, namely his great-aunt Margaret Swinton and Anne Murray Keith. That Scott describes rather than names his informant at this stage does not militate against such an identification: he had not yet portrayed Mrs Murray Keith as Mrs Bethune Baliol in *Chronicles of the Canongate*, nor Margaret Swinton in the (to some degree composite) figure of Aunt Margaret in 'My Aunt Margaret's Mirror'. Nor had he named either woman, in print at least, in relation to any of his published works.

As one of the sources for the story told in 'The Highland Widow',[87] Mrs Murray Keith might seem the more likely candidate; however, as the central event of the story occurred in Edinburgh this is not an important consideration. Certainly, Scott admired Mrs Murray Keith's lively mind. After her death, he mourned her as 'this excellent old lady; one of the few persons whose spirits and cleanliness, and freshness of mind and body, made old age lovely and desirable',[88] and reflected upon 'her virtues, her talents, her exquisite elasticity' and her 'clearness of intellect' which remained intact until the end.[89] If these assessments of Mrs Murray Keith appear to link her with the woman of 'sense, spirit, wit, and intelligence' who furnished the ghost story, Scott's description of his informant's dress shares elements with the portrayal of Mrs Murray Keith's *alter ego*, Mrs Bethune Baliol. Mrs Baliol's dress comprised a 'silk or satin gown of some colour becoming her age', which was 'garnished with triple ruffles'. It was, however, 'always rather costly and distinguished', mixing elements of past and present fashion, and she wore shoes with diamond buckles and slightly raised heels, as well as a 'very handsome' cap of Flanders lace and an array of rings, bracelets and other items of jewellery.[90] The overall impression of her appearance is perhaps rather too studied and too opulent for the old lady of 'Phantasmagoria', in her ' black silk gown, small haunch-hoop, and triple ruffles, . . . the apparel most proper to her denomination' (40.36–41.1). The date of Mrs Murray Keith's death may also argue against her identification as Scott's source. She died on 26 April 1818, and Scott was informed in a letter written from Balcarres on the following day.[91] He was therefore probably still ignorant of her death when promising 'Phantasmagoria' to Blackwood on 28 April, although he knew of it by the time he wrote to Daniel Terry two days later. If, as seems likely, Scott had already begun the story proper by 28 April, his informant, whom he clearly indicates to be deceased, cannot have been Mrs Murray Keith. And if he were writing up the story after her death, given the depth of his feelings we would expect some reference to the recent passing of his respected informant even if she were to remain unnamed.

Like Mrs Murray Keith, Scott's great-aunt Margaret Swinton was a well-born woman admired by Scott for her spirit and intellect. As he tells Joanna Baillie, he learned the story of the battle of Halidon Hill from 'Mrs Margaret Swinton sister of my maternal grand mother a fine old maiden lady of high blood and of as high a mind who was lineally descended from one of the actors'.[92] Similarly, in the Magnum introduction to 'My Aunt Margaret's Mirror' he describes her as 'a lady of eminent virtues, and no inconsiderable share of talent, one of the ancient and honourable house of Swinton'.[93] Mrs Swinton's dress, too, and its impact on Scott, strongly recall, colour excepted, his source for 'Phantasmagoria', as he describes how the story of Halidon Hill 'with many others of the same kind is consecrated to me by the remembrance of the narrator with her brown silk gown and triple rufles and her benevolent face which was always beside our beds when there were childish complaints among us'.[94] The portrait of the 'Aunt Margaret' of 'My Aunt Margaret's Mirror' might also be relevant, with her 'invariable costume' (50.9) of a 'brown or chocolate-coloured silk gown, with ruffles of the same stuff at the elbow, within which are others of Mechlin lace—the black silk gloves, or mitts, the white hair combed back upon a roll, and the cap of spotless cambric, which closes around the venerable countenance' (50.12–16), elements which together produce a timeless style 'peculiar to the individual Aunt Margaret' (50.17–18). However, Aunt Margaret is a composite and partly fictionalised figure based not only on Margaret Swinton but also on Scott's Aunt Janet and, as the above description suggests, perhaps even on Mrs Murray Keith.[95] By the time of 'Phantasmagoria' Margaret Swinton had been dead for nearly forty years, having been murdered in November 1780 by an insane female attendant, a shocking incident which left a deep mark on the young Scott.[96] That he was only 'about ten years old'[97] at the time of her death is no obstacle:

Margaret Swinton had by then provided him also with the story of Halidon Hill and the foundation of 'My Aunt Margaret's Mirror'. In the absence of any direct evidence, she is the likeliest candidate.

As he himself reveals, Scott's fantastical narrator bears the name of a minor character in *Henry IV, Part 2*; however, his general conception is also influenced by the eccentric narrators and characters featured in periodicals such as *The Mirror* and *The Lounger*. Further, some details pertaining to the Shadows, father and son, may probably be traced to two less well known periodical works, both of which were owned by Scott. Like Simon Shadow, whose 'conversation has lain much among old spinsters and widows' (40.5–6), the pseudo-editor of *The Looker-on*,[98] himself a Simon (the Rev. Simon Olive-branch, A.M.), explains how, though 'an old bachelor, and naturally of cold constitution', because of his temperament he has always been treated 'with a great deal of female anecdote, and female eloquence'.[99] And although Simon Shadow's appearance—his 'tall slim figure, thin stilts of legs, and disproportioned feet' (39.19), his 'general resemblance to a skeleton hung in chains' (40.7–8)—is primarily based on the elongated shadow created by the sun when low in the sky, it may owe something to Olive-branch's self-portrait as 'a little pinched-up old man' who looks as though he had been 'cased up and embalmed a century and a half' and who, with his unchanging appearance, seems 'to have stood in a sort of winter solstice' ever since reaching maturity.[100]

In his depiction of Simon's father, Sir Mickelmast Shadow, Scott may be indebted to *Salmagundi*, a periodical paper written by Washington Irving with his brother William and James Kirke Paulding, which appeared in New York in 1807–08. Salmagundi was reprinted in volume form in 1811 and in an edition revised by Irving in 1824. Although the Abbotsford Catalogue includes only the latter, Scott did in fact own the 1811 edition. It was given to him on 24 May 1813, through William Erskine, by Irving's friend Henry Brevoort, whom Scott had met in Edinburgh. Brevoort had already given him Irving's *History of New York, by Dietrich Knickerbocker*,[101] and Scott certainly read and admired both works. In 1819, in the course of enlightening Irving on publication practices in Britain, Scott predicts undoubted success for his *Sketch Book*, but worries that *Knickerbocker* and *Salmagundi*, being 'more exclusively American . . . may not be quite so well suited for our meridian'. However 'they are so excellent in their way, that if the public attention could be once turned on them I am confident that they would become popular'.[102] Given Scott's high opinion of Irving's work, it may be no coincidence that 'Mickelmast', although clearly a suitable name for a 'Shadow', is a near synonym of the surname of one of *Salmagundi*'s pseudo-editors, Launcelot Langstaff. Furthermore, like Sir Mickelmast Shadow, Langstaff is tempted outside in inappropriate conditions, with dire consequences. His feelings 'ever at the mercy of a weathercock', he is encouraged by the clement weather to take a morning stroll, only to be 'utterly discomfited, and driven home by a tremendous squall of wind, hail, rain, and snow',

cursing the fallibility of 'the almanac-makers'.[103] Langstaff's character
and his unlucky outing are more fully detailed than the corresponding
elements of Scott's story, but they could have influenced the thumbnail
sketch of Mickelmast's fatal excursion 'into the meridian sun' (39.10)
undertaken 'with the purpose of paying his respects to an eclipse,
which a rascally almanack-maker falsely announced as being on the
point of rendering our globe a visit' (39.11–13).

  If Scott has drawn on periodical literature to create the Shadows,
the whole conception of the character of the narrator owes most to
Scott himself. Simon Shadow, with his library of works on the supernatural and interest in the occult, as well as his reclusive and indistinct
presence, constitutes a teasing and satirical self-portrait which partakes
of the mystification concerning the authorship of the novels and the
'Great Unknown'. Scott is toying with his readers here: is the reference
to Guy Mannering (39.34), for example, a hint as to authorship, or a
rebuttal? The very next year he would end A Legend of the Wars of
Montrose, and the Third Series of Tales of My Landlord, with praise
for the author Susan Ferrier in the following terms: 'if the present
author, himself a phantom, may be permitted to distinguish a brother,
or perhaps a sister shadow, he would mention, in particular, the author
of the very lively work, entitled "Marriage".'[104] For readers who remembered 'Phantasmagoria' the pieces may have fallen into place.

'MY AUNT MARGARET'S MIRROR'

Informants and Sources. On 26 May 1824 Mrs Hughes of Uffing-
ton dined at Scott's house in Edinburgh. As seems to have often been
the case with dinner in the Scott household, he told a story of the
supernatural. According to the account Mrs Hughes recorded in her
diary,

> Sir W. told us admirably a story in which his grandmother had a
> part: her sister was married to Sir Archibald Primrose, a most
> wicked and abandoned man: after a series of ill conduct he left
> his family suddenly without giving any clue as to where he might
> be found: his wife desired her sister to accompany her to a con-
> juror of great celebrity who lived in the Canon gate: they disguised
> themselves in their servants' cloaths and plaids, but as soon as
> they entered, the wizard exclaimed, "Ladies this disguise is use-
> less with me; I know your rank, and I know your purpose: if you
> have the courage to remain perfectly still and silent I can inform
> you of what you wish to know, but remember the least deviation
> may destroy the spell and may also produce effects you may be
> unable to endure: weigh well your determination before you give
> it:" their curiosity prevailed and the promise of stillness and
> silence was given. A dark curtain was then withdrawn from a
> large glass: the wizard began his incantations and the glass which
> at first had been perfectly dark, began to clear and wear an
> appearance like the dawning of day: gradually the clouds formed
> themselves into masses and at last presented the appearance of a

large church thronged with people, an altar richly decorated, and Lady Primrose seen at the head of a long train of bride men and maids, her husband leading a very beautiful girl dressed in the Flemish style towards the Priest as if to receive the nuptial benediction: at this she uttered a faint exclamation, and the whole pageant *shimmered* and wavered, assuming the appearance of water into which a stone had been thrown: the Conjuror looked at her with a dark frown: she suppressed her feelings and continued to gaze: the forms again became distinct and to the spectators in the church were added three or four officers whose backs they only saw: these after a minute drew their swords and advanced to the altar in a threatening posture: then all seemed confusion and the glass ceased to exhibit any distinct forms: by the next mail Lady Primrose received a letter from her brother who was an officer in the *Scotch Dutch* (as they were called) and quartered at Dort. He said, "I can give you strange news of your villain of a husband: we had heard of a grand wedding to take place between an English stranger and one of our great Burgo Master's daughters: I went with two or three friends into the church, and guess my surprise at seeing in the bridegroom your worthless husband: my friends also knew him, and we so far forgot ourselves as to draw our swords and rush towards him: mischief was prevented and of course the marriage stopt."[105]

Here we have the story told by Scott in 'My Aunt Margaret's Mirror' but in an earlier form, without the disguise of the fictional names. Just as the unnamed narrator of the *Keepsake* story claims that this story is a family one, so Scott makes the same claim both to Mrs Hughes and in an entry in his journal for 13 April 1828 where, however, the family member taking part has moved back one generation, from grandmother to great-grandmother:

Amused myself by converting the Tale of the Mysterious Mirror into 'Aunt Margaret's Mirror', designd for Heath's What dye call it. Cadell will not like this but I cannot afford to have my goods thrown back upon my hands. The tale is a good one and is said actually to have happend to Lady Primrose, my great grandmother having attended her sister on the occasion.[106]

According to Mrs Hughes's account, Scott's source for the story was his mother:

Everybody exclaimed "And how Sir Walter could this be accounted for?" his answer was, "Troth I tell it you as I always heard it from my mother, and I can no other way account for it, but that my grandmother must have been just a liar."[107]

In the introductory note to 'My Aunt Margaret's Mirror' in the Magnum, however, Scott names a different source: 'I have only to say, that it is a mere transcript, or at least with very little embellishment, of a story that I remembered being struck with in my childhood, when told at the fireside by a lady of eminent virtues, and no inconsiderable share of talent, one of the ancient and honourable house of Swinton'.[108]

The further details he gives identify this lady as his great-aunt Margaret Swinton, the sister of his mother's mother, Jean Swinton. On the issue of the reliability of the tale he adds that his great-aunt

> entertained largely that belief in supernaturals, which in those times was not considered as sitting ungracefully on the grave and aged of her condition; and the story of the Magic Mirror was one for which she vouched with particular confidence, alleging indeed that one of her own family had been an eye-witness of the incidents recorded in it.
>
> "I tell the tale as it was told to me."[109]

It is very possible that Scott heard the story from both women, as was the case with the original story lying behind *The Bride of Lammermoor*, since this was apparently a story originating in the Swinton side of Scott's family.[110] Nevertheless, although Scott had sources in his own family, it is probable that the story was more widely known and two versions of it appear in different editions of Robert Chambers's *Traditions of Edinburgh*.[111] On the other hand Scott himself supplied information to Chambers for the *Traditions*[112] and he may have been the source of this story. Certainly it would appear that some of the details in Chambers's later and more elaborate version of the story, such as the fact that the ladies disguised themselves specifically with plaids, have been taken from 'My Aunt Margaret's Mirror'.

Scott's assertion that the *Keepsake* version is 'a mere transcript, or at least with very little embellishment' and that he has told the story 'as it was told to me' should be treated with some scepticism. 'My Aunt Margaret's Mirror' shows clear signs of elaboration, not least, as we shall see, in the incorporation of another story relating to different people. One obvious element of fictionality is the conversation between Lady Bothwell and Sir Philip Forester regarding Major Falconer: this is clearly intended to foreshadow the fatal duel between the two men which itself does not appear in Mrs Hughes's account. Another interesting variation between the two accounts is the change from implied synchronicity of vision and event (which Scott can only account for by supposing his grandmother to be a liar) and the delay of a couple of days which forces Aunt Margaret to 'maim' (72.3) a good story by admitting the possibility of a rational explanation.

Shortly after the appearance of 'My Aunt Margaret's Mirror' in *The Keepsake* Scott received a letter from G. P. R. James, a fellow novelist, acknowledging that a scene in his newly published book *Darnley, or the Field of the Cloth of Gold*[113] closely resembles the scene with the magician in 'My Aunt Margaret's Mirror' even though he had not read the story when he wrote the book. Eager to avoid any charge of plagiarism he tells Scott that 'The idea of the mirror and the Magician were both taken from the well-known deception, shewn to Lord Surry by Cornelius Agrippa, and though I daresay the world in general will not acquit me of this sort of literary highway robbery, I am sure that *you* will believe me innocent'.[114]

The resemblance was more than coincidental. Scott knew the incident referred to and had indeed himself used it as the basis for Fitz-raver's song in Canto 6 of *The Lay of the Last Minstrel* (1805). The source of the story is Thomas Nashe's *The Unfortunate Traveller* (1594) in which Jack Wilton, the traveller of the title, meets up with the Earl of Surrey in Germany. At the emperor's court they encounter Cornelius Agrippa and Wilton, on the Earl's behalf, asks Agrippa 'to see the liuely image of *Geraldine*, his loue, in the glasse, and what at that instant she did and with whome she was talking. He shewed her vs without anie more adoe, sicke weeping on her bed, and resolued all into deuout religion for the absence of her Lord'.[115] Scott takes the 'glasse' to be a looking glass but it is earlier described as a 'perspec-tiue glass'[116] which could cover either a telescope or an arrangement of mirrors. Scott's earlier use of this scene suggests he may have had it in mind in writing 'My Aunt Margaret's Mirror'. However the details in Nashe are meagre and Scott could well have turned to Cornelius Agrippa himself to supplement them. He owned a copy of *Three Books of Occult Philosophy*, an English translation, published in 1651, of Agrippa's *De occulta philosophia libri tres* (1533) and referred to the work in his *Letters on Demonology and Witchcraft*.[117] A fourth book appeared in 1565 and has been generally accepted as spurious but it provides details of the calling up of spirits which could have influenced Scott in his 'embellishment' of the original story.[118] In particular the magician's dress of linen (see 66.28) follows the fourth book's require-ment that the invocant of the spirit should be dressed in a linen gar-ment[119] and the description of the mirror as set behind 'a table, or rather a species of altar' (66.39) recalls Agrippa's injunction, in the description of the preparation of the place of invocation, 'let there be a table or altar placed therein'.[120] Further vestiges of Agrippa's instruc-tion can perhaps be discerned if we consider the earlier scene in *The Lay of the Last Minstrel* as an intermediate stage between Agrippa and 'My Aunt Margaret's Mirror' in Scott's mental development of the scene. The *Lay*'s 'hallow'd taper'[121] placed before the mirror closely parallels Agrippa's requirement of 'two consecrated wax-lights burn-ing'[122] but the parallel is more remote in the *Keepsake* version's 'five large flambeaux, or torches' (67.10) (although both in Scott's story and in Agrippa these are to be placed on 'each side' of the altar). If there is, as seems highly probable, a line of development from Nashe and Agrippa through the *The Lay of the Last Minstrel* and on to 'My Aunt Margaret's Mirror', then it is also clear that, however much he may owe to the germ of his ideas to those sources, Scott's enriching and embellishing imagination has been at work in this scene as in all parts of his retelling of this family tale.[123]

The final part of the story is from an entirely different source. Scott has concluded his tale by including a dramatic incident which he had heard from Mrs Murray Keith. In 1822 he published an edition of Lord Fountainhall's *Chronological Notes of Scottish Affairs, from 1680 to 1701* which includes an account of the murder of Joseph Johnston of Hilton by William Home (brother to the Earl of Home) in December 1683. To this Scott added a note relating an event from later in Home's life and citing 'the late excellent and accomplished Mrs Anne Murray Keith' as his authority:

> I have heard it related as a circumstance arising out of this tragic story, that the son of the slaughtered Johnston was many years afterwards, while at a public assembly, called out to speak with a person, who, it was said, brought him some particular news from abroad. The stranger met him at the head of the staircase, in a sort of lobby, which led into the apartment where the company were dancing. He told young Johnston of Hilton, that the man who had slain his father was on his death-bed, and had sent him to request his forgiveness before he died. Before granting his request, Johnston asked the stranger one or two questions, and observing that he faultered in his answers, he suddenly exclaimed, "You yourself are my father's murderer;" and drew his sword to stab him. Hume, for it was the homicide himself, threw himself over the balustrade of the staircase, and made his escape. Indeed he had taken this mode of endeavouring to ascertain whether he might venture to return to Scotland, without exposing himself to the vengeance of the friends of the man he had murdered.[124]

This story is clearly the source of the last part of 'My Aunt Margaret's Mirror'.[125]

Historical Characters and Background. If the story of the apparition in the magic mirror had any basis in historical reality it would now be impossible to discover what that was but the *people* involved are alleged to be historical figures and it may be possible to identify them. However Scott's sources of information were dead by 1824, the time of his first recorded telling of the story, Margaret Swinton having died in 1780 and his mother in 1819, and Scott's memory of the details could be defective. As we have seen, he was apparently inconsistent, claiming at one point (according to Mrs Hughes) that it was his grandmother who was involved and on another occasion in his journal that it was his great-grandmother. This looseness with regard to generations exhibits itself in the same year as Mrs Hughes's visit to Scotland when Scott, in a letter to his son discussing his plans to decorate the hall of Abbotsford with the escutcheons of his ancestors, remarks that 'The blazonry looks very well, but I have lost three of my grandmothers I fear irredeemably',[125] and tellingly he goes on to lament that 'My poor mother could have informd me but I fear no one living can'. Since there are three of them we must assume that Scott is thinking of great-grandmothers or even great-great-grandmothers. A few lines later he comments that 'Twelve or thirteen quarterings are however pretty well for a new Baronet as they are all real', which makes it clear he was seeking to display the blazons of his sixteen great-great-grandparents. Thus in relating his story to Mrs Hughes Scott may have been using the word 'grandmother' loosely, or he may have been genuinely uncertain which generation the story belonged to. Alternatively Mrs Hughes may have misremembered Scott's account.

On the other hand his journal and Mrs Hughes's diary agree that the principal protagonist was a Lady Primrose. Neither of his two grandmothers had sisters or sisters-in-law who bore that title but one of his great-grandmothers did. Anne Sinclair, who married Sir John Swinton in 1698 and was the mother of Jean (Scott's maternal grandmother) and Margaret Swinton (his great-aunt), was the daughter of Sir Robert Sinclair of Longformacus by his second wife, Margaret Alexander. Her elder half-sister, Elizabeth (born 1650), daughter of Robert Sinclair and his first wife Elizabeth Douglas, married Sir James Primrose (born 1645 and dead by the time his father died in 1679).[126] Although Scott's confusion between generations apparently extends to the Primroses (in Mrs Hughes's record the protagonist's husband is named as Sir Archibald Primrose, the name of James Primrose's father) it would appear that the two sisters central to the original story were Anne Swinton and Elizabeth, Lady Primrose.

However, there are two problems with this identification. Firstly, since the events must have taken place before the death of James Primrose (he was dead by 1679), Anne Sinclair, who was not married until 1698 and who was born after 1667, must have been a child at the time, probably too young to fulfil the role assigned to her in the story.[127] Perhaps it was another sister who accompanied Lady Primrose and then told Anne Sinclair about the supposed events. Secondly, Robert Chambers in his account identifies the protagonist as a quite different Lady Primrose, namely Eleanor Campbell (born about 1679, died 1759), daughter of the second earl of Loudoun and wife of another Sir James Pringle (died 1706) who was created Viscount Pringle in 1703. This must, however, be incorrect as this Lady Primrose did not have a sister who was either grandmother or great-grandmother to Scott.[128] After his death she married John Dalrymple, second earl of Stair (1673–1747). Lady Stair was a prominent figure in Edinburgh society and the subject of a number of stories and it may be for this reason that the story accreted to her over time. Alternatively Chambers, who was less well versed in Scottish family history than Scott, may have wrongly identified the Lady Primrose in question. It is also not impossible that Scott himself was the source of this apparently erroneous identification. In the version of the story he told to Mrs Hughes he does not identify her as the later Lady Primrose who became Lady Stair but it may be significant that in 'My Aunt Margaret's Mirror' the story of the disrupted wedding and the duel following it are confirmed to Lady Forester by 'the celebrated Earl of Stair' (71.5). It is possible that Scott associated the Earl with the story because he believed Lady Primrose later married him and that he introduced him into the fiction here because of this. The earlier Lady Primrose was a much less well known figure than Lady Primrose/Stair and Scott was certainly aware of a family connection between the Swintons and the Dalrymples since he notes with regard to his great-aunt Margaret that she was 'nearly related to the Lord President'[129] who was James Dalrymple, first viscount Stair (1619–95). Even though this connection is not relevant to the identification of the sisters, since it was only by a later marriage that Lady Primrose became a Dalrymple, it may have been enough to sow some confusion in Scott's mind, if indeed he was unclear about which generation the story belonged to and therefore about the exact relationship between Anne Sinclair and Elizabeth, Lady Primrose. If the dates in the fictionalised version of the story in 'My Aunt Margaret's Mirror' can be considered as any kind of evidence, then it is worth noting that Sir Philip Forester, the fictional equivalent of Sir James/Archibald Primrose, is said to have 'flourished about the end of the 17th and beginning of the 18th century' (54.37–38): these are precisely the dates for Viscount Primrose and are later than the dates for the earlier Sir James.

No other characters from 'My Aunt Margaret's Mirror' can be identified as derived from historical figures; a brother of Lady Primrose plays a part in Mrs Hughes's account but as Sir Robert Sinclair had several sons it has not been possible to identify which might have been the one referred to in the version of the story told to Scott.

There are neither dates nor precisely datable individual events in the version recorded by Mrs Hughes and the version in 'My Aunt Margaret's Mirror'. However, as already noted, 'My Aunt Margaret's Mirror' is located generally in the years around 1700; this allows Scott to have Forester take part in the campaigns of the Duke of Marlborough and also to have the magician suspected of being a Jacobite spy. Neither of these historical allusions, however, is central to the story.

'THE TAPESTRIED CHAMBER'

Versions of the Story. On 2 September 1831 Scott sent Cadell introductions for the *Keepsake* stories for inclusion in the Magnum. In the one intended for 'The Tapestried Chamber' he wrote that 'The original teller of the story was to me at least was the celebrated Miss Seward who among other excellencies possessed that delightfull talent which enables those who have it to read or recite with the greatest possible effect & upon whom it is needless to make any remark saving that she did so'.[130] In the story itself he had already noted that 'the present writer heard the following events related, more than twenty years since, by the celebrated Miss Seward, of Lichfield' (76.22–23), no doubt referring to his visit to her in Lichfield in 1807.[131] Scott's comment that, for him, Anna Seward was the 'original' teller of this story is significant since there are indications that he had also read and been influenced by other versions of the story.

In September 1818, there appeared in *Blackwood's Edinburgh Magazine* a ghost story entitled 'Story of an Apparition'.[132] Prefaced by a letter to the Editor subscribed 'A. B.', 'Story of an Apparition' is clearly the same story as Scott related as 'The Tapestried Chamber'. Because it is so close to Scott's *Keepsake* story the narrative is worth quoting in full:

About the fall of the leaf, in the year 1737, Colonel D. went to visit his friend Mr N. at his country seat in the north of England. As this country seat was the scene of a very singular adventure, it may be proper to mention its antiquity and solemnity, which were fitted to keep in countenance the most sombre events. The following circumstances were well known in the family, and are said to have been related by one of its members to a lady much celebrated in the literary world, but now deceased.

Upon arriving at the house of his friend, Colonel D. found there many guests, who had already got possession of almost all the apartments. The chillness of an October evening, and the somewhat mournful aspect of nature, at that season, collected them, at an early hour, round the blazing hearth, where they thought no better amusement could be found than the ancient and well approved one of story-telling, for which all mankind seem to have a relish. I do not mean the practice of circulating abominable slanders against one's friends, but the harmless, drowsy, and good-natured recreation of retailing wonderful narratives, in which, if any ill is spoken, it is generally against such as are well able to bear it, namely, the enemy of mankind, and persons who, having committed atrocious crimes, are supposed, after death, to haunt the same spots to which their deeds have attached dismal recollections.

While these tales went round, the evening darkened apace, and the windows ceased any longer to contrast the small glimmerings of external twilight with the bright blaze of the hearth. The rustling of withered leaves, casually stirred by the wind, is always a melancholy sound, and, on this occasion, lent its aid to the superstitious impressions which were gaining force by each successive recital of prodigies. One member of the family began to relate a certain tradition, but he was suddenly stopped by their host, who exhibited signs of displeasure, and whispered something to him, at the same time turning his eyes upon Colonel D. The story was accordingly broken off, and the company went to supper with their hair standing on end; but so transitory are human impressions, that in a few minutes they had all recovered their gayety, except the Colonel, who was unable to comprehend why any tradition should be concealed from him in particular.

When they separated to go to sleep, he was led by Mr N. (as the reader will probably anticipate), to a chamber at a great distance from the other bed-rooms, and which bore evident marks of having been newly opened up, after remaining long unoccupied. In order to dissipate the confined air of the place, a large wooden fire had been lighted, and the gloomy bed-curtains were tucked stiffly up in festoons. I have not heard whether there was tapestry in the room or not; but one thing is certain, that the room looked as dreary as any tapestry could have made it, even if it had been worked on purpose by Mrs Ann Radcliffe herself. Romance writers generally decorate their imaginary walls with all the wisdom of Solomon; but, as I am unable to vouch for the

truth of every particular mentioned in this story, I mean to relate
the circumstances faithfully as they were told me, without calling
in so wise a man to lend his countenance to them.

Mr N. made apologies to Colonel D. for putting him into an
apartment which was somewhat uncomfortable, and which was
now opened only because all the rest were already filled. With
these excuses, and other suitable compliments, he bade his guest
good night, and went away with a good deal of seriousness in his
countenance, leaving the door a-jar behind him.

Colonel D——, observing that the apartment was large and
cold, and that but a small part of the floor was covered with
carpet, endeavoured to shut the door, but found he could only
close it half way. Some obstacle in the hinges, or the weight of
the door pressing upon the floor, opposed his efforts. Nevertheless, being seized with some absurd fancies, he took the candle,
and looked out. When he saw nothing, except the long passage
and the vacant apartments beyond, he went to bed, leaving the
remains of the fire still flickering upon the broad hearth, and
gleaming now and then upon the door as it stood half open.

After the Colonel had lain for a long while, ruminating half
asleep, and when the ashes were now nearly extinguished, he
saw the figure of a woman glide in. No noise accompanied her
steps. She advanced to the fire-place, and stood between him
and the light, with her back towards him, so that he could not
see her features. Upon observing her dress, he found that it
exactly corresponded in appearance with the ancient silk robes
represented in the pictures of English ladies of rank, painted
three centuries ago. This circumstance filled him with a degree
of terror which he had never experienced before. The stately
garniture of times long past had a frightful meaning, when appearing, as it now did, not upon a canvass, but upon a moving shape,
at midnight. Still endeavouring to shake off those impressions
which benumbed him, he raised himself upon his arm, and faintly
asked "who was there?" The phantom turned round—approached
the bed—and fixed her eyes upon him; so that he now beheld a
countenance where some of the worst passions of the living were
blended with the cadaverous appearance of the dead. In the
midst of traits which indicated noble birth and station, was
seen a look of cruelty and perfidy, accompanied with a certain
smile which betrayed even baser feelings. The approach of such
a face near his own, was more than Colonel D—— could support; and when he rose next morning from a feverish and troubled
sleep, he could not recollect how or when the accursed spectre
had departed. When summoned to breakfast, he was asked how
he had spent the night, and he endeavoured to conceal his agitation by a general answer, but took the first opportunity to inform
his friend Mr N——, that, having recollected a certain piece of
business which waited him at London, he found it impossible to
protract his visit a single night. Mr N—— seemed surprised,

and anxiously sought to discover whether any thing occurred to
render him displeased with his reception; but finding that his
guest was impenetrable, and that his remonstrances against his
departure were in vain, he insisted upon shewing Colonel D——
the beauties of his country residence, after which he would reluctantly bid him farewell. In walking round the mansion, Colonel
D—— was shewn the outside of the tower where he had slept,
and vowed, mentally, never to enter it again. He was next led to
a gallery of pictures, where Mr N—— took much delight in
displaying a complete series of family portraits, reaching back to
a very remote era. Among the oldest, there was one of a lady.
Colonel D—— had no sooner got a glimpse of it, than he cried
out, "May I never leave this spot, if that is not she." Mr N——
asked whom he meant? "The detestable phantom that stared me
out of my senses last night;" and he related every particular that
had occurred.

   Mr N——, overwhelmed with astonishment, confessed that,
to the room where his guest had slept, there was attached a
certain tradition, pointing it out as having been, at a remote
period, the scene of murder and incest. It had long obtained the
repute of being haunted by the spirit of the lady, whose picture
was before him; but there were some circumstances in her history
so atrocious, that her name was seldom mentioned in his family,
and his ancestors had always endeavoured as much as possible
to draw a veil over her memory.

There may be differences in period, names and setting, but the plot
is the same, and the characters of the protagonists (including the
ghost) are almost identical to those of 'The Tapestried Chamber'.
Further, like Scott the narrator claims a source for his knowledge of
the story in a famous female author, now deceased, and affirms that
he will relate the story faithfully, as he heard it.[133] The similarities
between these two tellings of the story are so great that Coleman
Parsons believed, largely on these grounds, that Scott wrote 'Story of
an Apparition'.[134] However external evidence does not support his
opinion.

   The principal piece of evidence against Scott's authorship comes
from the pen of William Blackwood himself. According to Alan Lang
Strout, Blackwood recorded authorship of some *Blackwood's* articles in
two lists, of which only the second, covering from August 1818 to
March 1819 (that is, during his partnership with John Murray), is
relevant here. Strout makes two points about this list: firstly, that
Blackwood did not know the authorship of articles sent from London
by Murray, and secondly, that Blackwood groups under the heading
'Various' a few pieces whose authorship he may have known.[135] 'Story
of an Apparition' appears under 'Various' in this list, and it is very
unlikely that Scott would be one of the authors known to Blackwood
who would be designated in this way, as elsewhere in the same list he
appears under his own name. It is also unlikely that Blackwood would
have made a mistake in regard to Scott, of all people, given his

eagerness to recruit and retain Scott for his magazine.[136] Blackwood's categorisation, then, would seem to rule out Scott as the author of 'Story of an Apparition'. Scott's own Introduction to the story for the Magnum edition, as well as his opening comments in the story itself —in both cases lacking any mention of his writing up the story previously—could lead us to the same conclusion. However he might consider that the lapse of a decade between versions would render such information irrelevant to readers and furthermore he had specifically reserved the right to republish his contributions to *Blackwood's*.[137]

More interesting is Scott's remark that 'Miss Seward always affirmed that she had derived her information from an authentic source' (76.31–32), and that 'I will not avail myself of any particulars I may have since received concerning the detail of the localities' (76.33–35). This appears to imply his familiarity with other examples of the story which claim to derive from Anna Seward. Could Scott be referring to 'Story of an Apparition'? Its appearance in *Blackwood's* guarantees that he would have known it. Scott also tells us that 'Miss Seward suppressed the names of the two persons chiefly concerned' (76.31–32), and that she gave to the main protagonist 'the name of Browne, but merely, as I understood, to save the inconvenience of introducing a nameless agent in the narrative' (77.6–8). Given that he was prepared to use her designations here, he would presumably have done so in any earlier version. On balance, his comments imply that this was his first attempt at the story, but that he had seen at least one other version that may not have had its source in Anna Seward.

The strongest evidence in favour of Scott's authorship of 'Story of an Apparition' is, as Parsons noted, an incident described by James Hogg in his *Familiar Anecdotes of Sir Walter Scott*.[138] Writing in 1834, Hogg recalls Scott reading him a ghost story which, according to Hogg, he had been inspired to write by reading Hogg's recent similar work:

> there was one fore-noon he said to me in his study. "I have never durst venture upon a real ghost story Mr Hogg but you have published some such thrilling ones of late that I have been this very day employed in writing one. I assure you 'it's no little that gars auld Donald pegh' but yon Lewis stories of your's frightened me so much that I could not sleep and now I have been trying my hand on one and here it is." He read it; but it did not make a great impression on me for I do not know at this moment not having his works by me where it is published. It was about the ghost of a lady which and I think appeared in the Abbot or Monastry. He read me also a humorous poem in M.S. which has never been published that I know of. It was something about finding out the happiest man and making him a present of a new holland shirt. Paddy got it who had never known the good of a shirt. . . . I never heard what became of that poem or whether it was ever published.[139]

In mentioning these two novels Hogg must be thinking of the White Lady of Avenel, who figures prominently in *The Monastery*, begun in mid 1819 and published in 1820, and in passing in *The Abbot* (1820). However, Hogg's time scheme does not work: Scott cannot have been inspired to write his own story by Hogg's Lewis stories. In 1810 Hogg had published in two parts an early version of 'Basil Lee' in his periodical *The Spy*,[140] but although in this version the narrator briefly describes a period on Lewis, the 'Lewis stories' appear only in *Winter Evening Tales* (1820). Furthermore, the text in *The Spy* does not contain the line which, according to Hogg, Scott quoted from his story as 'it's no little that gars auld Donald pegh'; in the expanded version in *Winter Evening Tales* a form of these words is uttered by a Highlander who returns to Basil's shop to buy some more of the vitriol which he had earlier received instead of whisky.[141] Furthermore, it is possible that the story Hogg heard that day was not, as Parsons infers, 'Story of an Apparition'. The poem to which Hogg refers in this episode is clearly 'The Search after Happiness; or, The Quest of Sultaun Solimaun', which comprised *The Sale-Room*'s fifth number of 1 February 1817, and a careful examination of Hogg's statements may indicate that poem and story were read to him on the same occasion. Many of the items in *The Sale-Room*, to which Scott certainly contributed, remain unascribed, and it is at least theoretically possible that he was responsible for a letter on supernatural apparitions, signed H. F. A., included in the number for 22 February 1817. Embedded in this letter is a self-contained story about the ghost of a young lady. If Scott wrote this story it is far more likely that he read it to Hogg along with 'The Search After Happiness' than that he read 'Story of an Apparition'.

One notable coincidence between 'Story of an Apparition' and 'The Tapestried Chamber' is the claimed source of each. The narrator of 'Story of an Apparition' asserts that the circumstances of the story 'were well known in the family, and are said to have been related by one of its members to a lady much celebrated in the literary world, but now deceased', just as Scott claimed that his story was derived from another celebrated and deceased literary lady, Anna Seward. However, unlike Scott, the narrator of 'Story of an Apparition' does not claim to have had the story directly from the literary lady and his wording could be taken to imply that he was at one further remove. Similarly the prefatory letter merely claims that what follows 'is no invention of mine, but a ghost-story of natural growth, which I heard in conversation'.[142] Perhaps Scott, while not the author, was nevertheless the author's immediate source: in other words, a family member told it to Anna Seward, she told it to Scott, and Scott told it to the author.

If Scott was not the author, who was? The prefatory letter to the story is signed 'A. B.' For Strout, these initials suggest Alexander Blair.[143] However, not only are none of Blair's known contributions signed thus—they are either unsigned or occasionally over 'S. A.'—but Brian Murray has shown that another *Blackwood's* story by 'A. B.' and which Strout assigns to '?Alexander Blair' is actually by Thomas Mitchell.[144] Furthermore, Blair was not recruited to *Blackwood's* until 1822.[145] In any case these particular initials were often used as a pseudonym, and if we disregard them the possibility that Scott may have told the story to the author provides an alternative lead. Scott could have related the story to many people. Some such as Lockhart and Wilson, along with other *Blackwood's* regulars including William Laidlaw, are excluded by William Blackwood's 'Various'. Who else might it be? One person, who knew both Scott and this story, springs to mind. Washington Irving visited Scott at Abbotsford in 1817, made an agreement with William Blackwood to furnish articles for the magazine,[146] and, as we shall see, later published a version of the story under his own name as 'The Adventure of My Uncle'.[147] On the other hand, Blackwood himself complains that the arrangement with Irving has not borne fruit.[148] Although Blackwood might have been unaware of the identity of the writer if the article had been submitted through John Murray in London, it is worth noting that Irving's letters of July to September 1817 contain no reference to a story for *Blackwood's*.

'The Adventure of My Uncle', Irving's acknowledged version of Anna Seward's story, was written when Irving was living in Paris, and is set in France. There may be differences in setting and in the nature of the ghost, who returns as the victim rather than as the perpetrator of a sexual crime, but this is clearly Anna Seward's story despite its French dress and whimsical and sexually suggestive tone,[149] and it is significant that Irving acknowledges the borrowed nature of much of his material in his address to the reader, although failing to name his sources.[150] Scott, who must have known 'Story of an Apparition' from its appearance in *Blackwood's*, certainly knew *Tales of a Traveller*: he owned a copy of the first edition and also refers to it in his journal in 1832.[151]

A close comparison of 'Story of an Apparition', 'The Adventure of My Uncle' and 'The Tapestried Chamber' suggests that 'The Tapestried Chamber' is an amplified and more literary version of 'Story of an Apparition' and that in writing it Scott may have drawn on 'The Adventure of My Uncle'. While Scott's story is extremely close to 'Story of an Apparition', there are also elements common to 'The Adventure of My Uncle' and 'The Tapestried Chamber' which are either absent from or in direct contrast to the case of 'Story of an Apparition'.[152] Some of these similarities are unimportant in terms of plot or characterisation, but are significant in that they suggest a close relationship between the two tales. These include the unplanned nature of the visit in the course of a journey, the description of the mansion with its turrets, walled park, and different periods of construction, the fact that in each case the ghost is accompanied by sound and is dressed in high-heeled shoes and a sweeping, floor-length robe, and the atmospheric tolling of the castle clock. Correspondences such as these imply a definite link between the acknowledged versions of Irving and Scott. Could this result from Irving's version preserving details of the story as told to him by Scott? If so, this would seem to constitute further evidence against attribution of 'Story of an Apparition' to Irving. It seems more probable, however, that Scott borrowed, consciously or unconsciously, from Irving's version of the story when he wrote 'The Tapestried Chamber'. If conscious borrowing was involved, did Scott feel entitled to take from Irving's story because he had furnished him with it in the first place? If the debt was unconscious, could Irving's version have falsified his memory of the original story, so that he believed himself to be relating it more faithfully than he really was?[153]

It appears, then, that 'The Adventure of My Uncle' played a role in the elaboration and fictionalisation of Anna Seward's story as Scott presents it in 'The Tapestried Chamber', and this despite Scott's apparent claim to be telling the story exactly as he heard it from her. It is however clear that for Scott a story retained its identity even if significant details, setting or arrangement of material were substantially changed. He was prepared to describe *The Bride of Lammermoor* as an 'ower true tale',[154] and yet his own mother, one of his sources, told the Scotts of Harden that he had not been faithful to the facts.[155] Further, in the specific case of 'The Tapestried Chamber', Scott does not in fact claim to be reporting Anna Seward's exact words. Quite apart from the qualification 'so far as memory permits', he says only that he has related the story 'in the same character' as he heard it, and believes that he deserves praise or blame solely in relation to his judgment 'in selecting his materials', because he has 'studiously avoided any attempt at ornament which might interfere with the simplicity of the tale' (76.9–11). Scott is here merely claiming to have kept to the original storyline; he has not added incidents (as he did in 'My Aunt Margaret's Mirror') or made changes to the outcome (as in *The Bride of Lammermoor*).[156]

There is some internal evidence that Scott is embellishing Seward's account. He makes an anachronistic reference to the theories on apparitions current in his own day which is inappropriate to the period of the story itself and to Anna Seward as narrator of the story in 1807. This happens both when General Browne claims that upon regaining consciousness 'An hundred terrible objects appeared to haunt me; but there was the great difference betwixt the vision which I have described, and those which followed, that I knew the last to be deceptions of my own fancy and over-excited nerves' (85.36–39), and when Lord Woodville refrains from suggesting any of the 'fashionable' explanations: 'vagaries of the fancy, or deceptions of the optic nerves' (86.15). Scott is making clear reference here to the work of John Ferriar and Samuel Hibbert. In his *Essay Towards a Theory of Apparitions* (1813) Ferriar attributed apparitions to psychological causes ('deceptions of my own fancy', 'vagaries of the fancy'), whilst for Hibbert (*Sketches of the Philosophy of Apparitions; or, An Attempt to Trace Such Illusions to Their Physical Causes* (1824)) they arise when an excited bodily state bypasses the brain and acts directly upon the senses ('over-excited nerves', 'deceptions of the optic nerves').[157]

Ghost stories by their very nature as well as by their mode of transmission present particular problems in relation to authenticity. Apart from the fact that the original experience may have contained hallucinatory or at least imagined features, such stories easily acquire embellishment simply by passing through many hands. Scott himself highlights this in *Letters on Demonology*: 'it is upon the credit of one man, who pledges it upon that of three or four persons who have told it successively to each other, that we are often expected to believe an incident inconsistent with the laws of nature, however agreeable to our love of the wonderful and the horrible'.[158] He makes a similar point in relation to a 'haunted chamber' story communicated to him in writing by Lord Webb Seymour, claiming that it 'has appeared in print in different shapes & languages'.[159] Although 'The Tapestried Chamber' partakes of the conventions exhibited by such tales, it seems from Scott's account that in telling her story Anna Seward had a particular place in mind, although she did not reveal it to her hearers.

Stories of haunted chambers are attached to many of the castles and stately homes of Britain, and several share some elements with the story told in 'The Tapestried Chamber': for example, the rustling of a silk dress, and even the tap of high-heeled shoes, frequently accompany the movements of a female ghost.[160] A more significant similarity involves the castle of Berry Pomeroy in Devon, which numbers among its resident ghosts that of a fourteenth-century lady who is occasionally glimpsed mounting the staircase and entering the chamber where she murdered her own child, born of an incestuous relationship with her father.[161] This latter ghost appeared in the early nineteenth century to Sir Walter Farquhar (1738–1819), an eminent physician who, unaware of the tradition, was visiting the castle to deliver a baby.[162] In light of the woman's crimes of incest and murder, relatively rare among British female ghosts, it is tempting to postulate a link between Berry Pomeroy and the story which became 'The Tapestried Chamber'. Perhaps Farquhar's experience was the kernel of an incident such as Anna Seward related.

As we have seen, Scott's version of Anna Seward's story represents a creative fictionalisation of the facts upon which the story was based. More probably, it further develops Anna Seward's own fictionalisation of the original narrative. It is noticeable that in his opening remarks to 'The Tapestried Chamber' Scott does not claim to be telling a true story, and although he reports Seward's own claim 'that she had derived her information from an authentic source' (76.31–32), given his emphasis on her gifts as a story-teller and also, by implication, on her detailing to a spellbound audience 'the minute incidents' which serve to give a story 'authenticity' (76.18–19), it is likely that he suspected that she was herself embroidering the tale, and to a particular end. He was well aware of 'Another species of deception affecting the credit of . . . supernatural communications', namely that which 'arises from the dexterity and skill of the authors who have made it their business to present such stories in the shape most likely to attract belief'.[163] It is possible to interpret the detail of the family portrait as a device aimed at encouraging the listener's or reader's belief in the ghostly visitation described. For those who knew Farquhar or the original of General Browne, their personal and professional reputation would be sufficient; those at one further remove, with no personal knowledge of the protagonist, might need stronger proof. Perhaps Anna Seward 'authenticated' her story by the introduction of the portrait, thereby presenting the sceptics among her audience, and ultimately among Scott's, with an intriguing mystery.

'DEATH OF THE LAIRD'S JOCK'

Versions of the Story. The story of the Laird's Jock's death seems to have been somewhat of a favourite of Scott's and he recounted it in writing more than once. What is more he had considered it as a possible subject for a painting some time before he recommended it to Reynolds for *The Keepsake*. Scott's first account was written when, in the 1812 edition of *Minstrelsy of the Scottish Border*, he expanded an existing note on the Laird's Jock appended to the ballad 'Dick o' the Cow' by adding the following:

> Tradition reports that the Laird's Jock survived to extreme old age, when he died in the following extraordinary manner. A challenge had been given by an Englishman, named Forster, to any Scottish borderer, to fight him at a place called Kershope-foot, exactly upon the borders. The Laird's Jock's only son accepted the defiance, and was armed by his father with his own two-handed sword. The old champion himself, though bed-ridden, insisted upon being present at the battle. He was borne to the place appointed, wrapped, it is said, in blankets, and placed upon a very high stone to witness the conflict. In the duel his son fell, treacherously slain, as the Scotch tradition affirms. The old man gave a loud yell of terror and despair when he saw his son slain and his noble weapon won by an Englishman, and died as they bore him home. A venerable border poet (though of these later days) has composed a poem on this romantic incident. The stone on which the Laird's Jock sate to behold the duel, was in existence till wantonly destroyed a year or two since. It was always called THE LAIRD'S JOCK'S STONE.[164]

Scott does not identify the poet any further than this and the only poem we have found by an author who might fit this description is one by William Scott published in his *Border Exploits* of 1812 where a number of poems evidently his own work are contained within the prose text.[165] (William Scott's use of the ballad form in imitation of the ancient Border ballads may have prompted Scott to call him a 'border poet (though of these later days)' and, since he does not write as if he were a young man in 1812, he could reasonably be called 'venerable').[166] One of the poems (recounting, according to William Scott, a 'local tradition')[167] includes the following stanzas:

> Where Kershope 'twixt the kingdoms flows,
>   May still be seen the plain,
> Where brave Armstrong of Greenah fell,
>   And was by Foster slain.

Disputes between them ran so high,
　　Nought could allay their pride,
But Will of Greenah he must die,
　　Or Foster of Stongarthside.

A duel's set; the day arriv'd,
　　And both must take their fates;
For it was fix'd, whoe'er surviv'd,
　　Should heir both the estates.

To borrow Side's well proven sword,
　　Did Will of Greenah hie
Unto Heugh-head, where Jock lay sick,
　　Who gave't reluctantly.

Upon a stone near the Heugh-head,
　　Jock caus'd him rais'd to be;
That when the combatants engag'd,
　　He might the battle see.

With anguish he did soon behold
　　Base Foster's brandish'd sword;
Sure proof that Greenah was no more,
　　And he was Greenah's Lord.

By fraud did Foster gain the field:
　　Ere Greenah's sword was drawn,
He unawares did thrust him through,
　　Base coward! with his brand.[168]

In the surrounding prose text William Scott further identifies Will
Armstrong of Greenah as Jock o' the Side's brother.[169] The contest
of an Armstrong and a Foster, the ailing owner of the sword brought
to watch the combat from a stone, the location of the fight at Kersehope-foot, and the sword won by the victor through an act of treachery
—all these belong to both accounts and make it clear that William
Scott and Walter Scott are narrating the same basic story. It is highly
likely that it was the publication of William Scott's book in 1812
which prompted Scott to add to his existing note in the new edition
of the *Minstrelsy* which was published in the same year but not until
11 December.[170] However it would seem that Scott was already aware
of the story from some other source since he has information differing
somewhat from William Scott's. In William Scott's version the sword
belongs not to the Laird's Jock but to Jock o' the Side. Moreover the
defeated combatant is Will Armstrong of Greenah who is the brother
rather than the son of the sword's owner.

In 1821 Scott related the tale to the painter Benjamin Haydon
saying that Haydon might like to consider it as a subject for his art:

By the way, there is a tale of our county which, were the subject
well known, as it is but a local and obscure tradition, strikes me
as not unfit for the pencil, and I will tell it to you in three words.
In ancient times there lived on the Scottish frontier, just oppos-

ite to England, a champion belonging to the clan of Armstrong
called the Laird's Jock, one of the most powerful men of his
time in stature and presence, and one of the bravest and most
approved in arms. He wielded a tremendously large and heavy
two-handed sword, which no one on the west border could use
save himself. After living very many [years] without a rival, Jock-
of-the-Side became old and bedridden, and could no longer stir
from home. His family consisted of a son and daughter, the first
a fine young warrior, though not equal to his father; and the last
a beautiful young woman. About this time an English champion
of the name of Foster, ancient rivals of the Armstrongs, and
Englishman to boot, gave a challenge to any man on the Scottish
side to single combat. These challenges were frequent among
the Borderers, and always fought with great fairness, and attended
with great interest. The Laird's Jock's son accepted the challenge,
and his father presented him on the occasion with the large two-
handed sword which he himself had been used to wield in battle.
He also insisted on witnessing the combat, and was conveyed on
a litter to a place called Turner's Holm, just on the frontier of
both kingdoms, where he was placed, wrapped up with great
care, under the charge of his daughter. The champions met, and
young Armstrong was slain; and Foster, seizing the sword, waved
it in token of triumph. The old champion never dropped a tear
for his son, but when he saw his renowned weapon in the hands
of an Englishman, he set up a hideous cry, which is said to have
been heard at an incredible distance, and exclaiming, "My sword!
my sword!" dropped into his daughter's arms, and expired.

I think that the despair of the old giant, contrasted with the
beautiful female in all her sorrows, and with the accompaniments
of the field of combat, are no bad subject for a sketch *à la mode*
of Salvator, though perhaps better adapted for sculpture.[171]

Significantly in this letter Scott appears to identify the Laird's Jock
with Jock o' the Side (the sword's owner in William Scott's account)
although they are not identified with each other elsewhere. Indeed in
Minstrelsy of the Scottish Border Scott not only printed 'Jock o' the
Side' in which they appear as different people but also quoted Maitland
of Lethington's separate stanzas on the two men from his 'Complaynt
aganis the Thievis of Liddisdail' twice, once in Appendix III to the
Introduction (the whole poem) and once in the notes to 'Dick o' the
Cow' (the stanza on the Laird's Jock) and the introduction to 'Jock o'
the Side' (the stanza on 'Jock o' the Side').[172] Given that Scott was
aware that the Laird's Jock and Jock o' the Side were two different
people it is quite likely that at this stage he was unsure which of the
two the story was associated with. Either he was confusing his own
version with the one given by William Scott or he was beginning to
wonder whether William Scott's version was the correct one.

Having already thought of it as a potential subject for a painting
Scott was at no loss for an idea when Reynolds and Heath approached
him for a story that could be used in their illustrated annual. Writing

to Reynolds in March 1828, Scott suggests this story along with the
story of 'A Highland Anecdote', as being 'susceptible of pictural illustration' and thus appropriate for a possible contribution to *The Keepsake*. He relates the story briefly, explaining that it is

> a tradition connected with a large stone in Liddesdale, called the
> Laird's Jock's stone. It takes the name from a furious Scottish
> champion, called the Laird's Jock, because he was the eldest son
> of the Laird of Mangerton, chief of the clan of Armstrong. He
> succeeded his father in command of the warlike tribe to which
> he belonged. Frequent defiances at that time passed between the
> Scots and English on each side of the frontier, but the Laird's
> Jock's size and strength rendered him superior to all men in
> single combat, and he wielded a huge two-handed sword which
> no one could use but himself. At length he became old, decrepit,
> and finally bed-ridden, and was obliged to resign the command
> of the tribe to his son, a gallant young man, but far from being
> his father's equal. Of that the old man seemed sensible, for he
> never would resign possession of the sword which had won so
> many victories. At length a brave young Englishman, one of the
> Fosters, if I recollect right, sent a challenge to the best Scotsman
> on the opposite side of the Liddle, to fight him in single combat
> at what was called the Turney-holm—a flat space of ground used
> for such encounters. The old champion took great interest in
> this challenge, which was accepted by his son, and for the first
> time put him in possession of the favourite sword. He caused
> himself to be transported in a species of sledge, or litter, to witness
> the combat, and was placed on the stone, which still bears his
> name, wrapd up in blankets, and attended by his daughter, a
> beautiful young woman, who was her father's constant guardian
> and the nurse of his old age. The combat begun, and (by treach-
> ery, say the Scots, which is probably in that respect partial,) the
> young Armstrong fell, and the victorious duellist seizing the huge
> two-handed sword, brandished it aloft as the trophy of the field.
> At this distracting sight the old giant, who had long been incapable
> almost of turning himself in bed, started up, the covering falling
> partly from him, and showing the wreck of his emaciated frame,
> and uttered a cry so portentously loud, as to be heard for miles
> around. He was born back to his own tower of Mangerton, where
> he died in a few hours, which he spent in lamentations, not for
> his son, whom he never named, but for the loss of the noble
> sword which in his hands had won so many victories. If any artist
> should take this work in hand, he ought to forget there is such a
> thing as the Highland dress in the world, for it was never worn
> in my country. The moment would [be] the fall of the young
> chief, and the effect produced on the spectators, and particularly
> his father and sister. Cooper could do it admirably.[173]

Scott, it will be noted, reverts here to his original unequivocal identification of the sword's owner as the Laird's Jock but he no longer
suggests that the stone has been destroyed; either he had forgotten

this detail or had discovered that he was wrong.

As well as figuring in 'Dick o' the Cow' the Laird's Jock also plays a prominent role in 'Jock o' the Side' being described in both ballads as 'the gude Laird's Jock'.[174] In his original editorial material in *Minstrelsy of the Scottish Border* Scott records that 'Dick o' the Cow' and 'Jock o' the Side' were published in 1784 'in the *Hawick Museum*, a provincial miscellany, to which they were communicated by John Elliot, Esq., of Reidheugh, a gentleman well skilled in the antiquities of the Western Border, and to whose friendly assistance the Editor is indebted for many valuable communications'.[175] Perhaps it was from Elliot that Scott heard this story, or maybe it was related to him during one of the 'raids'[176] which he made in the 1790s with Robert Shortreed, Sheriff-Substitute of Roxburghshire, into 'the then wild and inaccessible district of Liddesdale', as Lockhart describes it, in order 'to pick some of the ancient *riding ballads*, said to be still preserved among the descendants of the moss-troopers'.[177] But whomever Scott heard the story from, the ultimate source of 'Death of the Laird's Jock' seems to be a traditional story regarding a contest between an Armstrong and a Foster which was known separately to William Scott and Walter Scott. In addition, as was his custom, Scott also brought other parts of his wide-ranging knowledge to bear and in this case introduced the story of Bernard Gilpin and the glove displayed in a church as a symbol of challenge which he had already quoted (from a life of Gilpin published in 1753) in his 1817 introduction to *The Border Antiquities of England and Scotland*.[178]

Historical Characters and Context. We have not been able to find any historical account of a combat between a Foster and either William Armstrong or the Laird's Jock's son which might have been the origin of the story known to Scott. However, both the Laird's Jock and Jock o' the Side, the two contenders for the role of the central figure in the story, the owner of the famous sword, were historical figures, as Scott was aware. In *Minstrelsy of the Scottish Border* he offers a sardonic note on Jock's honesty in which he cites various historical sources:

> The commendation of the Laird's Jock's honesty seems but indifferently founded; for, in July 1586, a bill was fouled against him, Dick of Dryup, and others, by the deputy of Bewcastle, at a warden-meeting, for 400 head of cattle taken in open foray from the Drysike in Bewcastle: and in September 1587, another complaint appears at the instance of one Andrew Rutledge of the Nook, against the Laird's Jock, and his accomplices, for 50 kine and oxen, besides furniture, to the amount of 100 merks sterling. See Bell's MSS., as quoted in the *History of Cumberland and Westmoreland*.[179] In Sir Richard Maitland's poem against the thieves of Liddesdale, he thus commemorates the Laird's Jock:—

> > 'They spuilye puir men of thair pakis,
> > They leif them nocht on bed nor bakis;
> > Baith hen and cok,

With reil and rok,
The *Lairdis Jock*
All with him takis.'

Those who plundered Dick had been bred up under an expert
teacher.[180]

Maitland's poem is not precisely dated but he did not begin writing
till the age of sixty which places it in the latter part of his long life
which stretched from 1496 to 1586. In addition to these references
we find Thomas Musgrave in 1583 providing a list of Borderers to
Lord Burghley which includes 'Joke Armestronge called the Lordes
Joke [who] dwelleth under Denyshill besydes Kyrsope in Denisborne'.
He was the son of 'Seme Armestronge lord of Mangerton [who]
married John Fosters daughter of Kyrsope foot'. Musgrave further
records that another Jock Armstrong, a nephew of the Laird's Jock,
also married a Foster.[181] Thus, as T. F. Henderson in his edition of
the *Minstrelsy* points out, if he 'did fight a duel with a Forster there,
his opponent must have been a near relative'.[182] (As Musgrave informs
Burghley, the Armstrongs were the dominant family in Scotland along
the Liddel north of the Kershope as were the Fosters in England to
the south of this point.) Scott's Laird's Jock is thus established as a
historical figure living in the late sixteenth century, provided that the
Laird's Jock spoken of here is the same as the one in Scott's story.
However Henderson argues that 'Jock o' the Side' relates the events
of a historically recorded incident of 1527 and that therefore the
Laird's Jock who figures in that ballad 'was probably the "Laird's
Jock" of an earlier generation, *i.e.* the son of Thomas, not of Sim,
Armstrong of Mangerton'.[183] Since, as Scott himself explains in his
story, the appellation 'the Laird's Jock' is one that can be applied to
any Jock who is the son of the Laird, it could obviously be used in
more than one generation.

Similarly Jock o' the Side would be a Jock Armstrong living at the
Side, a small hamlet in Liddesdale, and there was probably more
than one person who bore this name. Scott knew of at least one
historical Jock o' the Side, the subject of a stanza in Maitland's 'Complaynt' which he quotes in a note on the ballad bearing Jock's name:

The reality of this story rests solely upon the foundation of
tradition. Jock o' the Side seems to have been nephew to the
Laird of Mangertoun, cousin to the Laird's Jock, one of his deliv-
erers, and probably brother to Chrystie of the Syde, mentioned
in the list of Border clans, 1597. Like the Laird's Jock, he also is
commemorated by Sir Richard Maitland. . . .

'He is weil kend, Johne of the Syde,
A greater theif did never ryde;
He never tyris,
For to brek byris,
Our muir and myris
Ouir gude ane guide.'[184]

As with the Laird's Jock, Scott equates this later sixteenth century
Jock o' the Side with the one mentioned in the ballad which Henderson

believes to deal with events of much earlier in the century. If the ballad records the names of the protagonists correctly then there must have been an earlier Jock o' the Side as well as an earlier Laird's Jock. However Scott's dating of his story as 'about the latter years of Queen Elizabeth's reign' (90.18–19) suggests he was identifying the Laird's Jock in this story as the one written about by Maitland. If the events did originally take place at this later time then one piece of possible corroboration for William Scott's version of events (by which Foster as winner obtains or retains control of Greenah) is that in 1583 we find reference to a Will Foster of Grena in Liddesdale.[185]

Just as a story may have been transferred from one Jock to another, so the stone which Scott calls the Laird's Jock's stone may also have suffered transference. In *Minstrelsy of the Scottish Border* Scott describes the location of the combat as 'Kersehope-foot', in the letter to Haydon as 'Turner's Holm' and in the letter to Reynolds as 'Turney-holm'. Another note in the *Minstrelsy* is more specific and detailed: 'Kershope-burn, where Hobbie met his treacherous companions, falls into the Liddel, from the English side, at a place called Turnersholm, where, according to tradition, tourneys and games of chivalry were often solemnised.'[186] The variant form 'Turney-holm' is explained by implication in a further note, this time in the Magnum edition of *The Black Dwarf*, to the effect that 'There is a level meadow, on the very margin of the two kingdoms, called Turner's-holm, just where the brook called Crissop joins the Liddel. It is said to have derived its name as being a place frequently assigned for tourneys, during the ancient Border times'.[187] As we have seen, one of the interesting differences between Scott's versions is that, while in his expanded *Minstrelsy* note of 1812 he reported that it had been destroyed 'a few years since', in 'Death of the Laird's Jock' he notes that the stone on which the Laird's Jock was placed to view the combat at Turner's Holm 'is still called the Laird's Jock's stone', thus implying that it was still in existence in 1828 when he was writing the story.

At the spot described by Scott there is now no stone called the Laird's Jock's Stone but roughly in the same location there is a stone known as Will o' Greena's Stone described in the Inventory of the Royal Commission on the Ancient Monuments of Scotland as 'a short unhewn pillar of sandstone' about 55 cm high and 30 cm wide. The compilers of the inventory also suggest, on the evidence of earlier maps and because it is not earthfast, that it may have been moved from its original location.[188] This conjecture is supported in 1924 by James Logan Mack who describes Turner's Holm and notes that on 'this field stood, until a few years ago, a large stone which Sir Walter Scott designed "The Laird's Jock's Stone," and which is named in at least one map "Will o' Greena's Stane."' Mack, seemingly unaware of Scott's claim in the *Minstrelsy* note that it has been destroyed, laments that it has recently been moved 'on the trivial pretext of being an obstruction to the cultivation of the ground' and reports that a 'fragment of it was, however, preserved, and now rests alongside the railway line, about one hundred feet east of the spot on which it was originally erected'.[189] Given Scott's possible transfer of the story from Jock o' the Side to the Laird's Jock, it is conceivable that he knew that there was a stone associated with one of the key figures in the story (Will of Greenah in William Scott's version) and transferred the association with the stone to the figure who interested him most, the significant spectator whom he later identified as the Laird's Jock. This mental transference may have been assisted by a memory that William Scott offers the story as an explanation of a stone; however, the ballad actually continues on to relate other events which then provide an explanation of the nearby Millholm Cross, not of Will of Greenah's stone.

'A HIGHLAND ANECDOTE'

Sources and the Informant. As with 'Death of the Laird's Jock' Scott offered Frederic Mansel Reynolds a brief synopsis of 'A Highland Anecdote' in a letter before writing it up at greater length for *The Keepsake*. As this earlier account provides some extra information it is worth quoting in full. However, the original letter seems to be lost and it is given here as printed in the *Athenæum* for 1835, even although there are obvious transcription errors such as the placename 'Lettermore' appearing as 'Zittermur' and the misreading of 'Glenure' as the better known 'Glencoe'.[190]

The other story is highland, and I know the individual to whom the incident happened, and who had the character of having been the murderer of Callam Dearg, or Red Colin, in the wood of Zittermur. How that may [be], I know not; when I knew him he was lame of a leg and much disabled, which happened in this manner:—he was out in search of a goat, which had strayed from the flock, and as he was ascending by a steep and narrow path which ran slantingly upwards along the face of a huge precipice, which turned steeper and narrower every moment, he met a red deer stag coming butting down the same path which he was accending [*sic*]. What was to be done! the path was so narrow that the stag could not turn, and though the man might have done this, yet the odds were that before he could have [taken] many steps downwards, the stag, as they are very dangerous when brought to bay, would have charged and certainly pitched him over the precipice. To stand his ground was to incur a similar danger, and the country being disarmed after the affair of 1745, he had no fire-arms. My friend Duncan, therefore, laid himself flat in the path, in hopes that the deer would extricate them both from the dilemma, by walking over him. It was long, I think two or three hours, before the stag could settle what he would do, but at length he took courage, and advancing very cautiously, put his head down to snuff at Duncan ere he stept over his prostrate body. But the Highlander, greedy of game, and trusting to the apparent timidity of the creature he was dealing with, seized the deer's horn with one hand, and drew his dirk with the other.

The attempt had exactly the success which his want of faith, for there was an understood compact between the creature and him, certainly deserved. The stag sprung over the precipice, carrying Duncan along with him, who, with better luck than he deserved, fell uppermost. It was many hours after this adventure, that he was found by a party who were out in quest of him, lying above the dead animal, with his leg, thigh, and three or four ribs broken. I never could convince him that he was morally wrong in the whole affair; for my part I always thought the stalking down and shooting Glencoe, or Red Colin, was the more justifiable matter of the two; however, we remained friends all the same.[191]

In this letter Scott implies that he had heard this story from its protagonist; he certainly had discussed it with him. This is also implied in 'A Highland Anecdote' as printed (where Scott speaks in his own voice and not through a fictional narrator[192] and is confirmed by a deleted passage in the manuscript where he reports that the story was 'communicated to me by the sufferer'.[193] No other account of the central anecdote has been found.

In writing to Reynolds Scott does not name his informant and in 'A Highland Anecdote' he coyly refers to 'Duncan, as I shall call him' but in the journal entry of 11 March 1828 in which he records his sending the story to Reynolds he writes straightforwardly of 'the adventure of Duncan Stuart with the stag'.[194] Scott's circumspection about the name had a good reason: he tells us that Duncan was suspected of involvement in one of the most notorious killings of Scottish history, the so-called 'Appin Murder' in which Colin Campbell of Glenure, known as Red Colin, was killed in the wood of Lettermore on the Appin Peninsula on 14 May 1752. Scott's reference in 'A Highland Anecdote' to Duncan as taking part in 'a certain tragic affair, which made much noise a good many years after the rebellion' (94.18–19) is equally circumspect but in writing privately to Reynolds he was quite explicit in identifying this event as the Appin Murder. Still a well-known event in 1828 when Scott was writing this story (and due six years later to become the subject of a novel),[195] the murder has remained in the public eye more than many other unsolved cases partly because it figures in Stevenson's *Kidnapped* and partly because of the romantic legend that the secret of the identity of the killer is passed down from generation to generation of the chiefs of the Appin Stewarts. The story was one that connected strongly with Scott's personal interests. The Stewarts of Appin had been out in the Forty-Five under the leadership, not of their chief, but of Charles Stewart of Ardsheal, one of the main landowners in the peninsula. After the rebellion was suppressed Ardsheal fled to France and his estates were forfeited to the crown. Glenure was appointed factor of the estate and at first dealt leniently with the existing tenants using as his intermediary Ardsheal's half-brother James Stewart of Aucharn, known as James of the Glen (in Gaelic *Seumas a' Ghlinne*). Later, after some criticism that he was too lenient, he began to replace the tenants with members of his own clan. At the time of his murder Glenure was on his way to evict a number of tenants.

The identity of the murderer is the most controversial aspect of the murder and a great deal has been written in various attempts to identify him. At the time a number of people fell under suspicion including the secondary hero of *Kidnapped*, Alan Breck Stewart, who was in the area and escaped from Scotland shortly afterwards. James Stewart (of Aucharn, as he had now become) was hanged after being convicted of being 'art and part' (that is, an accessary) in the murder but it was clear that he was not the actual murderer since he was provably elsewhere when it was committed. It was the opinion of many people at the time that he was not part of any conspiracy to murder Glenure and was therefore unjustly convicted. Many, though not all, subsequent commentators have agreed with this.[196] Scott himself in the Introduction to the Magnum edition of *Rob Roy*, written in November 1828,[197] refers to this 'remarkable Highland story' and describes James Stewart as 'condemned and executed upon very doubtful evidence; the heaviest part of which only amounted to the accused person having assisted a nephew of his own, called Allan Breck Stewart, with money to escape after the deed was done'. He further claims that the conviction was 'obtained in a manner little to the honour of the dispensation of justice at the time'.[198] On the other hand the Campbells believed that a number of people were involved and there is no doubt that they were determined to find someone to punish for the murder of a prominent member of their clan.[199] Allan Breck drew attention to himself by fleeing, although as a deserter from the army he was in any case in a dangerous position.

Over time, and beginning with the days immediately after the actual murder, many rumours circulated about the identity of the murderer of Colin Campbell and Scott had evidently heard such a rumour in connection with the person who told him the story of the stag. In neither telling of the story does Scott claim unequivocally that Duncan was the murderer; rather he says in his letter to Reynolds that he 'had the character of having been the murderer of Callam Dearg, or Red Colin' and in 'A Highland Anecdote' that he 'was supposed by many to have been an accomplice, if not the principal actor' (94.16–17). Nevertheless Scott seems to have felt that there might be some truth in the allegation since in the printed version in *The Keepsake* he was careful neither to give Duncan's full name nor to name the event he was connected with, and in the manuscript he deleted his original comment that he had heard the story from Duncan himself. We know, then, from the *Keepsake* version that Scott had been told, possibly by Duncan himself, that he had been involved in the 1745 rising and further that he was suspected of the Appin Murder. Neither of these pieces of information can be relied on as historically accurate. Nevertheless Scott treats the allegations as plausible and, if we assume that they are features that could reasonably be ascribed to the person described, they can be used to provide some evidence as to the identity of Scott's informant.

In addition, we have it on Scott's own authority that Duncan was 'not a very aged man'[200] when he heard the story in his 'early youth' (94.14–15) about twenty years after the events it describes. If by 'early youth' Scott means something like the ages of ten to twelve this would fall in the years 1781 to 1783. If we take Scott's admittedly rather imprecise description of him as 'not a very aged man' to mean that he was about sixty this would have him born in 1721 to 1723 and place him in his early twenties in 1745, at about thirty in 1752 at the time of the Appin Murder and at about forty at the time of the incident narrated in 'A Highland Anecdote' which Scott tells us happened 'twenty years or more before I knew Duncan' (94.29). These ages are certainly compatible with the activities ascribed to him at these points in time, but they are based on imprecise information.

Unfortunately no Duncan Stewart met by Scott in his 'early youth' either in Edinburgh or elsewhere has been identified,[201] but other records are more helpful. While Duncan Stewart is a relatively common name, the range of possibilities can be narrowed on the assumption that he must have been in the Appin area in 1752 since only someone in that area would have been suspected of being involved in the Appin Murder. At the same time, assuming that he had indeed been out in the Forty-Five, we are also looking for someone who took part in the rising. For a resident of the Appin area the obvious regiment to join in 1745 was the Appin Stewart regiment commanded by Charles Stewart of Ardsheal. Of the nine Duncan Stewarts listed in the muster roll of the Appin Regiment compiled by Livingstone, Aikman and Hart,[202] three were killed at Culloden, one killed at either Falkirk or Culloden and one transported after Culloden, while another was from Glenlyon in Perthshire and thus unlikely to have been later involved in the Appin Murder. This leaves three possible candidates: a nephew to the laird of Ballachulish, wounded at Culloden; a changekeeper at Inverfola, Appin, also wounded at Culloden; and Duncan MacAlan Stewart, likewise wounded at Culloden. However, Duncan Stewart living in Inshaig in Appin in 1752 appears, in fact, to be one of the Duncan Stewarts supposedly killed at Culloden, a younger brother of the laird of Achnacone.[203] He thus must be added to the list, giving a total of four.

There are very extensive, though not complete, written records of the investigation of the murder and of the trial of James Stewart of the Glen which include a transcript of the precognitions of a large number of witnesses, the published account of the trial and the correspondence of the private and public figures involved in the prosecution. These documents contain references to a number of Duncan Stewarts. These include Duncan Stewart in Inshaig (already referred to above), Duncan Stewart in Achnacone in Glencoe, two Duncan Stewarts, elder and younger, in Cuil, Duncan Stewart, travelling packman in Arlarich in Rannoch, Duncan Stewart of Glenbuckie and Duncan Stewart of Glenfinlas. The last two can be excluded from consideration: they neither lived in the Appin area nor were suspected of the murder; they became involved in the investigation because Alan Breck had visited them before the murder and, in the case of Glenbuckie, because James of the Glen had stayed with him on the way back from Edinburgh a short time before the murder. The travelling packman can also be excluded as seemingly belonging to a different social class to Scott's Duncan; in any case the mention of him in the murder investigation arises solely from his encounters with Alan Breck Stewart in the days immediately after the murder: there seems to be no implication that he was involved in the murder itself.

As well as the extensive written records, the Appin Murder has given rise to a substantial body of folklore, of which Scott's references to the rumours about Duncan are some of the earliest recorded. In 1865 John Dewar collected a traditional account of the murder according to which Donald Stewart, nephew and son-in-law of the laird of Ballachulish, and the laird of Fasnacloich lay in wait for Colin Campbell and Donald fired the fatal shot.[204] Although there are certain discrepancies between this account and the written record recent writers on the murder have given some credence to the story especially as the letters of those investigating the crime show that they were aware of a shooting match at which the Stewart gentry were competing with each other and were anxious to find out more about it, although it seems they failed to do so.[205] Some details of the traditional story seem to be wrong (for instance, it is much more likely that it was the young Fasnacloich, James Stewart, than his father) but the presence of clearly inaccurate details need not invalidate the whole story. By association this story brings in another Duncan Stewart since the young laird of Fasnacloich had a brother of that name. However he subsequently became a lieutenant in the 74th Highlanders,[206] an outcome not compatible with Scott's story. Another Duncan Stewart, son of Robert Stewart of the mill at Duror, appears in a local tradition collected by David Mackay in the early twentieth century but, as the story has him with James Stewart when James was told of the murder, there is no suggestion that he was the murderer or associated with him.[207]

This leaves four Duncans: one in Inshaig, another in Achnacone in Glencoe and two more in Cuil. [1] Duncan Stewart in Inshaig meets the criterion of being connected with both the '45 and the murder. (For the purposes of this argument it is not necessary to prove that any of them was the murderer; it is enough that they could plausibly be suspected of it). His presence in the '45 in his role of younger brother of Achnacone has been noted and he was very much under suspicion at the time of the murder: one of the Campbells investigating the murder believed that 'Duncan in Insack knows more then he has yet discoverd'.[208] However he had a son, Alexander, who was married and old enough to play an active part in events preceding the murder (he was one of a delegation who went to Glenure's house in the hope of convincing him not to evict Stewart tenants from the Ardsheal estate) and is thus possibly too old to be Scott's Duncan. Duncan Stewart in Inshaig nevertheless remains a real possibility. [2] Duncan Stewart in Achnacone in Glencoe did not live in the Appin Peninsula but his home was only a short distance into Glencoe and thus not far from the scene of the murder. He came under suspicion of supplying Alan Breck Stewart with food and the investigators were keen to interview him and, in particular, his son.[209] Moreover James Stewart of the Glen visited him on his way to Edinburgh before the murder. In a recent article Angus Stewart suggests that he was the brother or nephew of Ballachulish and that he may have been the nephew of Ballachulish who was wounded at Culloden.[210] If so, he has a connection with both the murder and the rebellion. However, he too, with an adult son, also called Duncan, was probably too old to be Scott's protagonist—indeed it seems that he had died by 1762 since he had been succeeded by his son in the property of Achnacone by that time. On the other hand, if the elder Duncan was a *brother* of Ballachulish (otherwise unrecorded) his son would be Ballachulish's nephew, presumably the Duncan who is recorded as being wounded at Culloden. This would make the son both a participant in the '45 and, through his father, connected with the Appin Murder. As such he is a candidate for being Scott's Duncan. [3] Of the two Duncan Stewarts in Cuil, the elder was perhaps (like those in Inshaig and Achnacone in Glencoe) too old to be Scott's Duncan. [4] The younger, however, is a possibility. He owned a gun and took part in a shooting match along with James Stewart, younger of Fasnacloich, who, as we have seen, might be identified as one of the two men waiting in ambush for Glenure in Lettermore in the traditional account. Indeed, Holcombe, in her recent exhaustive study of the murder, suggests that the younger Duncan Stewart of Cuil may have been one of a number of men lying in wait for Glenure on the day of the murder although, as she notes, 'To judge by Duncan's surviving precognition, the prosecutors did not ask him to account for his whereabouts at the time of the murder'.[211] However, no evidence of the younger Duncan being involved in the events of 1745 has been found.

Altogether, then, there is more than one Duncan Stewart who could have been the one known to Scott, but a closer identification is not possible: this is not strange for the murderer of Colin Campbell of Glenure has been an unsolved mystery for more than 250 years and is unlikely to be solved now. At the same time, one other possibility remains. Scott's memory, though extraordinary, was not infallible. He may have misremembered the name of the man he knew. If that man's name was Donald rather than Duncan he could have been the Donald Stewart, nephew and son-in-law of Ballachulish, who is named as the murderer in the traditional account. However, another traditional story collected by Dewar gives details of Donald's later life which are not compatible with the events narrated in 'A Highland Anecdote', for according to this account Donald Stewart 'went to sea and did not return again until he was an old man'.[212] Nonetheless Scott's identification of a Duncan Stuart as the possible murderer does not solve the mystery of this famous murder but adds an intriguing extra element to the mix and gives a particular interest to this, the last of his stories to be published.

CONCLUSION

The stories in this volume fall into two groups. While 'The Inferno of Altisidora' and 'Christopher Corduroy' draw strongly on literary texts for their inspiration, 'Phantasmagoria', 'My Aunt Margaret's Mirror', 'The Tapestried Chamber', 'Death of the Laird's Jock', 'A Highland Anecdote' and much of 'Alarming Increase of Depravity Among Animals' can be described as traditional stories retold by Walter Scott. In this note the discussion of informants and other versions of the stories has in each case shown a line of transmission, while the investigation of historical sources, though not always leading to positive identification of actual historical events on which the story is based, demonstrates that tales seem to attach to a variety of events and a variety of people, and in so doing illustrates vividly the ways in which 'tradition' is created. To both groups Scott brings his extraordinarily wide reading so that, no matter how 'historical' the tale, it is deeply imbued with the influence of other texts. Taken together the two groups of stories remind us how much the telling of a story is an act of literary re-creation even when the author sets out explicitly to 'say the tale as 'twas said to me'.

NOTES

For shortened forms of reference see 229–30. All manuscripts referred to are in the National Library of Scotland unless otherwise stated.

1   'On the Present State of Periodical Criticism', *Edinburgh Annual Register for 1809*, 2 (2), 558, 559.

2   'On the Present State of Periodical Criticism', 564. The Latin means 'The judge is condemned if the guilty person is declared innocent'.

3   'On the Present State of Periodical Criticism', 578.

4   'On the Present State of Periodical Criticism', 578.

5   'On the Present State of Periodical Criticism', 579.

6   'Richard Cumberland', *Prose Works*, 3.211.

7   'On the Present State of Periodical Criticism', 579, 580.

8   'On the Present State of Periodical Criticism', 581.

9   *Prose Works*, 6.196.

10   *Minstrelsy*, 4.125–36.

11   *Sir Tristrem*, in *Poetical Works*, 5.91, 307.

12   *Letters*, 3.280, 2.149.

13   *Life*, 6.92.

14   *Journal*, 6.

15   *Letters*, 1.265, 4.535–36.

16   *Journal*, 94.

17   *Sir Walter Scott's Edinburgh Annual Register*, ed. Kenneth Curry (Knoxville, 1977), 119.

18   *Waverley*, ed. P. D. Garside (Edinburgh, 2007), EEWN 1, 363, 365.

19   *Scott on Himself*, ed. David Hewitt (Edinburgh, 1981), 28.

20   See R. S. Fergusson, 'Two Border Fortresses: Tryermain and Askerton Castles', *Transactions of the Cumberland and Westmorland Antiquarian*

and Archaeological Society, 3 (1876–77), 175–78.
21 See explanatory note to 17.2.
22 *Life*, 1.305.
23 *Journal*, 358.
24 John Frew, 'Scott, Abbotsford and the Antiquaries', in *Abbotsford and Sir Walter Scott: The Image and the Influence*, ed. Iain Gordon Brown (Edinburgh, 2003), 37.
25 Scott himself lived on familiar terms with Shetland, rather than Highland, ponies, among them 'a dwarf of the Shetland race', named Marion, who was his designated companion during his second recuperative period at Sandyknowe (*Life*, 1.90). Although Marion came into the house as she pleased and was fed at Scott's own hand, it is not recorded that she supplemented her regular meals by raiding the corn-chest.
26 See MS 3937, f. 7r.
27 See the discussion of MS 3937, ff. 8r–9v in Essay on the Text, 125–27.
28 See the High Court Minute Books—Series D held by the National Archives of Scotland (NAS), at JC.7/ 37, f. 49v. The trial is recorded on ff. 43r–96r and ff. 186v–199r.
29 This name appears in various other forms, including Murdiston and Murdistone (as in Laidlaw's manuscript, MS 3937, ff. 8r–9v), Murdieson (as in Scott's manuscript, MS 3937, f. 7r), Murdison, and even Murderson.
30 The only person of this name traceable through baptismal records was baptised in Drummelzier on 19 April 1727; the son of Andrew Murdison, he appears to have been the youngest of a family of two girls and four boys. It may be significant, then, that James Hyslop, the principal witness at the trial, stated that 'he knew Alexander Murdison the Prisoner, and his Brothers when Tenants in Drummelzier' (NAS: JC.7/ 37, f. 50r).
31 NAS: JC.7/ 37, f. 44r. The date appears to have been altered from '1771' to '1770'.
32 *Chambers's Miscellany of Useful and Entertaining Tracts*, 20 vols (Edinburgh, 1844–47), 2 (no. 15), 12. An account of Murdieston, Millar and Yarrow appears in an anonymous section entitled 'Anecdotes of Shepherds' Dogs', 12–15. The author quotes lengthy sections of 'Alarming Increase' without acknowledgement but includes additional information. This text is reprinted by Edward Jesse in his *Anecdotes of Dogs*, 2nd edn, (London, 1858), 222–28, where it is ascribed to 'Dr. Anderson' (222). Interestingly, Dr Robert Anderson, editor of *The Works of the British Poets* (1795), spent a night at William Laidlaw's house when Laidlaw was a farmer at Traquair Knowe; the company included William Wordsworth and James Hogg: see W. S. Crockett, *The Scott Country* (London, 1902), 188.
33 NAS: JC.7/ 37, f. 95r.
34 This can be deduced from the information supplied by William Chambers in his *Glenormiston: First Paper* (Edinburgh, 1849), 13.
35 NAS: JC.7/ 37, f. 44r.
36 Mostyn John Armstrong, *A Companion to the Map of the County of Peebles, or Tweedale; Published 20th June 1775* (Edinburgh, [1775]), 47.

37   William Chambers, *Glenormiston*, 13n. Chambers's belief that Murdieston was a 'young man' would conflict with a birthdate of 1727, but it is possible that he was mistaken, or that Murdieston's present problems originated in a 'disorderly' past.

38   For details see the lengthy indictment, which is reproduced in John Maclaurin (Lord Dreghorn), *Arguments and Decisions in Remarkable Cases, Before the High Court of Justiciary, and Other Supreme Courts, in Scotland* (Edinburgh, 1774), 557–66. It was not copied into NAS: JC.7/ 37.

39   *Chambers's Miscellany*, 2 (no. 15),13.

40   *Chambers's Miscellany*, 2 (no. 15),13; NAS: JC.7/ 37, ff. 49v–50r.

41   *Chambers's Miscellany*, 2 (no. 15), 13.

42   NAS: JC.7/ 37, f. 50r.

43   NAS: JC.7/ 37, f. 52r.

44   NAS: JC.7/ 37, f. 50r.

45   *Chambers's Miscellany*, 2 (no. 15),13.

46   NAS: JC.7/ 37, f. 52r.

47   See William Chambers, *A History of Peeblesshire* (Edinburgh and London, 1864), 266. Chambers is quoting from the Burgh Records relating to 27 July, where the provost of Peebles expresses his anxiety concerning the presence of Murdieston and Millar.

48   NAS: JC.7/ 37, ff. 47r, 54v.

49   NAS: JC.7/ 37, ff. 43v, 44r. In 'Alarming Increase' Dundas is named as the 'Advocate Depute'; see note to 32.24–25.

50   NAS: JC.7/ 37, ff. 48r–82v.

51   NAS: JC.7/ 37, f. 83r–v.

52   NAS: JC.7/ 37, ff. 84r–94v.

53   NAS: JC.7/ 37, f. 95v; *Scots Magazine*, 35 (1773), 105.

54   NAS: JC.7/ 37, f. 96r.

55   NAS: JC.7/ 37, f. 188r.

56   NAS: JC.7/ 37, 188v–189r; *Scots Magazine*, 35 (1773), 105.

57   *Scots Magazine*, 35 (1773), 105–07; NAS: JC.7/ 37, f. 189r.

58   *Scots Magazine*, 35 (1773), 105.

59   *Scots Magazine*, 35 (1773), 331; James Boswell, *Boswell for the Defence, 1769–1774*, ed. William K. Wimsatt, Jr, and Frederick A. Pottle (Melbourne, London, Toronto, 1960), 156.

60   Maclaurin, 581–94.

61   See Boswell, 156. Scott informed J. W. Croker, who was planning an edition of Boswell's biography of Johnson, that Boswell 'was very fond of attending on capital punishments, and . . . used to visit the prisoners on the day before execution with the singular wish to make the condemned wretches laugh by dint of buffoonery, in which he not infrequently succeeded' (*Letters*, 11.117: 30 January 1829).

62   *Scots Magazine*, 35 (1773), 331. Boswell was among the watching throng, and observed in his diary, 'Effect diminished as each went' (Boswell, 156).

63   NAS: JC.7/ 37, f. 67r/v.

64   MS 3925, f. 168v: Scott to [Blackwood], 24 April [1818]. This letter opens 'Dear Sir', and bears no address or year, but it is included

amongst a small collection of letters to various members of the Blackwood family.

65 Magnum, 35.197–99.

66 The manuscript of the note in the Interleaved Copy of *Redgauntlet* (MS
23027) begins on the leaf facing 467 and continues on the leaves facing
466 and 465.

67 For a detailed history of the Independent Companies see Peter Simpson,
The Independent Highland Companies 1603–1760 (Edinburgh, 1996).

68 Simpson, 115.

69 Magnum, 35.197.

70 Magnum, 35.198.

71 As the *Redgauntlet* note is in Scott's own voice, 'Donald' is unlikely to
result from fictionalisation of the story as Scott heard it, but perhaps
Scott had forgotten, or indeed never knew, the Captain's first name.
We are told in 'Phantasmagoria', where the name 'Donald' does not
appear, that the widow addresses him 'by his name and surname'
(44.12), that is, by his family name and designation.

72 The large companies originally consisted of about 70 men (increased
to about 110), while the small companies began with about 40 (increased
to about 70). For exact numbers see H. D. Macwilliam, *A Black Watch
Episode of the Year 1731* (Edinburgh and London, 1908), 1–5.

73 The orders for the raising of the six companies (12 May 1725), and for
their augmentation (27 January 1727), are reproduced in Macwilliam, 3–5.

74 Macwilliam, 2.

75 Simpson, 113; Macwilliam, 8 (note 5).

76 Simpson, 114, 201.

77 Simpson, 114.

78 The orders for raising the companies are addressed to the captain of
the company 'or to the Officer or Officers appointed by him to Raise
Voluntiers for that Company' (Macwilliam, 4).

79 Macwilliam, 2.

80 Simpson, 126–28, 151.

81 Alastair Campbell, *A History of Clan Campbell*, 3 vols (Edinburgh,
2000–04), 3.191.

82 David Stewart, *Sketches of the Character, Manners, and Present State of the
Highlanders of Scotland with Details of the Military Service of the Highland Regiments*, 2nd edn, 2 vols (Edinburgh, 1822), 1.250–54; Simpson,
118–19.

83 For the list see Andrew Ross, 'The Historic Succession of the Black
Watch', in *A Military History of Perthshire 1660–1902*, ed. Marchioness
of Tullibardine (Perth, 1908), 51–53; this list is reproduced in Simpson,
207–08. For Stewart's list see Stewart, 1.245–46.

84 Ross, 52.

85 Magnum, 35.197.

86 For details see Essay on the Text, 132–34.

87 See Magnum, 41.xxxiii; *Chronicles of the Canongate*, EEWN 20, 410.

88 *Letters*, 5.134–35: Scott to Daniel Terry, 30 April 1818.

89 *Letters*, 5.162: Scott to Mrs Lindsay [of Balcarres], 13
June 1818.

90   See *Chronicles of the Canongate*, ed. Claire Lamont, EEWN
     20, 62.8–17.
91   *Letters*, 5.161 (note 2).
92   *Letters*, 7.62: Scott to Joanna Baillie, [10 February 1822].
93   Magnum, 41.292.
94   *Letters*, 7.63: Scott to Joanna Baillie, [10 February 1822].
95   See Essay on the Text, 153.
96   *Letters*, 7.63; Magnum, 41.292–93.
97   *Letters*, 7.63.
98   *The Looker-on: a Periodical Paper, by the Rev. Simon Olive-branch, A. M.*
     was written by William Roberts in 86 numbers between 1792 and 1794
     (93 in the collected version), and was subsequently included in *The
     British Essayists*, ed. Alexander Chalmers, 45 vols (London, 1808; CLA,
     334), as volumes 41–44.
99   *The Looker-on*, no. 5 (24 March 1792); *The British Essayists*, 41.52–53.
100 *The Looker-on*, no. 15 (28 April 1792); *The British Essayists*, 41.144–45.
101 *Letters*, 3.259: Scott to Brevoort, 23 April 1813.
102 *Letters*, 6.46: Scott to Irving, 4 December 1819.
103 *Salmagundi; or, The Whim-Whams and Opinions of Launcelot Langstaff,
     Esq. and Others*, ed. from the American edn by John Lambert, 2 vols
     (London, 1811), 1.148. The relevant issue, 8, is dated 18 April 1807.
104 *A Legend of the Wars of Montrose*, ed. J. H. Alexander, EEWN 7b,
     183.20–23. In the very letter to Blackwood in which he heralds 'Phant-
     asmagoria' he thanks him for *Marriage*, praising it for 'the singular merit
     that the 3d and last volume is the best which seldom or never happens'
     (MS 3925, f. 168r). Later, in the Introductory Epistle to *The Fortunes
     of Nigel* (1822), Captain Clutterbuck reports the 'Author of Waverley'
     as saying, 'Let fame follow those who have a substantial shape. A shadow
     —and an impersonal author is nothing better—can cast no shade' (*The
     Fortunes of Nigel*, ed. Frank Jordan, EEWN 13, 8.29–31).
105 Mary Ann Hughes, *Letters and Recollections of Sir Walter Scott*, ed. Horace
     H. Hutchinson (London, 1904), 146–47.
106 *Journal*, 457.
107 Hughes, 148.
108 Magnum, 41.292.
109 Magnum, 41.293–94.
110 For Margaret Swinton as a source of the story in *The Bride of Lammer-
     moor* see Scott's note in *Peveril of the Peak* (Magnum, 28.92), and for
     his mother see *Letters*, 6.118–19.
111 For the earliest version see Robert Chambers, *Traditions of Edinburgh*,
     2 vols (Edinburgh, 1825), 1.251–52; for a later and more elaborate
     version in Chambers's last revision of the work, see *Traditions of Edin-
     burgh* (Edinburgh, 1869), 76–79.
112 See *Letters*, 9.180–81; *Traditions of Edinburgh* (1869), x.
113 G. P. R. James, *Darnley, or the Field of the Cloth of Gold* (London,
     1830).
114 Wilfred Partington, *The Private Letter-Books of Sir Walter Scott* (London,
     1830), 236.
115 Thomas Nashe, *The Works of Thomas Nashe*, ed. Ronald B. McKerrow,

rev. F. P. Wilson, 5 vols (Oxford, 1958), 2.254.

116 Nashe, 2.253.

117 Henry Cornelius Agrippa (1486–1535), *Three Books of Occult Philosophy*, trans. J. F. [John French] (London, 1651): *CLA*, 148. See Walter Scott, *Letters on Demonology and Witchcraft* (London, 1830), 186, 190.

118 An English translation of this work, entitled 'Of Occult Philosophy, or, Of Magical Ceremonies: The Fourth Book', appeared in a one-volume collection of similar works entitled *Henry Cornelius Agrippa, His Fourth Book of Occult Philosophy*, trans. Robert Turner (London, 1655), 32–71.

119 Agrippa, 'The Fourth Book', 60.

120 Agrippa, 'The Fourth Book', 60.

121 *The Lay of the Last Minstrel*, Canto 6, stanza 17, in *Poetical Works*, 6.201.

122 Agrippa, 'The Fourth Book', 60.

123 Scott also made use of this story of the magic mirror in *The Bride of Lammermoor* where one of the charges against Ailsie Gourlay is 'that she had, by the aid and delusions of Satan, shewn to a young person of quality, in a mirror glass, a gentleman then abroad, to whom the said young person was betrothed, and who appeared in the vision to be in the act of bestowing his hand upon another lady' (ed. J. H. Alexander, EEWN 7a, 241.13–17).

124 Sir John Lauder, Lord Fountainhall, *Chronological Notes of Scottish Affairs, from 1680 to 1701*, ed. Walter Scott (Edinburgh, 1822), 33–34. According to Fountainhall's account Home was later killed 'in the wars abroad' (Fountainhall, 33).

125 *Letters*, 8.250: 6 April [1824].

126 The escutcheons on the ceiling of the hall at Abbotsford include those of his three other maternal great-grandparents but not that of the Sinclairs, suggesting that Scott was unaware of this part of his ancestry.

127 A birth date for Anne Sinclair has not been found but since she was a child of the second marriage it must have been after 1667 when her father had a child by his first marriage.

128 Two of Scott's great-grandmothers were Campbells but neither belonged to the family of the Loudon Campbells.

129 Magnum, 28.92.

130 MS 911, f. 271r. For Scott's letter to Cadell see MS 15980, f. 162r.

131 See *Life*, 2.121.

132 *BEM*, 3 (September 1818), 705–07.

133 We have adopted the masculine pronoun for convenience; we do not preclude the possibility of the author's being a woman.

134 C. O. Parsons, 'Scott's Prior Version of "The Tapestried Chamber"', *Notes and Queries*, 107 (1962), 417–20. Parsons believed that he was following Andrew Lang in this opinion. Lang's view is expressed, however, somewhat ambiguously. In his introduction to the relevant volume of the Border Edition he writes that '"The Tapestried Chamber" is a fair example of the conventional ghost story. Scott may have forgotten that it had been published before in "Blackwood's Magazine" for 1818' (*Chronicles of the Canongate*, ed. Andrew Lang (London, 1894), x). For Parsons's reading of Lang's comment, see 'Scott's Prior Version of

"The Tapestried Chamber"', 417.

135 See Alan Lang Strout, 'The Authorship of Articles in *Blackwood's Magazine*, Numbers xvii–xxiv (August 1818–March 1819)', *The Library*, 5th series, 11 (1956), 187, 199–200. The two lists seen by Strout have now disappeared.

136 See Essay on the Text, 116–19.

137 MS 4937, f. 75r: Scott to William Blackwood, 18 October 1817.

138 See Parsons, 417.

139 James Hogg, *Memoir of the Author's Life and Familiar Anecdotes of Sir Walter Scott*, in James Hogg, *Anecdotes of Scott*, ed. Jill Rubenstein (Edinburgh, 1999), 55–56.

140 *The Spy*, no. 3 (15 September 1810) and no. 4 (22 September 1810): see James Hogg, *The Spy: A Periodical Paper of Literary Amusement and Instruction*, ed. Gillian Hughes (Edinburgh, 2000), 21–29, 32–43.

141 James Hogg, *Winter Evening Tales*, ed. Ian Duncan (Edinburgh, 2002), 11. This last story, however, may be a traditional one; it appears, for example, in George Wallace Crabbe, *Scottish Humour, Songs and Lore* (Melbourne, *c.* 1905), 23, in a version which does not appear to derive from Hogg, as the setting is Falkirk Tryst, the shopkeeper a pharmacist, and the emphasis on the buyer rather than the seller of the vitriol. Did Scott in fact use a traditional, almost proverbial, expression in his conversation with Hogg, an expression which led Hogg to incorporate the story itself into his expanded version of 'Basil Lee'?

142 *BEM*, 3 (September 1818), 705.

143 See Alan Lang Strout, *A Bibliography of Articles in "Blackwood's Magazine" Volumes I through XVIII, 1817—1825*, Library Bulletin no. 5, Texas Technological College (Lubbock, Texas, 1959), 45.

144 See Brian M. Murray, 'More Unidentified or Disputed Articles in *Blackwood's Magazine*', *Studies in Scottish Literature*, 9 (1971–72), 108.

145 See MS Acc 12200, f. 1r–v (John Wilson to Alexander Blair, 4 June 1822): 'Before I left Edinr I lookd over the printing of last No of Ebony who was in London. He cast me an article in your handwriting but as I think written by your Sister. Such articles do good to a Magazine, and it interests me: but it is very dry & dusty; & Ebony, who is a shrewd man, asked me if I thought it was done by yourself. Tell your excellent & most gifted Sister to make her articles a little more amusing. . . . Why do you not write, my good Alexander Blair? Ebony is in great spirits about Maga and it sells beyond all the others. It seems to be less detested & indeed less detestable than formerly; & may settle down into a good Periodical Work.'

146 Irving's letters provide evidence of his dealings with Blackwood; see especially his letters to Peter Irving of 1, 6 and 22 September 1817, in Washington Irving, *Letters*, ed. Ralph M. Aderman, Herbert L. Kleinfield and Jenifer S. Banks, 4 vols (Boston, 1978–82), 1.501, 503, 506.

147 Washington Irving, 'The Adventure of my Uncle', in *Tales of a Traveller*, 2 vols (London, 1824), 1.16–41.

148 See Blackwood's letter to William Maginn ('RTS') of 18 October 1820, in Margaret Oliphant, *Annals of a Publishing House: William Blackwood and His Sons*, 3rd edn, 2 vols (Edinburgh, 1897), 1.378.

149 In draft form Irving's story may have been even closer to the original,
     for it is clear from his journals and notebooks that he worked hard at
     lengthening and improving it. See Washington Irving, *Journals and Note-
     books*, 5 vols (Madison, Wisconsin, 1969–86), Vol. 3 ed. Walter A.
     Reichart, 3.294, 305, 318, 321, 329, 332. Irving also borrowed works
     on French history from the Bibliothèque nationale in order to enrich
     his tale. See Judith Giblin Haig's introduction to *Tales of a Traveller*
     (Boston, Massachusetts, 1987), xviii.
150 See *Tales of a Traveller* (1824), 1.xi–xiii.
151 *CLA*, 201; *Journal*, 708.
152 Neal Frank Doubleday briefly discusses 'The Adventure of My Uncle',
     finding its events and circumstances 'surprisingly parallel' to those of
     'The Tapestried Chamber', in 'Washington Irving and the Mysterious
     Portrait', in his *Variety of Attempt: British and American Fiction in the
     Early Nineteenth Century* (Lincoln, Nebraska, and London, 1976),
     41–42, 47–48 (note 4).
153 For Doubleday, 'since it seems unlikely that Scott would have pub-
     lished his tale in the form we have it had he realized its great likeness
     to Irving's', an unconscious memory of Irving's tale must have been
     involved. See 'Washington Irving and the Mysterious Portrait', 48
     (note 4).
154 *The Bride of Lammermoor*, EEWN 7a, 262.21–22.
155 See *Letters*, 6.119.
156 Scott was notorious for his oral embellishment of other people's anec-
     dotes. According to C. R. Leslie, he 'amplified, digressed, and in relating
     anything he had heard, added touches of his own that were always
     charming'. When Lord Eldin remonstrated with Scott that he had stolen
     one of his stories and 'decorated' it to such a degree that it was almost
     unrecognisable, Scott replied, 'Do you think . . . I'd tell one of your
     stories, or of any body's, and not put a laced coat and a cocked hat
     upon it?': Charles Robert Leslie, *Autobiographical Recollections*, ed. Tom
     Taylor, 2 vols (London, 1860), 1.237.
157 John Ferriar, *An Essay Towards a Theory of Apparitions* (London, 1813);
     Samuel Hibbert, *Sketches of the Philosophy of Apparitions; or, An Attempt
     to Trace Such Illusions to Their Physical Causes* (Edinburgh, 1824).
158 *Letters on Demonology and Witchcraft* (1830), 357–58.
159 MS 911, f. 51r.
160 The manor at Creslow in Buckinghamshire, for instance, is believed to
     house the ghost of a 14th-century lady who is seldom seen but whose
     movements may be traced by the rustling of her silk dress. See *The
     Other World; or, Glimpses of the Supernatural*, ed. Frederick George
     Lee, 2 vols (London, 1875), 2.92–96. Sabine Baring-Gould's mother
     used to recount hearing the high-heeled shoes of the White Lady of
     Lew Trenchard House, known as Madame Gould, proceeding down
     the corridor. See William Henderson, *Notes on the Folk-Lore of the North-
     ern Counties of England and the Borders* (London, 1866), 277.
161 In view of the location of this tradition in Devon, it is interesting that
     Scott changed the setting of 'The Tapestried Chamber' from the 'mid-
     land' to 'western' counties in the manuscript.

162 See Joseph Braddock, *Haunted Houses* (London, 1956), 48–51. Far-quhar (1738–1819) numbered among his patients Lord Melville and the future George IV.

163 *Letters on Demonology and Witchcraft* (1830), 391–92.

164 *Minstrelsy of the Scottish Border*, 5th edn, 3 vols (London and Edinburgh, 1812), 1.225 (*Minstrelsy*, 2.91–92).

165 William Scott, *The Border Exploits* (Hawick, 1812).

166 Scott's name appears in the list of subscribers to *The Border Exploits* (379), and he may have had some contact with its author.

167 William Scott, 227.

168 William Scott, 228–29.

169 William Scott, 234.

170 See William B. Todd and Ann Bowden, *Sir Walter Scott: A Bibliographical History, 1796–1832* (New Castle, Delaware, 1998), 31, citing the *Morning Chronicle*.

171 *Letters*, 6.332–33, with alteration of Grierson's punctuation in the first sentence.

172 *Minstrelsy*, 1.189, 2.91, 2.93.

173 *Athenæum* (1835), 55–56.

174 *Minstrelsy*, 2.80, 103.

175 *Minstrelsy*, 2.71.

176 *Life*, 1.200.

177 *Life*, 1.194. Shortreed, however, makes no mention of the Laird's Jock's stone in his account of the 'raids' as recorded by his son; see MS 8993, printed as J. E. Shortreed, 'Conversations with my Father on the Subject of his Tours with Sir Walter Scott in Liddesdale', in W. E. Wilson, 'Robert Shortreed's Account of His Visits to Liddesdale with Sir Walter Scott', *Transactions of the Hawick Archaeological Society* (1932), 57–63.

178 *Prose Works*, 7.96–97.

179 See Joseph Nicolson and Richard Burn, *The History and Antiquities of the Counties of Westmorland and Cumberland*, 2 vols (London, 1777), 1.xxxi.

180 *Minstrelsy*, 2.91.

181 *Calendar of Papers relating to the affairs of the Borders of England and Scotland (The Border Papers)*, ed. Joseph Bain, 2 vols (Edinburgh, 1894), 1.121.

182 *Minstrelsy*, 2.92.

183 *Minstrelsy*, 2.96.

184 *Minstrelsy*, 2.93.

185 *The Border Papers*, 1.123.

186 *Minstrelsy*, 2.116.

187 Magnum, 9.101n.

188 Royal Commission on the Ancient Monuments of Scotland, *An Inventory of the Ancient and Historical Monuments of Roxburghshire* (Edinburgh, 1956), 1.95.

189 James Logan Mack, *The Border Line* (Edinburgh and London, 1924), 163.

190 The error is unlikely to be Scott's as both names appear in the correct forms in Scott's introduction to *Rob Roy* (Magnum, 7.cviii).

191 *Athenæum* (1835), 56.

192 Although the story appears in *The Keepsake for 1832* with the author's name given as 'Sir Walter Scott, Bart.', the usual ascription (as in 'Death of the Laird's Jock') was 'The Author of Waverley', even although he had acknowledged his authorship in 1828.

193 University of London Library, MS SL V 27, f. 4r.

194 *Journal*, 442.

195 George Robert Gleig's *Allan Breck*, 3 vols (London, 1834), tells the story of Allan Breck and of the Appin Murder under different names and with some variation of the historical details.

196 Compare, for example, John Cameron's claim that 'it is in the highest degree improbable that in fact James Stewart had any antecedent complicity in the crime, whoever was the actual assassin' ('The Appin Murder: A Summing Up', *Scottish Historical Review*, 33 (1954), 98) with the opinion of Sir James Fergusson: 'the question . . . is whether James Stewart knew that an attempt was to be made on Glenure's life. To me this seems impossible to doubt' ('The Appin Murder Case', in *The White Hind and Other Discoveries* (London, 1963), 155).

197 *Rob Roy*, EEWN 5, 380–81.

198 Introduction to *Rob Roy*, Magnum, 7.cviii.

199 For example, Mungo Campbell, Glenure's nephew who was present at the murder, wrote to an unnamed correspondent that 'From Glenure's words and the situation of the place where I saw one of the villains there's reason to believe that there were more than one on the spot'. He also suggested that Allan Breck 'was made the instrument but numbers were his associates.' (Letter of 23 May 1752, printed in *Highland Papers*, ed. J. R. N. Macphail (Edinburgh, 1911–34), 4.127, 128 (Publications of the Scottish History Society, third series, 22).)

200 The manuscript reads 'not a very old man' (University of London Library, MS SL V 27, f. 4r).

201 It is possible that Scott met him in Appin although the reference to streets renders this unlikely. On the disputed dating of Scott's visit to Appin see Angus Stewart, 'Sir Walter Scott and the Tenants of Invernenty', *The Stair Society: Miscellany Four*, ed. Hector L. MacQueen (Edinburgh, 2002), 233–42.

202 *Muster Roll of Prince Charles Edward Stuart's Army 1745–46*, ed. Alastair Livingstone, Christian W. H. Aikman, and Betty Stuart Hart (Aberdeen, 1984), 12–16.

203 That Duncan Stewart in Inshaig was the same as the Duncan who was younger brother of the laird of Achnacone seems to be confirmed by two tombstones at a graveyard near Tynribbie in the Strath of Appin. The first reads, 'Sacred to the memory of Duncan Stewart third son of Dougald Stewart Esq. of Achnacone. Of Ann Stewart his spouse, daughter of John Stewart Esq. of Fasnacloich. Of their son Alexander Stewart late tenant of Isiag and of Elizabeth Stewart his spouse and their children. This stone is placed here by order of Duncan Stewart Esq. Capt of the 35th Regt. of Foot, son of Alexander and Elizabeth Stewart, from a pious regard to the remains of these intered underneath. Anno Domini 1818'. The second reads, 'Sacred to the memory of the

descendants of Duncan Stewart late tacksman of Isaig, third son of
Dougald Stewart Esqr of Achnacon. This stone is placed here by Dun-
can Stewart Esqr. late Captain in His Majesty's 35 Regt. of Foot. Anno
Domini 1819'. See Dorothy Stewart Linney, 'Notes on Some Stewart
Burying-Places in Appin', *The Stewarts*, 8 (1947–50), 320–21.
Although Linney repeats the commonly held opinion that 'Duncan
Stewart, third son of Dugald, sixth of Achnacone, was killed at Culloden'
it is clear that he was the Duncan Stewart who was tacksman of Inshaig
in 1752 since, if he had died in 1746, his son Alexander alone would
have been named in the documentation surrounding the Appin Murder
whereas in fact both are named.

204　　*The Dewar Manuscripts*, ed. John Mackechnie (Glasgow, 1964), 201–03.

205　　See John Campbell's letter of 2 September 1752 to Campbell of Bar-
　　　caldine: 'I much wish some thing coud come out of the Shooting Match',
　　　printed in Appendix 18 to *Trial of James Stewart*, ed. David N. Mackay
　　　(Edinburgh, 1931), 386.

206　　John H. J. Stewart and Duncan Stewart, *The Stewarts of Appin* (Edin-
　　　burgh, 1880), 156.

207　　Mackay, 367.

208　　MS 315, f. 61v–62r: Captain Alexander Campbell to John Campbell
　　　of Barcaldine, 31 July 1752.

209　　From an unsigned memorandum prepared by one of those investigating
　　　the case and listing actions to be taken; MS 315, f. 120v.

210　　Angus Stewart, 'A Memorial and Opinion of 1762 Given by Robert
　　　McQueen, Later Lord Braxfield', *The Stair Society: Miscellany Three*,
　　　ed. W. M. Gordon (Edinburgh, 1992), 202.

211　　Lee Holcombe, *Ancient Animosity: the Appin Murder and the End of
　　　Scottish Rebellion* ([Bloomington, Indiana], 2004), 521.

212　　*The Dewar Manuscripts*, 216.

EXPLANATORY NOTES

In these notes a comprehensive attempt is made to identify Scott's sources, and all quotations, references, historical events, and historical personages, to explain proverbs, and to translate difficult or obscure language. (Phrases are explained in the notes while single words are treated in the glossary.) The notes are brief; they offer information rather than critical comment or exposition. When a quotation has not been traced this is stated: any new information from readers will be welcomed. When quotations reproduce their sources accurately, the reference is given without comment; verbal differences in the source are indicated by a prefatory 'see', while a general rather than a verbal indebtedness is indicated by 'compare'. References are to standard editions or to the editions Scott himself owned. For Scott's novels a reference is given to the EEWN text by page and line number where possible, and otherwise to the volume, page and line numbers of the first edition. Books in the Abbotsford Library are identified by reference to the appropriate page of the *Catalogue of the Library at Abbotsford* (*CLA*), preceded by the word 'see' if Scott had a different edition from the one cited. Biblical references, unless otherwise stated, are to the Authorised Version. Plays by Shakespeare are cited without authorial ascription and references are to *William Shakespeare: The Complete Works*, edited by Peter Alexander (London and Glasgow, 1951, frequently reprinted). Unless otherwise stated, manuscripts referred to are in the National Library of Scotland.

The following publications are distinguished by abbreviations, or are given without the names of their authors, in the notes and essays:

BEM   *Blackwood's Edinburgh Magazine.*
CLA   [J. G. Cochrane], *Catalogue of the Library at Abbotsford* (Edinburgh, 1838).
Corson   James C. Corson, *Notes and Index to Sir Herbert Grierson's Edition of the Letters of Sir Walter Scott* (Oxford, 1979).
EEWN   The Edinburgh Edition of the Waverley Novels (Edinburgh, 1993–).
Journal   *The Journal of Sir Walter Scott*, ed. W. E. K. Anderson (Oxford, 1972).
Kinsley   *The Poems and Songs of Robert Burns*, ed. James Kinsley, 3 vols (Oxford, 1968).
Letters   *The Letters of Sir Walter Scott*, ed. H. J. C. Grierson and others, 12 vols (London, 1932–37).
Life   J. G. Lockhart, *Memoirs of the Life of Sir Walter Scott, Bart.*, 7 vols (Edinburgh, 1837–38).
Magnum   Walter Scott, *Waverley Novels*, 48 vols (Edinburgh, 1829–33).
Minstrelsy   Walter Scott, *Minstrelsy of the Scottish Border*, ed. T. F. Henderson, 4 vols (Edinburgh, 1902).
ODEP   *The Oxford Dictionary of English Proverbs*, 3rd edn, rev. F. P. Wilson (Oxford, 1970).
OED   *The Oxford English Dictionary*, 2nd edn, ed. J. A. Simpson and E. S. C. Weiner, 20 vols (Oxford, 1989).
Poetical Works   *The Poetical Works of Sir Walter Scott, Bart.*, ed. J. G. Lockhart, 12 vols (Edinburgh, 1833–34).

230   EXPLANATORY NOTES

Prose Works   *The Prose Works of Sir Walter Scott, Bart.*, 28 vols (Edinburgh, 1834–36).
Ray   J[ohn] Ray, *A Complete Collection of English Proverbs*, 3rd edn (London, 1737): *CLA*, 169.

EXPLANATORY NOTES TO 'THE INFERNO OF ALTISIDORA'

1.10   a new book fairly bound   i.e. Miguel de Cervantes Saavedra, *Don Quixote*, Part 2 (1615).

1.12   Motteux' Translation   the English version of *Don Quixote* used by Scott in the 'Inferno' is the translation first published 1700–03 by Peter Motteux (1663–1718) and others, as revised by John Ozell (d. 1743). The revised version first appeared in 1719; Scott owned the reprint of 1766 (*CLA*, 317).

1.18–19   a bachelor of fifty, or, by'r lady, some fifty-five years standing   see *1 Henry IV*, 2.4.410.

1.23   beau garçon   *French* fine fellow, fop.

1.23   Lady Rumpus   minor character in *The Lounger*, a periodical edited by the novelist Henry Mackenzie (1745–1831) between 1785–87; see especially no. 4 (26 February 1785).

1.23–24   Miss Tibby Dasher   not identified; her name suggests a character from a play or a periodical such as *The Lounger*, but she is possibly Scott's invention. *Tibby* is a Scots diminutive of both Elizabeth and Isabella, while *Dasher* implies that she dresses well and fashionably.

1.24   oyster parties   small private gatherings revolving around the consumption of raw oysters and porter, followed by dancing, which took place in taverns known as 'oyster cellars', which were numerous and fashionable in Edinburgh in the 1780s.

1.24   the lovely Lucy J——   Lucy Johnstone of Hilton (1765–97), an Edinburgh belle, noted also as an amateur composer and celebrated by Burns in 'O wat ye wha's in yon town' (1796; Kinsley, no. 488).

1.25   St Cecilia's Hall   built in the Cowgate 1761–63 as a concert hall for the Edinburgh Musical Society; also a popular venue for dances in the 18th century.

1.26   Miss B——t   Elizabeth Burnett (1765–90), second daughter of James Burnett, Lord Monboddo, Scottish judge and Enlightenment anthropologist. Burns praised her beauty in stanza 4 of his 'Address to Edinburgh' (1786; Kinsley, no. 135) and wrote an elegy for her after her early death from consumption (1791; Kinsley, no. 324).

1.26–27   as the learned Partridge pathetically observes, non sum qualis eram   in *Tom Jones* (1749) by Henry Fielding (1707–54) Partridge remarks 'non sum qualis eram' (I am not what I was), quoting the words of Horace (Quintus Horatius Flaccus, 65–8 BC), in *Odes*, 4.1.3, both to Tom (Bk 15, Ch. 12) and to Squire Allworthy (Bk 18, Ch. 5).

1.29   the New Theatre Royal   the first Theatre Royal in Edinburgh opened in 1769 in Shakespeare Square, at the east end of Princes Street on the site of the former Post Office building. Scott became a trustee and shareholder in 1809.

1.30–31   selected as a proper beau to the General Assembly   the annual meeting in May of the General Assembly, the supreme governing body of the Church of Scotland, was also an important social occasion.

2.3   beadles   minor parish officers who kept order in church, punished offenders, and attended upon the minister.

2.4   Ruling Elder   one of a group of officials appointed in each parish of the Church of Scotland (which is Presbyterian in government) to manage

church affairs and maintain moral discipline in conjunction with the minister.
2.4 Argyle's square once part of a fashionable district on the site of the Royal Scottish Museum in Chambers Street, Edinburgh, which developed S of the Old Town in the 1730s, prior to the construction of the New Town to the N.
2.5 petits soupers *French* small informal supper-parties.
2.16–17 Mr Creech's shop the High Street shop of William Creech (1745–1815), Edinburgh bookseller and publisher, a popular meeting place for the literati. The shop was at the E end of the Luckenbooths, which were in the High St on the N side of the High Kirk (St Giles Cathedral).
2.20 Adam Smith philosopher and political economist (1723–90), author of *The Theory of Moral Sentiments* (1759) and *The Wealth of Nations* (1776), and generally regarded as the founder of modern economics.
2.20 Ferguson Adam Ferguson (1723–1816), philosopher and historian, author of *An Essay on the History of Civil Society* (1767) and *The History of the Progress and Termination of the Roman Republic* (1783).
2.20 Robertson William Robertson (1721–93), historian, author of the widely praised *The History of Scotland during the Reigns of Queen Mary and of King James VI* (1759) and *The History of the Reign of Charles V* (1769), and Principal of the University of Edinburgh from 1762.
2.20 both the Humes David Hume (1711–76), philosopher and historian, best known for *A Treatise of Human Nature* (1739), *An Enquiry Concerning the Principles of Morals* (1751), and his hugely popular *The History of England, from the Invasion of Julius Caesar to the Revolution in 1688*, completed in 1762; and John Home (1722–1808), Church of Scotland minister and author of *Douglas* (first performed 1756). David Hume changed the spelling of his name but both spellings are pronounced 'Hume'.
2.21 Lord Kaimes Henry Home (1696–1782), made a judge of the Court of Session as Lord Kames in 1752, a writer on law, ethics, history, literature and agriculture.
2.22–23 the Man of Feeling, and other distinguished members of the Mirror Club Henry Mackenzie (1745–1831) was known as the Man of Feeling after publishing the novel of that name in 1771; he was the prime mover and editor of *The Mirror* (1779–80) and *The Lounger* (1785–87), supported by other members of the Mirror Club most of whom were afterwards judges of the Court of Session, such as William Craig (1745–1813), Alexander Abercromby (1745–95), and William Macleod Bannatyne (1744–1833).
2.23–24 Johnie M'——n perhaps John McGowan, Scottish lawyer and antiquary (d. 1803); see *Letters*, 11.262.
2.24 the facetious Captain Grose Francis Grose (1731–91), English antiquary, draughtsman, and lexicographer. He published *The Antiquities of England and Wales* (1772–83); his *Classical Dictionary of the Vulgar Tongue* (1785) and *A Provincial Glossary, with a Collection of Local Proverbs, and Popular Superstitions* (1787) were at the time the largest collections of non-standard words. He visited Scotland in 1788, 1789 and 1790 for antiquarian research, which resulted in *The Antiquities of Scotland* (2 vols, 1789–91); Burns's 'Tam o' Shanter' was published for the first time in Vol. 2. From 1765 Grose was a captain in the militia, and he was apparently a very amusing man, which may account for 'facetious'. But 'the facetious Captain Grose' seems to have been a stock phrase, e.g. used by W. H. Ireland (1777–1835), in *Stultifera Navis* (1807), 239n, and again by Scott in *Letters on Demonology and Witchcraft* (1830), 370.
2.26–27 hearing the tremendous Dr. Johnson . . . North British literati Samuel Johnson (1709–84), lexicographer, poet, critic, and man of

letters, visited Scotland in 1773, as documented in James Boswell's *Journal of a Tour to the Hebrides with Samuel Johnson, LL.D.* (1785). For the nervous silence of Scottish professors in his presence, especially at Aberdeen and Glasgow, see Boswell's entries for 23 August and 29 October 1773. *North British* was often used to designate matters Scottish in the 18th century.

2.28–29 Slender . . . chain see *The Merry Wives of Windsor*, 1.1.268–70. Sackerson was a bear kept in Paris Garden, in Southwark on the S side of the Thames, in Shakespeare's time.

2.35 the High School the High School of Edinburgh, whose origins as a burgh school go back to at least 1519. Scott was a pupil 1779–83, when the school was located near the E end of the Cowgate. The building, now part of the University of Edinburgh, stands in High School Yards in Infirmary St.

3.6–23 the account which Altisidora gives . . . contented see Cervantes, *Don Quixote*, Part 2 (1615), Ch. 70, in the Motteux and Ozell translation (see note to 1.12).

3.11 Flanders lace fine lace made in Flanders (the W half of modern Belgium), where the flax was of very high quality.

3.32–33 the high-way to the place of perdition . . . neither broad, nor flowery, nor easy Scott here conflates the descriptions of the path to hell in several sources, such as Matthew 7.13, Virgil's *Aeneid*, 6.126, *All's Well that Ends Well*, 4.5.48–49, and 'Thomas the Rhymer', in *Minstrelsy*, 4.88.

3.33–35 In steepness, indeed, and in mephitic fragrance . . . the descent of Avernus see Virgil, *Aeneid* (29–19 BC), 6.236–42. Here and in the following lines Scott depicts the approach to Ballantyne's printing-house, which was situated at Paul's Work at North Back of Canongate and could be entered from the Canongate by 'the long, narrow, and steep Coull's Close' ([W. L. Carrie and W. T. Dobson], *The Ballantyne Press and its Founders 1796–1908* (Edinburgh, 1909), 21).

3.36–37 the more ancient part of our good city the Old Town of Edinburgh extending between the Castle and Holyroodhouse, as opposed to the fashionable New Town laid out to the N in the later 18th century. 'Good city', or more often 'good town', is a regular sobriquet for Edinburgh.

3.40 no iron-heeled beau of the present day dandies of the Regency period such as 'Beau' Brummell (1778–1840) had iron clips fitted to the heels of their shoes or boots in order to draw attention to themselves.

3.41–42 a very large building, with a court-yard in front Ballantyne's printing house, a large building formed from several adjoining houses, was entered from a small courtyard: see [W. L. Carrie and W. T. Dobson], *The Ballantyne Press and its Founders 1796–1908* (Edinburgh, 1909), 144, and illustration facing 143.

3.42 Tartarus in classical mythology, the deepest region of the underworld, where punishment was exacted.

4.1 neither Minos nor Æacus, neither Belial nor Beelzebub i.e. neither the judges of the dead in classical myth, nor the devils of Christianity. Minos, the king of Crete, and the Greek hero Æacus were believed to have become judges of the dead in the underworld. 'Belial', a name traditionally associated with Satan, is used for one of the fallen angels in Milton's *Paradise Lost* (1667, revised 1674), 2.108–18. Beelzebub, a Philistine deity, was the 'prince of the devils' (Matthew 12.24; Mark 3.22), and Christian commentators identify Beelzebub with Satan on the strength of Matthew 12.24–27, Mark 3.22–26, and Luke 11.15–20; in *Paradise Lost* he appears among the fallen angels as Satan's second-in-command (1.78–81).

4.2–4 the building . . . Pandemonium . . . abode of Hela i.e. the building resembled James Ballantyne's printing house more than Satan's palace in Milton's *Paradise Lost* (see especially Books 1 and 2), the classical underworld as described by Virgil (see *Aeneid*, Bk 6) or the Scandinavian Helheim.

4.4 Cerberus in classical mythology, a monstrous three-headed dog which guarded the entrance to the underworld. The entrance to Ballantyne's printing-house was 'guarded' by the time-keeper, for many years a Mr Smith (see [W. L. Carrie and W. T. Dobson], *The Ballantyne Press and its Founders 1796–1908* (Edinburgh, 1909), 144–45).

4.7 an English bull-dog in 1803 Scott was offered 'a monstrous sort of bull-dog' called Cerberus which was alleged to be the offspring of his own dog Camp (*Letters*, 1.205–06).

4.10 the fetters and chains in front of Newgate the twin portals of Newgate Prison in the City of London, as designed by George Dance the Younger (1741–1825), were surmounted by iron fetters and chains. The original prison was replaced in 1770–78, destroyed in the Gordon Riots in 1780, and again rebuilt to Dance's design in 1780–83; the building was demolished in 1902–03.

4.32 Astaroth goddess of war and sexual love in the ancient Middle East, and one of the fallen angels in *Paradise Lost* (1.437–46).

4.32 Belphegor Moabite god of licentiousness in the Old Testament and a demon of medieval legend.

4.35–37 one old gentleman . . . bare-faced Richard Cumberland (1732–1811), author of close to fifty plays and three novels, edited *The London Review* (1809), a short-lived critical journal intended as a rival to the *Quarterly*, in which he broke with convention by introducing signed articles.

4.37 Entellus the Sicilian involved in a boxing match with the Trojan Dares in Virgil's *Aeneid*, 5.368–460.

4.38–39 his few and awkward partners Cumberland's collaborators included H. J. Pye (1745–1813), Horace Twiss (1787–1849), Thomas Young (1773–1829), and the brothers James Smith (1775–1839) and Horatio (Horace) Smith (1779–1849).

5.3 printers' devils errand boys in printing offices.

5.14 battledore and shuttle-cock game in which two people strike a shuttlecock from one to the other by means of small rackets, or battledores; it was the forerunner of badminton.

6.1 play booty play badly in order to lose.

6.18 phlogiston according to the theory developed by Georg Ernst Stahl (1660–1734) and first published in 1702, all inflammable substances contained 'phlogiston' which was released during combustion. This theory was disproved by Antoine-Laurent de Lavoisier (1743—94) who demonstrated in 1776 that in combustion a substance combines with oxygen.

6.34–35 cæteris paribus *Latin* other things being equal.

6.41–42 crown octavos, and duodecimos books in which a crown sheet of paper (measuring 38×51 cm) is folded to produce respectively 8 leaves (16 numbered pages), and 12 leaves (24 pages).

6.42 small deer *King Lear*, 3.4.135: 'But mice and rats, and such small deer', where *deer* retains its original meaning of *animals*; it is used humorously here in reference to small sized books.

7.1 upon the wheel wheeling.

7.5 throwing doublets thrice running at backgammon in the board-game backgammon, where two dice are used, a player throwing the same number on both dice scores double their total value.

7.22 Tempus *Latin* time.

7.29 none has a tenant at the bar justices of the peace were landowners, and their own tenants would sometimes appear before them.

7.29–30   inexorable as the same bench when dinner-time draws near
compare Alexander Pope (1688–1744), *The Rape of the Lock* (1712; revised
1714), Canto 3, lines 21–22: 'The hungry judges soon the sentence sign,/
And wretches hang that jury-men may dine'.
7.42   Lethé   *Greek* forgetfulness; in the Roman poets, one of the five
rivers of the underworld, whose waters were drunk by the Shades in order to
forget their earthly existence.
8.19   Madoc   (1805), a poem in blank verse by Robert Southey
(1774–1843); it had been scathingly reviewed by Francis Jeffrey in the *Edinburgh Review*, 7 (October 1805), 1–28.
8.21–23   a poem . . . an old blind man . . . some gay courtiers   *Paradise
Lost* (1667; revised 1674), the epic in blank verse by the 'old blind man'
John Milton (1608–74), was denigrated by William Winstanley (d. 1698).
Winstanley, who abhorred Milton's republican politics, claimed of him that
'his Fame is gone out like a Candle in a Snuff and his Memory will always
stink' (*The Lives of the Most Famous English Poets* (London, 1687), 195).
Winstanley was not a courtier, but perhaps his royalist politics made Scott
think that he was.
8.34–36   verses subscribed Amyntor . . . verses to Lydia   i.e. poems
to Lydia signed 'Amyntor'. These classical names suggest an old-fashioned
style of poetry which would have been current in the narrator's youth towards
the end of the long vogue for classical imitation in the century from 1650.
Horace provides a Roman classical model for a poem addressed to Lydia
(*Odes*, 3.9), while the poem 'Amyntor from beyond the Seas to Alexis' (1649)
by Richard Lovelace (1617–57) is an example of English neoclassicism using
names from the Greek classical world.
9.10–12   for Love esteems . . . Entire affection scorneth nicer hands
see Edmund Burke (1729–97), 'Speech on presenting to the House of Commons (on the 11th February, 1780) a Plan for the Better Security of the
Independence of Parliament, and the Economical Reformation of the Civil
and Other Establishments', where Burke claims: ' "Love," says one of our
old poets, "esteems no office mean,"—and with still more spirit, "Entire affection scorneth nicer hands" '. Scott owned a copy of the individual speech
(London, 1780; *CLA*, 312) as well as *The Works of the Right Honourable
Edmund Burke*, 14 vols (London, 1801–22; *CLA*, 193). See *The Writings and
Speeches of Edmund Burke*, Vol. 3: *Party, Parliament, and the American War*, ed.
W. M. Elofson (Oxford, 1996), 512. Burke misremembers 'No office mean
or base she doth refuse', where 'she' is Mercy, which appears in Robert
Aylett (*c.* 1582–1655), *The Brides Ornaments* (London, 1625), Meditation 3
'Of Mercy', line 210, a poem written in Spenserian stanzas; he quotes Spen-
ser's *The Faerie Queene*, 1.8.40, line 3, which runs 'Entire affection hateth
nicer hands'.
9.16   Herrick   Robert Herrick (1591–1674), English poet and Anglican
minister, author of *Hesperides: or, The Works both Humane & Divine of Robert
Herrick Esq.* (London, 1648).
9.16   Derricke   John Derricke (dates unknown), an English engraver and
versifier, best known for his poem *The Image of Irelande* (1581), which Scott
reprinted in his edition of *A Collection of Scarce and Valuable Tracts [Somers
Tracts]*, 13 vols (London, 1809–15), 1.558–621.
9.27–29   to the types of Bensley or Bulmer, . . . dying speeches   the
quality typefaces commissioned by the London printers Thomas Bensley
(1759–1833) and William Bulmer (1757–1830), together with those of
James Ballantyne in Edinburgh, are here contrasted with the rough typefaces
used for broadsides.
9.33   in stature and complexion, the identical "wee reekit devil" . . .

Burns see Burns's 'Kellyburnbraes' (1792; Kinsley, no. 376), stanza 10: 'A reekit wee devil looks over the wa''.' Lockhart identifies the small smoky devil as Francis Jeffrey (see *Peter's Letters to His Kinsfolk*, 2nd edn, 3 vols (Edinburgh, 1819), 1.60). Jeffrey (1773–1850) founded the *Edinburgh Review* in 1802 with Sydney Smith (1771–1845) and Henry Brougham (1778–1868), became its editor in 1803 and held the position for 25 years; he became a judge in 1834, as Lord Jeffrey. His short stature was noted by Lockhart (*Peter's Letters*, 1.60), and his 'dark complexion' by Henry Cockburn (*Life of Francis Jeffrey*, in *Lord Cockburn's Works*, 2 vols (Edinburgh, 1872), 1.386).

9.34–37 ambidexter . . . alternately in different directions Jeffrey often alternated praise and censure within a review, leaving the reader uncertain of his position until the very end.

10.9–10 like Ismael . . . every one's against him see Genesis 16.12.

10.10–11 A dæmon . . . a jockey whip for the racket William Gifford (1756–1826). He first attracted public notice with his satires *The Baviad* (1791) and *The Maeviad* (1795), and was editor of the *Anti-Jacobin, or Weekly Examiner* 1797–98, and of the *Quarterly Review* 1809–24.

10.25 ardent spirits strong and fiery-tasting alcoholic spirits.

10.30 Pit-water an allusion to the views of the English statesman William Pitt the Younger (1759–1806), Prime Minister 1783–1801 and 1804–06. Pitt began as a reforming Tory Prime Minister, but after 1793, in attempting to control the impact of the French Revolution in Britain, his government passed much repressive legislation, and he was characterised as a 'loyalist', i.e. someone who supported the crown and the political status quo.

10.31 Hollands Hollands (or Hollands gin), a grain spirit. The principal reference is to the whig views of Charles James Fox (1749–1806), second son of the first Baron Holland, who was the most brilliant whig of the last part of the 18th century, and of his nephew Henry Richard Fox (1773–1840), third Baron Holland. The latter's seat, Holland House in Kensington in London, was the centre of whig politics for the first 40 years of the 19th century. Charles James Fox was bitterly opposed to the interventions of the King, George III, in parliamentary rule, and consistently favoured the French attitude to political legitimacy.

10.33 French liqueur double distilled i.e. brandy.

10.33 Burdett Sir Francis Burdett (1770–1844), the most radical politician of his time; his political activity was greatest in the period from 1807 when M.P. for Westminster. Slogans such as 'Burdett and Liberty' and 'Burdett and Independence' were staple features in early 19th-century political vocabulary.

11.1 a very peculiar tone of voice Jeffrey's distinctive voice is described by Lockhart as a 'sharp, shrill, but deep-toned trumpet' (*Peter's Letter's to His Kinsfolk*, 2nd edn, 3 vols (Edinburgh, 1819), 2.60; see also 1.60).

11.6–9 the occupation of Anchises in the shades . . . Lustrabat when Aeneas came upon the shade of his father Anchises in the underworld, 'he was inspecting the souls now confined there but destined to go to the light of the world above' (Virgil, *Aeneid*, 6.679–81).

11.16–17 A racqueteer . . . my obliging informer's back-game Sydney Smith (1771—1845), an Anglican clergyman, who co-founded the *Edinburgh Review* and wrote for it for 25 years. He championed reforms in a variety of areas, including prisons, Parliament, and the position of Roman Catholics.

11.21–22 another . . . had torn and dirtied his band response to Sydney Smith's attack on Oxford education in a review of R. L. Edgeworth's *Essays on Professional Education* in the *Edinburgh Review* , 15 (October 1809),

40–53, was led by Edward Copleston (1776–1849) in *A Reply to the Calumnies of the Edinburgh Review against Oxford, Containing an Account of Studies Pursued in that University* (Oxford, 1810). Copleston held various positions at Oxford, as well as ecclesiastical appointments, and ultimately became Bishop of Llandaff.

11.24 the urbanity of this goblin Henry Cockburn describes Jeffrey's 'urbanity' and 'kindly liveliness' in *Life of Francis Jeffrey*, in *Lord Cockburn's Works*, 2 vols (Edinburgh, 1872), 1.378.

11.26–28 like the liberal-minded Sancho . . . good sort of people even in hell itself see *Don Quixote*, Part 2, Ch. 34, where Sancho Panza is impressed by the Christian sentiments of a post-boy claiming to be the devil.

12.7–9 Corelli . . . his celebrated piece of music . . . the Devil's Concerto the 'Trillo del Diavolo' by Giuseppe Tartini (1692–1770), rather than Arcangelo Corelli (1653–1713), was claimed by the composer to be a poor shadow of the sonata played to him in a dream by the devil himself. Tartini described the circumstances of the sonata's composition to the astronomer Joseph Jérôme le Français de Lalande (1732–1807), who included this account in his *Voyage d'un François en Italie*, 8 vols (Venice, 1769), 8.292.

12.15–16 if my vision really issued from the Gate of Horn i.e. if my vision represented the truth. According to Virgil (*Aeneid*, 6.893–96), dreams are sent to the living by the Shades, those that are true coming through a gate of horn, and the false through a gate of ivory; the idea is based on Homer's *Odyssey*, 19.562–67.

12.18–19 some others in my budget . . . offer to you next year in a letter to James Ballantyne of 23 October 1810, Scott had proposed imitations of Southey, Wordsworth, and possibly 'Monk' Lewis in addition to those which finally appeared (*Letters*, 1.412); he also told Joanna Baillie on 4 August 1811, shortly after the publication of the 'Inferno', that if it proved successful Ballantyne wanted him to provide an imitation of her own work (*Letters*, 2.526).

12.22 Caleb Quotem a character in George Colman the Younger (1762–1836), *The Review; or, The Wags of Windsor* (first performed 1800).

12.23 April 1 i.e. April Fool's Day. Captain Clutterbuck's Introductory Epistle to *The Fortunes of Nigel* is similarly dated: *The Fortunes of Nigel*, ed. Frank Jordan, EEWN 13, 17.26.

12.28–29 sage . . . the rights of man a probable allusion to Thomas Paine (1737–1809), who, in his *Rights of Man* (1791–92), supported the French Revolution.

13.1 buckskin'd justices i.e. magistrates wearing the buckskin breeches of a country squire.

13.2 Wire-draw the acts that fix for wires the pain i.e. draw out inordinately the laws fixing the penalties for poaching.

13.9 one poor Easter chace the annual 'common hunt' held in Epping Forest on Easter Monday, during which a loosed deer was pursued by large crowds of Londoners; possibly instituted in 1226, it lasted until about 1882.

13.10–11 as free . . . the Parisian train following the storming of the Bastille on 14 July 1789, French peasants flocked to every chateau, burning hunt registers, and forcing their masters to sign away their feudal rights; when the National Assembly ratified the annulment of feudal privileges on 4 August, peasants all over France began hunting the game in the parks and forests for themselves (see Erich Hobusch, *Fair Game: A History of Hunting, Shooting and Animal Conservation*, trans. Ruth Michaelis-Jena and Patrick Murray (New York, 1980), 188). Chantilly, about 40 km from Paris, was the site of the magnificent chateau of the dukes of Condé, with its old and extensive hunting forest; it was razed during the Revolution.

13.16 La Douce Humanité *French* gentle humanity. Edmund Burke in his *Letter to a Noble Lord* (1796; see *CLA*, 193) described those who planned to rise against their unsuspecting masters as having 'nothing but *douce humanité* in their mouth': *The Writings and Speeches of Edmund Burke*, Vol. 9: *The Revolutionary War: Ireland*, ed. R. B. McDowell (Oxford, 1991), 175.

13.19 vive la liberté! *French* long live freedom! (a catchcry of the French Revolution).

13.20 But mad Citoyen, meek Monsieur again on 19 June 1790 the National Assembly in France abolished both nobility and the associated titles; as a consequence the form of address 'monsieur' was replaced by 'citoyen' (citizen). Napoleon, as emperor, restored titles of nobility in 1808, and the addressive 'monsieur' came back into use.

13.21 With some few added links resumes his chain for Scott, Napoleon's empire was more oppressive than the monarchy which, after an interval of republican rule, it had replaced.

14.5 that shrouds the native frore i.e. that shelters the frore (freezing) American Indian.

14.21 sweeping net large fishing-net capable of enclosing a wide area.

14.41–42 an antique stirrup . . . "The Red King" William II (called Rufus; born *c*. 1060; ruled 1087–1100), was killed on 2 August 1100 while hunting in the New Forest, probably by an arrow from one of his companions, Walter Tyrrell. 'The Red King' is an original ballad on the death of William II by William Stewart Rose (1775–1843), English poet and translator and a friend of Scott's, which appeared along with his translation of *Partenopex de Blois* in the volume of the same name (London, 1807). Stanza 40 tells how 'still, in merry Lyndhurst-hall,/ Red William's stirrup decks the wall'. Scott and Rose made 'a long circuit through the forest' on horseback together in April 1807 (*Letters*, 12.105). Referring to this visit, Lockhart quotes from Rose's 'Gundimore': 'Here Walter Scott has woo'd the northern muse;/ Here he with me has joy'd to walk or cruise;/ And hence has prick'd through Yten's Holt, where we/ Have called to mind how under greenwood tree,/ Pierced by the partner of his "woodland craft,"/ King Rufus fell by Tyrrell's random shaft' (*Life*, 2.119).

15.8 grouse or partridge massacred in March i.e. outside the shooting season. The Act of 1773 (13 Geo. III, c. 54), in force in Scott's time, determined the close season for game birds, which for grouse was 10 December–12 August, and for partridge 1 February–1 September.

15.10 no wicket in the gate of law i.e. no small door set within the bigger gate through which simple access could be given to a secure place.

15.17 Edward Mansell a very different character of this name appears in *The Fortunes of Nigel* as the 'punctilious old soldier and courtier' Sir Edward Mansel, who is himself possibly based on the Edward Mansel (d. 1595) knighted by Queen Elizabeth in 1572 (see *The Fortunes of Nigel*, ed. Frank Jordan, EEWN 13, 335.13 and note). The baronetcy expired in 1750.

15.31 robs the warren or excise i.e. steals game birds from the enclosures in which they have been bred, or smuggles liquor thus stealing from the state by not paying excise duty.

15.39 the revenue baulked, or pilfered game i.e. tax evasion (probably through smuggling) and poaching.

16.1–2 Around the spot . . . midnight round according to tradition, on the anniversary of William Rufus's death his ghost follows the trail of blood which flowed from his body as it was transported to Winchester for burial.

16.11 Malwood-walk formerly an administrative area of the New Forest in Hampshire.

17.2 Triermain a castle about 4 km W of Gilsland in N Cumbria, known to Scott from his time in Gilsland in the autumn of 1797 when he met his wife. Medieval in origin (its exact date is unknown), it was described as partly 'fallen down and decayed' in 1580. In Scott's time substantial ruins remained but a further portion collapsed in 1832: see W. T. McIntire, 'Triermain Castle', *Transactions of the Cumberland and Westmorland Antiquarian and Archaeological Society*, n.s. 26 (1926), 247–54.

17.23 Plantagenet name given by later historians to the descendants of Matilda and Geoffrey of Anjou who ruled England 1154–1399, with reference to Geoffrey's badge, a sprig of broom (in Old French, *plante geneste*). The first three of these kings (Henry II, Richard I and John) are, however, sometimes termed the Angevins, the name Plantagenet being reserved for their successors, ending with Richard II.

17.27 Sir Roland de Vaux see Historical Note, 177.

18.3 Glaramara rocky mountain ridge rising to a height of 783m about 4 km S of Borrowdale in Cumbria. Despite its height it would not be visible from Triermain and in later editions it was replaced by the nearer and higher Skiddaw.

18.23 Richard de Brettville a fictitious character, although a Richard de Bretevill is mentioned in relation to a London property in the late 12th century (see Derek Keene and Vanessa Harding, *Historical Gazetteer of London before the Great Fire* (Cambridge, 1987), 355–56).

18.35 Philip of Fasthwaite a fictitious character and place, although Scott introduced a similar fictional name for a farm in *Waverley* (ed. P. D. Garside, EEWN 1, 300.40 and note), locating it on Ullswater. The name, especially its suffix, is characteristic of the region; though no such actual location has been discovered, there is a Finsthwaite Parish at the S end of Lake Windermere.

19.5 the sack of Hermitage Hermitage Castle, Roxburghshire, 10 km NE of Newcastleton. Begun in the 13th century and much modified over time, it was, as a major Border castle, often attacked.

19.8 the Nine-stane Hill the Nine-Stane Rig, a prehistoric stone circle, stands on a hill about 2 km NE of Hermitage Castle.

19.14 Lyulph's tow'r a small modern Gothic castle, built on the ruins of an existing peel tower above the northern shore of Ullswater by the Duke of Norfolk in 1780. He belonged to the Howards of Greystoke in Cumbria and named it after Lyulph (Ligulf), the father of the first baron of Greystoke from whom he was descended. (Some authorities give Ligulf's name as Sigulf.)

19.19 Arthur's and Pendragon's praise *Arthur* was a legendary Romano-British king of the late 5th or early 6th centuries, who became a hero in the pseudo history of the kings of Britain (*Historia Regum Britanniae*) by Geoffrey of Monmouth in the 12th century, whereas *Pendragon* was a title given to an ancient British or Welsh chief holding or claiming supreme power. According to legend, Uther Pendragon was the father of Arthur.

19.20 Dunmailraise according to legend, a cairn on Dunmail-Raise, a high point on the road between Thirlmere and Grasmere in Cumbria, marks the spot where Dunmail, king of Cumbria, was buried after being defeated in battle in 945, supposedly by Edmund, King of the Saxons, and Malcolm I, King of Scots.

19.22–23 characters . . . Graven deep what this refers to has not been discovered; Scott climbed Helvellyn (see next note) with Wordsworth in 1805.

19.24 Helvellyn the third highest peak in the Lake District (at 950m); it overlooks Ullswater to the east and Thirlmere to the west.

19.41 Irthing river flowing W through northern Cumbria to join the Eden SE of Carlisle.

20.1 Kirkoswald town beside the Eden about 12 km N of Penrith in Cumbria.
20.2 Eden river flowing N through Cumbria to the Solway Firth.
20.3 red Penrith's Table Round a prehistoric earthwork near Eamont Bridge just S of Penrith in Cumbria, known as King Arthur's Round Table although it substantially predates the legendary King Arthur. Scott in a later note recorded the conjecture 'that the enclosure was designed for the solemn exercise of feats of chivalry' (*Poetical Works*, 11.34). Many of the buildings of Penrith are constructed of the local red sandstone: according to Camden the name, 'if derived from the British language', means '*Red Head* or *Hill:* for the soil and the stones of which it is built are of a red colour' (William Camden, *Britannia*, trans Richard Gough, 2nd edn, 4 vols (London, 1806), 3.246: *CLA*, 232). Camden's *Britannia* was written in Latin and first published in 1586.
20.5 Mayburgh's mound and stones of pow'r prehistoric earthwork with standing stones just S of Penrith. Only one stone remained when the poem was written but Scott noted later that 'Two similar masses are said to have been destroyed during the memory of man' (*Poetical Works*, 11.35).
20.7 Eamont river flowing out of Ullswater to join the Eden near Penrith.
20.8 Ulfo's lake Ullswater in Cumbria; the name is derived from 'Ulf's lake' (see Eilert Ekwall, *The Concise Oxford English Dictionary of Place-Names* (Oxford, 1936), *Ullswater*).

EXPLANATORY NOTES TO 'CHRISTOPHER CORDUROY'

21 motto Greek ἕως, ὅτῳ ἀιεὶ θέλει εἶναι, ἤν until it existed in whatever way it always wants to exist. This 'quotation' does not occur in the works of the comic poet Menander (for whom see note to 21.9) or his much later namesake Menander the Rhetor (dates unknown), or in any other Greek text. The text here follows its base text; diacritics have not been inserted in the text, although necessary, because of the vagueness in Scott and his contemporaries about what was required.
21.9 a beautiful fragment of Menander the Athenian dramatist Menander (*c.* 342–292 BC) wrote over 100 plays; excepting one, all are known only through fragments or adaptations.
21.11–20 strange and fantastical systems ... its own end cosmogonies involving spontaneous generation from inert materials are associated with Thales of Miletus (*c.* 624–547 BC) and his followers Anaximander (*c.* 610–*c.* 546 BC) and Anaximenes (died *c.* 528 BC), rather than with the philosophers of Menander's time.
21.21 αυτοποιητον παν Greek αὐτοποίητον πᾶν everything created by itself: untraced. The concept of spontaneous generation from inert materials does appear in the works of the writers in the previous note, but not the word 'αὐτοποίητον', which is not found in the works of Greek philosophers. It is possible, then, that Scott has had the idea of spontaneous creation and either he or a friend generated a readily understandable Greek equivalent. For the diacritics see the note to 21.motto above.
21.25 the misery which flesh is heir to see *Hamlet*, 3.1.62–63: 'The heart-ache and the thousand natural shocks/ That flesh is heir to'.
22.6 The oracles of Delphi and Dodona the oracle of Apollo in his temple at Delphi was consulted by many rulers, among them Midas (King of Phrygia in the 8th century BC), Gyges (King of Lydia *c.* 685–*c.* 657 BC), Croesus (King of Lydia *c.* 560–546 BC) and the Roman emperor Julian (ruled AD 355–63). The oracle of Zeus, in an oak grove at Dodona in modern Ipeiros in NW Greece, was consulted by Croesus, as well as by the

Roman emperors Hadrian in AD 132, and Julian two centuries later.

22.20   Abon Hassan   in 'The Story of the Sleeper Awakened' from *The Arabian Nights' Entertainments*, the caliph Haroun Alraschid fulfils the wish of Abon Hassan to be caliph for a day by drugging him and having him transported to his court. Abon Hassan wakes to find himself dressed in the Caliph's clothes, is treated as if he were caliph, and finally comes to believe that he is caliph. Scott apparently writes from memory, drawing on the two slightly different versions available to him: the traditional English translation from the French of Antoine Galland (1646–1715) as found in Henry Weber's *Tales of the East*, 3 vols (Edinburgh, 1812), 1.131–40, from which he took the form 'Abon Hassan' for the hero's name; and Jonathan Scott's revised and corrected translation from the Arabic, *The Arabian Nights' Entertainment*, 6 vols (London, 1811), 4.177–283, on which he drew for other details. Both versions are in Abbotsford (*CLA*, 43).

22.24–25   the teeth of Mesrour ... his true condition   believing he is dreaming, Abon Hassan asks, not Mesrour, the chief of the eunuchs, but both a lady and a court officer to bite him to test whether he is awake. Although he becomes convinced that he is caliph, he never believes himself to be Haroun Alraschid himself.

22.26–27   to the great displeasure of his wife   in the original story it is his mother, not his wife, that Abon Hassan upsets in this way when he returns home believing that he is indeed caliph.

22.27–28   call about him for ... Moon-face   in the English translation of Galland, Abon Hassan summons the ladies who entertained him in the Caliph's palace by calling 'Cluster of Pearls! Morning star! Coral Lips! Fair Face!' (Weber, 1.234). However in Jonathan Scott's translation the last woman is called 'Moon-face' (4.215) and 'Soul's Torment' is the name of another of the women Abon Hassan meets in the Caliph's palace (4.209). For full references to Weber and Scott see note to 22.20.

22.29–30   Aristotle, in his book De Mirabilibus Auscultationis   see *De mirabilibus auscultationibus*, in Aristotle, *Minor Works*, ed. and trans. W. S. Hett, Loeb Classics (London, 1936), 250–51. In this work, no longer attributed to Aristotle, the scene of the imaginary performance is Abydos rather than Agrigentum.

22.38–41   he considered himself as Lord ... hornfulls of small-beer   no character with these particular delusions has been traced, but characters afflicted with different kinds of 'phrenzy' occur in periodical literature; see for example Henry Mackenzie's periodical *The Mirror*, no. 17 (23 March 1779) and no. 93 (28 March 1780).

22.42   Lord Peter   see Section 4 of Jonathan Swift's allegorical satire *A Tale of a Tub* (written *c.* 1696; published 1704), where, in comic allusion to the Roman Catholic practice of serving only bread at communion, and to the belief that when consecrated the bread and wine become in substance the body and blood of Christ, 'Lord' Peter (the Roman Catholic church) suffers from the delusion that a loaf of bread, i.e. the communion wafer, may truly be both a leg of mutton and a bottle of claret.

22.42   Chateau-Margout   one of the greatest of red wines, from Margaux in the Gironde in France.

23.3–4   a late celebrated High-German Doctor ... lose his nose   not traced; certainly there were many quacks allegedly of German origin in Britain, and some of these claimed that their nostrums were efficacious against syphilis, which commonly destroyed the sufferer's nose: see C. J. S. Thompson, *The Quacks of Old London* (London, 1928).

23.8–11   Dr Spurzheim ... the shape of her skull   Johann Kaspar Spurzheim (1776–1832), a German doctor who, with his teacher Franz

Joseph Gall (1758–1828), developed the theory and practice of phrenology, whereby it was alleged that a person's character could be read from the shape and protuberances of the skull. Phrenology was ridiculed in the anonymous burlesque poem *The Craniad* (Edinburgh, 1817), probably the work of Francis Jeffrey and John Gordon, which is itself the subject of *The Sale-Room*, no. 20 (17 May 1817), 153–59; Spurzheim's theory is further referred to in *The Sale-Room*, no. 25 (21 June 1817), 199.

23.13   a commercial town at no great distance   Glasgow, 70 km W of Edinburgh.

23.15   novi homines   *Latin* new men; men who have made money but who do not belong to an 'old' family. Originally the phrase was applied to plebeians who managed to enter the Roman Senate to which, traditionally, only patricians could belong; the concept of the new man has been the subject of a considerable literature through the ages.

23.16   the vanity of human wishes   the phrase forms the title of a poem (published 1748) by Samuel Johnson (1709–84) which was a favourite of Scott's. The idea of the emptiness of human aspirations is drawn from the Bible, and particularly Ecclesiastes.

23.23–24   in the first number of your paper   i.e. in your next issue.

23.32   arrived some years ago at the dignity of the magistracy   i.e. he became a *Baillie*, or member of the town council with powers as a magistrate.

23.38   some time in the West Indies   throughout the 18th century and into the 19th century the Scots had a substantial presence in the British colonies in the Caribbean; for a useful summary see T. M. Devine, *Scotland's Empire* (London, 2004), 221–49.

23.42   Nisbett's Heraldry   *A System of Heraldry, Speculative and Practical* (Edinburgh, 1722) by Alexander Nisbet (1657–1725).

24.21–26   Our family name of Corduroy ... Cœur du roy   the name of the material *corduroy* may have its source in the surname *Corderoy*, which does indeed derive from the French *cœur de roi* (king's heart). However, *Corduroy* does not exist as a variant of the surname, and the younger Christopher's theory concerning its origin is therefore more plausible than his uncle's. See *A Dictionary of Surnames*, ed. Patricia Hanks and Flavia Hodges (Oxford, 1988) and *A Dictionary of English Surnames*, ed. P. H. Reaney, 3rd edn (Oxford, 1995).

24.28–29   the Douglasses wear a heart with a king's crown on it   the crowned heart in the Douglas arms commemorates Robert the Bruce's dying request to Sir James Douglas to take his heart to Jerusalem for burial. Although there are conflicting accounts of his journey it seems likely that he was slain in Andalusia on his way east, fighting against the Moors. See also note to 25.22.

24.30–31   the clan of the Macgregors ... for the best part of a century   following the massacre of the Colquhouns by the Macgregors at Glen Fruin in 1603, an Act of the Privy Council proscribed the use of the names Gregor and MacGregor. The proscription was lifted by Charles II but reimposed by William III and was not finally removed until 1774.

24.32–33   the Register-office   the place where all Scottish state and official records are kept, including wills; the institution is now known as the National Archives of Scotland. Searchers were paid to find legal documents in the archive.

24.42   wafers, and the old signet stamp   wafers, or thin disks of adhesive material such as flour and gum, or gelatine, were used to seal documents and were stamped with signets, or small seals.

25.1   tandem triumphans   *Latin* victorious in the end. The Douglas motto is 'jamais arrière' (*French* never at the rear). Others of the name of Douglas use other mottoes but not 'tandem triumphans'. Christopher's choice may imply Jacobite leanings: according to some historians, this motto was displayed on the banner of Prince Charles Edward Stuart during the Jacobite rising of 1745.

25.4 at last eventually.

25.22 the good Sir James Douglas also known as the Black Douglas, this loyal follower of Robert the Bruce died in Spain in 1330 and was buried in Melrose Abbey.

25.22–23 Archibald Bell-the-Cat Archibald Douglas, fifth Earl of Angus (d. 1514). *Bell the cat* is a proverbial utterance used of a dangerous mission, from the fable of the mice who agreed to hang a bell round the cat's neck, but were each too afraid to do it (*ODEP*, 44). Angus acquired the nickname after killing the low-born favourites of James III, in response to Lord Gray's query 'Who will bell the cat?' at a council of Scottish nobles called to discuss disposing of the king's minions.

25.25 the Antiburghers members of the section of the Secession Church (which had seceded from the Church of Scotland in 1733) who in 1747 left the rest of that church (the 'Burghers') over the question of taking the burgess oath. It was much debated whether the oath, required of all wishing to become a burgess in the major burghs, involved the upholding of the established Church of Scotland, which the antiburghers as seceders felt they could not do with a good conscience. The two sections were reunited in 1820.

25.26–27 the Episcopal chapel ... the genteeler religion in 1690 bishops were removed from the established Church of Scotland, but one group continued in a non-established church with bishops; this episcopal church was favoured by many upper-class Jacobites in the 18th century and continued to draw upper-class support in Scott's time.

25.30–31 he had his arms taken out regularly in the heralds' book i.e. he had applied to the Lord Lyon King of Arms for the grant of a coat of arms which was then duly registered in the Public Register of All Arms and Bearings in Scotland.

25.37 session-clerk's office prior to the law requiring the registration of all births, marriages and deaths which took effect in Scotland in 1855, the only records in these matters were those of the parishes of the established Church of Scotland; the records for each parish were maintained by the session clerk.

25.42 circuit the High Court of Justiciary, Scotland's highest criminal court, normally convened in Edinburgh but also went on circuit to hold trials in specified places: Jedburgh was on the south circuit.

26.31–32 erected into a barony legally reconstituted as lands held by baronial tenure directly from the crown; this would make the holder a feudal baron entitled to be referred to as a laird.

26.32–33 supporters would not stand him above L. 100 applying for supporters (in heraldry a pair of figures standing either side of a shield in a coat of arms) would only cost him £100. This represents a further heightening of his pretensions since they were only granted to limited categories of people.

27.13–14 the "εν εαυτω τελειος και καταφρονητης των ἐξω" of Antoninus *Greek* ἐν ἑαυτῷ τέλειος καὶ καταφρονητὴς τῶν ἔξω the man who is perfect within himself and contemptuous of external things. This phrase does not appear in the *Meditations* of the Roman emperor Marcus Aurelius Antoninus (AD 121–80), nor in any other Greek text in its full form. The first three words occur together only in the *Commentarium in Parmenidem* ('Commentary on the Parmenides [of Plato]') of the 5th-century Neoplatonist Damascius, at 142.11.

27.14–15 observations of old John of Gaunt ... summer's heat? on

Bolingbroke's being exiled by Richard II, his father, John of Gaunt, suggests that his son pretend while in exile that the sights and sounds of nature are courtly pleasures (see *Richard II*, 1.3.287–93), but Bolingbroke takes a materialist position and rejects his advice (1.3.294–99).

27.24 Q. E. contributors to *The Sale-Room* followed the convention of using pseudonyms, usually initials, which were apparently chosen either at random or with some private, and now unrecoverable, significance.

EXPLANATORY NOTES TO
'ALARMING INCREASE OF DEPRAVITY AMONG ANIMALS'

29 motto *Latin* our parents' era, more wicked than that of our grandparents, has produced us who are even viler, and who will soon bring forth a generation more depraved again: Horace (65–8 BC), *Odes*, 3.6.46–48.

29.17 slipper'd pantaloons see *As You Like It*, 2.7.158. The phrase denotes feeble old men reduced to wearing slippers rather than outdoor shoes.

29.20–21 Parliamentary Reports upon Mendicity a Select Committee of the House of Commons published a report on the 'State of Mendicity [i.e. begging] in the Metropolis' in July 1815, with an appendix in 1816.

29.21–22 Mr Colquhoun's Essay on the Police of the Metropolis Patrick Colquhoun (1745–1820) was a police magistrate at Worship Street police office, Shoreditch, from 1792–1818; his *Treatise on the Police of the Metropolis* went through seven editions between 1796 and 1806.

29.24–25 Mr Owen . . . impracticable remedy for an incurable disease in 1817 the social reformer Robert Owen (1771–1858) was advocating the creation of 'Villages of Unity and Mutual Co-operation' for the unemployed (*Selected Works of Robert Owen*, ed. Gregory Claeyes, 4 vols (London, 1993), 1.174). He himself established a model community at New Lanark in Lanarkshire (where he managed the cotton mills from 1800–25) and later in the United States, Ireland, and elsewhere in Britain.

29.25–26 the public ear has been crammed compare *The Tempest*, 2.1.100–01.

30.6 the eighth commandment 'Thou shalt not steal' (Exodus 20.15).

30.6–7 benefit of clergy the privilege, allowed initially to the clergy but afterwards to anyone who could read, of claiming exemption from the jurisdiction of a secular court or, later, from the execution of its sentence. This privilege was abolished in Scotland at the Reformation, but survived in England in modified form until 1827.

30.7–8 two melancholy instances of depravity in the newspapers for details of the newspapers and issues concerned see Essay on the Text, 124–25.

30.9 our Chronicle of Remarkable Events the 'British Chronicle' section of the 'Register' which concluded each number of *Blackwood's*.

30.11–25 Shadwell Office . . . St George's in the East . . . Hatton Garden there were magistrates' courts, with up to a dozen constables attached, in High Street, Shadwell and at Hatton Garden; St George's in the East is a parish adjacent to Shadwell.

30.28–29 St Pancras Church situated on Pancras Road, it has been known as St Pancras Old Church since the consecration of a new church in the area in 1822.

30.29 Battle Bridge now known as King's Cross (from a monument to George IV, erected 1836, dismantled 1845), Battle Bridge was a district beside a former bridge over the River Fleet; according to *The London Encyclopedia*, ed. Ben Weinreb and Christopher Hibbert (London, 1993), 435, the name does not, as commonly believed, commemorate a battle between the Romans and the Iceni under Boudicca, but represents a corruption of Broad Ford Bridge.

30.37 the Veterinary College later the Royal Veterinary College. It was established in the parish of St Pancras in April 1791, on the present-day site of the College's Camden Town Campus.

31.5–7 the Houyhnhnm himself . . . an absolute yahoo in Book 4 of Jonathan Swift's *Gulliver's Travels* (1726), the Houyhnhnms, a race of rational horses, rule over a brutish race of humans called Yahoos.

31.9–10 his alliance with . . . the fox and the wolf referring to the common ancestry of the dog, the fox and the wolf, all ultimately members of the dog family.

31.13–16 Gilbertfield, that "Imp of fame" . . . Bonny Heck 'The Last Dying Words of Bonny Heck, a Famous Grey-Hound in the Shire of Fife', attributed to William Hamilton of Gilbertfield (*c.* 1665–1751). Although Burns mentions him frequently, he does not appear to have called him, after Pistol, an 'imp of fame' (*Henry V*, 4.1.45).

31.29–30 a Highland pony . . . one of that kind ourselves see Historical Note, 219, n. 25.

31.31–32 pull the bobbin till the latch came up . . . Red Riding-hood herself see Robert Samber's translation of Charles Perrault's 'Le petit Chaperon Rouge' in *Histories; or Tales of Past Times* (London, 1729), 5.

31.35–37 as late antiquaries of the Gothic race . . . the name of Man John Pinkerton (1758–1826), historian and antiquary, was the principal detractor of the Celts in favour of the Goths, or Germanic peoples. In *An Enquiry into the History of Scotland Preceding the Reign of Malcom III. or the Year 1056*, 2nd edn, 2 vols (London, 1794; see *CLA*, 9) he characterises the Highlanders as 'mere savages, but one degree above brutes' (1.268), contrasting 'these Celtic cattle' (1.341) who are 'indolent, slavish, strangers to industry' with the Lowlanders who are 'acute, industrious, sensible, erect, free' (1.340).

32.4 stouthrief and sorning robbery and sturdy begging.

32.7 poors' box a box, usually placed at the entrance to a church, for holding contributions for the relief of the poor.

32.12 some will hund their dog whare they dar'na gang themsel untraced: some will drive their dog where they don't dare to go themselves.

32.17 elucidated in the sequel i.e. explained by what follows.

32.18–19 the celebrated case of Murdieston and Millar for details of the crimes, trial and execution of Alexander Murdieston and his shepherd John Millar see Historical Note, 179–81.

32.22–23 Braxfield or Monboddo . . . passed sentence upon them Robert Macqueen, Lord Braxfield (1722–99), was one of the advocates acting for Murdieston; he was not raised to the bench until 1776. James Burnett, Lord Monboddo (1714–99), pioneer anthropologist and author of *Of the Origin and Progress of Language*, 6 vols (Edinburgh, 1774–92), and a judge from 1767, was not involved in the trial or sentencing of Murdieston and Millar.

32.24–25 Lord Melville . . . Advocate Depute Henry Dundas (1742–1811), first Viscount Melville from 1802, was involved in the prosecution of Murdieston and Millar as Solicitor-General, which made him deputy to the Lord Advocate.

32.26 a farm on the north bank of the Tweed the farm tenanted by Murdieston, which is named elsewhere as Ormiston; Laidlaw includes the name in his notes (MS 3937, f. 8r), but it was not carried over into the *Blackwood's* story. Renamed 'Glenormiston', the farm was 'improved' by successive owners including the publisher William Chambers (1800–83), the grandson, ironically, of William Gibson, the farmer responsible for the arrest of Murdieston and Millar (see William Chambers, *Glenormiston: First Paper* (Edinburgh, 1849), 13).

32.27 **the ancient baronial castle of Traquair** Traquair House, which dates from the 12th century although largely rebuilt in the 17th century, near Innerleithen.

32.28 **Minion of the Moon** this phrase, which originally signified a night-watchman (see *1 Henry IV*, 1.2.25) came to mean, as here, a night-robber.

32.34–35 **the ridge of mountains . . . Leithen from the Tweed** the range includes the hills of Lee Pen, directly north of Ormiston, and Lee Burn Head.

32.38 **weather-gleam** the sky just above the horizon; the phrase is italicised probably because it is Scots and northern English, and does not form part of the standard English lexicon.

32.42 **Yarrow** apparently a common name for a dog; see *Marmion* (Edinburgh, 1808), Intro. to Canto 4, line 95, in *Poetical Works*, 7.179.

33.5 **peel houses** small fortified towers, often built in the 16th and early 17th centuries in the Borders.

33.6–7 **placed alternately along the north and south bank** Ormiston peel tower (or peel house), the residence of the Dicksons of Ormiston in the 16th and 17th centuries, was one of a chain which included those at Cardrona, Nether Horsbrugh, and Horsbrugh Castle. Already a ruin in Murdieston and Millar's time, Ormiston peel tower was demolished in about 1805 (see Royal Commission on the Ancient and Historical Monuments of Scotland, *Peeblesshire: An Inventory of the Ancient Monuments*, 2 vols (Edinburgh, 1967), 2.263, 289–90).

33.9–10 **in the vault of this tower . . . conceal the sheep** the ground floor of peel towers, which had a vaulted roof, was used as a store-room or a refuge for animals as need arose.

33.18 **of the fancy** engaged in like pursuits.

33.26 **haunts of men** a phrase in frequent use in the 18th and early 19th centuries. Scott might have read it in Nathaniel Lee (*c.* 1650–92), *Lucus Junius Brutus* (1681), Act 3, scene 3 (the earliest example); Thomas Blacklock (1721–91), 'Ode on the Death of Mr Pope', line 70; Tobias Smollett (1721–71), *The Expedition of Humphry Clinker* (1771), Matthew Bramble to Dr Lewis, 8 June; Thomas Campbell (1777–1844), *The Pleasures of Hope* (1799), 1.332; George Crabbe (1754–1832), *The Borough* (1810), 1.8; Anna Seward (1742–1809), 'Pastoral Ballad', line 27, in *Poetical Works* (1810) which was edited by Scott; Lord Byron (1788–1824), *Lara* (1814), Bk 1, line 96; and Thomas Moore (1779–1852), *Lalla Rookh* (published May 1817), 'The Fire-Worshippers', 2.220.

33.27 **Wallace's hill** a hill on the S side of the Tweed, W of Traquair and almost opposite Ormiston.

33.28 **a pool in the river Tweed** probably the 'dirt-pot', a deep and dark pool at a bend in the Tweed below Nether Horsbrugh: see William Chambers, *A History of Peeblesshire* (Edinburgh and London, 1864), 377 (note 1), and James Walter Buchan, *A History of Peeblesshire*, 3 vols (Glasgow, 1925–27), 2.377.

34.7 **where sheep shou'd na be** untraced.

34.9 **keel** red mark made on sheep with iron ore, glossed by Laidlaw as a 'stain with soft iron ore that stains the wool' (MS 3937, f. 8r); however witnesses at the trial mention newly applied tar-marks rather than keels.

34.13 **told the story to a respectable sheep-farmer** see Historical Note, 179.

34.15 Murdieston and Millar suffered death they were executed on 24 March 1773.

34.16 dying speech the last speech of a person being hanged. Dying speeches were a literary kind, sold as broadsides following an execution, and purporting to be the condemned's last words uttered on the scaffold. Of course their authenticity was always doubtful.

34.18–19 a person unexpectedly reprieved ... purchasing his own last speech a common occurrence, as last speeches were normally printed before the execution itself.

34.22 purchased by a sheep-farmer elsewhere (note to *St Ronan's Well*, Magnum, 34.247) Scott specifies that the farmer was from 'Leithen', by which Innerleithen is probably meant.

34.39 the Spartan art of privately stealing in the austere military state of Sparta, stealing was encouraged, and the thief punished only if caught in the act.

35.27 ride post i.e. ride hired horses. A horse would be hired at each post (i.e. a coaching inn) and exchanged for a fresh horse at the next post; posts were generally around 12 miles apart.

35.32 Smithfield area in London formerly just outside the City walls, celebrated as a horse and cattle-market.

36.1 Finchley Common notorious haunt of highwaymen, then N of London.

36.28 malice prepense *legal French* malice aforethought, or criminal intent.

36.29–34 the dog of Islington ... bit the man see stanza 5 of Oliver Goldsmith, (1728?–74), 'An Elegy on the Death of a Mad Dog' (1766).

36.36 Houyhnhnms see note to 31.5–7.

36.37–38 find a bill for murder i.e. declare that there is sufficient evidence for the suspect to be tried for murder.

36.38 species facti *legal Latin* the particular nature of the thing done; the precise circumstances attending any crime or civil wrong.

36.43 more sinned against than sinners see *King Lear*, 3.2.59–60: 'I am a man/ More sinn'd against than sinning'.

EXPLANATORY NOTES TO 'PHANTASMAGORIA'

38.2 Veiled Conductor the designation of the elusive editor of *Blackwood's Edinburgh Magazine* used in the Notices in the number for March 1818, alluding to the image of the veiled editor in Ch. 2 of the 'Chaldee Manuscript' (*BEM*, 2 (October 1817), 92).

38.12–13 "make faith," ... civilians to 'make faith', or to affirm or give surety, is a phrase used by 'civilians', that is, practitioners of civil law.

38.15–16 on the tenth part of which ... guilty of felony crimes committed in London and in Middlesex were tried at the Old Bailey by separate juries drawn from the relevant area. Perhaps because of the pressure generated by a greater number of trials, Middlesex juries had a reputation for severity: e.g. see Ch. 46 of *Roderick Random*, where Bragwell claims to avoid killing an opponent in a duel only because 'I know better things than to incur the verdict of a Middlesex jury': Tobias Smollett, *The Adventures of Roderick Random*, ed. Paul-Gabriel Boucé (Oxford, 1979), 272.

38.17 Sadducee in origin the name of a member of a Jewish sect which denied the resurrection of the dead and the existence of angels, but the term enjoyed wide currency after being used by Joseph Glanvill (1638–80) in his *Saducismus Triumphatus* (1681) to indicate those who did not believe in the existence of spirits (see *CLA*, 150).

38.19 pitched faggots and tarred barrels burning on a pile of wood covered in tar, or within a barrel which had contained tar, was a method used to execute witches.

38.20 the golden mean the avoidance of extremes; the phrase translates Horace's 'aurea mediocritas' (*Odes*, 2.10.5).

38.21–22 Gines de Passamonte's ape ... partly true and partly false in *Don Quixote*, Part 2 (1615), Ch. 25, the ape belonging to the puppeteer Gines de Passamonte supposedly informs Don Quixote about his experiences in the cave of Montesinos, saying 'part of those things are false, and part of them true'. The wording is that of the translation by Peter Motteux (first published 1701) and of the revision of Motteux's translation by J. Ozell, which first appeared in 1719 (see *CLA*, 317).

38.22–28 Dr Ferriar of Manchester ... faulty or diseased organs John Ferriar (1761–1815), who moved to Manchester after training as a physican in Edinburgh, was one of the first to argue, in his *Essay Towards a Theory of Apparitions* (London, 1813), that apparitions resulted from psychological rather than supernatural causes.

39.6–9 Simon Shadow ... Sir John Falstaff ... hot day's march see *2 Henry IV*, 3.2.122–23.

39.16–17 leave your bower ... the veiled prophet of Moore in 'The Veiled Prophet of Khorassan', the first story told by the disguised King of Bucharia in *Lalla Rookh* (1817) by Thomas Moore (1779–1852), the false prophet Mokanna spends each night in a bower with a member of his harem.

39.21 Michael Scott Michael Scott (*c*. 1160–*c*. 1235), a Scottish scholar who studied and taught at many European universities. His original works on astrology and alchemy led to his reputation as a wizard.

39.21–22 the wizzards of old ... stolen the shadow this superstition appears to originate in the ancient and widespread belief in a link between a person's shadow and their soul. Charles Kirkpatrick Sharpe mentions that the opponents of Charles II believed that his bishops were 'cloven-footed, and had no shadows' (Robert Law, *Memorialls; or, The Memorable Things that Fell out Within this Island of Brittain from 1638 to 1684*, ed. Charles Kirkpatrick Sharpe (Edinburgh, 1818), lxxix).

39.26–27 like the farther end of the bridge in Mirza's vision see Joseph Addison, 'The Vision of Mirzah', first published in the *Spectator*, no. 159 (1 September 1711); in the vision, life on earth is seen as a bridge covered by black cloud at both ends: *The Spectator*, ed. Donald F. Bond, 5 vols (Oxford, 1965), 2.121–26 (see *CLA*, 334).

39.30–32 of the divining rod ... talismans, and spells paraphernalia connected with astrology, alchemy, and other magical practices. A divining-rod was a forked stick used for tracing underground water and minerals; the magical mirror (or 'magic mirror') was believed to display future events or distant scenes (as in Scott's 'My Aunt Margaret's Mirror'); a weapon-salve was an ointment believed to heal a wound by sympathetic agency when applied to the offending weapon; in astrology, lamens were thin metal plates of various uses, while sigils were signs believed to have mysterious powers; pieces of rock crystal (like the more familiar 'crystal ball') displayed scenes to seers, while a pentacle was a star-shaped figure, usually with five points, used as a magical or occult symbol.

39.33–34 an astrologer, like the valiant Guy Mannering see *Guy Mannering*, ed. P. D. Garside, EEWN 2, Ch. 4.

39.37 March beer strong beer brewed in March, when the temperature was ideal for brewing; it kept well over the summer months.

39.37–39 This goblin shall hammer ... to Castle Girnigo between Hermitage Castle, Roxburghshire, in the S. and Castle Girnigoe,

Caithness, in the N. lies most of Scotland. Hermitage was said to be haunted by a spirit confined there by Lord Soulis; Girnigoe, the home of the Sinclairs, Earls of Caithness, is not associated with any particular spirit although a horrific murder, that of John, Master of Caithness, by his father, took place there in 1576.

39.40   play or pay   sporting expression meaning that failure to 'start' in a race or match is counted as a loss for betting purposes.

39.41–40.1   goblins ... Oberon, and all his moon-light dancers spirits of popular superstition. Night-mares were female spirits believed to settle upon sleepers causing a feeling of suffocation; hags were malicious female spirits; break-necks (untraced) were probably spirits such as brags and kelpies which took the form of horses and threw their riders over a cliff or into a pond; black men were bogeys invoked to intimidate children; green women, or green ladies, were spectres attached to solitary places; puck-hairies were mischievous and often malicious spirits (such as Puck, or Robin Good-fellow); and Oberon was king of the fairies, appearing first in English literature in the translation by Lord Berners of *Huon of Bordeaux* (1534) and popularised in *A Midsummer Night's Dream*.

40.1   The wandering Jew   legendary Jew condemned to wander the world until Christ's return, as punishment for goading him as he walked to Calvary.

40.1   the high-priest of the Rosy-cross   the head of the Rosicrucian Order, a secret society which originated in Germany in the early 17th century and which espoused a blend of theosophical and occult traditions. Its emblem is a gold cross with a red rose in the centre.

40.1–2   the Genius of Socrates   the divine voice which Socrates claimed guided him in all his actions.

40.2   the dæmon of Mascon   the demon which, according to the French priest François Perreaud, haunted his house in Mascon (Mâcon) in Burgundy (see his *Démonologie, ou Traitté des Démons et Sorciers. Ensemble l'Antidémon de Mascon* (Geneva, 1653); *CLA*, 146).

40.2–3   the drummer of Tedworth   in an alleged case of haunting a drum was frequently heard playing a tattoo, and objects moved about with no visible agency, after a drummer was imprisoned in 1661 and his drum taken to the house of John Mompesson, of Tedworth, Wiltshire, who was responsible for his arrest. The case was popularised in Joseph Glanvill's *Saducismus Triumphatus* (1681; see *CLA*, 150) and George Sinclair's *Satan's Invisible World Discovered* (1685; *CLA*, 142).

40.12   in the snuff   burnt down to the candle-end.

40.17   the darksome bourne   in this allusion to *Hamlet*, 3.1.79–80, where *bourn* probably means 'frontier', Scott uses the term in the sense 'realm'.

40.22–23   supp'd full with horrors   *Macbeth*, 5.5.13.

40.31   Come like shadows—so depart   see *Macbeth*, 4.1.111.

41.4   purple robes   as worn by Scottish judges in the highest civil court, or Court of Session. In the High Court of Justiciary, the highest criminal court, the judges wear scarlet.

41.5   cocked hats   either the three-cornered hats with turned-up brim fashionable at the end of the 18th and beginning of the 19th century or a style of military hat.

41.5   three-tailed periwigs   the wigs of advocates.

41.33   independent companies   see Historical Note, 184–86.

41.36   Sidier-dhu   *Gaelic* black (or dark) soldiers; the independent companies formed in 1725 appear to have assumed the Campbell tartan (predominantly black, blue and green) now familiar as the 'Black Watch' tartan (see H. D. Macwilliam, *The Black Watch Tartan* (Inverness, 1932), 40).

41.37   Sidier-roy   *Gaelic* red soldiers; the regular British forces wore a red uniform (originally madder red, then scarlet) up to the end of the 19th century.

41.38–40 a marching regiment . . . **the Black Watch** the decision to embody the independent companies was taken in 1739, and the regiment, originally known as the 43rd Regiment of Foot, was assembled in 1740 under the Earl of Crawford; it became the 'Forty-Second' only in 1749.

42.2 the Brunswick government the first Hanoverian monarch, George I (1660–1727; reigned 1714–27), was descended from the Dukes of Brunswick and Lüneburg. The use of this term implies that the story-teller is a Jacobite.

42.28 the country of Lochiel the land of Cameron of Lochiel; Lochiel is the area around Loch Eil, W of Fort William.

43.16 their forefathers lived . . . **in flats** during Scott's lifetime, the middle classes moved from *flats* in the tenements of the Old Town into the terraced houses of the New Town.

43.25 belted plaid a plaid is a length of twilled woollen cloth, often bearing a checked or tartan pattern, now associated specifically with Highland dress but formerly worn in all parts of Scotland and the north of England in the place of a cloak. A *belted plaid* worn by Highland men, was secured to the body by means of a belt; 'While the lower part came down to the knees, the other was drawn up and adjusted to the left shoulder, leaving the right arm uncovered, and at full liberty' (David Stewart, *Sketches of the Character, Manners, and Present State of the Highlanders of Scotland with Details of the Military Service of the Highland Regiments*, 2nd edn, 2 vols (Edinburgh, 1822), 1.74; *CLA*, 332).

44.13–14 The apparition instantly answered ghosts are traditionally believed to be unable to speak until addressed.

44.17–18 the Father of the fatherless and Husband of the widow see Psalm 68.5: 'A father of the fatherless, and a judge of the widows, is God in his holy habitation'.

EXPLANATORY NOTES TO 'MY AUNT MARGARET'S MIRROR'

47 motto not identified: probably by Scott.

48.2–3 myself . . . **afflicted by early infirmity** . . . **have outlived them all** no doubt autobiographical; Scott was lame from childhood, and all of his siblings were now dead.

48.15 monotrochs Scott here jocularly applies the name coined for a one-wheeled gig to the wheelbarrow.

48.23–26 this little range of pasturage . . . **diminished fortune** there are parallels here with the experiences of Scott's great-uncle Robert Haliburton, who had become bankrupt and lost the estate of Dryburgh through commercial ventures; significantly, these misfortunes were recounted by Scott in his own autobiography, which he revised in 1826: see *Scott on Himself*, ed. David Hewitt (Edinburgh, 1981), 5.

48.33–34 sold for an old song out of the ancient possessor's hands a combination of the proverbial 'sold for a song' (*ODEP*, 220–21) and the phrase used by Lord Seafield on signing the Act of Union in 1707, 'there's the end of an auld song'.

48.33 My comforters Job's comforters. See Job 16.2: 'Miserable comforters are ye all'.

48.39 Earl's Closes i.e. the name of the estate: see 49.38, 42.

48.42–49.4 poor Logan: The horrid plough . . . **summer shade** see *A Tale* (1781), lines 309–12, by John Logan (1747/48–88), poet and dramatist, and minister of the Church of Scotland. He was 'poor Logan' because of his lifelong struggle with depression and alcoholism, and because he was forced to resign his parish in 1785 after writing his tragedy *Runnamede* (1783), which was banned from the stage at Covent Garden because the government considered its speeches on behalf of liberty too inflammatory (although it was published in 1783 in London, and the next year performed in Edinburgh). Scott quotes these lines in his journal entry for 4 April 1826 in describing his feelings about the clearing of trees around Ashestiel, his former home.

49.6–8   the adventurous spirit . . . the subsequent changes   the period of financial prosperity followed by the recession of the winter of 1825–26 in which Scott himself became insolvent.

49.13–16   the stile . . . shout and bound   this may well be autobiographical, as Lockhart certainly believed (see *Life*, 1.98). Scott was lame in the right leg, as a result of what was probably poliomyelitis contracted in his second year.

49.25   die under Nelson's banner   i.e. die in the Napoleonic Wars while serving in the British Navy under the command of Lord Nelson (1758–1805). This is not autobiographical: Scott's eldest brother Robert was a sailor, but died in 1787 at the age of 20 in the service of the East India Company.

49.31–32   comparison between the thing I was and that which I now am   see *2 Henry IV*, 5.5.57–59.

49.33   in face of   in front of.

49.35   made a study   contrived.

49.37   entablature   in classical architecture, that part of a building resting on the columns, comprising architrave, frieze and cornice; however the term is apparently here used by Scott of a similar feature above a window.

50.1   moving not unwillingly to the grave   an allusion to Shakespeare's schoolboy, 'creeping like snail/ Unwillingly to school' (*As You Like It*, 2.7.146–47).

50.8   by'r Lady   *1 Henry IV*, 2.4.410.

50.9   some fifty-six years   this relates to Scott's own age at the time that he completed the original version of this story; however, see Essay on the Text, 153–54.

50.13   Mechlin lace   lace of fine quality produced at Mechlin (Mechelen) in northern Belgium.

51.6   Clayhudgeons   as to *hudge* means to pile up, the name reflects its possessor's earthmoving activities.

51.11–12   The chapel . . . considered as common ground . . . used for a penfold   Scott's journal entry for 30 June 1828 records his visit, during a Blair Adam Club outing, to a supposed cell of the Culdees which had been converted into a pinfold (a pen for sheep or cattle). This visit seems too late to have inspired Scott here, as he finished the story in late April (see Essay on the Text, 154), but a visit to the chapel may well have been discussed before the outing.

51.20–21   My house has been long put in order   see Isaiah 38.1.

52.1–2   his old Mumpsimus to the modern Sumpsimus   the story of this old English priest is told in Richard Pace's *De Fructu Doctrinae* (Basel, 1517), 80. Having fallen into the habit of using *mumpsimus* for *sumpsimus* in the Mass, he refused to change to the newfangled pronunciation. Scott also alludes to the story in his journal entry for 25 January 1827.

52.4–5   a piece of   somewhat of.

52.7–12   George the Fourth . . . to arms against his grandfather   the Jacobite rising of 1745 took place under George II (1683–1760) who reigned 1727–60; he was the great-grandfather, rather than the grandfather, of George IV (1762–1830, reigned 1820–30).

52.14–15   They fought . . . with hearts unsubdued   not identified.

These lines are probably not by Scott as he uses a form of them in the second 'Letter on the Proposed Change of Currency' by 'Malachi Malagrowther' originally published in the *Edinburgh Weekly Journal*, 1 March 1826 (*Prose Works*, 21.325).

52.29 the Stuart right of birth George IV was a descendant of the Stuart kings through Elizabeth, daughter of James VI and I.

52.30 the Act of Succession under the terms of the Act of Settlement of 1701 (Scott's 'Act of Succession') and after the death of Queen Anne without surviving issue in 1714, George, Elector of Hanover, and his descendants became kings of Great Britain.

52.34–35 the will of the nation, as declared at the Revolution following the invasion of William of Orange in November 1688, James VII and II fled the country at Christmas, without abdicating. Early in 1689 the Parliaments of England and Scotland separately declared the throne vacant and invited William (a grandson of Charles I) and his wife Mary (daughter of James VII and II, and so a granddaughter of Charles I) to take the thrones of the two countries.

52.35 jure divino *Latin* by divine right, i.e. by divinely ordained right rather than the 'will of the nation' as expressed through Parliament.

52.39 Whimsicals in Queen Anne's reign, a section of the Tories sympathetic to the Hanoverian succession.

53.6–7 the Gaelic song . . . Hatil mohatil, na dowski mi *Gaelic* Tha mi am chadal 's na dúisgibh mi (I am asleep and do not waken me), the first line of a refrain to a song by Silis Nighean Mhic Raonaill who lived in the later 17th and earlier 18th centuries. See *Sar-Obair nam Bard Gaelach: The Beauties of Gaelic Poetry and Lives of the Highland Bards*, ed. John Mackenzie (Edinburgh, 1841), 60. However Scott's phonetic rendering of the Gaelic suggests for the first words *Cha til mo chadal* (My sleep will not return) or, closer in sense but not as close in sound, *Cadal, mo chadal* (Sleep, my sleep).

53.10–11 what your favourite Wordsworth calls 'moods of my own mind' 'Moods of My Own Mind' forms a section of the second volume of William Wordsworth's *Poems, in Two Volumes* (London, 1807).

53.28–30 the translator of Tasso . . . the magic wonders which he sung William Collins, 'Ode on the Popular Superstitions of the Highlands of Scotland' (written 1749–50; published 1788), lines 198–99. The overall context shows that these lines refer to the Italian poet Torquato Tasso (1544–95) rather than to Edward Fairfax (1568?–1635), who translated Tasso's *Gerusalemme liberata* (1575) as *Godfrey of Bulloigne* (1600); however, the immediate context suggests that they apply to Fairfax. Scott interprets Collins's lines similarly in *Letters on Demonology and Witchcraft* (1830), 247–48.

53.34–35 that your ears . . . your complexion . . . like that of Theodore see lines 88–96, and especially line 94, of John Dryden's 'Theodore and Honoria', in his *Fables* (1699).

54.20–22 the spells of Hallowe'en . . . peeping over our shoulder see Burns's 'Hallowe'en' (1786; Kinsley, no. 73), stanza 13 and note, which describes certain actions to be performed before a mirror in order to allow a glimpse of one's future spouse, 'as if peeping over your shoulder'.

54.27–28 a story . . . from my grandmother see Historical Note, 190–92.

54.34 Chartered Libertine *Henry V*, 1.1.47–48: 'when he speaks,/ The air, a charter'd libertine, is still', where the phrase means 'a person licensed to go their own way'. Scott is however using *libertine* in the sense of a licentious man.

54.38–39 the Sir Charles Easy and the Lovelace of his day and country Sir Charles Easy is a chronically unfaithful, but ultimately repentant, husband in Colley Cibber (1671–1757), *The Careless Husband* (1705); Robert Lovelace is an unscrupulous man of fashion who brings about the death of the eponymous heroine in Samuel Richardson (1689–1761), *Clarissa* (1748).

55.3–4 if laws were made for every degree see John Gay (1685–1732), *The Beggar's Opera* (London, 1728), Act 3, scene 13, air 26.

55.10 plenary indulgences i.e. full pardons.

55.12 Sillermills area in Stockbridge in Edinburgh, then N of the city.

55.12–13 made work for the Lord Advocate the Lord Advocate is the chief law officer of the Crown in Scotland and the principal prosecutor; the Lord Advocate appears only in the highest courts in the most important cases. Rape was one of the four crimes which had to be tried in the High Court of Justiciary, the highest criminal court in Scotland, and so the implication is that Forester raped Peggy Grindstone but was not charged.

55.15 the Duke of A—— a likely allusion to John Campbell, 2nd Duke of Argyle (1680–1743), a key figure in Scotland at the period in which the story is set.

55.22 King's-Copland apparently an imaginary estate.

55.34–35 some political matters . . . more wisely let alone by implication, the Jacobite cause.

56.15–16 any Sir Philip . . . Falconbridge himself a reference to the Bastard Faulconbridge in *King John*.

56.24–25 she spoiled his market i.e. he could have done better elsewhere.

56.38 menus plaisirs *French* little amusements.

57.4 beau garçon *French* fine fellow, fop.

57.25 from Leith to Helvoet Leith is the port of Edinburgh and Hellevoetsluis is a port in the south of the Netherlands near Rotterdam.

57.35 the Gazette either the *London Gazette* (first published as the *Oxford Gazette* in 1665) or the *Edinburgh Gazette* (first published 1699), the official organs for government notices.

59.13 par voie du fait *legal French* by violent means.

59.39 taking on becoming worked up.

60.4 the campaign part of the war of the Spanish Succession (1701–13) in which Britain, the Dutch Republic, various German states, and Austria fought against France and its allies. The scene of the most important engagements was Flanders, where John Churchill, first Duke of Marlborough (1650–1722), commanded the British forces.

61.23–25 the Paduan doctor . . . that famous university the University of Padua, founded in 1222, was particularly celebrated in the 15th to 18th centuries for its research in medicine, astronomy, philosophy and law.

61.30 Doctor Baptista Damiotti Scott's choice of 'Baptista' is perhaps influenced by the name of the Italian natural philosopher and inventor of the camera obscura, Giambattista della Porta, also known as Giovanni Battista della Porta (d. 1615), author of *Magiæ Naturalis*, first published in 1558, and expanded to 20 books in 1589; see *CLA*, 108.

61.33–34 a seeking of health . . . Egypt see Isaiah 19.3, 31.1.

61.36 set these imputations at defiance outface these imputations.

61.37–38 the city of Edinburgh . . . abhorrence of witches and necromancers for an account of Scottish witch-hunting, especially severe from the 16th to the 18th centuries, see Letter 9 of Scott's *Letters on Demonology and Witchcraft* (1830). Recent research concludes that 'witch executions per head of population in Scotland may have run at ten times the English level' (James Sharpe, 'Witch-Hunting and Witch Historiography: Some Anglo-Scottish Comparisons', in *The Scottish Witch-Hunt in Context*, ed. Julian Goodare (Manchester and New York, 2002), 182).

62.7 man of art man of skill, expert. In this context, however, there may be implications of 'black art'.

63.29 philosophical utensils *philosophical* is here used in the now obsolete sense of 'scientific'.

64.31–32 there is still a previous inquiry i.e. I need to ask you something before we proceed.

65.5 Put up lay aside.

65.5 an adept needs not your gold an adept, or alchemist who has learned the secret of turning base metals into gold, has no need of the gold of others.

66.11–14 The music . . . of the harmonica . . . later period in life the *harmonica* was an instrument developed by Benjamin Franklin (1706–90) in about 1762 as an improvement on the 'musical glasses' in vogue in the 17th century. The sound of this family of instruments was reported as having a powerful effect on both performer and audience, and it may be relevant to Scott's story that Franz Mesmer (1734–1815) induced a receptive state in his hypnotic subjects by playing the harmonica to them. Since the story is set early in the 18th century, Lady Bothwell could have heard the true harmonica as an old lady, although the instrument used by Damiotti would have been an earlier form of the musical glasses.

67.1 The master—to use the Italian phrase the Italian *maestro* is applied to an expert and was also formerly used of a doctor; either sense is appropriate here.

67.40 the Geneva gown and band black gown with a collar or neckband extending into two square-ended strips of white linen; originally the dress of the Calvinist clergy of Geneva, it was later adopted by other Protestant churches.

69.27 composing draught sedative.

70.19 the graduate applied to the family physician, suggesting that he has a medical degree.

70.34 What comes from Italy after their expulsion from France following the Treaty of Utrecht (1713), the Old Pretender (the son of James II and VII) lived first in Lorraine, then in Avignon (both outside France at that time), and from 1717 in Rome.

70.34–35 what comes from Hanover see note to 52.30.

70.36 whig and tory names for the two parties which dominated the House of Commons. The term *whig* was derogatory, and originally used of Scottish Covenanters, i.e. Presbyterians who rebelled against the rule of Charles II over issues of religious conformity. The term *tory* was also derogatory, derived from an Irish word for an outlaw and applied to those fighting for James II in Ireland after 1688. Whigs were largely responsible for ousting the last Stuart king, James VII and II, in 1688, were supporters of the Protestant Succession, and tended to be non-conformists (i.e. they did not worship in the Church of England). Tory politicians tended towards Jacobitism, i.e. to support the Stuarts and their hereditary rights to the crown, and were High Churchmen, believing in the Church of England as the English successor to the Church of Rome. The rivalry of whig and tory was particularly fierce during the reign of Queen Anne (reigned 1702–14).

70.37–38 a Carolus . . . a Willielmus a *Carolus* (*Latin* Charles) was a gold piece struck in the reign of Charles I, while a *Willielmus* (*Latin* William) was a gold coin used in the Netherlands. The doctor is thus saying that he is happy to be paid by tories (supporters of the Stuart descendants of Charles I) and whigs (supporters of William III and the Protestant succession).

70.41 you had best set him down a Jesuit, as Scrub says see Act 3, scene 1 of *The Beaux Stratagem* (London, 1707) by George Farquhar (*c.*

1677–1707). Scrub applies the term 'Jesuit' to the newly arrived gentleman Aimwell, after declaring that others believe him to be a spy or a mountebank.

71.5   the celebrated Earl of Stair   John Dalrymple, 2nd Earl of Stair (1673–1747), soldier and diplomat, who fought under Marlborough in Flanders 1703–11.

71.7   the Scotch-Dutch   the Scots Brigade, or brigade of Scottish soldiers which was in the service of the government of the Netherlands from the time of William the Silent in the 16th century until 1782.

71.12   at play   at the gaming table.

72.12   the Chevalier St. George   name for the Old Pretender (1688–1766), son of James VII and II, and thus the Jacobite claimant to the British throne.

72.14   the Protestant succession   the succession of the Protestants William III and Mary, Anne and George I, rather than the Roman Catholic descendants of James VII and II.

72.22   to cut the Gordian knot   to solve a problem directly, or with force: see *ODEP*, 328–29. According to a prophecy, whoever could undo a complex knot tied by Gordius, a Phrygian king, would rule Asia. In 333 BC Alexander the Great is said to have cut through it with his sword.

72.27   the silver greyhound   the badge worn by the King's messengers, whose duty it was to arrest prisoners of state.

72.27–28   made, as we say, a moonlight flitting   *proverbial* left one's residence, by night or by stealth, usually without paying debts of some kind. See *ODEP*, 542.

72.31   Galen or Hippocrates   Galen (*c.* AD 129–200) and Hippocrates (*c.* 460–*c.* 375 BC) were both celebrated Greek physicians.

72.35–37   we Scots . . . one or two little barleycorns of vice   untraced, although the 'it is said' may apply to 'rarely forgive, and never forget'.

72.38   we rarely forgive, and never forget, any injuries received   possible allusion to the Latin phrase *perfervidum ingenium Scotorum* (very fiery character of the Scots), founded on the 'Scotorum præfervida ingenia' of George Buchanan (1506–82): see Buchanan, *Rerum Scoticarum Historia*, in his *Opera Omnia*, ed. Thomas Ruddiman, 2 vols (Edinburgh, 1715), 1.321. See also the proverbial 'hard-hearted as a Scot of Scotland' (Ray, 223; *ODEP*, 353).

72.39–40   an idol of our resentment, as poor Lady Constance did of her grief   see *King John*, 3.4.90–105.

72.40–41   Nursing our wrath to keep it warm   see Robert Burns, 'Tam o' Shanter' (1791; Kinsley, no. 321), line 12.

73.5   Fastern's E'en (Shrovetide)   a Scots term, literally 'eve of the fast', i.e. Shrove Tuesday, the last day before Lent.

73.6   full and frequent   assembled in great numbers.

73.7   the lady patronesses   ladies who presided at public assemblies, i.e. gatherings of people in 18th-century polite society for the purposes of conversation, dancing, and gaming. For details of the organisation of the Edinburgh assemblies see Robert Chambers, *Traditions of Edinburgh*, 2 vols (London, 1825), 2.27–31.

74.22   I have given no mercy, how then shall I ask it?   see Matthew 5.7: 'Blessed are the merciful: for they shall obtain mercy.'

74.30   the worms which thou hast called out of dust   an allusion to the creation of Adam from 'the dust of the ground' (Genesis 2.7) and to the frequent biblical terminology depicting human beings as worms (e.g. see Job 25.6, Psalm 22.6, and Isaiah 41.14).

76.21–23 the celebrated Miss Seward, of Lichfield Anna Seward (1742–1809), 'the Swan of Lichfield', corresponded with Scott from 1802. In accordance with her final wishes he published her poems in 1810, with a memoir. She no doubt told him this story when he visited her in 1807 (see *Life*, 2.121), since he goes on to state that he heard it from her 'more than twenty years since'.

77.1 the American war the American War of Independence (1775–83).

77.1–2 Lord Cornwallis's army, which surrendered at Yorktown the British army, under Charles, Earl (later Marquess) Cornwallis (1735–1805), surrendered to the combined American and French forces at Yorktown, Virginia, in October 1781, an event which was instrumental in ending the war.

77.6 general officer name commonly extended to all officers above the rank of colonel.

77.12 morning stage the interval (often about 12 miles) between posts (inns) where the horses were changed, covered in the course of a morning.

77.27 a castle, as old as the wars of York and Lancaster a castle built during the Wars of the Roses (1455–85), when the families of York and Lancaster disputed the English throne.

77.29 Elizabeth and her successor Elizabeth I (1533–1603) reigned 1558–1603; her successor, James VI and I (1566–1625), held the Scottish throne as James VI from 1567, and the English throne as James I from 1603.

78.2 was determined to decided to.

78.11–12 a nobleman . . . Lord Woodville the Woodvilles (whose title was however Earl Rivers) were prominent in the reign of Edward IV (reigned 1461–83), and this choice of name may be a consequence of Scott's reference to the Wars of the Roses.

78.15 the same with one and the same as.

78.23 Eton famous English school, near Windsor. A *fag* was a junior pupil who performed menial tasks for a senior.

78.24 Christ Church a college at Oxford.

79.28–29 the Bush, as the Virginians call it probably borrowed from the Dutch *bosch, busch*, the phrase *the bush* is first recorded in the United States, although it is now particularly associated with Australia.

79.29 light corps army corps, lightly equipped to ensure mobility.

79.29 like Diogenes himself Diogenes (*c.* 412–323 BC), a Greek Cynic philosopher who, according to tradition, lived in a tub or large earthenware jar.

79.42 back settlements outlying settlements.

80.2 conduce to promote.

81.43 huddled on hastily put on.

82.16 post horses horses hired to pull a coach over the next stage (normally around 12 miles, 20 km) to the next post, i.e. an inn where horses could be changed.

83.17 with consent of the owner i.e. if the owner had had a say in it.

84.23–26 a sacque; that is, a sort of robe . . . a species of train as Scott later specifies in relation to the portrait, the sacque was 'the fashionable dress of the end of the seventeenth century' (88.8–9).

85.17–18 I felt my hair individually bristle . . . my life-blood arrested echoes the ghost's claim that he could tell Hamlet a tale which would make 'each particular hair to stand an end' (*Hamlet*, 1.5.19) and 'freeze thy young blood' (*Hamlet*, 1.5.16).

87.24 Vandyke the great Flemish portrait painter Antoon Van Dyck (1599–1641), whose name was anglicised as Anthony when he was knighted and appointed Court Painter by Charles I in 1632.

87.39–42 Cavalier ... Round-head the Cavaliers fought for Charles I, and the Roundheads for Parliament, in the English civil war of 1642–51.

87.43 the exiled court at Saint Germain's when James VII and II fled to France in 1688, he, and later his son James 'VIII and III' (the 'Old Pretender', i.e. claimant, to the British and Irish crowns), held court at the chateau of St Germain near Paris under the protection of Louis XIV, until they were obliged to leave France in 1713 by the Treaty of Utrecht.

87.43–88.1 one who had taken arms for William at the Revolution a supporter of William of Orange against James II in the Glorious Revolution (1688–89).

88.2 Whig and Tory see note to 70.36.

88.3–4 cramming ... 'against the stomach of his sense' see *The Tempest*, 2.1.100–01.

88.26 to be unmantled to have its furnishings removed. This is the only use of *unmantle* noted in the *OED*.

EXPLANATORY NOTES TO 'DEATH OF THE LAIRD'S JOCK'

89.2 the editor of The Keepsake Frederick Mansel Reynolds (d. 1850), editor of *The Keepsake* 1828–35 and 1838–39. For details of Scott's strained relations with him see Essay on the Text, 148–49.

89.7 sicut pictura poesis *Latin* a poem is like a picture; see Horace (65–8 BC), *Ars Poetica*, line 361.

89.29 rearing up fostering the growth of.

89.31–32 The well contested ground,/ The warlike Borderland *Albania; A Poem Addressed to the Genius of Scotland* (London, 1737), lines 13–14. Scott possessed a copy of the original folio edition of this anonymous poem (*CLA*, 13), which was reprinted in *Scotish Descriptive Poems*, ed. [John Leyden] (Edinburgh, 1803), 157–69; *CLA*, 162.

89.33–34 the union of the Crowns in 1603 on the death of Elizabeth, James VI, King of Scots, became King of England. Although Scotland and England remained independent countries until 1707, there was no further war between the kingdoms (although Scots armies invaded England in the course of the English Civil War 1642–51, and Cromwell's army invaded Scotland), and cross-border raids and skirmishes died out. If enough had been said and sung about the Borderland, it was Scott himself who was responsible in *Minstrelsy of the Scottish Border*, 2 vols (Kelso, 1802), *The Lay of the Last Minstrel* (Edinburgh, 1805), and *Marmion* (Edinburgh, 1808).

89.37 every dale had its battle, and every river its song see *Marmion*, Intro. to Canto 2, lines 70–71, in *Poetical Works*, 7.80: 'Nor hill, nor brook, we paced along,/ But had its legend and its song'.

90.3 Bernard Gilpin, the Apostle of the North rector of Houghton-le-Spring, County Durham, Bernard Gilpin (1516–84) acquired a large following through his missionary journeys in Tynedale and Redesdale in the English Border regions.

90.11 Reach it to me hand it down to me.

90.18–19 about the latter years of Queen Elizabeth's reign around the end of the 16th century: Elizabeth (1533–1603) reigned 1558–1603.

90.19 Liddesdale valley on the Scottish side of the border with England NE of Carlisle.

90.21 a small river either Liddel Water or the Kershope Burn, both of which mark the border for a time.

90.25–26 the sept or clan of the Armstrongs ... the Laird of Manger-ton for Scott's account of this clan see his introduction to 'Johnie Armstrang' in *Minstrelsy*, 1.330–51; he describes the ruins of the castle at Mangertown, or Mangerton, in the introduction to 'Hobbie Noble' in *Minstrelsy*, 2.115–18.

90.34–36 Some of his feats . . . contemporary chronicles for details see Historical Note, 209–10.

90.37 singular combat a variant of 'single combat'.

90.38–39 Cumberland, Westmoreland, or Northumberland the English border counties prior to the local government reorganisation of 1974.

90.42 Durindana or Fushberta the swords of Orlando and his cousin Rinaldo in Ludovico Ariosto (1474–1533), *Orlando furioso* (first published 1516, completed 1532).

91.1 the foes of Christendom the Saracens, against whom Orlando and Rinaldo fight.

91.3 Hobbie Noble see 'Jock o' the Side' and 'Hobbie Noble', in *Minstrelsy*, 2.93–109, 115–29.

91.32 one of the name of Foster see Historical Note, 210–11.

91.38 a neutral spot, used as the place of rencontre variously identified by Scott as Turner's holm, Turney-holm, and Kershope-foot. For details see Historical Note, 205–08.

92.6–7 a fragment of rock, which is still called the Laird's Jock's stone for details see Historical Note, 211–12.

92.17–18 antediluvian giant . . . the destruction of the deluge see Chapters 6 to 8 of Genesis, and in particular Genesis 6.4.

92.39 at once simultaneously.

93.10 thrown into perspective shown extending away from the viewer.

93.15–17 the pennon of Saint George . . . and that of Saint Andrew the respective flags of England and Scotland, which display the crosses of their patron saints.

EXPLANATORY NOTES TO 'A HIGHLAND ANECDOTE'

94.8 the spirited engraving of the Gored Huntsman the illustration to 'The Gored Huntsman', an anonymous story in *The Keepsake for 1828* (London, 1827), 21–32; the engraving, which faces p. 31, is by William Finden (1787–1852) from a painting by Abraham Cooper (1787–1868). (The painter's name appears in the 'List of the Plates' at the beginning of the volume as 'A. Cooper, Esq. R. A.' but under the engraving as 'R. Cooper, R.A.', a clear error as no 'R. Cooper' was a member of the Royal Academy). Abraham Cooper specialised in animal and battle paintings, and was much admired by Scott (see *Letters*, 10.98–99, 380, 394, and 11.88), who chose him as one of the illustrators of the Magnum (*Letters*, 10.457, 11.292–93).

94.15–18 Duncan . . . the affair of 1746 . . . a certain tragic affair for details of Duncan's identity, his participation in the Jacobite Rising of 1745–46 which culminated in the battle of Culloden on 16 April 1746, as well as his possible involvement in the 'Appin Murder', see Historical Note, 212–17.

95.7 whistling the Gathering of his Clan whistling the tune used to summon the clan's fighting men.

95.26–27 come by the worst be defeated.

95.31–32 a rock which would have suited the pencil of Salvator the Italian artist Salvator Rosa (1615–73) pioneered a style of landscape painting depicting wild natural scenes; his works were highly esteemed in Britain in the late 18th century and throughout the 19th century.

96.13 although, as Dangle says, he was my friend in the opening scene of Richard Brinsley Sheridan (1751–1816), *The Critic* (London, 1781),

Dangle repeatedly concurs with Sneer's criticisms of Sir Fretful Plagiary, adding however on each occasion 'tho he's my friend'.

96.14   a hart of grease   a fat deer, fit for the table.

GLOSSARY

This selective glossary defines single words; phrases are treated in the Explanatory Notes. It covers archaic and technical terms and occurrences of familiar words in senses that are likely to be strange to the modern reader. For each word (or clearly distinguishable sense) glossed, up to four occurrences are normally noted; when a word (or sense) occurs more than four times in the stories, only the first instance is given, followed by 'etc.'. Orthographical variants of single words are listed together. Occasionally the most economical and effective way of defining a word is to refer the reader to the appropriate explanatory note.

abate reduce 35.37
abide endure 65.34
adept alchemist who has attained the secret of turning base metal into gold 65.5 etc.
adventure hazard 48.26
advices letters of introduction 57.25
alliance kinship 31.9
alloy inferior metal added to one of greater value 51.26
ambidexter ambidextrous 9.34
amry-sneck pantry latch 31.21
annoy vex, disturb 57.7
apartment room 43.35 etc.; *pl.* suite of rooms 2.4, 8.29–30, 43.17, 62.37
artist magician 72.7
aspin aspen 20.18
awful awe-inspiring 90.41
back-game return game 11.17
back-shop private shop behind the public one 24.3, 25.32
back-stroke return stroke, 'return' 6.8
baillie member of the town council with powers as a magistrate 25.28
battery pieces of artillery grouped for combined action 83.40
beadle minor parish officer 2.3 (see note)
beat beaten 6.27
beldame hag 11.40
betted bet 7.5
bickering flickering 80.37
bilk avoid paying 12.33

bill indictment 36.37
billet note 73.14
bobbin piece of wood attached to string tied to the latch on the other side of a door, thereby raising it 31.31
bruiser boxer 15.16
buckskin'd clothed in buckskin trousers 13.1
budget bag, wallet, brief-case 12.18
buffet beat, thump 6.15
burgess citizen of a burgh 25.24
burgomaster member of the governing body of a municipality 71.14
burthen burden 7.43, 74.11
candour impartiality 56.17, 83.39
chace *noun* chase, hunt 13.9; hunting-ground 14.24
chace *verb* chase 5.22
chafts jaws 31.22
champaigne champagne 22.42–43
chance-medley blend of accidental and human causes 36.36
character reputation 11.26, 31.26, 41.12; status, rank 47.31, 61.38, 63.3–4, 76.30
charter-chest chest for storing documents 26.9, 88.17
cheer countenance 17.8
chimney-stalk chimney-stack 77.34
chords violin strings 15.20
christal piece of rock crystal used by seers 39.31
circuit see note to 25.42

civilian practitioner of civil law 38.13

claymore two-edged broadsword used by Highlanders 52.17

clerk lay officer assisting the minister 67.41, 90.8, 90.11

close alleyway leading from the street to tenements or outbuildings 3.36

cognosce pronounce insane 26.35

common-sewer main sewer of a town or city 9.4

concourse throng 5.11, 68.3

conjure implore 44.12, 83.4

controversy dispute 77.4

conversazione private gathering devoted to discussion of the arts or sciences 11.34

cordial stimulating drink 10.22

counter upper part of a horse's breast 36.6

country district 41.24 etc.

crape piece of crape (thin, transparent fabric) covering the face as a disguise 14.16, 18.2

creagh plundered cattle 42.30

crisis vital stage 54.3, 63.15

crow crow-bar 14.16

crutch-headed (of a walking-stick) having a transverse handle like the head of a crutch 49.30

cry proclaim for sale, hawk 34.17

curst cursed 9.23

dar'na dare not 32.12

declension decline 8.8

decyphering deciphering 25.38

denomination kind, sort 41.1

derange throw into confusion 6.22

designation person's place of residence, added to their name for purposes of identification 41.31

detach send off (from main body) for a special purpose 71.23

devote designate 48.11

devoted doomed 48.17

diablotin *French* imp 5.17

dinted dented 17.31

dirk short dagger carried by Highlanders 43.25, 96.2

disengaged unoccupied 35.3; free of engagements 82.27

dismal dire 15.43, 71.41

doublet two dice showing the same number 7.5

dram-bottle bottle holding a small draught of whisky or other spirits 10.22

dreadfully in such a way as to cause dread 91.30

drift intention 31.18

dub-a-dub *verb* drum 39.38

dull listless 47.23

dullness sluggishness 21.14

duodecimo for 6.42 see note to 6.41–42

duskish somewhat dark 43.20

earmark mark in a sheep's ears indicating ownership 33.13

ecstacy ecstasy 16.32

eidolon phantom 11.15

elucidate explain 32.17

empiric quack 61.28, 65.7

end portion of a match, such as a 'game' in tennis 10.37

endear render attractive 81.16

entablature in classical architecture, that part of a building resting on the columns 49.37 (see note)

entertainer host 87.32

equipment fitting out 42.22

event outcome, consequence 92.11, 92.21

exalt enhance 57.3

expectant person who expects to receive something 6.29

fa befall 31.22

fag junior pupil at an English public school who performs menial tasks for a senior 78.23

fairly handsomely 1.10

falchion sword 91.1

fashion usage 54.8; fashionable society 57.5, 73.6; standing as a man of fashion 81.40

fatal fateful 88.18, 90.10, 93.9

field-piece light cannon used on the battlefield 13.13

flesh inure 15.40

flocks tufts of wool or cotton, or of cloth, used as stuffing 3.15

forgot forgotten 8.32, 9.17

frore freezing 14.5

frost-fog frozen mist 18.1

gambols tricks 47.9

gamester player 3.17 etc.

gang go 32.12

gathering air played on bagpipe or drum to summon the members of a clan 95.7

gentry folk 5.42

germain germane 70.23

ghastly pale 82.3
glee joy 88.24
gorgon-face gorgon's head, representation of the head of Medusa 4.8
grin grimace 85.7
hand-maiden personal maid 54.23
haunch-hoop hoop of whalebone or steel, or a structure of such hoops, used to hold out a woman's skirt 40.37
higgler itinerant dealer who buys poultry and dairy produce and supplies petty commodities 14.27
hornfull the amount held by a drinking-horn 22.41
hund drive 32.12
hutch hut 14.26
intrust entrust 91.29
jubilee rejoicing, acclamation 7.36
justify vindicate, excuse (a person) 56.19
kaill-pot-lid soup-pot lid 31.20
kateran marauder 42.27
keel ownership mark on a sheep 34.9 (see note)
kennel gutter, drain 9.8
label moulding over a window 49.37
lamen thin metal plate used in astrology 39.31
legend account 55.20
like likely 39.8
lists barriers around an area enclosed for a tournament or other contest, or the area itself 6.17 etc.
longitude length 4.25
low-browed low 3.38–39
lubbard clumsy, stupid 5.37
make noun form, shape 92.16
marriage-lines marriage certificate 26.8
masque mask 4.33
match ally oneself in marriage 17.5, 17.20
mendicity the existence, state, and number of beggars 29.21
mephitic foul-smelling 3.34
meridian mid-day 39.10
merrymen companions in arms, followers 18.16
messuage house-site 48.18
monotroch wheelbarrow 48.15 (see note)
moonlight cant smuggled spirits 14.25
mortification use of self-inflicted

pain to control one's desires 4.12
murrey-coloured purplish red 80.32–33
near nearly 81.37, 90.43
nearly closely 84.4
noise rumour, talk 72.29, 94.18
nonentity figment of the imagination 38.35
nostrum quack medicine or remedy 23.2
nurse nurse-maid 7.36, 22.13
octavo for 6.42 see note to 6.41–42
o'erawe, overawe intimidate 2.3; hold sway 14.1
overset overthrow 6.22
packet packet-boat 57.25; parcel of mail, dispatches 70.2
padding highway robbery 32.3
particolour particoloured, displaying two or more distinct colours 77.39
patter make a quick succession of tapping sounds 80.30
peccant sinning 56.12
peck measure of capacity for dry goods which varied according to commodity 72.37
peculiar distinctive 11.1, 55.42, 63.29, 63.31
peculiarly especially 2.3, 95.9
pentacle star-shaped figure, usually with five points, used as a magical symbol 39.31
period end 50.25, 68.43
pet tantrum 7.37
phantasmagoria series of optical illusions 38.1, 40.30, 72.19
philosophical scientific 63.29 (see note)
phrenzy frenzy, fit of insanity 25.18
pibroch piece of music for the bagpipe, generally martial or mournful in tone 52.17
pica 12 point type 5.1
piece put back together 8.17
plaid length of cloth worn in place of a cloak 43.25 (see note) etc.
plait pleat 84.25
plight condition 17.31
polisson French scamp 4.28
portion dowry 55.27
pre-occupation prejudice 86.43
pretend claim, profess 4.30–31 etc.
prevailing influential 53.29
prick ride 17.29

professor one making a profession of a particular art or science 55.9

proné *French* extolled 72.15

puff praise in inflated terms 70.40

puffing extravagantly commendatory 24.13

quarto book in which there are 4 leaves per gathering 6.38, 8.18

quit move out of tenanted property 48.20

quo' quoth 31.23

racqueteer tennis-player 5.43, 6.22, 11.16

rally take (an animal) in hand 36.10

range *noun* stretch 48.23, 94.31

reasonably in the normal fashion 63.36

recal recall 73.42

receipt formula for medicine 61.25

reconcile become reconciled 42.17

recover recover from 71.40

rectify flavour (spirits) during re-distillation 10.26

redeem regain 76.30

reekit sooty 9.34

regret express sorrow 86.17

regularly formally 25.30

relique relic, object venerated for its association with a holy person 5.20

rencontre encounter 91.38, 95.14

rencounter duel 71.39; encounter 86.4

research careful search 94.35

reunion reuniting 84.12

review inspection of troops 5.21

ridicule reticule, small handbag usually of woven material 30.33

rive tear 90.22 (see note)

roll round pad of hair or other material 50.15

rug tug roughly 90.22 (see note)

run smuggle 14.25

sackless innocent 36.15

sate sat 18.25, 50.18, 51.10, 92.31

scarce scarcely 13.13 etc.

sconce bracket-candlestick fastened to a wall 63.36

scutcheon shield displaying a coat of arms 67.36

selle saddle 20.20

sept sub-division of a clan 90.25

sequel remainder of a narrative 32.17

session-clerk secretary of a kirk-session, the governing body of a parish in a Presbyterian church 25.37

sexton parish officer responsible for grave-digging 90.12

shift prank 31.19

shin sharp slope 33.8

shiver smash 9.38

shivers small fragments, 'smither-eens' 6.15

sigil in astrology, a sign believed to have mysterious powers 39.31

small-beer weak beer made from hops and malt that had already produced one brew 22.41

solemnize celebrate 5.26, 13.18

something *adv* somewhat 11.10, 64.19

sorning act of exacting free board and lodging by intimidation 25.43, 32.4

spell make out, decipher 8.19

stage distance covered without stopping for rest or change of horses 77.12

stand cost 26.33

stedfast steadfast 22.1

stopt stopped 36.6

stouthrieff, stouthrief robbery with violence 25.43, 32.4

strain lineage 17.4, 17.24

stub-nails old horseshoe nails and other scraps of metal used for making stub-iron 9.8

stump'd stumped, truncated 31.37

sunk sank 3.28, 43.39

supporters *heraldry* pair of figures standing either side of a shield in a coat of arms 26.32

surname person's place of residence added to their name for purposes of identification, designation 44.12

tale-teller story-teller 89.13

teaze irritate by a persistent and annoying action 34.35

temperature disposition 54.3–4

tenement large house divided into sections for a number of tenants 23.33; large house occupied by only one household 49.38

themsel themselves 32.12

thift theft 31.22

toilette act of dressing 54.8, 80.31; dressing-table 82.2

toils nets into which game is driven

14.23
toupee topknot on a wig, or such a wig itself 2.33
tradition information handed down, especially orally, from one generation to the next 2.32 etc.
trencher-cap academic cap, 'mortar-board' 11.21
twelve-mo book in which there are 12 leaves to a gathering 6.35
ungenial (of weather) unpleasantly cold or damp 81.29
unlucky unfortunate for the opponent 9.39
unmantle remove furnishings from 88.26 (see note)
untented not probed and cleansed 74.20
unwieldy clumsy 4.38
urchin mischievous youngster 2.35, 5.3
villany villainy 62.25, 71.34

vizard mask 4.29
wading (of the moon) intermittently covered by cloud 16.6
wafer adhesive disk for sealing documents 24.42 (see note)
watch-word word or phrase used as a signal 14.37
water-flag yellow flag (*Iris pseudacorus*), a common British species 49.24
weather-gleam sky just above the horizon 32.38
whare where 32.12
whilome whilom, at some time in the past 39.35
wilder'd bewildered, perplexed 15.5
willing desirous 35.27, 65.8
wire-draw draw out to an inordinate length 13.2
wizzard wizard 39.21
wold open country 15.2
wreathed twisted 77.33